Saving Nia

G.B. Jones

authorHOUSE

AuthorHouse™
1663 Liberty Drive
Bloomington, IN 47403
www.authorhouse.com
Phone: 1 (800) 839-8640

Published by AuthorHouse 07/07/2017

ISBN: 978-1-4772-8136-9 (sc)
ISBN: 978-1-4772-8137-6 (hc)
ISBN: 978-1-4772-8135-2 (e)

Library of Congress Control Number: 2012919603

Print information available on the last page.

This book is printed on acid-free paper.

Chapter 1 Nia's Abduction

Nia was six years old when her world crashed.

When she heard her mother call her, she became so happy that she ran down the stairs. She had been sitting on the top step, which was where she usually sat while her mother talked to a social worker. But that day her life changed, she saw her favorite teddy bear in the social worker's hand and her suitcase on the floor.

Mrs. Patterson watched her daughter's eyes dart from the teddy bear in the social worker's hand to the suitcase. When her little girl's eyes clouded over in understanding, it took everything in her to stop herself from grabbing her daughter and running out of the house. Invading thoughts of the law backing the social worker helped her to maintain control.

Nia turned and ran back upstairs. "No! No! No! No!" tumbled from her mouth as she ran into her room and looked in her closet. All her clothes were gone! She crawled under her bed and started screaming. She couldn't stop. She screamed, "Momma, Momma, Mommy!" She could barely catch her breath between screaming and crying. Tears streamed down her face as her body shook uncontrollably.

The social worker rushed up the stairs and into Nia's room. She peeked under the bed and tried to talk Nia into coming out. After nearly fifteen minutes of trying unsuccessfully, she called out, "Mrs. Patterson, can you help me?"

Nia's mother entered the room. She felt numb as she lay on the floor looking at her daughter. She reached for Nia's arm and, coaxing her, said, "Come on, baby. Mother's here. Come on out from under the bed."

Nia inched out, yielding to her mother's soft voice and gentle pulling. She climbed into her mother's lap as her mother sat on the floor, and she held tightly onto her mother with her arms stretched around her neck. She pressed her face into her mother's chest. Her mother rocked her from side to side as they sat on the floor. "I want you to be a good girl," her mother whispered into her ear while kissing her. "You know you'll always be my little girl. You know I told you about your birth mother whose belly you came out of. She wants you to be with her now."

Mrs. Patterson fought panic from overtaking her as she carried her baby down the stairs and out of the house. There was a thick fog all around her as she slowly sat Nia into the backseat of the worker's car and fastened the seat belt as she whispered, "I'll always love you." She felt as if she was part of a nightmare as she moved out of the car and closed the door to the upheld arms and frantic screams of her baby. Her stomach erupted, and she turned her head toward the ground because she felt as if she would vomit. As she stood and watched the car move farther and farther away, she felt her heart being pulled out of her body toward the car. She wanted to run behind the car. She screamed out, "No …," which was all she could do to catch up with the vehicle. She grabbed the railing along the steps barely in time to break her fall as her knees gave out, and she lowered her body onto the steps. She sat with her head down nearly in her lap sobbing until neighbors' voices and hands rubbing her arms and back broke through her desolation.

When she entered her house, the emptiness overtook her. She sat in her rocker, Nia's favorite chair. As she rocked, events that had twirled around them the last few weeks and lead to this tragic day replayed in her mind. She saw her little girl sitting on the steps and it was just like she was watching a movie.

***

Nia sat on the steps. Although she was supposed to be in her room, she would sit on the steps so that she could watch until the social worker stood up to leave. She would then run down the stairs and go into the kitchen. The kitchen was where she knew her mother would go to after the social workers visit. Nia would sit at the kitchen table and draw pictures, color, and play with her doll babies, all the while talking and laughing with her mother as her mother cooked, washed dishes, did laundry, and did whatever else she found to do that kept her in the kitchen for so long.

She had been used to social workers coming to her home and talking with her mother. They would ask questions about her. Sometimes her mother would call her to come and talk with the social worker. Then her mother would go into the kitchen while the social worker asked Nia questions as they sat at the dining room table. Nia would eat the cookies and drink from the glass of milk that her mother would have placed on the table before returning to the kitchen. The social worker would say, "Mrs. Patterson … umm … your foster mother says you're doing very well." Some of the questions seemed silly to Nia.

"Are you happy?" the social worker would ask, to which Nia would respond, "Yes!" Nia would jump as she answered the question.

"Is your foster mommy a good mommy?"

"You mean my mommy?" Nia would blurt out. Her eyes would be fixed on the social worker.

"Yes, I mean your mommy, the social worker would respond."

"Yep! She's a good mommy." Nia would giggle and then yell out, "The best mommy in the whole world!"

"How often does your mommy take you to the park?"

"Every day!"

"When you do something wrong, what does your mommy do?"

"She kisses me."

"Your mommy kisses you when you do something wrong?" The social worker's voice would have a surprised tone.

Nia would nod her head. "Uh huh. She tells me I did something bad and she doesn't want me to do it anymore. Then she tells me she loves me and that's why she wants me to do things good. Then she kisses me."

After the social worker would leave, Nia would ask, "Mommy, why are they always asking questions?"

"Because you're so special, and everyone loves you and knows what a strong little girl you are."

Mrs. Patterson had told Nia how the doctors didn't think she would live after she was born. She would tell her the story over and over again because Nia liked hearing the story.

"Sweetie, when I first saw you I didn't know what to think. You was so small and so sick. All sorts of tubes—some bigger than you—were all over your body. When I looked at your little face, you looked like an angel. You looked so sweet and peaceful. I knew you was strong. I said to myself, *We'll show them.* So I brought you home from the hospital. I had to do a lot of things to help you breathe, and you were on all kinds of medicines. When we'd go to the doctors, they'd say bad things. They told me you had only a few months to live. That made me cry, but I thought to myself, *I'm gonna make you the happiest baby until God calls you to be with him in heaven.* See, I was believing the doctors, but God had something else in mind."

She put her hands on her hips and smiled. "Now look at you! You my big little girl, and they said you would live only a few months. And the good Lord took you off all those medicines!"

Nia had asked how she got to be such a sick baby.

"You were born with poisons in your body."

"But how did the poisons get into my body, Mommy?" Nia had inquired, a puzzled look on her face.

"They got in you because they was in your birth mother's body."

"What's a birth mother?" Nia's eyebrows would crinkle as her eyes squinted when she didn't quite understand something as they did when she had asked that question. Her mother told her that her birth mother was the lady whose belly she was made in. When she grew too big for that lady's belly, the doctors took her out.

"Oh!" Nia had said the first time she'd heard the story. She'd been quiet for moments. Then she had looked up at her mother and asked, "How did the poisons get into my birth mother's body?"

Nia's mother did not respond for such a long time that Nia tapped her shoulder. Then her mother said, "She took the wrong medicine, and they hurt her body."

"Why did she take bad medicines that hurt her body?"

"Because she was sick and she was confused. She was too sick to take care of herself or you. That's why the social worker asked me to take you from the hospital and bring you to our home. You cried all the time when I first brought you home, so I would hold you in my arms and sit in the rocking chair and rock back and forth, and then you would stop crying. I'd sit with you in my arms in that chair for hours.

Even as Nia grew bigger and stronger, she loved to sit on her mother's lap in that rocker. She'd lay her head on her mother's chest and let her body go limp as her mother's big, warm arms would enfold her. It was as if their bodies flowed together as they rocked in the chair. As Nia got older, every evening when she'd hear the music that told her the news was coming on, she'd drop her dolls or whatever she was busy doing, and run into the living room. It was her special time to sit on her mother's lap because, while the news was on, her mother, who was normally very busy, would sit in the rocking chair and watch the television. Not too long after the news was over, they would walk upstairs. Nia would have a bath. When she was in bed, her mother would sing her a song, and then they'd say prayers together.

Things began to change when a social worker came to their home and stayed a long time talking to Mrs. Patterson. Nia was playing with her dolls at the top of the stairs. She really wanted to be downstairs, but she stayed at the top of the stairway, which was as close as she could be to her mother, since she had been directed to stay upstairs until the meeting was over. She was trying to be quiet, but her doll baby kept talking. So she had to whisper into her doll baby's ear, "Shush. Be quiet, Titi." But Titi was noisy and kept walking down the banister with Nia's hand clasped around her waist. She was a teenage doll baby, so she didn't want to listen. Nia had to tell her, "Stop! You can't go down there!" She sneaked down a few steps to keep Titi from going farther down the banister.

She heard that lady who was talking to her mother say, "Visits will begin this Saturday. Nia needs to get to know her family." There was such a long time when nobody spoke that Nia stepped down a step, bent forward, and peeked into the living room to make sure the lady was still there. When she saw the lady, she pounced down and sat on the step above the one she had been standing on. She was tired of being upstairs. It was time for her to go to the park and play. She and her mommy went to the park every day. Her mother would push her on the swing, and she would swing and swing and swing. It was as if she was a bird flying … as the swing would take her up into the sky. When she put her chin down onto her chest as she came back down, she'd feel the air swishing past her, and it would feel so good.

As Nia reflected on being at the park on a swing, she heard her mother say, "Go back upstairs, Nia!" She stomped up the steps. Now she really wanted that lady to leave!

Nia sat down on the top step with Titi. She told Titi, "I want that lady to leave!" Then she heard her mother say, "Please, let me tell her." When she heard the lady say, "Good-bye, Mrs. Patterson," Nia tiptoed down a few steps and peeked into the living room. She watched them go out the door. Immediately Nia ran down the stairs into the living room. She jumped on the couch and stared at the open porch door. Her mother came back into the house and locked the door behind her. Slowly she walked into the living room and sat in the rocking chair. Nia got off the couch and sat in her mother's lap.

"Nia," her mother said, very softly, "remember when I told you that I went to see you in the hospital? You were so tiny, as tiny as my hand. See my hand?" her mother said, holding up her palm for Nia to see.

"That tiny?" Nia held her hand to her mouth as she giggled.

"And you had tubes attached to your body?"

"Yep, like the pipe baby." Nia arched her back and tossed her head back.

"Don't lean back so far, Nia," her mother warned. "You could fall. Pay attention. Remember I told you the doctors said you was too sick and too tiny to live? But I brought you home and fed you every hour and gave you the medicines and rocked you in my arms all day long? And you got stronger and stronger. You a fighter. You a big girl now! We showed them, didn't we?"

"Yep!" Nia yelled, and she began rocking from side to side as her mother tried to talk to her.

"Be still, Nia, and listen!"

Nia stopped rocking. Her mother had turned her head away from her. She had seen her mother do that before when she was sad about something, so sad that tears would drop from her eyes. Nia patted her mother's chin with her hand so her mother would turn back and look at her. Her mother turned back toward her. Her eyes were glassy. Her mother closed her eyes and she opened them and her voice was low. She held out her hand and told Nia again how she'd looked when she first came home from the hospital. Nia giggled at the image of herself lying in her mother's arms like a doll. She was filled with warmth. She listened to the story she always loved—about how precious she'd been to her mother. She heard that term again—*foster mother*—and this time it caught in her head and felt heavy.

"I'm your mommy because I love you, and I been caring for you since you was a baby, but you know, precious, I'm your foster mother. Your real mother's family wants a chance to enjoy your too. You understanding me, baby?"

Nia answered jubilantly, "Yep!"

"Guess it's selfish of me to want to keep you all to myself." Nia's mother took in a sharp breath, and her belly quivered. Her mommy began crying. Nia was not sure why her mother was crying. She hugged her mother tightly.

"Oh, Mommy, don't cry. Everything's going to be okay." Quickly thoughts flowed through her mind of how she could make her mommy happy. She rubbed her mother's back with her hand as she shouted, "I'm going to go to dancing class, Mommy." Her mother had been telling her about starting dance lessons and had even taken her several times to visit the studio, but Nia had refused to go inside, so her mother had brought her back home each time.

That Saturday, a few days after the social worker's visit, and on the two Saturdays that followed, the social worker took Nia to the home of a woman and left her there. She was told the woman was her grandmother. Each time she returned home after a weekend visit, Nia would have nightmares and would wake up crying. She'd tell her mother how everyone was mean to her at that house. Nia told her that one lady, who everyone said was her Aunt Tina, looked at her and laughed. Aunt Tina looked strange to Nia because she had yellow hair with orange streaks in it sticking out all around her head. The hair came down all around her shoulders. Aunt Tina had huge round gold earrings hanging from her ears, and her lips were bright red. Nia had thought they were bleeding and had looked in horror at her as she was talking. Aunt Tina had turned away from her, wiggled her body, and said to a lady named Eva, "She a little strange acting, ain't she? She look terrified. I don't know what they do to her in that foster care."

Eva had smiled and said, "She okay. The foster mother she had took good care of her. It's a wonder how messed up I was with all that stuff I was putting into my body when I was carrying her, that she a normal little girl. She pretty, too."

Aunt Tina had added, "It's okay to be skinny when you an adult but little children should have some meat on their bones."

Eva, who everyone at Grandma Vern's house told her was her mother, laughed as she said, "She skinny just like me!"

Nia told her mother that the lady they told her to call Grandma Vern scared her when she had said to Eva, in a rough growl, "You was a skinny thing all your life. You was a skinny child, and you's a skinny grown-up. You skinny now 'cause you don't eat. You still putting them drugs into your body instead of food."

Eva, who had been sitting down, got up and pointed at Grandma Vern. "You have to go there! Don't you see my child right here? I'm eating here right now." Eva's voice got louder. "I'm eating all this food my big sis Tina cooked. You don't see me eating now? Don't you see this plate in my hand?"

The people in Grandma Vern's house were always fussing, Nia told her mother. And she told her that Grandma Vern would scream at her for no reason at all. Grandma Vern said that Nia acted as if someone was supposed to wait on her. She made her wash dishes and had her sweeping the kitchen floor every day. A girl they said was her cousin laughed at her and would say, "You not a princess here." She took Nia's doll, Titi, and popped her head off.

***

Mrs. Patterson let out a loud moan as the painful events leading to this tragic day continued to flash before her mind. She looked at the dining room table. Just yesterday she and Nia had sat at that table. Nia had listened as she called the social worker and told how the people at the home she'd been taking Nia to, were treating her.

The social workers words clamored through the phone, "It's normal for Nia to reject her family because she doesn't know them, but given time she'll find things she has in common with then. I'm glad you called because I planned to call you to let you know that the Family Court judge mandated that Nia be reunited with her family. I'll be coming tomorrow afternoon to move her."

She had dropped the phone as her body went limp. Nia had rushed around the table and put her arms around her, hugging onto her as she kept repeating, "It's O.K. mommy. It's O.K. Don't be afraid!"

Mrs. Patterson saw a dark veil covering over her. Again she felt ice clogging up her veins. It was the same feeling she had felt as she had washed and ironed Nia's clothes the past night as she had carefully packed her suitcase. She had to fight to keep moving then. And now, as she sat in the rocking chair staring … her body was frozen. She could not move.

Chapter 2 Nia's Initiation

Pulled out the front door of Grandma Vern's house, Nia nearly fell as she stumbled down the concrete steps outside the house. Her legs were awkwardly moving to keep up with the fast pace of Grandma Vern. Nia's arm flung through the air and knocked against a slender tree. She grabbed onto a branch of the tree as she twisted her other hand and snatched it from her grandmother's grip. She threw that arm around the tree and held tightly onto the tree. "No! No! I'm not going with you! I'm not going with you! I want my mommy," Nia screamed. Fear was imprinted on her face. Her eyes were wide open and glassy, and her gaze rapidly shifted from side to side. Her cheeks were puffed, and her lips were slightly parted and trembling as she struggled to breathe.

Grandma Vern quickly turned toward Nia and tried to grab her hand. But Nia held tightly onto the tree. She pressed her body into it so that the rugged surface of the tree was imprinted on her face. "No! no! I'm not going with you!" Then Grandma Vern yanked her arm so forcefully that her hand scraped across the tree. Blood oozed out of her hand.

Grandma Vern bent down in front of her and looked into her face. "Look at me!" She pushed Nia's chin up.

Nia tried to look at her grandmother through the wetness in her eyes. Although the face in front of her looked muddy, she could see the woman's lips moving. Grandma Vern's voice lowered, "Whether you like it or not, you're living with me now, and I don't play with children. I didn't play with my own, so I ain't taking no foolishness from you. I have a mind to break off that branch that you were hanging onto so tightly and tear your butt up with it. That's how I do children." Her voice was raspy. "Let me see that hand!" Grandma Vern stared at the hand for a moment then opened her handbag and removed a tube of ointment and some tissues. She put some ointment on the tissues and placed them into Nia's bleeding hand. "Now hold those tissues tight, and you keep that hand in your pocket! Come on, before we miss the bus. I don't want no more trouble out of you, you hear?" Nia tried to nod her head while sniffling and trying to catch her breath.

Grandma Vern raised her voice, "Do you understand me?"

"Yes." The word finally escaped from Nia's lips.

Nia shivered from the cold while she stood in one spot waiting for the bus. Her hand was aching. Even though she tried hard to stop crying, because she feared Grandma Vern would hit her, tears kept seeping out the corners of her eyes. The sharp chill in the air also caused tears to seep from her eyes. She felt as if she was dreaming. It was as if she was outside of herself watching everything going on as she climbed the huge steps onto the bus alongside Grandma Vern. Surely her mother would wake her up any moment and rock her in her arms.

When they got off the bus they walked and walked. To Nia it seemed as if she would never stop walking. Finally Grandma Vern led her into a big building and into a large room that was packed with people. Nia ran alongside her grandmother, who tightly held her hand as she rushed to get a seat. A man seated next to the seat they were headed toward got up, and as her grandmother sat down, she pulled Nia into the seat the man had emptied.

"Vernetta Glenn!" boomed above the noise in the room.

Grandma Vern got up and grabbed Nia's hand. They followed a lady to an office. Once in the office, Grandma Vern let go of Nia's hand and pointed to a chair and said, "Sit there!" Nia sat in the chair.

"Hello, Mrs. Glenn. I'm Hazel Chapman. I'm the caseworker assigned to your case." The worker sat down in the seat behind the desk. "Mrs. Glenn, you called this office saying your granddaughter is now living with you. This is your granddaughter?" Vernetta Glenn nodded.

"Do you have her birth certificate?"

Nia's grandmother opened her handbag, shuffled through some papers, and pulled out an envelope, which she handed to Ms. Chapman. Ms. Chapman opened the envelope and stared at the paper she had unfolded.

"When did she come to your home?"

"She been coming on the weekends for three weeks now."

"But what day did she come to live permanently?"

"The social worker brought her yesterday."

"I need the name of the social worker and her agency so I can verify this information."

Vernetta Glenn dug into her pocketbook again and handed Ms. Chapman a piece of paper. "This here's her information."

"Are there any other changes in your household?" Ms. Chapman asked.

"No."

"How's your daughter doing? Is she sticking to the rehab program?"

"She doing just fine."

"Well, maybe getting to know her daughter will help her." Ms. Chapman looked at Nia. "Is she okay? Is she crying?"

"Yes, ma'am. She been crying since she woke up."

Nia could feel the worker staring at her, although she kept her head down and her hand in her pocket clinched around the tissues, as she had been told to do. Ms. Chapman's voice grew soft. "Hello, Nia." Nia did not respond. "You're not going to speak to me?" Nia remained silent.

The worker turned her focus toward Vernetta Glenn. "Since your granddaughter is now residing in your home, an increase in your benefits will be reflected on your next check, and a medical card for her will be mailed to you. Is there anything else, Mrs. Glenn?"

"How much will the increase be? This child's growing. She was very sick when she was born, and sometimes she's sick now. She takes a lot of care."

"You will get the welfare benefit for another child."

"That ain't enough. Why don't I get what you give the foster parents? You give foster parents hundreds of dollars a month to take care of children. That woman who was taking care of her was getting almost a thousand dollars a month."

Ms. Chapman said, "Ms. Glenn, that's another state agency with their own criteria. You'll have to go to them for the answers to those questions."

Silence covered over the room for a few moments. Nia looked up to see the worker staring at Grandma Vern. Then the worker spoke. "Mrs. Glenn, this is York County Social Services. Your grant is based on the number of dependents in your home. If you get foster care money, Nia will come off your welfare grant. Were you told you would be getting money for foster care services for Nia?"

"No."

"Did they tell you to come here for help?"

"Yes, the lady told me Nia would make my amount increase."

"I'm not real knowledgeable about the child welfare foster care programs, but it sounds to me that they did not consider you as a foster parent, or they wouldn't have referred you to this office. I suggest you check with the child welfare social worker who told you to come here."

"Well, I took her in because I thought I could get that kind of assistance like the foster parents get. She got all kind of problems. She got emotional problems. Look at her. She cry all the time."

"She is your grandchild. Do you want me to hold off on your application until you find out whether you can get foster parent assistance?"

"No! No! Leave that be." Grandma Vern got up and grabbed Nia's hand. Nia's other hand swung out of her pocket, and the bloodied tissues fell on the floor.

The social worker looked shocked, "What's wrong with her hand?"

"Got it scratched up playing round a tree." As they walked out of the welfare office, Vernetta Glenn squeezed Nia's hand till it hurt as she mumbled to herself, "They tell me one thing then they say something else. I should have known not to trust these lying ..." She didn't finish her sentence, but Nia knew she meant something bad.

Nia stopped walking. She saw a car that looked like her mother's car. Vernetta Glenn quickly stooped down in front of her and said, "Do you think I have time for your foolishness? I'm your Grandma Vern. You keep up with me when I'm walking."

As they walked, Grandma Vern continued to mumble complaints directed at the welfare caseworker. They stopped suddenly where there was a group of people standing, and they waited along with them for the bus.

After boarding the bus, Nia sat in a small space next to her grandmother. Her heart raced as she stared expectantly at people getting onto the bus who seemed to be the size and complexion of her mother. But as each person headed toward the back of the bus, she'd see that that person wasn't her mother. Neither Nia nor her grandmother could stop Nia's tears as she rode the bus back to her grandmother's house.

Chapter 3 Grandma Vern's House

At Grandma Vern's house, Nia wasn't allowed to say anything about the only mother she'd known, Mrs. Patterson. Twice she got smacked when she asked her grandmother if she could go to her mommy.

"No!" her grandmother snapped. "Eva will come by when she can."

"No!" Nia snapped right back. "I want to see my *real* mommy. I want my mommy!"

Her grandmother hit her again and said, "Your real mommy is Eva. Go to your room and stay there until I tell you when to come out."

Nia went to the room and got into the bed she had slept the night before. The room that was now her room was depressing. It had dirty white walls. Clothes and broken toys lay all over the floor. There were two other beds in the room. Tiffany, who she was told was her cousin, slept in one of the beds. She was told that Tyron, another cousin whom she hadn't met yet, slept in the other bed. There was one dresser that had a drawer missing.

She thought about her home where she had her own room with pink walls with faces of rabbits, turtles, baby chicks and other animals that her mother had painted on the walls because her mother was artistic. Nia and her mother loved animals. Since she was very young she used to look at pictures of animals in storybooks that her mother would read to her. When she got excited about a particular animal, like a giraffe because of its long neck and spotted body, next thing she knew, her mother would get up and go to the closet next to the stairs. She'd pull out brightly colored paint cans and brushes, and they'd head upstairs. Nia smiled as she remembered how she'd sit on the floor and watch her mommy move her arm back and forth splashing paint onto the wall until she'd see the animal coming right out of the wall! That huge giraffe was overlooking her bed smiling down at her. All the animals her mother drew on her walls had smiles on their faces. And there were all sorts of stuffed animals in her room. Her favorite was Barney Bear who was just about as big as she was. He sat on the floor next to her bed. Even the curtains in her room had animals printed on them.

Nia lay on the bed with her face to the wall rocking back and forth as she whispered, "Mommy! Mommy! Mommy!" Tiffany heard her and laughed at her. She then ran out the room loudly repeating, "Mommy, mommy, mommy. She's calling her mommy."

A boy's voice overpowered Tiffany's. "You my new cousin? Yeah, you my new cousin 'cause you in the new bed. My name is Tyron."

Nia stopped rocking.

"Why you calling your mommy? I had another mommy too. Look … look … look …" Tyron said excitedly. Nia turned toward him.

Tyron had his shirt lifted up, and she saw a strange black drawing. "I got a tattoo! My real mommy did this. That's why they took me and Tiffany away from her. They said my mommy was bad for doing this, so they gave us another mommy. When we'd come to see Grandma, she didn't like us calling our foster mommy 'mommy' either. She'd shout, 'Your mommy's Tina!' Then Grandma Vern came and got us and brought us here with her. Don't be sad. Grandma's not so mean. Tomorrow my real mommy's coming. My mommy can cook real good. Come here. I want to show you something." He patted her arm. Nia got off the bed.

"Can you read?" Tyron asked as he sat on the floor and picked up a book that was on the floor. He tugged at her pants and said, "Come on. Sit down." Nia sat next to him on the floor and stared at the picture in the book.

"That there's a dog." A big smile spread across Tyron's face, and his eyes glittered. "I'm gonna have a dog one day. Mommy says when she gets a house, I'm gonna move with her, and we're going to have a big dog. You like dogs?" Nia nodded. "Then you can come and live with us too."

Nia's eyes shifted and stared ahead, yet she was not seeing anything. Then a tear sat in the corner of her eye. Her focus suddenly shifted back to Tyron because of the excitement in his voice, "Look! Look! Look! You see that big elephant? I want to ride on an elephant's back one day. Do you?" Nia looked at the elephant and nodded. She felt as if she was in a strange place with a little boy who kept pulling her to go with him. He was a nice, friendly boy, and she let him lead her. They sat looking at the pictures as Tyron turned the pages and explained each picture. He turned to her. "How old are you?"

"Six years old," Nia responded.

Tyron smiled and said, "I'm older than you. I'm seven years old. So I'm your big-brother cousin, right?"

The door swung open. Grandma Vern held the doorknob as she looked down at them. "You kids put down that book and come on and eat your lunch." Nia began to cry.

"What you crying for now? Shut up that crying," Grandma Vern roughly commanded. Nia tried to stop, but she had a hard time catching her breath. "Wash your hands first," her grandmother ordered as she left the room.

Tyron looked at her. "Why you crying? You scared of Grandma? Don't be scared. She won't bother you if you don't do nothing wrong. Come on." Tyron was trying to lift Nia up from her seated position on the floor. When Nia stood up, she wiped her nose and eyes with her arms. Tyron took her hand and they went to the bathroom. Tyron turned on the water, and they both held their hands over the sink.

Tyron giggled, "You can't just hold your hands out. You have to rub them like this." Nia's stared at his hands as he quickly moved them back and forth.

Then Tyron took her hands, rubbed the soap bar against them, and instructed her, "Move your hands." Nia rubbed her hands feeling very strange and sad. Her mother had always been around her when she was washing her hands.

Tyron turned around in the small bathroom and began wiping his hands on a towel that hung from a rack. "Now pat your hands dry. I see I'm gonna have to teach you everything." Tyron shook his head. "You don't know nothing. Why they didn't teach you when you was here before? I would have taught you if I was here." He smiled widely. "But I'll teach you now 'cause you my new cousin."

Nia followed Tryon into the kitchen. The scent of toast and the sight of tomato soup reminded her of home, and for a moment she felt warmth flow through her. They walked toward the table and sat down. Normally Grandma Vern's cooking was so different from her mother's. Grandma Vern mostly gave them cereal out of boxes for breakfast, peanut butter and jelly sandwiches for lunch, and mostly beans and franks or hamburgers for dinner. Lots of times she opened things from cans and put them into a pot to warm up. She'd spoon food out of the pots into their plates. There had been a few things Grandma Vern cooked that Nia liked, but she could never get a second helping of what she liked. Grandma Vern didn't believe in second helpings.

Nia looked at Tyron's plate after she had finished her food.

"You want my toast?" he asked.

Nia continued to stare at his toast. He put his toast on her plate.

"You want some of my soup?" Nia nodded. Tyron put his plate by hers and was beginning to spoon soup into her bowl when Grandma Vern's arm suddenly appeared between them. She shifted Tyron's bowl back in front of him. "You eat your own food. She had the same amount you had!" Nia began to cry. Her grandmother snapped at her. "Shut up and finish eating your food!" Nia stared at the toast until Grandma Vern left the kitchen. Then she slowly ate the piece of toast.

Nia hurried to her room when she finished eating. She wanted to get back into bed and go to sleep. Everything was strange to her now. She felt as if she was in an unending nightmare. She wanted to sleep because, when she was asleep, she would dream about her mother. When she got into the bed, she rocked back and forth and whispered, "Mommy, Mommy. Where are you, Mommy? I been looking all over for you! I love you, Mommy. I want to be with you in our rocking chair, hugging you, Mommy. I'm your baby. I'm your strong little girl. I'll go to the dance school. I'll be good. I'll listen to you, Mommy. I promise."

Tiffany's voice overpowered her thoughts. Nia turned away from the wall and sat up, her legs dangling with her toes barely touching the floor. Nia watched Tiffany jump onto her own bed and begin playing with her dolls. Suddenly, she began screaming at her dolls. The two dolls she had in her hands began fighting each other. Then Tiffany threw both dolls down onto the floor, barely missing Tyron, who was sitting on the floor reading. Tiffany moved off her bed and walked around the room on tiptoe. She twisted her hips and tossed her head back and forth, which made her long braids swing from side to side. Nia stared at her. Tiffany turned toward Nia and nearly closed her eyes as she glared at her. "What you looking at?" Nia dropped her eyes and stared at the floor.

As she sternly looked at Nia, Tiffany pointed her finger at papers on the floor. "Pick up those papers and throw them in the trash." Quickly Nia moved to where the papers were and picked them up and put them in the short trash basket in the room. Then Tiffany said, "Get back over there and make up your bed." Nia went to her bed and began fixing the covers.

Tyron looked up from his book and said to Nia, "You don't have to listen to her. She's not your mother!"

"You shut up before I kick your ass!" Tiffany quickly returned.

"Ooh, I'm telling," Tyron shouted. "Grandma said you not supposed to say that!"

He ran toward the door, but Tiffany grabbed his arm. "Please, please, please. Don't tell Grandma. Look I got some money. I'll give you some if you don't tell."

Tyron yanked his hand from her, "I'm telling!" he yelled. Tiffany punched him. "Ouch!"

Grandma Vern appeared in the room with a strap in her hand and started hitting everyone. Terror ran through Nia as the belt struck her arms and legs. She didn't run around like the others. It didn't occur to her to run, because she had never been hit before. Grandma Vern raised her voice over their screaming, "I ain't putting up with all that noise that was going on in here. There's to be no fighting. I'm the only one who does any fighting round here. You hear?" Tiffany and Tyron nodded their heads through their tears and cried out, "Yes, Grandma." Nia was silent as she scooted back toward the wall and crossed her arms over her aching, trembling body.

***

Even through the darkness of the room, Nia could see the outlines of the calendar that was above Tiffany's bed. Tiffany had gotten one of their uncles to nail it onto the wall. She had done this so that she could cross off each day, and she would know when the day was Saturday. On that day there would be no school, and she and Tyron would likely visit her mother. But Nia knew how to know days from a calendar too because her mother had shown her, teaching her about how each new day had a name and how each week started with the day called Sunday. She had loved Sundays with her mother, who would sing as they made their way to the park. And now three Sundays had passed since she'd lived in this place.

Nia squeezed her eyes shut, wishing she could just sleep. She knew the beds across from her would remain empty for a few nights because her cousins had gone to visit their mother, and the silence felt heavy, like a blanket over her face.

A dull, clamoring sound emerged over the stillness that surrounded her. At first she thought it was the sound from her dreams. Then she opened her eyes as she realized she was awake, and that was the sound from her mother's car. When her mother turned the key off, the car would start making clinkering, knocking, noises, as if it was mad it had been turned off. That's what her mother had said, and they had always laughed when the car started those noises. Yes, she knew that sound, and it was here. A bubble of joy rose through her, and she popped up from the bed. She had known this nightmare couldn't last!

As quietly and carefully as she could, Nia inched out of her room and peeked into the living room, feeling somehow that she had to move just right. She saw Grandma Vern open the door, and she heard her mother's voice say, "Please let me just hug her."

Nia raced through the living room toward the front door, but Grandma Vern had closed it. When Nia got to the door, she banged on it and reached for the knob. Grandma Vern grabbed at her, but she kicked at her grandmother and screamed as she frantically tried to open the door.

"Mommy! Mommy! Mommy!" she yelled, and then ran to the window and swished the curtain aside. She saw her mother wipe her eyes as she got into the car. Nia banged at the window. She felt her grandmother's hand on her arm, and she screamed and kicked and flung her hands around as hard as she could. Suddenly she felt her body flying through the air.

***

When Nia opened her eyes, a woman's bright face was smiling at her. "Well, little lady, I'm happy to see that you are doing better. I'm just going to check your temperature. Open your mouth so I can put the thermometer in." Clamping down on the thermometer, Nia looked around the room. She saw bright yellow wallpaper and some pretty toys piled up in a corner. She was someplace different. The lady took the thermometer out of her mouth and held it up. "You're doing great." Her eyes followed the lady, who picked up a folder that was attached to the end of the bed. She scribbled on it and set it back down. Nia felt happy inside. She thought that she had been brought to this place for her mother to pick her up. Her mother used to tell the story of how she'd brought her home from a hospital.

A man Nia guessed was a doctor came into the room and said, "You gave us a scare." He picked up the folder and studied it for a while, then set it back down. "I have good news for you. You'll be able to go home as soon as you eat something."

Nia felt excitement rush through her. The nurse raised the bed and placed a tray in front of her. "Eat up. Your family's here to take you home." Nia quickly turned her head toward the door. She saw her grandmother standing by the door. She began to cry.

"Now what caused this?" the nurse asked, putting her hands on her hips. "Don't you like to eat?" Nia continued to cry. The nurse turned to her grandmother and said, "Maybe you can calm her down." The nurse left the room.

Nia's grandmother came toward her and leaned over the bed. In a low-toned voice she said, "Girl, you better eat some of this food so we can get on up out of here." Nia struggled to take a bite of the sandwich, but she couldn't stop crying, and the food tumbled out of her mouth. Her grandmother shook her head and whispered, "If you don't hurry up and eat this food, I'll tear your butt up some more when you get home." Then Grandma Vern sat down on the chair next to the bed.

Chapter 4 School

When Nia started school, she did exactly what her teacher told her to do. Quietly she would sit at her desk and complete all the work she was assigned. She wouldn't move unless she was told to move. She studied what she was told to study.

The class she was in was not orderly when she began her school year. Her first grade teacher, Ms. Chaney, had a hard time getting some of the children to stay at their desks and remain quiet. One little boy in particular couldn't stop fidgeting. At times he would suddenly jump up out of his seat and run around the classroom.

Nia could hear the complaints of the parents as they stood outside the partially opened door of her classroom waiting for the dismissal of their children. At times their angry faces flashed before her.

"Our children black and ghetto!" a mother shouted.

Turning her head and twisting her lips in annoyance, another mother said, "She's scared of our children! She too busy yelling at the kids and running after them. My child ain't learning a thing."

With a determined look on her face, a third parent quietly commented, "I'm gonna complain to the principal. He needs to put my son in another class so he can learn something! There's enough things he gonna have to fight through in life to make it. He needs his education!"

A few weeks after school began, as Nia sat at her desk listening to the fragmented sentences of her teacher, who would always stop her discussion to tell some student to behave, a dark-brown-skinned, heavy-set woman, who walked with a sway to her body, strode into the classroom. The moment she walked in, a hush fell over the class, and the children followed her with their eyes. Ms. Chaney introduced her as Miss Bertha and told them Miss Bertha was a teacher's assistant, and she would be helping out in their classroom. Miss Bertha kept a stern look on her face all the time. She never spoke. All she did, all day long, was sit, arms folded, in a chair beside the coat closet that was along the wall on one side of the classroom. Although Miss Bertha didn't have a strap in her hand, something about how she looked and held herself suggested to the children that she did have a strap somewhere under her skirt and that she would not hesitate to use it. With her presence, the class was magically transformed. Everyone sat in his or her seat and didn't move unless the teacher told them to move. On a few occasions, Jared, the one boy who seemed to have a particularly hard time sitting still, jumped up. The whole class would laugh except Nia who never laughed. Miss Bertha never said a word. She would go over to Jared, grip his elbow firmly, and march him out of the classroom. What the class imagined was happening to Jared terrified them. They kept quiet and kept their eyes focused on the blackboard. Everyone knew that Miss Bertha would soon return and that Jared wouldn't be with her.

All of Nia's grades were one hundred. Ms. Chaney liked her and often used her as an example when she talked about good students. Grandma Vern liked the reports that came from her school. She'd say, "Look at that. She smart. She get all these one hundreds like her grandma. I got high grades too when I was your age." That was as far as Grandma Vern went in making compliments.

Children in Nia's class were always trying to make friends with her because they thought she was smart. When Candice jumped in front of her smiling and giggling and then whispered, "James likes you," Nia just stared at her until she ran off. Something had closed down inside of her so that she felt like a statue. She couldn't laugh. She couldn't run around and play games and skip and hop and jump around like the other children. And she didn't want to.

There was one girl, however, who, like Tyron, pierced through the invisible barricade that surrounded her. While walking to the bus stop one morning, she heard footsteps running behind her, and they slowed down next to her and walked alongside her. After that morning, she would hear the footsteps every day. The girl would walk with her and stand beside her at the bus stop. Neither girl spoke. The other children at the bus stop would yell, curse, pop bubblegum, and chase one another.

At the beginning of the second week, the girl turned as they stood at the bus stop and said, "My name is Razonya. What's your name?"

"Nia." Her own voice startled her.

Even when Razonya's family moved away from Nia's street, she was still on the same bus route as Nia. Razonya would board the bus a few stops after Nia's. When the bus pulled up at Razonya's stop, Razonya would look along the windows of the bus until she saw Nia, then she would smile at her. Nia never smiled back, but she would continue to stare at Razonya. There were a lot of children at Razonya's bus stop, and like Razonya, they were Hispanic. Yelling in Spanish and English, they would bring onto the bus a new wave of noise. But Razonya would quietly move through the bus to where Nia was seated and sit beside her.

Nafesia, who was a girl in Nia's class, kept threatening her. She'd call Nia stuck up, and some others in her class would pout and say, "Yeah! Yeah! She stuck up." In the schoolyard during recess, Nafesia would point her finger at Nia and say, "You think you so smart. You ain't smart. I bet you can't even fight." She'd circle around Nia, mocking her walk and laughing at the clothes she wore. "Oh, you think you 'Miss It.' Look at them sorry shoes. About to get left behind they so tired looking." The other children, particularly two girls who hung around Nafesia, would laugh. Nafesia picked on her nearly every day, yet Nia never responded. She didn't feel anything. She didn't feel anger or fear, not even embarrassment. Although she saw the girl hobbling around her, the words the girl yelled out dissolved in mid air. Nia would just stare at her. Nafesia interpreted Nia's lack of response as a snub.

As the weather warmed, jackets flew onto the schoolyard ground during recess. "On your mark, get set … go!" commanded attention. Girls danced around in groups preparing for dance competitions. An excitement filled the atmosphere as the warming air brought endless outdoor activity for everyone.

Nia and Razonya were about to board the homebound school bus one afternoon. Razonya was breathing hard because she had run fast so that she wouldn't miss the bus. She'd had to hurry because she had been in a racing competition with a few other girls, and she had won. Cheering voices were still screaming out her name. Nia was about to board the bus when she felt a thump on her back. As she turned to look around, she saw Nafesia right behind her. Before she could even think about what was happening, she saw Razonya grab Nafesia's braids and yank them so hard that Nafesia fell to the ground. Razonya jumped on Nafesia and began smacking her and punching her in the face. Then she put her hands around Nafesia's throat and banged her head onto the concrete pavement. Nia shook her head. Inside she was screaming, "No! No! No! Stop! Stop!" But the words would not flow out of her mouth. Suddenly an exchange formulated in her mind and she envisioned her grandmother yanking at her and banging her head onto the ground.

The bus driver rushed off the bus and lifted Razonya off Nafesia. Strangely, Razonya was not told to go to the office, and, except for one boy, Angelo, who was a fat boy with a big mouth, nobody even said anything about the fight. Angelo turned to Nafesia and said, "You better not come over here. I'll get Razonya to beat your butt again." Nia and Razonya sat next to each other on the bus quietly as they always did.

When Nia stepped off the school bus, she walked slowly toward her block. When she turned the corner to her street, her eyes opened wide and her heart pounded hard as she strained to look down the block at the front window of the house where she lived. Her entire body relaxed as the dread of going home lessened when she saw that the curtains were closed. The closed curtains meant Grandma Vern was not home.

Placing one foot squarely in front of the other, she walked along the street. A tinge of warmth trickled through her as she thought of Razonya protecting her. Soft air wisped across her face, and a quick vision flashed before her mind of her swinging high into the sky. And with the vision of swinging, she saw her mother behind her pushing the swing back into the air each time it lowered. Instantly she rolled up her hands into fist and put them over her eyes. She stopped walking. When she removed her fist from her eyes, they were wet. She looked up at the tree standing beside her. It was so big and strong and never moved. She stood by the tree a few minutes. Then her vision jumped from tree to tree along her street. There were only three, and tiny, light-green leaves were sprouting on their branches. Her head slightly turned as her eyes followed the pattern of the houses up one side of the street and down the other. The houses on that street were two-story brick houses, most of which were attached to one another. There were a few houses, like Grandma Vern's, that were unattached, although they were square like the others. Those houses had two families living in them, one upstairs and one downstairs. All the houses had four steps leading to the front door and small yards to one side of the steps.

It was garbage collection day. Nia walked past empty trashcans on the sidewalk, some standing and some toppled over into the street. The lids were tossed everywhere. She wrinkled her nose because of the stench of trash that had missed its mark and was lying on the street.

Quickly Nia crossed the street. Her heart beat hard. Out of the corner of her eye, she watched, because she was approaching a yard where a vicious dog lived. He would often bark at her. Even though there was a fence around that yard, Nia was frightened by how angry the dog sounded. She thought that one day the dog would jump over the fence and eat her up.

As she walked toward a house that was just a few front yards before her home, her mind flashed on the elderly lady who would always tap at the window as she was passing by. She had seen the lady briefly, but she had never stopped or spoken to her. Now she cautiously slowed down watching from the corner of her eye, because the lady was sitting on her porch, and she spoke. "Well, Miss Nia. Isn't it a beautiful day? I love springtime. The sweet soft breeze puffing all around. The birds tweeting."

Nia froze in her tracks. Slowly she turned her head, surprised that the lady knew her name. Nia watched the lady's face crinkle into a smile. "Well, I finally got your attention, little lady. My name is Mrs. Peters."

Nia stared at Mrs. Peters. Mrs. Peters had long lines down each side of her dark face, and her small body was curved forward as she sat in her wheelchair.

"I know a secret," Mrs. Peters said in a soft wavering voice. "I'll tell you if you won't tell anyone." Nia stood motionless. "Well, since you're still here, I take it that means you want to hear it. I knew your mother when she was a little girl."

Nia's heart pounded. She wanted to walk away, but somehow Mrs. Peters kept her attention with her shaky, whispering voice. "She never listened. That's how she got into all the trouble she got into. Your grandmother would beat her something fierce. Neighbors would bang on the door after hearing the lashing and the child hollering. I was one of them. We'd shout to her, 'Stop beating that child!' Your grandmother would yell back, 'Mind your own damn business!'" Mrs. Peterson began laughing, a soft laugh. Her whole body shook slightly. She stopped suddenly and her voice got firmer, "But she'd stop beating on your momma. Once or twice someone mentioned calling child protective services, but no one ever made the call. We was all scared of your grandma. Everyone knew she had a gun, and she was mean." Mrs. Peters sighed. "But I can see you're a good girl. You not like your mother or your grandmother. You can come to visit me anytime.

I'll tell you lots of stories." She leaned back into her wheelchair. "Bye, now. Go on home. Go on. I don't want you to get in trouble for being late." She shook her head and added, "I know how your grandma is."

Nia stared at Mrs. Peters as she walked away. She knew she didn't have to rush, because her grandmother was not home. She almost fell over a trashcan lid, but she looked down quickly and moved her foot back in time.

Nia sat down on the steps in front of her house. She pulled out her books to do her homework, which was what Grandma Vern had told her to do until either she or Tiffany came home. After she did some of her homework, she looked up at the sky. She was glad it wasn't raining, snowing, or freezing cold. When it was, she would huddle in the corner against the door covering her face with her backpack. If someone from the family upstairs came home, they would let her inside so she could sit on the hallway steps. The lady of the house upstairs generally worked late, but when she was home, she'd come down, open the front door, and say, "Nia, you'll freeze out there. Come on inside. Do you want to come up to my apartment while you wait for your grandmother?" Nia always shook her head. Her grandmother had told her that she was never to go into anyone's house unless she was with her.

Nia wished Tyron would come. Sometimes Tyron would join her on the steps, but it was not often because, most of the time, he'd return home from school later than Tiffany. Grandma Vern would try to get out of him why he was always so late. He would tell her that the teacher let him out late. Then she would ask Tiffany if his story was true. Tiffany would look up at her grandmother and say, "Sometimes, Grandma, his teacher lets him out late because he has to stay for detention." The matter would be dropped until the next time Tyron came home extremely late. Tiffany's response to any situation seemed to calm Grandma Vern, even though she was often lying.

Although it was true that Tyron got many detentions that caused him to return home from school late, he would often hang out with his friends after school. At night he'd whisper in the dark what he'd been up to. He'd talk excitedly about what had happened during his day, because he knew Nia would be awake, and he knew Tiffany would be asleep. Tiffany could not keep her eyes open once she went to bed. In fact, often they could hear her softly snoring.

Tyron would go to his friends' houses where they would eat, roughhouse, or play video games. Tyron had told Tiffany that the mother of one of his friends always gave them snacks and even helped him and her son with their homework. When Tyron saw how his grandmother didn't complain when he was over at that boy's house, he would tell her that he had been at that boy's house no matter what he'd actually been doing.

As she sat on the steps, Nia felt a spark of excitement ripple through her when she saw Tyron's figure emerge onto their street. He was walking with Ricky, who lived near the middle of their street. As they always did, Tyron and Ricky laid their book bags on the ground and stooped down. Tyron yelled out, "On your mark, get set, go!" They raced side by side to Ricky's fence. It looked like a tie to Nia, as it always did. Even though they could hardly catch their breath, they laughed as they slowly walked back to their book bags.

"I won!" Ty yelled out, looking at Ricky.

"No, I won!" Ricky shouted back.

They never agreed on who had actually won. The boy waved at Tyron as he walked into his front yard. Tyron swung his arm up and waved back. Nia watched him toss around his book bag and jump over trashcans. Then he furiously ran along the sidewalk, trying to outrun cars.

A wide grin spread across Tyron's face as he approached their front yard. Nia felt her insides glowing. Sitting on the steps with Tyron was her favorite time. Tyron seemed to enjoy trying to make her smile, because normally she'd never smile. Now he jumped in front of her and shouted, "What am I now?" He made a long tube out of his notebook and held it in front of his nose. Slowly he moved his head up and down and tossed his body sluggishly from side to side. Nia couldn't stop the laughing bubbles that erupted from inside her belly and tumbled out of her mouth. Then Tyron threw his book down, bent his knees, and dangled his hands along the ground. He started scratching his body while hobbling around.

After his silliness, he plopped down on the step next to Nia and laid his head on her shoulder. Immediately he fell asleep.

Much as she thought she would stay awake, she always fell asleep along with Ty when he rested his head on her shoulder. The sound of footsteps and people talking woke her up. She looked up thinking it was Grandma Vern and Tiffany coming, but she looked into the faces of strangers—a man and a woman who smiled at her as they walked past her. She peeked down at Ty, whose mouth was open because he was so deeply asleep. She felt warmth with Ty right next to her. Ty liked her even if nobody else in her new family did. Her mind drifted into a twilight; she was somewhat awake and somewhat asleep. She replayed what one of her aunts had said, laughing, "Eva, what ugly man you been with make that ugly child? Don't you got more sense than to lay up with a ugly man, 'cause you get caught holding an ugly baby? That's why you threw the child away." They all thought it was so funny. "Wasn't about no drugs," her aunt had continued. "You just didn't want to bring that ugly baby home. I saw her when she was born. I went up there to the hospital. She look like a rat."

Tiffany's loud voice woke her up. "You look like two little twin lovebirds." Then Tiffany kicked Tyron's foot. "Wake up, Ty."

When they walked into the house, they went into their bedroom. It was what Grandma Vern had told them to do when they returned home from school and she wasn't there. "Go to your room and do your homework until I come home." Her words always hung in the air hovering over them. Grandma Vern came home moments after they'd settled in their room, and there were people with her, some of their relatives. Tiffany rushed out of the room, and Nia listened to her hurried talk about needing to practice for a class play with one of her classmates. She soon left the house. Nia was relieved she was gone. It was quiet when Tiffany wasn't in their room.

Nia sat on the floor in front of her bed with her legs crossed and a book in her lap. She watched Ty as he marched tiny toy soldiers along the wooden floor. The relatives all thought she and Tyron looked alike. Sometimes they'd tease their mothers and say something funny had been going on. They'd say to Aunt Tina, "Who you say Tyron daddy is?" They'd turn around to Eva and say, "Who you say Nia daddy is?" They'd laugh. "Them two brother and sister for sure!" Tiffany would get mad and stomp out the room. Ty began calling Nia his little sister. Nia didn't like to hear their talk about looks, because everyone other than her mother said she was homely.

Eva would fuss back at them. "Shhh, she can hear you. Don't talk about my child like that. She'll be fine. Anyway, I'd rather a homely, mind-her-own-business child than a smart-behind pretty child who think she's grown."

Yet, even though they all agreed that Nia and Ty looked just alike, there was never a word said about Ty being ugly or homely. Instead, they'd say, "Ty, my little man," or, "Ty got it going on. Ty take care of business."

Ty got his reputation of being a "hustler" early on, because he would rush around the house when relatives were over, picking up papers and napkins that were always falling on the floor and cleaning out ashtrays that brimmed over with ashes and cigarette butts. He emptied wastebaskets that filled up quickly with soda cans, beer cans, and candy wrappers. He tied up and took out the garbage in the kitchen regularly when someone—generally Aunt Tina—was cooking. They'd give him fifty cents, sometimes even a dollar. Someone would say, "Look at that straight-up hustler."

Tyron stopped marching his soldier men along the floor near his bed and began talking excitedly commanding his men around, "Take cover … take cover! Boom! Boom!" Nia turned her head. She did not want to think of fighting. She didn't want to have dreams about fighting, and she didn't want to be afraid.

That evening as she sat on her bed with her back against the wall, her eyes followed shadows that passed along the wall. They were ghosts trying to take her with them. Tiffany entered the room. "What you trembling like that for?"

"Ghosts." The whispered word escaped from Nia's lips. Tiffany looked at the shadow and ran to the window. "Silly girl, that's only the shadow of a car going by." Nia wasn't convinced.

Tiffany ran out the room. There was a new wave of noisiness in the living room. She heard some of her relatives' voices. Then she heard Tiffany say, "Nia is a silly child. She thinks ghost are in the room."

Later that evening, while alone in her room, because both Tyron and Tiffany had gone to spend the night with their mother, Eva emerged in front of her. "Hi, baby."

Nia cast her eyes down. Sadness overtook her. She didn't want this person in front of her who everybody said was her mother. She mumbled, "Hi."

"The lighting is so dim in this room. I'm gonna talk to your Grandma Vern about putting more lighting in this room so you kids can see." She was quiet for a few minutes as she looked around the room. When she turned back facing Nia, she said, "Look up at me." Nia looked at Eva. "You keep your head up. Don't pay no mind to the dumb family we got. They don't know what they talking about." Then it seemed as if Eva stood in front of her and stared at her for a long time. Nia felt as if a heavy weight overshadowed her. "I'll see you later, baby," finally she said. She walked out of the room. Nia listened to her footsteps continue walking. Then she heard the front door slam.

"Is that Eva who left?" someone asked and then added, "She can't never say good-bye to no one."

Nia knew Eva wouldn't show up at the house again for months. But she felt relief when she left.

Chapter 5 Therapy

When Nia was nine, her teacher, Ms. Frisby, told her to wait after class because she wanted to talk to her. As she stood in front of Ms. Frisby, who was seated at her desk, Ms. Frisby grasped her hands. "Nia, I want to know if someone is hurting you at home." Nia didn't respond. Her teacher continued. "You never smile, Nia, and you don't play like the other children. I'm going to call your grandmother." Ms. Frisby got up and pulled the chair by the closet to her desk. "Sit down, Nia." Nia felt fear ripple through her as Ms. Frisby dialed her number, which she had written down on a paper on her desk. She could hear her grandmother's growling voice jumping through the phone, "Who you say you are?"

"Ms. Frisby. I'm Nia's teacher. I'm concerned about Nia, because she never smiles and doesn't mingle with the other children. Is she like that at home?"

"That's who she is. Don't call here wasting my time with silly questions!"

"Well," said Ms. Frisby, "I intend to refer Nia to the school counselor."

Grandma Vern raised her voice even louder, and shouted, "You do whatever you intend to do!" The phone clicked.

The day following Ms. Frisby talking to Nia's grandmother, Ms. Frisby told Nia to go to the school office. Nia had a note in her hand that Ms. Frisby had given to her. She handed it to the lady at the desk in the main office. The lady told her to sit in one of the three chairs to the right of the entrance doorway. Nia didn't look at anyone while she waited. After she had waited for a long time, one of the doors that lined one side of the main office area opened. A tall lady in a gray suit stood in the doorway.

"Sorry you had to wait so long, Nia. You can come into my office now." The lady's gray suit, her thick-heeled gray shoes, her hair pulled back into a bun, and her height projected sternness, and Nia expected that she would be harsh. But she had a warm voice and a pleasant smile as she looked at Nia and said, "Have a seat." Nia sat in the chair beside the desk. The lady sat behind the desk. She looked at Nia and began asking questions: "How old are you? Do you like school? Who's your best friend? How many girlfriends do you have? What do you do when you're not at school? Did anyone ever do something to you that was not nice?"

Nia rarely talked, so if the questions couldn't be answered with a simple yes or no, she didn't answer. Afterward she was sent back to class.

***

"I ain't got time to be playing these games," Grandma Vern barked into the phone. "You get paid to sit around all day and meet. I'm busy. I ain't got no time for meeting. I been to your school meetings with my own children. You don't listen to the parents. You act like you listen, then you do what you want to do."

Nia shuddered. Slowly she walked toward her room as she tried to force from her mind the image of her grandma's shrill words slamming into Ms. Frisby or the school counselor.

"Depression! You want to put a nametag on her—'depression'—'cause she don't talk? Too much talking going around as it is. Leave the child alone. She get good grades. Ain't that enough? Ain't you people glad you got a child doing good, getting good grades and don't fuss and fight? Oh, you can't tell me about depression. I got depression. We all got depression where I come from. You ain't got it 'cause you got all the money. Give me your money and then tell me if you don't get depression! No! I'm not coming up to the school for no meeting. We meeting right now. You want her to see a therapist, then you get her to the therapist. I'm a diabetic. I'm homebound. You get someone to take her to your therapy and bring her back home. So this here is your meeting. Bye." Grandma Vern slammed the phone down.

"I'm sick of them school teachers," she fumed. "They ain't got nothing better to do than call folk and worry them. They make me sick. They want to raise our children. Most of them who be worrying folk ain't got no kids of their own and always telling peoples how to raise their children."

Nia heard Grandma Vern's footsteps move from the living room to the kitchen. She heard the refrigerator open, slam shut, and then the sound of the bottle cap being popped off. She had seen the scene before, so she knew her grandmother was sitting in a chair staring at the wall while drinking out of her can of beer.

"Nia!"

Quickly Nia got off her bed. She went into the kitchen and stood in front of her grandmother with her head bowed. Her eyes stared at the floor.

"I don't need them people snooping around my house. Don't you say nothin' to them school people." Grandma Vern knew that Nia hadn't said anything to the school counselor or her teacher. She knew that Nia never talked. She got up from the table, tossed her beer can into the trash, and walked away from Nia, muttering, "They ain't got nothing better to do than start messing with folks."

***

Every Monday, at the end of the school day, a driver waited for Nia at the school office. Nia would follow him out the school building to his taxi, and he'd drive her to a building with a sign on the lawn that read "Stanton Family Counseling Services." The first time the driver walked in with her, but after that he would simply turn to her where she sat in the backseat, look at her, and say, "Okay, Ms. Nia. You know where to go. I'll see you when you're done."

After that first time, Nia learned to go into the building and sit down in the lobby to wait for Miss Watkins, who would shortly come out from one of the offices. Miss Watkins, who was the therapist, always said the same thing each Monday. "Nice to see you, Nia. Come on and join the group." Nia would follow Miss Watkins to where the other children sat in a circle on the floor. "Make room in our circle for Nia," Miss Watkins would say. Nia would sit in the spot that was opened up for her.

When Miss Watkins asked her direct questions, she wouldn't answer. Even when they played a game of "telling the truth," in which each child would say something that was true, Nia wouldn't say anything.

A girl named Tonai, who was much bigger than the other children, would say, "She don't have nothing to say. That's what she's saying. Why you trying to force her to talk? Some people like to talk and some people don't. She quiet. It's okay to be quiet!" Tonai would nod her head forcefully as if trying to convince everyone.

Although Tonai was only twelve, she seemed a lot older than everyone else in the group, probably because she was so outspoken and taller than everyone, even some of the counselors. She had a round face; a complexion the color of caramel candy; large, bright, brown eyes; and perfectly shaped, full, red lips. Though pretty, she was rough, and she was always talking, usually loudly. But unexpectedly one day, words that boomed out of Tonia's mouth startled Nia: "You took me from my mother and father. That's why I'm mad!"

Those words Tonai shouted out paralyzed Nia for a moment, and she began to hurt and wanted to cry. Miss Watkins called it "group therapy" and said it was supposed to help, but for Nia, it hurt to remember how she had suddenly been taken from her mother. It seemed that something inside of her had been trying to patch over the wound in her heart caused by the loss of her other life, but now the bandages had been ripped open, and she was bleeding again!

"Tonai," Miss Watkins softly said as she leaned forward in her chair that was centered within the group. "Often people like policemen and judges make decisions that affect us and our families, and sometimes the decisions make us feel bad or make us feel that we were treated wrong, but often we don't understand why things happen. We have to trust that the judges and the courts made decisions for good reasons. Tonai, and all of you children, must be strong and still do the things you need to do like go to school and do well in school and listen to the adults who care for you. Things will work out. They have a way of working out. Does everyone agree?" All the children nodded their heads up and down, even with exaggerated motions—except Nia and Tonai.

Miss Watkins stood up and clapped her hands once. "This part of the therapy session is now ended. You know that we talk for thirty minutes and then we play for thirty minutes. We are now beginning playtime."

Carlos was the first to jump up. He ran to the corner where a hoop was set up and grabbed a basketball. He shot the ball into the hoop. One of the other boys joined him. Carlos would always get too wild. He shouted excitedly, "No you didn't! You just took the ball from me. That ain't fair. You can't knock the ball out of my hand!" The therapist walked over and put her hand on Carlos shoulder. "Carlos, you have to learn how to calm down and play fair. I saw the whole thing. The ball belongs to Tony. Now play fair. It's no fun winning by cheating." As soon as Miss Watkins turned to walk back to her seat, Carlos nodded his head roughly and made wide motions with his mouth so that anyone looking knew he had responded with, "Yes it is!" Carlos then turned around and ran to retrieve the ball that Tony had thrown into the basket.

Nia was sitting in one of the chairs that were lined up against the wall. She watched the children do whatever they wanted to do, and she saw that the two counselors who had been in the room the whole time were watching the children play and writing notes on their pads.

There were all types of games and toys in the room. One girl ran toward a toy bin, picked up a doll, and dashed to the area where a play kitchen had been set up. While holding the doll on her hips, she scrambled make-believe eggs in a tiny pan on the small stove. Every few minutes, she'd hit the baby doll and shout, "Be quiet!" One girl was playing with a puzzle. A few of the children were playing board games together. A group of girls were unwinding a long rope. One girl got on each end and they doubled the rope, held one side of the rope in each hand and began turning, quickly gaining speed, their heads bobbing in motion with the swinging rope. A girl ready to jump was swaying along with the rhythm of the rope, and then she jumped in. The girls took turns jumping into the fast-swinging ropes.

Nia watched Tonai go around the room butting into whatever everyone else was doing. She grabbed the ball as it bounced off the floor, swished it around Carlos, and then shot the ball into the hoop. She put her thumbs up and waved her hand over her head as she walked away. For a few moments she watched the children playing board games then shouted out that they should have done this or that. Suddenly, she turned around and yelled to the girl in the kitchen, "Stop beating that baby!" Moments later she went over to the girls jumping rope and began swaying her body to the rhythm of the rope. She jumped in and skipped as the girls counted—ten, twenty, thirty, forty, fifty, sixty, seventy, eighty, ninety, a hundred, a hundred ten, a hundred twenty—until her foot stomped on the rope.

When she'd finished her rounds, Tonia flopped down next to Nia, as Nia had known she would. "Why don't you talk?" she asked, her face close to Nia's. "What they do to you that you don't talk?" As usual, she paused for a moment as if today might be the day that Nia responded. Then she said, "Well, you my friend. I'm a good secret keeper. You can tell me anything."

In the silence that followed, Nia listened to the thump, swish of Carlos's ball and the smack against the doll's behind. "I don't want to be in foster care. You in foster care?" she heard Tonia saying. Nia wasn't sure what foster care was, though she had certainly heard the words often enough at home, but she nodded because she had heard Tonia say they had taken her from her mother.

"I knew it!" Tonai shouted. "It makes you so sad. Everyone in my family is sad except one of my brothers. He's happy. He got a new family. He's the only child in his new family. He likes it. They his family now."

The loud smack of the therapist's handclap stopped all activity. There was a scramble of feet and a clashing sound of toys being placed into the toy bin. "What are we going to do?" the therapist yelled out.

"Listen and think," the group replied.

Tonai hugged Nia as they exited the room and walked to meet their drivers. Tonai walked right up to Nia's driver and asked, "Can you take me home after you take Nia home? I want to see where she lives 'cause we're friends."

The driver, who was standing alongside the car, shook his head, "No, baby. One of the social workers has to approve that. You need to talk to your social worker." He opened the door for Nia, and Nia got into the car. As she sat down, she saw Tonai put her hand up, palm toward the driver, to signal him to stop. She yelled, "Wait!" and ran back into the building.

The driver was checking to make sure all the doors were locked when Tonai shouted, "Here she is." She was pulling one of the therapists toward the car.

The therapist asked the driver, "Are you able to drop Tonai off after taking Nia home? I think it would be good for Nia."

"You the boss!"

"Yeah, boss lady," Tonai added.

Nia watched Tonai struggle to get the car door open. The therapist calmly said, "Let me get it," and she put her hand on the door handle. Before she opened the door, she looked at Tonai. "Now remember our agreement. I extended myself to you, and what are you supposed to do?"

Tonai mumbled, "Follow the rules." Tonai jumped into the backseat as Nia moved over. Nia felt excitement ripple through her as the car began to move forward.

Tonai moved close to Nia, "Do you live far?" Nia shook her head. "I don't live that far either, but I think from the way he's going we live in the same direction." Tonai had so much to say. She had lots of brothers and sisters who were in different foster homes. But she told Nia that she'd be going back to her real home soon.

The car slowed as it entered Nia's street. Tonai yelled out, "I know this area. I don't live far from here. Oh, I'm going to come and visit you, Nia."

Nia felt fear flutter through her. "Bye," she said as she stumbled out of the car. She rushed up the steps to her house hoping Tonai would forget where she lived. She knocked on the door and waited. When Grandma Vern opened the door, the driver pulled off. Nia could hear Tonai yelling, "Bye, Nia! Bye Nia!"

***

Nia was awake lying on her bed looking at cracks in the ceiling. She remained in bed because it was Saturday morning. Nia and her cousins had been instructed to remain quiet in their room until their grandmother got up. It was easy for her cousins to be quiet because they slept late on the Saturday and Sunday mornings that they were home, just like Grandma Vern. Grandma Vern liked to sleep late on Saturday mornings because she generally held a drinking party on Friday nights. In addition, Grandma Vern was very irritable after her Friday or Saturday night parties, so they had to be especially careful not to aggravate her. It would be time to get up when Grandma Vern widely opened their slightly cracked door and would say, "Get up. Wash up and come and get some breakfast."

Nia knew her grandmother was up, because she heard the slow, sliding sound of slippers, then the shutting of the bathroom door. She heard a rough, hacking noise, then the gurgle of mucus being coughed up, followed by the flushing of the toilet. There was the sound of running water and splashing.

Suddenly, Nia heard a knock at the front door. The knocking started out faint, but became louder and more insistent. Nia thought it might be Tonai because only Tonai would be so persistent. Nia pressed her lips together. She wanted to run to the door, but she wasn't allowed to open the front door without permission.

"Stop that knocking!" Grandma Vern yelled out. The knocking continued. Nia listened to the slow, sluggish dragging of Grandma Vern's slippers. Grandma Vern was never in a hurry to answer the door. Often she wouldn't move, and then the knocking would stop.

Quietly Nia moved off her bed and knelt down at the slit in her door, opening the door slightly more. Carefully, she peeked out. Although she had only a momentary glimpse, because Grandma Vern stood in the doorway, she saw that it was Tonai. For seconds her whole being filled with excitement as she imagined that she would be able to be with Tonai. Then she heard Grandma Vern growl, "This too early!" Grandma Vern roughly added. "Don't come here on Saturday. She got work to do. You should be home cleaning your mother's house. Ain't you Ben's daughter? Huh! Your foster mother know you here?" Grandma Vern slammed the door shut.

Nia quickly got up and rushed to her bed, barely making it before Grandma Vern swung the door open and shouted, "You kids get up and go brush your teeth for breakfast. It's Saturday morning, and you got to clean up this house." She said nothing about Tonai's visit and went about her morning routine.

Nia sat at the table staring ahead. Nearly every day followed the same pattern. She and her cousins sat quietly at the table. The kitchen was old fashioned. For years there had been only one cabinet attached to the wall next to the stove. Because there wasn't enough storage room, dishes and even food cans were piled on the side of the table by the wall. Grandma Vern had gone to the Friends of Families program that gave out used clothing, furniture, canned vegetables, and outdated bread—all their bread came from that program—and she got a large, white, second-hand, two-door kitchen cabinet. But even that cabinet wasn't big enough. It was soon crammed with pots, dishes, cereal boxes, and canned goods, and still there were cans of food and food boxes and bread piled up on the side of the kitchen table that was against the wall.

Grandma Vern turned on the faucet. She took a pot out of the dish drainer and filled it with water. Once again they heard the familiar sound of the pipes knocking as Grandma Vern turned off the faucet. She put the pot on the stove to boil. Grandma Vern grabbed three bowls out of the dish drainer and slammed them onto the table. She snatched three spoons out of the utensil part of the dish drainer and dropped them onto the table, one next to each bowl. Then she turned the oatmeal box upside down until three packets fell out. She tore open the packets and shook the contents into the bowls. Finally, she turned around and grabbed the small pot of boiling water. She poured water into each bowl and pushed the bowls to where each of the children sat.

They quietly and quickly ate their meal. They were disciplined to do this because, during the weekdays, they had to be on time for school. Ty and Tiffany had long walks, and Nia had to catch a bus. And on Saturdays they had to spend their late mornings and early afternoons cleaning, although very little cleaning would actually get done.

When Grandma left the kitchen, Ty began talking. "You got work to do this morning, Tiff, so you can't go over your girlfriend's house." Ty liked to stir Tiffany up.

Tiffany raised her voice, "I'm going. You watch and ..." Grandma Vern appeared in the doorway. "Just eat. No need for all that talking."

After breakfast, as Nia swept the hallway, she heard Grandma Vern's strong coughing. It didn't seem to bother Tiffany and Ty, but Nia felt her grandmother would die from the intensity of her hacking. As she swept in front of the bathroom door, she could see Grandma Vern bent over the sink coughing, and she saw thick, brownish stuff come out of her mouth.

Chapter 6 Grandma Vern's Parties

Standing over the kitchen sink, Nia reached for and dried the last pot that had been in the drainer. She stooped down and placed the pot on the bottom shelf of the cabinet. The kitchen had become her safety ground because nobody else particularly liked being in it. They'd enter the kitchen to get something and quickly leave. She had always been very careful not to do or say anything that would upset Grandma Vern. She simply stayed out of her way as much as possible. So working in the kitchen had its advantages as it minimized her interacting with Grandma Vern, Tiffany and their guests.

Aunt Tina entered the kitchen with both arms full of groceries. As she set the bags on the kitchen table, she yelled out, "Mama, this is a sorry house. How you gonna have these children grow right if you never have the right food in here to feed them? I don't know how you'll survive."

Since she was around eight years old, when Aunt Tina would visit, Grandma Vern would tell Nia to go to the kitchen to help Aunt Tina. Aunt Tina began teaching her how to cook. So just as she had always done, Nia went to the bags and began putting away the food.

"We gonna make stuffed peppers, rice, and red cabbage," Aunt Tina sang while nodding her head.

Nia got out the items needed for the meal. She was careful with the knife, just as Aunt Tina had in times past instructed her. She chopped onions, mushrooms, and tomatoes into tiny pieces and sprinkled seasonings on the beef just as her aunt had showed her in the past.

It was established that Nia was Aunt Tina's cooking assistant. In the beginning when she was learning to cook, Nia would do exactly what Aunt Tina would tell her to do. It wasn't long before she could prepare the meals herself. Aunt Tina would sit at the kitchen table with her legs up on a chair. She would drink beer while watching Nia prepare the entire family meal. Occasionally Aunt Tina would offer some instruction. When Nia had nearly finished cooking the meal, Aunt Tina would appear next to her. She'd open the pots and use the lids to swirl the aroma toward her nose. Often she'd take a large spoon and stir the food around in the pot. Now Aunt Tina wouldn't even stay in the kitchen.

So Nia became the family cook and had to wash the dishes as well because Tiffany hated dishwashing and would come up with some excuse to get out of it. She always had cheerleading practice, or a book report, or some vague but enormous homework assignment, or she simply wasn't feeling well. Tyron would run out of the house after dinner. Nia got in the habit of washing the big pots and dishes as she cooked so there wouldn't be much to wash after everyone ate.

When the meal was ready, Nia fixed a plate for Aunt Tina, who always returned to the kitchen just when the meal was done, as she did this day. Aunt Tina sat down at the table. She took a bite out of the cornbread and a forkful of cabbage, then used the fork to push in a portion of cabbage that hadn't quite made it all the way into her mouth. She sliced the stewed pepper and scooped some of the rice onto the fork and put that into her mouth. She had her eyes closed as she chewed. She looked up at Nia. "You must be my real daughter. I could tell from the time you first started helping me, you had cooking in your blood." She shook her head so that her hair—streaked red, blonde, black, and bright orange—fluffed back and forth. With the nail of her pinky finger, she cleared a small piece of meat that had got stuck between her teeth. Then she picked up her beer can and slowly walked toward the living room.

"The meal's ready. It's grubbing time," she announced, holding up her beer can.

Nia went back to the sink and focused on washing the dishes. She was hurrying with the cleaning because she wanted to get out of the kitchen before Grandma Vern's guests came. It was, after all, Friday night. Grandma Vern came into the kitchen and tasted the food on the plate that

Tina had fixed out and handed to her. She looked at Nia and said with a rough voice, "So you *can* do something right around here."

Aunt Tina, who had come to like Nia, turned toward her mother. "Is that your way of saying to the child that she did a good job? You treat that child so bad. She's your grandchild too." Grandma Vern twisted her lips and turned her head and sashayed out of the kitchen holding her plate in her hand.

Nia heard voices growing louder in the living room. She rushed to wipe around the sink and wring out the dishcloth so she could get to her room to avoid interacting with anyone. But then she heard the clicking sound of heels coming into the kitchen. "Where are the glasses?" Nia turned and pointed to the cabinet. She was glad she didn't know the woman, because she didn't want to have to answer questions. The woman opened the refrigerator and then the freezer door and threw ice cubes into her glass. As she turned to leave, without looking at Nia, she slightly nodded her head. Nia knew people would be drifting in and out of the kitchen, because Grandma Vern's guests smoked, drank, and ate all night. As Nia was exiting the kitchen, she heard Grandma Vern yell out above the noise, "The food in the refrigerator is for the chil'ren. You can eat these here chips and snacks, but don't go snooping around in my 'frigerator. I don't want nobody's nasty hands picking and poking through my 'frigerator, 'cause I don't know where your hands been, and I got chil'ren I'm raising."

Nia closed the door to her room. Still she could hear them. She picked up a comic book that was on the floor by Tyron's bed. She looked at the pictures and tried to read, but the noise kept disrupting her focus. Nia stood up. She had been trying to hold out, but she had to go to the bathroom. Quickly she moved along the hallway to the bathroom. Quietly she clicked the door closed and hurriedly got onto the toilet. She flushed the toilet and washed her hands, then carefully opened the door. She glanced into the living room. She was careful so that no one would see her, but she could see them. They looked stupid to her. Their faces seemed shiny. Some of them moved with exaggerated body movements, with arms flung wide into the air as they shouted to get their points across. Others were slumped down along the couch, arms hanging limp over the furniture. Their talk sounded foolish. She heard fast, short, slurred words that reminded her of Donald Duck talking. Food wrappers lay around. The guests were noisy, sloppy, and greedy. A fog enveloped the entire living room. Suddenly Nia felt as if the smoke would choke her. There were different scents of smoke wavering throughout the house. As she stared into the living room, she saw a man she had been told to call Uncle Bobbie. When he caught sight of her, he seemed embarrassed and said, "Oops," and his hands began shaking as he tried to shift what looked like a thin cigarette from his lips to behind his back. Nia turned and rushed back into her room and closed the door, trying to hurry so Grandma Vern, who seemed to know everything that was going on all the time, wouldn't accuse her of sneaking around.

As usual, Nia was alone in the room. Tiffany always used the occasion of Grandma Vern's party to ask if she could visit a girlfriend. One of the relatives had driven her to her girlfriend's house. Nia's ears perked up. She heard Tyron's voice, "I got this. I'll clean it up."

Grandma Vern confronted him. "Ty, where you been?"

Nia knew he'd been at a friend's house and probably came home to get something he needed. Most likely he wanted a couple of dollars, which he'd normally get while cleaning up during Grandma Vern's parties.

"Hey, Grandma," she heard him say. Nia could imagine him because she had actually seen it so many times—Tyron rushing over and kissing Grandma Vern. Now at twelve years old, he hardly ever answered her questions. He'd generally tell her how he was helping her out. "I'm cleaning up for you, Grandma. I'm gonna take this trash out." Nia could see him in her mind, quickly moving through the crowd with a bag dumping ashtrays and picking up paper from the floor.

"Thanks for emptying out my ashtray. Here!" It was the voice of Uncle Bobbie likely giving Ty a dollar. She heard different voices addressing Ty—"Take this for your trouble."

"Here Ty." "You doing a good job Ty," a jolly woman's voice swung through the air.

"Yeah! I'm the clean-up man." Now Ty was pointing to himself and doing a little dance. Nia knew his routine. Laughter burst through the house.

"Here, baby." "Here baby." "Buy yourself a soda and chips, love."

Soon Nia no longer heard Ty's voice. She knew he had left the house, managing to slip past the folks who were dancing, playing cards, arguing, or sleeping, and would not return until the morning.

She wanted the party to end, but the gruff voices of the men and the shrill voices of the women got louder and louder and reached out into the street. She could hear the sounds from the living room coming in through her bedroom window.

Finally, the noise simmered down, and Nia began drifting off to sleep. But suddenly her eyes flung open because of loud banging sounds and chairs roughly scraping the floor. Covering her head with her blanket, she began shaking. There would be a fight, because that generally happened when they played cards. She heard a loud thump, and she thought a table had been slammed onto the floor. She heard a man shout, "I said you did!"

Another man answered him. "What you trying to call me? I ain't no cheat!"

"What, you think? I'm a fool? I'll cut your throat!" the first man said. Then a woman screamed.

Nia covered her ears when she heard Aunt Tina's loud, screechy, threatening voice. Aunt Tina liked to fight! When Nia's hands slipped down from her ears, she thought she heard Eva and maybe Uncle Bobbie arguing with someone. Then she heard Grandma Vern's calm yet chilling voice say, "Put that gun away! Put that knife down! There'll be no cutting up in here tonight! You's a sore loser. We all here watching. He ain't cheated or we'd all seen it. If you can't take being beat, you need to leave. Shut your mouths. Ain't no cops coming here tonight!"

Nia envisioned Grandma Vern standing with her big gun pointing at them. Nia had seen that gun once when her grandmother was cleaning it. Nia and her cousins had been sitting together on the floor in the living room watching TV when Grandma Vern had instructed Nia to get a cleaning rag. She'd gone into the kitchen and opened the broom closet and got a cleaning rag out of a bag at the bottom of the closet. When she returned to the living room, she'd held the cleaning rag up in front of Grandma Vern. She'd seen her grandmother holding the gun up toward the ceiling and blowing into it. Nia had stood in front of her for a few moments, holding the rag. She had learned that, if Grandma Vern seemed absorbed with something, she should just set whatever she had asked for next to her. Nia learned this because Grandma Vern had snapped at her more than once, "What you standing there staring at me for? Set it on the table and go sit down." So as Grandma Vern had continued to blow into her gun, Nia had carefully placed the rag on the table and sat back down in her spot beside her cousins in front of the television.

Nia, who had been listening in fear, was now relieved by the way Grandma Vern had calmed everyone down. Soon Nia could tell that they had gotten back to playing. Not long afterward she heard what sounded like someone stomping on the floor. A man's hard voice boomed, "I lost all my money. I can't go home. My wife ... she gonna kill me!"

"Your wife!" a voice belonging to one of her aunts yelled out. "What you talking about your wife for? You ain't going home to your wife. You here with me, fool. So if anyone should be mad 'cause you lost all your money, it should be me." Nia knew her aunt would have her lips curled up in annoyance and she'd be looking around from face to face for heads nodding in agreement.

"Oh yeah, baby. You right. You right," the man said lowering his voice sounding confused. Laughter erupted and vibrated throughout the house.

Nia tried hard to go to sleep so that when she woke up everything would be over. Then everything was quiet. She cuddled her head more comfortably by the wall, and her whole body seemed to take a deep breath and relax. The sound of the door to her room opening pierced through her sleep. As usual she stayed still in her bed. She always knew when her door opened because it squeaked. Tiffany had instructed her to put oil in the door, but when she was down on her knees trying to put oil in the hinges, Grandma Vern had stopped her. Grandma Vern said she liked the door the way it was. She told Tiffany the squeak wasn't that loud, and it let her know when the children were coming and going.

Surely Tyron was sneaking back into the house. She tightened her eyes thinking it had to be morning, and she didn't want to see light. But the footsteps were too sluggish and too slow for Tyron. Nia froze, terrified, as she sensed a huge figure hovering over her. Suddenly she heard Grandma Vern's dry-sounding voice float into the room from the hallway. "If you don't get out of that room right now, I'm gonna put a bullet up your ass."

Nia envisioned Grandma Vern standing at the door with her big gun.

The heavy footsteps retreated quickly out of her room, through the living room, and out the front door. She heard Grandma Vern shouting from the front doorstep, in a blood-curdling voice, "Don't you come over my house no more or I'll blow your brains out."

Chapter 7 Isaiah's Beating

Friday and Saturday nights at Grandma Vern's house weren't all raucousness. There were times Grandma Vern would tell sobering stories about the family's past. While she told the stories, sometimes Nia would hear laughter, but more often she'd hear crying. Nia would hear things she couldn't imagine were true, like the story of what happened to Isaiah. But something in Grandma Vern's voice, and the quietness and seriousness of everyone in the house while her grandmother told the stores, had her believe the stories were true.

As she had begun to do when the story telling started, Nia got off her bed, cracked her door, and sat on the floor. Then she carefully scooted out and peeked into the living room. She knew she couldn't be seen because she watched them through the bottom legs of a wooden chair that one of her aunts sat on.

As she often did when she had too much to drink, Grandma Vern stood in the middle of the room with one hand on her hip and the other pointed toward her grown children. She talked in her heavy, low-toned, unwavering, voice. "You all had it good. I didn't do to you like my mother, your Grandma Ellie, did me. You never met her. Good thing. You wouldn't be doing no drinking in front of her. Oh no! And you surely wouldn't be doing drugs. Guess why not? Because the first time she caught you, she'd slap the taste right out of your mouth. The second time, you'd better run because, just as sure as I'm standing here, she'd go get that shotgun she kept behind the door to her room. She'd come out pointing that shotgun at you, and she'd pull the trigger if you didn't move fast enough. My brothers be gone the minute they saw her going to her room. She'd say a child that'd defy her was no child of hers!"

"Say that!" one of the men yelled out.

"Oh, Mama, do we have to hear this?" Aunt Tina twisted her lips as she turned her head.

"Ellie would go get her shotgun," Grandma Vern continued as if she hadn't heard anyone else speak. "She'd shoot you. She'd look you in the eye and say, 'I brought you into this world. I'll take you out.'"

"See this?" Nia watched as her grandmother raised her sleeve over one arm and showed the scar that Nia had seen many times.

"I got this because I thought I was grown. She burnt me! My mama burnt me with a hot straightening comb. You know how bad it was 'cause you can still see the imprint after all these years. All I said was, 'That hurt!' because my mama was tugging hard at my hair. When she got still, I knew I was in big trouble. She hit me with that hot comb. Then she said, after she burnt me, 'You don't talk to me in that tone.'

"I was raised in Mississippi. You ain't never had a day when you didn't eat. Well, I had plenty. If my daddy didn't have money for food, and the crops didn't grow, we just didn't eat. There weren't these programs you could go to and get a bag of food." Grandma Vern stopped talking. The room was gravely still. "The best we could do was dream about food. That's the closest we got to it in them days.

"And we didn't live in warm houses like this. We lived in a wooden-planked, four-room shack that stood on a dirt road. There were other little houses lined up alongside our house on that dirt road. Them small houses had been used for families during slave days. There was no toilet in the house. To relieve ourselves, we had to leave the house and walk a short distance to a wooden enclosure that had a box with a hole in it set above a deep pit in the ground. When it was rainy and the ground was muddy, we had to dip out water from a barrel that had been set out to catch the rain and rinse off our feet before entering the house. Most of the winter we had no heat. We didn't have to suffer too long because it never got cold like up North.

Ellie had twelve children. She always showed big in her belly early on in the pregnancy, so it seemed as if she was always pregnant. Everyone smiled at her when she was young before she became bitter. They would nod their approval because she was young, plump, pretty, and married, and her pregnancies were a sign that she was an obedient wife. We tagged alongside her or behind her, holding our heads down, and we spoke only when we were spoken to. That was also deemed a sign of her skill as a mother. In the days when Ellie walked to town, men sitting on benches outside the stores would jump up as she approached so she could sit down and get some relief from her heavy burden. Women would turn their fans from themselves onto her to cool her off."

Grandma Vern explained that the town that Ellie walked to, which the surrounding colored communities relied on for most of their business needs, was dusty and shabby and consisted of four small stores. The buildings were slightly better constructed than the shacks the people from the area lived in. There was a grocery store, a barbershop, a dry goods store, and a small candy store. A church stood about half a mile down the road from the stores. Ellie had said the town had barely changed since she was a child. It was the best that blacks could do to accommodate themselves living in the South at a time when white people didn't want them around other than as servants and laborers.

Every few months every family had to conduct business in the big city. Someone in every family had to go to pay taxes and buy postage stamps and other items that they couldn't find in their small town. Of course women would save on food prices because food was cheaper in those big stores in the city.

Nia listened and learned about times back then. She kept reflecting on the subject of slavery, which she had learned about in school. Her heart would hurt when she'd hear about injustices. And although she had grown used to Grandma Vern's monotonous, slow-moving voice, when Nia listened to her grandmother's stories of her past, the words brought on vibrant visions before Nia's eyes.

Grandma Vern explained why going to the city was an especially dangerous undertaking for black men, which was why most black men avoided going there. It was a time in Mississippi when black folk had to walk with their eyes cast to the ground. It had been like that since the time of slavery.

"If anyone of us were walking around during slavery times," Grandma Vern raised her voice, "We'd better have a pass from our owner if we came to the city. And it seemed like it got worse just after slavery ended and on up into the fifties. Black man had to be quick to respond, 'Yes, sir,' or 'No, ma'am,' whenever a white person asked them a question. That's how Uncle Isaiah got in big trouble and was beaten to within an inch of his life. His mother took him with her shopping in the white folks' city, and he was looking all around … couldn't keep his head bowed and his eyes set on the ground like his momma kept telling him.

"In them days," said Grandma Vern, "all it took was one drunken white man, or someone who was angry that his life was in shambles, to call a black man 'boy' and to harass him. That black man's survival would depend on how good he was at acting like a fumbling child or an idiot so as to confirm the white man's image of a black man. White men would toss pennies into the street and order the black man to fetch them. He would have to hobble, grin, nod his head, as he moved toward the pennies saying, 'Yessir! Yessir! Yessir!' Grandma Vern would describe how the white men, feeling that things were back in their right place, would finally shake their heads. Their faces would be beet-red from laughing. The man who started it would feel a sense of power and control. Someone in the group would finally say, 'Go on home now, boy.' The black man would hobble off scratching his head and face, twisting around in circles as he went, acting as if he didn't understand what was going on. A new wave of laugher would ripple through the group of harassing men."

In those times, being around white folks was dangerous for every black person. Often it was simply a matter of being in the wrong place at the wrong time. Every so often, a group of white men would come on foot or in a vehicle to a small black-folk community. Sometimes the men would come with white sheets over their heads and torches or bats in their hands. Generally they would march toward someone's house and call out a man's name. At other times they would stream by one small black community and head for the next small black village. Everyone would know they were coming. Someone up the road would see them, and word of their approach would spread like lightning. People would rush to knock on doors of relatives and neighbors, calling out, "Lynch mob coming!" Sometimes it was known who they were looking for. Any males in that family over five years old were sent to neighbors' houses. That poor man's family would do the best they could to get him out of the area. The wanted man would run while family members would cover for him at the risk of their own lives.

Sometimes the mob would break down the door to a house. The women would be huddled together in a corner with the children looking into the face of the mob with shotguns pointed toward them. After a few moments of rampaging through the tiny home, breaking and knocking down things, the mob would leave. "He can't be far!" someone would yell out. The barking of dogs would come from the darkness, and the mob would rush from the house to meet up with the other men who were following the trail of the sniffing dogs. Most of the time, they would find the man they were looking for. On rare occasions, however, some man, generally a stranger, would be unfortunate enough to be caught in their path. They would take him as the man they were looking for. He'd be strung up to a tree. Sometimes he'd be hung by the neck. Other times, they would tie his hands together at the wrist and then attach them to a strong tree branch so that his body would dangle. They would beat him to death with sticks and bats.

There were men who would not allow their families to risk their lives for them. They would tell their families that, if they escaped and the mob couldn't find them, they might return to attack their families, and they wouldn't be able to live knowing their loved ones had suffered for them. Those courageous men would go out and face the mob when they heard their names called. All the families could do was cry out in prayer, "Please, God, spare his life. Please, God, if he must die, let it be quick. Let him not suffer." Every minute would be torture for the family. Their night would be filled with visions of the tortures those hate-filled men were inflicting on their beloved husband, father, son, brother, uncle, or nephew.

The sentence for an alleged crime was harsh. If a black man looked at a white woman, and certainly if he touched one, his genitals would be cut off, and he would be hanged. If the accusation was stealing, his hand might be chopped off. If the accusation was that he had beaten up a white man, he would face a brutal death by beating.

When the mob finished up their business, everyone listened for the footsteps and voices of the white men's retreat. As soon as they cleared the area, a few men would venture forth cautiously through the fields and wooded areas to find the body. Every now and then a man survived. Folks would say it was the hand of God that saved him. On the rare occasions that they brought the man home hanging onto life, the whole community would get involved in the fight to save him. Folks would bring all the medicinal items and bandages they had. If they needed more, someone would go to the store for supplies. The storeowner in their small town, who sometimes had to open up in the dead of night, would give everything that was needed. He would have to wait a few months before ordering new supplies because he knew that his suppliers might notice if he suddenly increased his order of bandages. Since both the white and black communities would have heard about the lynching, it was necessary to do everything to ensure that no one suspected the man was still alive.

That was how the community acted when Isaiah was attacked. People contributed whatever they could to save Isaiah. Isaiah was Grandma Vern's uncle. Her father, Amos, and Isaiah were brothers. Grandma Vern said that everyone thought that Isaiah was ahead of his time. It was speculated that he should have been born a hundred years later. He was outgoing and outspoken, and he understood everything without having to be told more than once.

Isaiah's father had died when he was four years old. His mother, Beatrice, was a strong, God-fearing woman. Her life centered on raising her children, attending church, talking about her Lord Jesus, and cooking. Since childhood, she had been known as Queen Bee, partly because she was taller than the other children, but also because she had a way about her. She was very organized, addressing what needed to be done in an efficient, competent, and calm manner. Although it was not talked about openly, everyone knew that men were always trying to please her in the hope of winning her affections because she was pretty as well as personable. Even when she was a child, boys carried her things for her and would fight to walk alongside her. Her charm came naturally. It was in the way she gazed thoughtfully at people while listening to them, her lips giving a slight hint of a smile. It was in the way she shrugged her shoulders when gossiping woman tried to engage her in malicious talk. She got them to stop their talk without feeling offended. It was in the way she sat with her body slightly angled to one side with her knees pressed together, her legs crossed at the ankles, and her head tilted. When she walked she seemed to take her time, even when she said she was in a hurry. She took elegant steps and held her chin up and her chest out. She was one of the few people in the community who didn't work for white folks. When her husband died, she kept right on working part-time in the grocery store in their small town. She didn't try to go somewhere else to get higher wages. Since she owed nothing for her house, she managed to live on the meager salary she received from the store.

Her three children, as she often told them, were the Lord's blessings to her, so they were first as far as anything going on in her life. Beatrice took Amos, her eldest; Isaiah; and Patricia, her baby, who was nicknamed Peaches, to church with her nearly every evening during the week, and they stayed at church all day on Sunday. That's how it was for blacks in Mississippi then. Church was their sanctuary. It was a place of peace away from the scuffling and tension that went on in their world. At church folks laughed and cried as they stomped their feet. Some whispered, others yelled out that Jesus would take care of them. The minister would talk about how much Jesus loved them and about loving their enemies. "Stay focused on Jesus," he would say. "He'll make it all right."

The small church stood like a monument in their community. It was well designed and looked as good as any church in the white community. It made the people feel that they were equal in the eyes of God. Poor as they were, they had poured all they had into their church. It was a nicely constructed log building. Stained glass with pictures of angels covered the windows. Chandeliers hung from the natural wood beamed ceiling. The floor was beautifully finished hardwood. Long benches that were perfectly spaced behind one another had royal red cushions on them. The church could comfortably accommodate a hundred people. People from neighboring black communities walked long distances to attend the Sunday service.

The church had felt like a safe haven until the day when a mob in white sheets set fire to it. The building was leveled to the ground. The community immediately began to rebuild. It was as if everyone in their small town and the neighboring communities had their heart set on getting their church back. It was quickly rebuilt.

Beatrice had taught her children to love everybody just as she has been taught. She told them that it was what Jesus called them to do. Even Isaiah's sister had asked her, "Why are we supposed to love those people who burnt our church down to the ground?"

"Why do white people hate us so much?" Isaiah had added with a confused look on his face.

She answered them, "All white people not the same. It just look that way because where we live was slavery before and now there's no more slavery, so white folks is mad because they don't have nobody to work the plantations for them for free no more. White folks not the same up North. They treat us more equal up there is what I heard." Then she smiled as she added, "God said, 'Vengeance is mine!' We got to be obedient and just love folks. If other people want to burn in hell for all eternity, that's their decision. Me and mine, we serving God!"

Beatrice kept her children close to her whenever they left home. On the rare occasions that she had to go to the city, she instructed them to stay next to her, keep their heads down, eyes on the ground, and say nothing except, "Yes, ma'am" or "Yes, sir," or "No, ma'am" or "No, sir," if anyone addressed them. Isaiah would look up, and his mother would shake his hand firmly and whisper, "Put your head down," as they walked along. Isaiah would put his head down, but would tell his mother, "I can't see where I goin' looking down at the ground." Despite his mother's warnings, Isaiah would take quick peeks at the buildings and the surroundings as they walked along.

One day early in the 1920s, they were walking home. Isaiah was in his teen years, and he told his mother that he wanted to see the world. He had read books and seen pictures of big buildings. Beatrice believed that Isaiah was acting cocky because his teacher, Miss Emily, was putting wrong ideas in his head. Beatrice even suspected that Miss Emily wanted to relive missed opportunities through Isaiah.

Everyone had heard about how smart Miss Emily was. She had learned to read on her own. They said that, when she was a toddler, she picked up pieces of newspaper or flyers and asked what each word was. And they said she taught herself math too. She was always counting as a child. Seeing her count became a fun game to her uncles, and everyone in town knew about it. People used to place bets to see if she could add different amounts of money. If she counted right, the person who won would get paid off and would have to give her some of his or her money. People in the town from which she came talked about how she had been working and bringing in money to her parents since she was a baby.

Miss Emily began to teach school out of the shack she lived in. A couple of rich white women took an interest in Miss Emily and her efforts to educate black children. They built a schoolhouse for the black children right next to Miss Emily's house. They even paid her a salary to teach and brought in two other teachers, educated black women from up North, to help her. They say Miss Emily traveled all over the world. She never married, which stood as proof in everyone's eyes of how devoted she was to educating their children.

Miss Emily came to Beatrice's house one afternoon and told her that Isaiah had a gift. Beatrice did not understand exactly what the teacher meant because she had not seen any gifts in Isaiah like the Bible tells about gifts—like the gift of seeing into the spiritual world, or the gift of prophesy, or the gift of healing people like Jesus did. But she listened while Miss Emily explained that Isaiah was good with numbers and that he liked to study the structure of buildings. Miss Emily sat in Beatrice's living room and told her that Isaiah could be an architect someday.

"Hush! Don't put those thoughts in my boy's head," Beatrice had whispered. "You know how things is!"

But Miss Emily had seemed determined to talk about what Isaiah could become. She had papers with her—an application for him to go to college. She said he had a right to go to the state college for free because he would get a scholarship. She kept saying that things were changing. But all Isaiah's mother could envision was a shotgun being pointed at Isaiah's head and the trigger being pulled. Finally, Beatrice stood up and said, "You have to leave now!"

Of course, Beatrice had told the pastor about her conversation with Miss Emily. He shook his head and said to her, "Maybe Isaiah has had enough of that schooling!" The minister mentioned it during Sunday service, "Folks, it's important to know your place! Don't go getting big ideas that'll get you killed."

As they walked along one day, shortly after Miss Emily had spoken to his mother, Isaiah kept talking excitedly about traveling all over the world. Beatrice tried to help him keep to what she knew was real for him. "Things different here, son. There's mean people we live around who don't like us. If they think we not being respectful, they get mad. If they hear about our man-child going off to some college, they might get mad. They may get real mad if they think we saying our children smart. They can hurt us because they in charge of everything. You can't step out of place. Get those ideas out of your head. You try to go to that white state college, and they shoot you." Beatrice had been seriously considering sending Isaiah up North. It soon became evident that she had delayed too long.

Mother Nessie came to Beatrice's home the day Isaiah nearly died. Mother Nessie had been around as long as anyone living could remember. Even the elders in the community who had "gone on to glory" had told stories about Mother Nessie before they died, and they had referred to her as "old." Nobody knew her age, and it seemed by the way she walked and by the way she talked that she was as old as time itself. Mother Nessie could see spirit things. Everybody, including the pastor, believed that she was a prophetess from God. She rarely brought good news, though, so when Beatrice opened the door, her heart sank. She stared at Mother Nessie then quickly composed herself and greeted her. She searched Mother Nessie's face for some clue about the message she was bringing. Mother Nessie seemed to look past her emotions. In her usual monotone voice, she said, "Hello, Queen Bee." Mother Nessie's expression never changed, which always created more tension in folks when she visited them. Beatrice was glad that her children were at home. Amos, her eldest, and his wife, Ellie, had left moments before Mother Nessie knocked at her door. If something had happened that quickly to them, she would have already heard about it. She thought, "How bad can the news be?" Perhaps one of her relatives had died. She braced herself for such news and said to herself, "Jesus strengthen me!"

"Come on in, Mother Nessie," Beatrice said a bit too loudly, then quickly she led Mother Nessie to a chair at the kitchen table. She hastened to get some tea and doughnuts for Mother Nessie and placed them in front of her. It was well known that Mother Nessie liked a good meal. Beatrice nervously rolled her hands over and over each other in front of her as she stood by the stove. "There's some fried chicken and rice sitting in the pots. Would you like some, Mother Nessie?"

"No, dear. The tea and doughnuts are fine. Sit down, dear."

Beatrice felt tears welling up in her eyes. Mother Nessie surely had really bad news! Mother Nessie, who loved a full meal, had refused it. It would be just plain sinful to sit at a person's table, eat their food, and then give them real bad news. Maybe it was her sister. Yes, something must have happened to her sister. They were particularly close, and her sister had visited them not too long ago. Beatrice glanced nervously at her son and daughter, who were seated together on the couch and were staring at Mother Nessie.

Mother Nessie leaned over the table toward Beatrice and whispered, "Have your children to go into the back room and close the door."

Beatrice looked at her children. She pressed her lips tightly together in a desperate attempt to stop them from trembling. Then as calmly as she could, she said, "You'll go to the back room and close the door." The children got up and left the living room. Unconsciously Beatrice grasped the fabric of her blouse right over her heart and continued to squeeze it tightly. She stared at Mother Nessie as the prophetess ate a doughnut and sipped the tea.

When she had finished the doughnut and taken a few more sips of tea, Mother Nessie put her cup down on the saucer. "That was very nice, dear." She looked around the room. "You keep a nice house. You's a good mother and a credit to the community." Beatrice's eyes were locked on Mother Nessie. "But there's a darkness overshadowing your home."

Beatrice let out a cry and then quickly covered her mouth with her hands. She didn't want her children to hear her crying.

"Your son, Isaiah … they coming to get him."

"Who?" Beatrice whispered as her whole body trembled.

It was as if Mother Nessie hadn't heard her. She continued to speak softly. "They will beat him badly … with whips." Mother Nessie stared unblinkingly at nothing that Beatrice could see.

Beatrice shook her head and cried out, "No ... no ... no ... He hasn't done anything wrong! He's here with me all the time." She could feel her entire body shaking. "I'm getting him out tonight," Beatrice whispered as she held her trembling hand to her mouth. "I'll put him on a bus."

"It's too late." Mother Nessie's unblinking stare did not change.

"Tonight. I'll put him on a train tonight."

Mother Nessie repeated firmly, "It's too late!"

Beatrice said through the tears that were now streaming down her face, "Mother Nessie, why didn't you come by earlier and tell me?"

"It don't work like that. With me, it works like a puzzle. Sometimes I see one piece ... like I seen your boy's face this morning. Sometimes the pieces get put together quickly, sometimes very slowly. I didn't see nothing else but the face. I kept waiting to see more to find out what was going to happen. But nothing more came. I'm here because sometimes when I come near to who I seen, I see the whole story. I just seen the whole story." For a moment she was quiet. Then in a dry voice she added, "God's the one decides the timing of my seeings. There's no more time."

Beatrice's cry came from deep within her stomach. Tears streamed from her nearly closed eyes. She did all she could do to brace herself as she whispered, "Is he going to die?"

Mother Nessie never answered. She got up. "I have to go now."

Queen Bee knew it was no use asking any more questions. She stood up to walk Mother Nessie to the door, but her body was trembling so badly that she couldn't move. "Thank you, Mother Nessie," she finally blurted out hoping that her words would catch up with the woman, who had already walked outside, leaving the door open, and was walking down the porch steps. She really didn't want Mother Nessie to go. She was hoping Mother Nessie could tell her that she saw something else ... something good!

Instead, after she got down the porch steps, Mother Nessie turned around to her and said, "Pray, daughter. Pray!"

As soon as she closed the door, Beatrice rushed to the room where her children were. "Isaiah, you have to leave now. You have to run!" She began to pull him off the bed and shove him out the back door. "You have to go, son. Bad men are coming to get you. Run!" Isaiah looked into his mother's eyes, and then he turned and ran out the back door.

Shortly after Isaiah had left, a man's voice called from the street. It was the cry that the whole community feared, "White sheets headed this way! White sheets headed this way!" The voice trailed off into the distance as the man ran to warn people in the next community.

They kicked open the door. Beatrice and her daughter, Peaches, held tightly onto each other, crying and trembling. The men yelled at them. "Where's your boy?" Beatrice shook violently at the sight of the white sheets and hoods and passed out. Her weight pulled Peaches to the floor so that Peaches was bent over her mother's body. Looking at her mother she began to scream. The men went through the house and smashed everything in their path. They had dogs with them, and the dogs were sniffing and barking all over the house. The men and dogs went into the children's room. One of the men brought out a shirt. Holding the shirt, the man went over to Isaiah's sister and roughly lifted her chin with his hand.

"This belong to Isaiah?" the man yelled as he waved the shirt in front of her.

Trying to wipe her eyes with her hands so that she could focus on what the man was demanding, she looked at the shirt and nodded her head. The man then pushed the shirt in front of the dogs' noses. Peaches' eyes rolled back in her head until only the whites showed. Her head dropped onto her mother's body. The men left through the back door following the tracking dogs.

A few minutes after the mob left, Beatrice lifted her chest. Her body movement brought Peaches back to herself. Immediately Peaches put her arms around her mother and tried to help her up. Beatrice struggled to her knees. She patted her daughter's arm to let Peaches stop trying to lift her. Then Beatrice bowed her head to the floor and prayed through her tears. Peaches knelt beside her. After an hour of praying, Beatrice told her daughter to go to bed. Beatrice would stay watch. She was determined to remain on the floor pledging with God until her son returned.

Isaiah hadn't gotten too far. He had grown tired and hungry, and he began to wonder why he was running. He had dozed off under a tree when he heard dogs barking in the distance. His insides trembled. "God help me. I can't outrun them dogs and there's no water around here where I can lose my scent." Isaiah looked up at the sky through the trees. He started climbing the tree under which he had been lying. Soon the dogs led the men to that tree, stood at its base, and barked furiously. He could see men coming toward the tree. Between the branches he saw five men robed in white holding guns pointing up toward him. He could see them. He knew they couldn't see him.

One of them called to him. "Isaiah, you up there, boy?"

Isaiah neither answered nor spoke.

"You answer me, boy. You already in big enough trouble." Isaiah remained silent.

"Now!" the man demanded. He seemed to be chewing on something. His voice was rough. He turned his head a bit, spat onto the ground, then continued, "You can come down that tree or we'll sit right here until daylight and then shoot you down. Or, we might just start shooting now. One way or another you coming down."

Through the branches, Isaiah watched as the man who spoke looked at the other men and then they all laughed. "Are you going to kill me?" Isaiah asked in a high-pitched voice.

"Now see there. This is why we coming to get you, boy, 'cause you ask questions. We the law. We ask the questions."

"I'm not coming down if you gonna kill me."

After a moment of silence, the mob's spokesman said, "We ain't gonna kill you, boy. We gotta teach you a lesson, that's all. Black boys can't go around acting like they own stuff. And we heard you act like you think you in charge of things, so we nipping it in the bud. Now come on down. We ain't got all day!"

Isaiah began to descend. As soon as they could reach his legs, they seized them and pulled him down. His body scraped painfully against the rough bark of the tree. As he yelled, "Ouch!" he instinctively turned his head toward them and saw Matt Turner, Mr. Sam Turner's son, trying to put his white hood back on. He had played with Matt when they were children. They used to sit together in the cornfields, splitting off corn leaves and chewing on cornhusks. Under the blazing sun, they would sit on the ground underneath the tall corn stalks while chewing corn and laughing at everything. They had even laughed at worms occasionally crawling out of cornhusks. They would grab the worms, throw them on the ground, and stomp on them. Matt was four or five years older than Isaiah, and it was Matt who had taught him to read. He was four years old at the time, and Matt was nine. Matt would point from word to word in his own book. After two years, Isaiah was reading as well as Matt, and they both discovered that in return Isaiah could help Matt understand his math. Matt had told him, "Hey, Isaiah! You came from slaves, and I came from the master, and you're smarter than me." Every day they used to meet so Isaiah could help Matt with his math because Matt just couldn't seem to get it from sitting in class.

They played together constantly until Matt's eighth year of school, which was when Mr. Turner told Matt that he was old enough to learn how to supervise the plantation. Matt, who was fourteen then, had told Isaiah that he hated what they were teaching him. "They telling me to be mean to niggers and sharecroppers, Isaiah," Matt had said. Isaiah didn't quite understand, but one day Matt stopped coming to their meeting place without even an explanation. Since then, Isaiah hadn't seen Matt, but he had heard about him. There was a lot of talk around the colored community about the white folks they worked for and all the devilment they kept themselves up to. Matt kept getting in trouble, got some girl pregnant, and his daddy sent him off to boarding school in another state.

Now, Isaiah's eyes locked onto Matt's. One of the men yelled, "String him up! Hang him!" Then Matt yelled, in a rough voice, "No. Whip him. Everybody 'round here will hear him yelling. We won't have no more trouble out of niggers 'round here no more." The men agreed.

Matt hadn't wanted to go with the lynch mob, but his father and the men in his family were among the leaders. The men said that blacks had been causing all kinds of problems in town lately. At town meetings, it was said that blacks were trying to get into their schools so they could sit next to their girls and bring shame upon their women. They were trying to take over voting. They had been taking jobs from white men because big factory owners from up North who had relocated to the South liked to hire them. It was agreed that people from up North—white liberals and their black cohorts—came down and stirred up trouble, not only by encouraging coloreds to think they were equal, but also by trying to change laws to make it so that Negroes would be treated as if they were equal.

The subject that came up most often was black men taking white men's jobs. Some white men were already unemployed because some plantations had closed down. Smaller plantation owners couldn't compete with all the latest machinery that harvested crops efficiently. Someone stated that black men had taken jobs from white men because black men would work for lower wages. That was money taken away from white women and children and diverted to black women and children. The only way to keep black people from stepping beyond their boundaries was to scare them. Black men needed to stay and work the cotton fields and watermelon patches and keep on singing the songs that soothed the soul while they worked. That was the way things had been, and that was the way things needed to stay.

Since the leader of the lynch mob was Matt's brother-in-law, Lou, it was expected that Matt would go along with the group. When Matt found that they planned to go after Isaiah, he tried, without looking suspicious, to get out of it. Then his own wife lied and told her brother, Lou, that Isaiah had looked at her in a bold and disrespectful way. His brother-in-law then signaled for Matt to come along. Someone got him a hood and a robe.

Matt knew that his wife had spitefully set him up, because she knew his fondness for Isaiah. He had told her of their childhood friendship because he had been trying to make a point that not all black people were as dumb as everyone liked to think. She had agreed with him, but then again, she had agreed with everything Matt said before he married her. But she had changed after they got married.

Matt felt trapped by his marriage. He didn't love his wife, whom he thought of as a stupid and manipulative woman. His father had told him that she was not good to be around soon after he had started seeing her, but he had been younger then and hadn't been able to see things beyond what was in front of him. Before they were married, she had become pregnant, not once, but twice, and had borne both children. Lou had come marching out onto the field where Matt had been supervising his workers. Shotgun in hand, Lou accused him of shaming his sister. Matt married his children's mother that week. He had already been caught in several affairs since the marriage. Lou, who was built solid like an ox and had an explosive temper, had already told him, "Mattie, I like you, but you gonna make me kill you one day." So when Lou motioned for him to get into the hood and cloak that were brought to him, Matt put them on and left the house with him.

Isaiah's eyes stayed on Matt until the men's roughness with his body caused them to close. The men stretched out Isaiah's arms, pulled them around the tree and knotted ropes around his wrists. They pulled the ropes taut, tying them together so tightly that Isaiah's face was smashed against the tree trunk. Another rope was thrown around his waist and firmly knotted against the other side of the tree. His shirt was quickly stripped off his back. Lou said, "Yeah. I want to see my work." Matt had no choice but to hand Lou the whip. The tail of the whip trailed along the ground as Lou hauled it back. He brought it forward with all the strength and anger in him.

"Ahhhhh," Isaiah yelled. His scream echoed through the woods. "Stop, please stop!" he pleaded. "Ahhhhh."

Matt watched as Isaiah's blood ran down his back. Lou did not stop lashing. Matt saw that every strike on Isaiah's back was digging toward his bones and ripping out flesh when it was pulled back for another strike. Isaiah's screams seemed to come from the depths of his soul. He screamed out, "You said you wouldn't kill me. I won't do it no more. I won't ... I won't."

Matt jumped in front of his brother-in-law. "Come on, Lou. Let me have a few lashes. Your arm must be tired anyway."

Lou nodded and said, "Yeah, you're right."

Matt knew he wasn't as strong as Lou, so his taking over would work to Isaiah's advantage. He consciously slowed down the pace of the lashes. It was a small gesture, but it was the only thing that he could do at that point to save Isaiah's life.

As Isaiah began to drift in and out of consciousness, his mind played tricks on him. He drifted back to when his uncle had beaten him when he was six years old. He had been visiting his relatives and had slept in the bed with his uncle. In the morning when he awoke, he sat up in the bed. He watched his uncle, who stood over a basin, spread white foam from a container all over his face. His uncle then glided a razor down his face. He'd place the razor at the top of his face in another area and glide it down. Afterwards, his uncle splashed water over his entire face than patted it dry with a towel. When his uncle returned to his side of the bed, he bent over to put his boots on. Isaiah edged out of the bed and went to the basin. He picked up the container and shook out some of the foam. The white froth looked so funny on Isaiah's face and hands that he began to laugh. In what seemed like a single leap, his uncle lunged to where Isaiah stood and snatched the container from him. "Boy, this stuff cost, and you wastin' it!" Isaiah couldn't remember his reply, but his uncle had clearly felt that he had been disrespectful and began to beat him with a belt. When Isaiah cried and said he was sorry, his uncle stopped beating him. But now he couldn't understand why his uncle wouldn't stop beating him. And the belt felt like knives being sliced into his skin.

Isaiah lost consciousness. His head hung, and his body sagged against the ropes that held him to the tree. Matt stopped whipping him. Lou, shouted, "What you stopped for?"

"He's dead! I know a dead nigger when I see one," Matt yelled back.

"Okay, okay. Let's get out of here." Lou responded. "I don't know when these niggers gonna learn!"

Matt went to Dr. Zocoff after the attack and asked him if he would treat Isaiah. He said he'd pay him. He broke down and told the doctor everything that happened but asked the doc never to tell Isaiah about the arrangement. Dr. Zocoff, who was from Germany, didn't like the way of race relationships in America. He told Matt he would treat Isaiah, and he could keep his money. Dr. Zocoff didn't feel he betrayed the trust, because he told the story only to Beatrice. And Beatrice, of course, in time, told the story to Isaiah.

Chapter 8 Saving Isaiah

"Tweee! Tweee!" The birdcall came from the man who had been positioned near the lynch mob. It was the signal to let the other men, who were hidden in the bushes, know that the lynching party had left. The men rushed out and ran toward Isaiah. The marks on his back were so bad that the one boy who was with them, who was about Isaiah's age, began vomiting. "Shhh," one of the men hissed at him. "These woods got ears." One of the men went quickly around the tree. Facing Isaiah, he snapped open his jackknife and cut the rope tying Isaiah's hands around the tree. He then cut through the rope around his waist. Isaiah's body fell into the hands of the men positioned on each side of him. Carefully they eased his body to the ground. They placed him on his side while one man squatted in front of Isaiah and put two fingers on his neck. Everyone held his breath as the man felt for the pulse beat of life. The man excitedly whispered, "He's alive!" The men quickly lifted Isaiah up. One said to the young boy, "Run and fetch Millie."

Beatrice had not moved from her living room, crying and begging God to spare her son. Still on her knees praying, Beatrice had heard a blood-curdling yell that she was sure was Isaiah. Difficult as it was to take, although his yelling meant horrendous pain, it also meant he was alive. As she prayed, she found herself struggling to listen for yelling. After a while she heard no sounds at all. She then fought to keep on praying through tears and visions of his hanging from a tree. When she heard rustling noises and men's low voices, she got up off her knees and peeked out her window. The men were carrying her son toward the house. She felt faint as she flung the door wide open. As they hauled Isaiah into the house, one of the men whispered as he passed Beatrice, "He's alive."

Carefully the men laid Isaiah face down on the couch. His back looked like a chopped-up T-bone steak. Blood bubbled out from the slashes. Tears streamed down Beatrice's cheeks as she held her arms crisscrossed over her chest and cried, "My son! My son! Oh, my son!" Every now and then, though, she would lift up her head and look toward the ceiling and whisper, "Oh, thank you, Lord. Oh, thank you. Thank you. Thank you. Thank you, Jesus, for bringing him home alive!"

Millie, upon whom their small community relied for any type of emergency medical care, came in behind the men who had carried Isaiah into the house. After they laid Isaiah down, the men quickly cleared items off a small table and set the table and a stool next to the couch. Millie sat on the stool and began to pull out bandages, ointment, a bottle of pills, and other medical items from her large black bag. These she placed on the table. In a loud whisper, she instructed Beatrice to bring her clean rags. Someone placed a bucket of water on the floor by her feet. She poured some peroxide into the water, placed the rag that Beatrice handed to her into the pail, fluffed it around, squeezed the water out of it, and began patting Isaiah's back. She returned the bloodied rag to the pail, quickly swished it around, wrung it out, and again began patting Isaiah's back. Millie continued this process over and over. The men were quick to change the water when it turned bright red. One of them would grab the pail as soon as Millie finished wringing out the rag. He'd run and toss the water out back. He would scoop the bucket into the barrow of water that sat on the back porch and run back into the house so that the bucket would be alongside Millie when she was ready to dunk the bloodied rag into it. Almost without looking, Millie grabbed each item she needed from the table: the bottle of hydrogen peroxide, ointment, bandages, scissors, tape. Everyone stood quietly watching the operation.

Millie carried herself with such confidence that their small community relied on her when anyone was ill. She wasn't a real nurse. She had learned her skills from watching nurses attend to her mistress. She was so gifted that her mistress let her nurse go and just let Millie take care of her. Friends of her mistress were always trying to get her to send Millie to see about their aging mother or their ailing loved one, but Millie's mistress wouldn't let her wait on anyone but herself. The talk was that it was Millie who kept her mistress alive for years after the doctor had told the family to make funeral preparations.

The day of Millie's mistress' funeral, a white lady left the main group of mourners and walked a short distance back to where the Negro mourners stood. She whispered into Millie's ear as they lowered Millie's mistress into the ground, "You can come work for me now, Millie." And so that lady became Millie's new mistress.

Millie attended to Isaiah for hours before she returned to her home to get ready to go to her mistress' house. However, she checked on him periodically throughout the day. In the long stretches between Millie's visits, Beatrice sat on the stool by Isaiah and watched him. Every time he moved, she whispered, "Thank you, Lord." Peaches sat on the floor beside her. Two neighbors, a man and a woman, stayed with them throughout the first night and most of the next day, their heads nodding as they dozed off in their chairs.

Beatrice looked into the face of her son. Scratches and lash marks marked it so that the skin had puffed out all around his mouth and eyes. Millie had told her that his face would heal with time and that the scars would disappear. As Beatrice stared at her son, she couldn't help wondering why God had allowed this to happen. She went to church. She was active at church. If they had special services or revivals where a guest minister would come, she would be there with her children. She believed everything God said. He said the angels would protect her children. Beatrice shook her head and looked upward as she felt new tears well up in her eyes. As if they were her own words, she whispered words she had read in her Bible, "Though you slay me, yet, I will trust you." Immediately she heard a soft voice whisper in reply, "I have saved your son." She looked around the room and saw everyone else sleeping. She held her hands to her mouth and rocked herself as she said through tears, "Thank you, dear God. Thank you, Jesus. I don't understand why things happen the way they do, but thank you so much, Lord, for saving my son's life. Thank you."

The sound of Isaiah moaning awakened Beatrice. Isaiah opened his eyes and murmured, "Mother ... Mother ... Mama." Beatrice put her face to his, careful not to touch any swollen areas. She kissed him on his eyes and nose as she used to when he was small. He closed his eyes and mumbled, "I hurt bad, Mama."

Heartened to hear her son strong enough to complain, Beatrice whispered, "I know. It's gonna go away soon! I got a pain pill. Miss Millie left it for you 'cause she knew you'd be needing it. I'm gonna put it in your mouth. I'm gonna get you some tea to help you swallow it."

The woman who stayed overnight handed Beatrice a cup of tea just as she had leaned away from Isaiah so she could get up to go to the kitchen. Beatrice smiled at the woman as she took the cup. The tea had remained hot as it had been simmering on the stove all night.

Beatrice's face was nearly touching Isaiah's face as she blew into the cup and placed it to her son's lips. "Open your mouth, so I can set the pill into your mouth, and then take a sip of this tea to help it go down."

Isaiah raised his head and groaned. He put his head back down and closed his eyes tight. The man who had stayed with Beatrice throughout the night stood up, looking to see if she needed help with Isaiah.

"I know, baby," Beatrice whispered into Isaiah's ear. "Just open your lips a little. You got to get this pain pill down in you. It'll make you sleep." Isaiah barely opened his mouth. Beatrice was able to get the pill into it. "Hold on, sweetie. Here! Just sip a little bit of tea." After swallowing the pill, Isaiah immediately fell asleep.

Beatrice stood up and held her arms out as she walked toward her neighbors. The appreciation she felt toward them could be seen in the warmth of her eyes and heard in the softness of her voice. "You like angels. Thank you for staying with me. I'm okay now. Go on home and get some sleep. Stretch out in your beds." The man and woman smiled at Beatrice. They knew that she was feeling better. She hugged each of them as she added with a tone of confidence, "I'll be fine now." The woman told Beatrice that she would check on her and Isaiah periodically. Beatrice smiled and nodded while continually thanking them as they left.

***

Isaiah wasn't the same after that beating, even after his skin grafted back together. He was slow about things. He lingered while walking and moved his arms and hands as if they were stiff. His mother figured, as she watched him walk, that he had to get used to the tightness of his skin. When he was spoken to, he generally wouldn't respond or he'd simply say "um." Even at church he kept a blank stare on his face. Folks began to speculate that his beating had left him brain damaged. Even his mother was not sure how much he understood. But Beatrice kept her mind on the words she heard spoken to her that night they brought him home. That night she had sat in front of Isaiah for hours staring at him. As she looked at him all cut up, she had to fight thoughts of his dying. She had to fight off feeling betrayed by God. She believed that God was her Father who looked out for her and always worked things out for her. Why would He have allowed her son to be beaten? Then she'd remember the whispered voice, "I have saved your son." If God saved her son, He would not give him back to her broken. Beatrice would smile knowing she simply had to wait to see what God had in mind.

A day came when she had to take Isaiah to the city. An elderly doctor had sent word through his maid that he wanted to take a look at Isaiah. He had told his maid to tell Beatrice that she didn't have to pay him anything. The doctor also relayed that, if anyone asked what business they had entering his building, she should say that Dr. Zocoff had sent for the boy to do some work.

It became a challenge for Beatrice to hold onto the way her God told her to be—forgiving and loving toward everyone, even her enemies. She had to fight anger and bitterness because she knew that some of the men who stared at Isaiah as they walked toward Dr. Zocoff's office had nearly beaten him to death. Two men in particular stared hard at Isaiah as they walked past a grocery store. One of them called out, "Hey, boy." Isaiah never changed his empty expression. He lifted his eyes a bit and said, "Yessir." Anyone could see the listlessness in his eyes. Beatrice had to fight thoughts of dying with her son. She knew in her heart that she would fight these men even to her death if they tried to attack her son again. She would surely hurt one of them because she knew that she would have the strength of a bull. Beatrice kept her eyes down and bit her lip as she tightened her grip around Isaiah's hand.

The man who had spoken waved his hat as if granting them his consent to continue on their way. A familiar voice floated through the air. "You doing okay, Isaiah? You all right?" It was Matt whose figure suddenly appeared in the doorway of a small shop.

"Yessir," Isaiah answered.

Matt stood for a moment staring at Isaiah. Then, as quickly as he had appeared in the doorway, he was gone.

When Dr. Zocoff examined Isaiah, he said it was a miracle he had survived. He gave Beatrice medicine that he said would help. He told her that, when she needed more, she should let his maid know. He'd send the medicine through his maid, and there'd be no cost.

***

It took two years for Isaiah to come back. On the day he came back to himself, as his family tended to think of it, a few men and ladies from the church were seated in the house around the kitchen table. Beatrice made tea for them and occasionally checked on Isaiah, who sat silently in an armchair in the living room. The church people were adding up profits from a raffle they had held earlier that week. They were figuring how many Bibles they could buy with the money, but they couldn't get the right count. Every time they recounted, they got a different figure. Then an unfamiliar man's voice said, "Fifteen." When the churchgoers realized that the voice was Isaiah's, it was as if the very air in the house stood still. Isaiah continued, "One raffle ticket hasn't been used yet. A couple of you keep putting that into the count. It keeps throwing off the correct figure for the Bibles."

It was as if Jesus himself had suddenly appeared. Everyone in the kitchen, including Beatrice, rushed into the living room. They stepped past the chair that had been knocked down in their haste to get to Isaiah. They surrounded Isaiah's chair. Tears ran down the women's faces as they hugged him. His mother kissed his forehead while crying and laughing at the same time. One man stood behind Isaiah's chair and stroked his head. Another man patted his shoulder.

Beatrice looked to the ceiling and pointed her finger. "Maybe I missed two years of watching him grow up, Lord," she said, before dropping her head, "but I am so, so, so thankful to you for saving my son."

Everyone began talking to Isaiah at the same time. It was as if they wanted him to get caught up on two years' worth of news that he had missed. Isaiah stood up, and Beatrice saw that even his posture was better. He looked like the confident person he had been before the beating. She began to dance around her son, singing, "Onward Christian soldiers, marching on to war!"

Isaiah was heralded in the community. It was as if he was a walking legend. "Hey, Isaiah!" "Good morning, Isaiah!" "It's good to see you, Isaiah!" Wherever he went, he was welcomed. Boys shyly saluted him when they passed him on the street.

Isaiah quickly earned money from working odd jobs. Beatrice soon realized that, in the past two years, when everyone assumed he was "gone," he hadn't been gone after all, despite his near silence. He had looked empty on the outside, but on the inside, his mind was taking in all sorts of information. Now he could fix anything that needed fixing. He could do carpentry, fix pipes and kitchen drains, secure fallen planks back onto houses, and do electrical wiring. Any other thing that was broken, he'd fix, and it would stay fixed.

When it came to storytelling, Isaiah's beating was the most popular topic in their small community. The talk was that he had braved horrendous torture. He was held in high esteem, thought of as a captured soldier who refused to betray his country. People told how there had been quiet, hidden, black eyes watching the beating. That man who was positioned dangerously close so that he could give the signal when the white men had cleared the area was one of the ones who'd tell the story. He told how Isaiah had come down the tree on his own to face his assailants. No, his attackers hadn't had to go up after him!

Sometimes children wanted to see Isaiah's back. Their parents would hush them, but when the parents weren't around, Isaiah would bend down to a child's height and lift up his shirt.

"Whoa!" one child would say. "It's like crisscrossed all over." Another would run his finger lightly across the scars and ask, "Do it hurt when I touch it?" And Isaiah would pull his shirt down over his back and say, "Not anymore!"

***

A few months after Isaiah had come back to himself, he looked at Beatrice as they sat at the kitchen table eating breakfast. "Mother, I got something to tell you."

"Yes, I'm listening." Beatrice smiled as she always did when he spoke, because the miracle of her son being alive still sizzled in her mind. She looked at him intently. His face had indeed healed. He had grown tall and was so handsome, and it was a manly handsome. Possibly he wanted to tell her he had a girlfriend. It was that time.

"I'm going to New York City."

Beatrice's smile fizzled into a questioning frown. "New York City?"

"Yes. I already wrote cousin Eddie, and he wrote me back." Isaiah pulled out a ticket. "He got me a seat on a bus from his end. All I have to do is board the bus."

Although she felt sad, Beatrice did not let herself become overtaken with sadness, because she knew it was best for him. Isaiah was too smart and too full of life to be caught up by the constraints on their lives that he had to experience in their part of the world. She didn't want him to become discouraged or feel hopeless. And, of course, she didn't want him killed. Now that he had come back to himself, she wasn't sure that Isaiah would continue to hold his head down among white folks, keeping his eyes glued to the ground and answering as simply as possible any questions they asked him. And she knew that there was even a worse fate that could happen to a man who had suffered what Isaiah had suffered. He could become bitter and have hatred burning within his heart. She didn't want her son's heart to change.

"When are you planning on leaving, son?" Beatrice asked.

"Soon. Very soon," he responded. As his mother stared at him, he added, "This week."

Beatrice shook her head. "Why didn't you tell me sooner so I could ..." She didn't know how to end the sentence, and held her hands in front of herself, as if to conjure up the words. "At least I could have helped you pack," she said finally.

"I didn't want to mention it if it wasn't gonna happen. Eddie's talking to his boss man about hiring me. Whether he hires me or not don't matter. I'll find work if I have to go house to house and work free to show people what I can do."

Seeming to come from the depths of her soul, a smile emerged on Beatrice's lips. She was so proud of her son, and she could feel her heart burning with admiration for him. With the Lord's help, she had raised a hardworking man who had values. Her mind was singing, "Thank you, Jesus. Thank you, Jesus."

"And, Mother," Isaiah said, "I'll be saving my money. I want you and Peaches to come up there."

His mother nodded and said, "Oh sure, son. It would be so good to visit you."

"No, Mother. I mean for you and Sis to come live up North, to move up there with me."

Beatrice hadn't seriously thought of leaving the small Mississippi community she'd been born and raised in. She said the first thing that came to her mind, "What about Amos?"

"Mother, Amos is married. I talked to Amos. You know his wife not gonna be willing to separate from her kinfolk down here. Amos supposed to be the man, but you know how that goes."

They looked at each other and nodded, knowing there was no need for further talk. Beatrice smiled at her son and nodded and then whispered, "Yes, we comin'."

No one was surprised to hear that Isaiah was going up North. Everyone nodded agreeably when they heard the news. They knew that Isaiah was destined to achieve something great and that he needed to be free to move toward his destiny.

Before he traveled north, Isaiah asked all the people who had employed him to write a letter about his work. Since a few of the older folks he'd worked for couldn't read or write, Isaiah would write down what they said about his work and they'd put their mark representing their signature at the end of the letter. Beatrice swelled with pride as Isaiah showed her the letters folks wrote about him. He placed the pile of recommendation letters into a large envelope.

At an evening church service, Beatrice proudly showed some of Isaiah's letters to her good friend who was the church secretary. The secretary's daughter, Anita, who was sitting beside her mother said, "They'd look much better typed, wouldn't they, Mama?"

Her mother agreed. "They be much better typed, but I don't know how to fit it in my time. With the church note taking and my job cleaning Mista Jimmy house and tending to your father and taking care of you chil'ren when I gets home, I got no time."

"I can type them, Mama."

"You right. You can type. You do it for Isaiah, baby. You can type them, and then Isaiah can get the people to sign them. That would be very nice."

Anita was beautiful. She had baby-smooth, chocolate-brown skin; large, lucid, light-brown eyes; full, pink-toned lips that had the shape of a kiss; and thick, black hair that stood like a crown over her head. She was tall and graceful. Isaiah had tried to avoid Anita, partly because he was shy concerning girls and partly because he had determined in his mind that he would be leaving, and he didn't want anything tugging at him to stay. Anita was hard to avoid, however. Their families sat next to each other at church, and Anita would look at him until she caught his eye, and then she would smile. Her smile would go right through him causing his heart to beat fast.

Knowing that the letters would look better typed, Isaiah went to Anita's house in the afternoon so she could work on them. Once they were in the house alone and working so closely together, Isaiah could no longer deny his attraction to her. She kissed him first as he leaned over her to check a letter she had typed. Isaiah could not control responding to her kiss. She was soft and succulent like flowing honey.

Much as Isaiah liked Anita, he knew he was too young to be a father. He had seen boys he had grown up with barely emerging from their own childhood before they became trapped by fatherhood. His mother had talked to him often about being careful of such traps that could change his life and take him in a direction that he didn't want for himself. Isaiah wanted to see the world. He wanted to leave the community where he had been born and raised and never return. When he said good-bye to Anita, she was upset, and she let him kiss her only on her cheek.

Chapter 9 Leaving Mississippi

After arriving in New York City, Isaiah was hired immediately at the beverage company where his cousin Eddie worked. During the interview, the owner asked him to describe the work he could do. Holding his hat in his hand as he sat opposite the man, Isaiah looked him in his eyes and said, "I can do any kind of work, sir."

"Can you drive?"

"Yes, sir."

"Can you load?"

"Yes, sir."

"Can you mop?"

"Yes, sir."

"Can you paint?"

"Yes, sir."

"Can you read?"

"Yes, sir."

The man then sat back and became quiet as he stared at Isaiah. Then he asked, "Can you do plumbing?"

"Yes, sir."

"Can you do electrical work?"

"Yes, sir."

"Do you have references?"

"Yes, sir." Isaiah pulled out the letters he had folded in his suit pocket and gave them to the owner. He watched as the owner scrutinized each reference slowly and carefully.

"Oh, you even have experience with concrete and masonry work," the man said as he looked up at Isaiah.

"Yes, sir."

The owner stood up. "I'll pay you a dollar and thirty-five cents an hour. Can you start tomorrow?"

"Yes, sir!" Isaiah excitedly responded.

Isaiah was faithful to his promise to his mother. He stayed with his cousin, gave him five dollars a week, and saved nearly all his money. Within six months he could afford his own apartment—a small one—in Brooklyn. It wasn't the best location, but it wasn't the worst, either. He really wanted to live in Queens because the houses were mostly single-family homes with grass and trees around them. To Isaiah, Queens felt closer to home than any other place in New York City. Isaiah kept a vision of the home he wanted in his mind. He figured that his sister could get a job, while his mother could market her cooking skills. He'd noticed how lots of city folks didn't have the time to cook or couldn't cook, at least not nearly as well as his mother.

He took the steps to make his vision a reality. He wrote to his mother and sister, told them how well he was doing, and asked them to come live with him. Beatrice wrote back to say that they would come! It would take them several weeks to pack. They would have to give things away to reduce to the bare minimum what they would take, since they were limited to what they could carry on the train. She would give the house to Amos, whose wife had a baby on the way.

***

Waves of nostalgia mixed with fear of what the future might hold washed over Beatrice as she looked around her home in the last few moments before she left for good. The sun shone through the light-orange curtains, casting a warm glow over the living room. Orange was her favorite color. She felt like sitting right back down in that big, fluffy orange chair opposite her brown couch. She could sit in that chair, kick off her shoes as she had done so many times, and feel the threads of the fluffy brown rug tickle her toes. She looked around at all the small, pretty ornaments she had on glass shelves against the wall on one side of the room. She couldn't bring herself to look into the kitchen. It would bring back too many memories. Family, friends, and church folk had all sat at her table and been served by her. There had been so much laughter and so many happy occasions.

Beatrice's heart grieved as she and Peaches rode in a taxi through town. They had to travel to the city where the train station was. It was Sunday evening. Neighbors sat out on their porches watching the taxi. Beatrice took out her handkerchief and waved as she passed groups of people. They waved their own handkerchiefs back at her. Beatrice was amazed at how everybody came out to watch her and Peaches leave town.

This was the only town she had lived in, and it had its own unique smell. It was the aroma of chicken being barbecued in someone's backyard, or chicken frying on someone's stove. It was the scent of candied yams and sweet potato pie wafting through the air as they baked. It was the sweet scent of baby powder drifting from the windows. Above all, it was the powerful smell of the richness of the earth after a rain shower. Beatrice had to fight to keep her emotions under control, but she broke down and cried in the taxi. How could she replace the sweet evening air that had enveloped her little family as they sat on the front porch to watch the fireflies? Other children would be running around a tree playing. She would send her children to join them. Neighbors could talk from their porches. Everybody watched the children. Those times were always sweetened when one of the men from the church would come by and sit on the bottom step of her porch. She could always tell when a man liked her. He'd bring her something sweet to eat. She'd eat the chocolate candy or pastry that he brought, but she wouldn't encourage him in any way. She had children to raise. She had made up her mind that she would not be with a man again until her children were grown and on their own. Later, as her children grew up, she contemplated how peaceful things were without a man in her life, and she dismissed any thought of having one. She was determined to live without one until the Lord called her home. She wanted no new worries and certainly no pain, not even tempered by love.

As the taxi passed the church, Beatrice lowered her hands from her eyes in time for one last look at the graveyard behind it. Her husband was buried there. Four years was all they'd had together. He had been run over by one of the reaping machines in the field, or so they said. She didn't believe it. Nobody in town said anything to her about it, but she knew no one believed it. She had put fresh flowers on his grave earlier that day.

A song rhythmically flowed through Beatrice's mind as a breeze came in through the cab windows: "Goin' home. Goin' home … to a place where I belong. Goin' home. I be loving you and I be missing you, but I goin' to a place in the sunshine where I be free. I goin' home. I goin' home. I goin' home!" Beatrice wasn't sure if she was really hearing the song, which she had never heard before, or whether she was imagining it, but she began humming it and then singing it. The song calmed her. As she rode by people, they added to the song, either with words or by humming in deep melodious voices. She felt much better to think that this song was moving with them all the way to the city of Jackson where they were to board the train.

***

When Beatrice and Peaches got off the train at Grand Central Station in New York City after a journey that seemed to have lasted forever, they put down their bags. A stampede of well-dressed white businessmen carrying attaché cases rushed around them from all directions. Not knowing what to expect, they hugged each other tightly burying their faces into each other's shoulders.

There had been some other black folks in the section of the train in which they had been riding. Although they had all slept most of the time, there had been times when they had talked and even shared food. But those folks disappeared so quickly when they got off the train that Beatrice and Peaches were soon the only two colored people standing on the platform. When they saw that no one was approaching them, Beatrice raised her head and looked into the faces of the bustling hordes of people. Everyone's eyes were set ahead. She realized that she and her daughter were invisible to them. They all were rushing to go somewhere, and the only thing that seemed important to them was to get to where they were going. It was as if they were in a different world. Until this moment Beatrice could never have imagined what it would be like to stand in the middle of a crowd of white people who paid them no mind.

Suddenly Beatrice heard the raised voice of her son. Then she saw him waving. He was near the top of the escalator, and he began descending amid a crowd of people. People were even stepping down and off the escalator as it moved. It appeared as if they were tumbling down the steps and getting dumped onto the ground. Even so, they walked off quickly. Once Isaiah was on the train platform, he seemed to make himself thin enough to squeeze through the narrow spaces between people. When he reached them, he hugged Beatrice and Peaches tightly. It had been a whole year since they had seen one another. Isaiah quickly swept his hand over his eyes and wiped the moisture off his face in attempts to regain his composure. He picked up their two large suitcases. "Hold onto my arms," he told them. "We gotta move. We got a train to catch." Positioned on either side of Isaiah, Beatrice and Peaches held on tightly to his arms and found themselves running down more steps. It was hard not to knock into the suitcases Isaiah carried as they moved alongside him. Finally they stopped. Isaiah put the suitcases down. They stood on a platform and waited for a train. Beatrice wondered why they were getting on another train. She could tell from Peaches' eyes that she wondered why as well, but they said nothing. She could handle one more train now that Isaiah was with her. Beatrice was bursting with joy at being with Isaiah again. She felt as if she was living in a wonderful dream. When her husband had died, she had thought about moving up North. But she had babies and a meager income, so she hadn't been able to move. She made herself content with where she was. But now, finally, she had moved up North!

As they stepped onto the train, Isaiah quickly ran ahead of them and covered three seats with the suitcases as everyone scrambled for seats. When Beatrice and Peaches caught up to him, he moved the suitcases out of the way, and the three of them sat down. Beatrice was exhausted from the long journey, and she could tell that Peaches was as well. Beatrice felt her eyelids grow heavy and happily laid her head on Isaiah's shoulder. Soon she and Peaches were sound asleep.

Chapter 10 The Restaurant

Beatrice and Peaches walked with Isaiah into an old multi-story brick building. "It's quiet in here," Beatrice said with a smile that sparked a smile from Peaches. There had been so much noise while they walked through the streets that Beatrice had thought her eardrums would burst. A chill ran through her when she saw dirt caked around ledges and corners of the floors as they waited for the elevator. Entering an elevator along with other people, Beatrice and Peaches were silent as they road up to the fifth floor. They stood quietly behind Isaiah as he unlocked the door to the apartment.

Their eyes widened as they entered and were surprised at the space that was such a contrast to the small rooms of their former home. The kitchen, which was to the right as they entered the apartment, was narrow but had cabinets all around. One side had a counter that overlooked the living room. They followed Isaiah down a short hallway into a bedroom on the left side of the hallway. There were two twin beds in the bedroom with bed coverings on them and near the window was a dresser. Isaiah sat their suitcases down. Beatrice smiled. She was so exhausted that she knew if she lay down on one of the beds, she'd fall off into a deep sleep, clothes on and all.

"This is nice, Isaiah. And you put this all in place by yourself?"

Isaiah smiled, "Let me show you the rest of the apartment.'

A few feet beyond their bedroom was a door. Beatrice held her hands over her mouth when Isaiah opened the door. She and Peaches exchanged glances and nearly at the same time hugged Isaiah. It was a bathroom. They'd had no bathroom in her home in Mississippi, only an outhouse out back. She went inside and touched the ivory-white sink. She looked into the toilet, then flushed it, and her eyes widened more as she stared at the bathtub.

On the other side of the bathroom was another bedroom, which was Isaiah's. They went back into the living room and sat on the couch. Moments later, Beatrice got up and went into the kitchen and began opening up cabinets. Dishes were in the cabinet. Pots were underneath the sink, and utensils were in the drawers. Beatrice shook her head. She looked up and whispered, "Thank you, Jesus." It was a good beginning.

Isaiah laid out his vision of a home in Queens. Beatrice and Peaches agreed to work together to save any money they didn't need for rent, food, and carfare. The day after they arrived in New York City, Isaiah showed Peaches how to look for a job. He went with her through the telephone book and gave her addresses of employment agencies. Within two weeks of coming to New York City, Peaches was hired as a housekeeper at a large hotel.

Cooking and wrapping plates of food consumed Beatrice's entire day. Isaiah got the ball rolling by bringing his mother's hot food plates to his job every day and eating her scrumptious meals during his lunch break. The men got to talking about the food. "Man, Isaiah, your mother can burn!" Someone else would yell out, "Isaiah, you putting my peanut butter and jelly sandwich to shame."

Isaiah was quick to respond. "Mother will make you a plate. She only charge a buck and a quarter." Soon Isaiah had to buy a large picnic basket to carry in the lunch orders. When his cousin Eddie came by in his truck to pick him up for work in the morning, he would load the basket into the back of the truck.

Beatrice purchased a long folding table to accommodate her orders. She put it in the living room up against the kitchen counter. She would turn around from the stove holding a plate that she had filled with food, set it down on the counter, wrap it and reach over the counter and place it on the table. On his way out the apartment, Isaiah would grab the plates and pack them into his picnic basket.

It got so that Beatrice was working day and night because the neighbors began requesting plates of food after they smelled the aroma of her cooking flowing through the hallways. Neighbors, their friends and relatives, and Isaiah's coworkers continually ordered plates. To get some relief, she put a sign on her door: "Closed Sunday."

Footsteps coming from the ceiling had Beatrice stop as she wiped off the table and stare up at the ceiling. "Whee," was all she could say as she shook her head and pressed her lips together. Loud voices erupted near her door, people yelling at one another. She shook her head as she thought, *where I come from neighbors don't yell at one another.* She nodded as she whispered, "I have to get used to the difference. I have to get used to families living around me, underneath me and over top of me." She was up in the sky, and she couldn't simply open her door and be outside. When she did open the door to the apartment, just to escape the boxed-in feeling, she often found herself looking into the faces of strangers. She'd nod and quickly close the door. Isaiah had told her, "Don't open the door when I'm not here. This is not like our hometown. People steal here and will hurt you to get what they want."

Beatrice was cooking one day when she began to breath rapidly and felt she couldn't catch her breath. She could feel her heart racing. Small sweat bubbles formed along her forehead. She knew she would get relief if she could just step out and breathe fresh air. The fact that she couldn't step barefoot out of her house and feel the vibrations of the earth, as if it were talking back to her, added to her closed-in feeling. She forced herself to focus on the family goal, and she fought off the suffocating anxiety that was trying to claim her. She started humming and repeating "Thank you, Jesus" until her breathing calmed. She went back to cooking.

***

Beatrice stepped through the doors of the apartment complex into the ethereal, muted light of dawn's onset and breathed in the now-familiar odor that had at first smelled of trash and was now simply the scent of New York City. The sense of freedom returned to her after she began taking walks. She loved being on these nearly empty streets enjoying the quiet, especially on a morning like this when rain was in the air. She turned a corner and stopped for a moment, closed her eyes so she could listen to the birds talk, letting the drizzle pour over her skin. Even though the air didn't have the sweet scent of Mississippi, she enjoyed feeling it drift across her face. She noted her time because she wanted to return to the apartment before the streets got flooded with people. She felt relaxed and realized that walking relieved her from the anxiety she felt from being hemmed in, and she determined that she would walk as often as she could.

Making her way homeward again—she had to get back and start the day's cooking—she passed an interesting tree. The few trees in the neighborhood weren't much to look at. They were withered and boxed into small patches of earth surrounded by bricks. But this one seemed to be pushing out of its box, its roots peeking out of the soil and touching the box's edges. *The earth is underneath it all*, she reminded herself as she walked on the concrete sidewalks and tarred streets.

Too soon, she pushed her way back inside the apartment.

"Mama," Isaiah scolded lovingly, "you all wet. You'll catch cold."

She smiled and took the towel he handed her.

"Why you want to go out in the rain like that?" he asked.

She took in a deep breath and let it out slowly. "Because I can feel God's life … the rain, the sun, the air, and smell the scent of the earth, even though it's underneath all that concrete."

New York City was more vibrant than Beatrice had imagined from talk she had heard in Mississippi. There was always something new to look at. She looked at people and enjoyed seeing all the different cultures, personalities, and lifestyles that were reflected in their accents, mannerisms, and dress. She would stare at billboards and street signs. She always scanned the windows of produce stores and meat markets. Sometimes she'd watch children playing while she sat on a bench in a park. Watching the children always delighted her even though she noticed that the children were bolder and acted older than children their ages down South. Their giggling and shouting would take her back to when she used to sit on her porch and watch her own children play hide and seek. She used to laugh loudly as she watched their small bodies flinging about as they excitedly rushed to find places to hide.

One evening, as she walked looking for food bargains, she turned a corner from the main street and walked onto a side street that was full of stores. She walked along for some time, lost in thought, so that she didn't realize that she had passed beyond the stores. What caught her attention, however, was music coming from a building. The sound was soft and soothing, and people were humming along with it. Beatrice's ears perked up. It was the kind of music that, in its tone and rhythm, reminded her of her church in Mississippi. She stood still. Carefully listening, she crossed the street and followed the music to a one-story building that was scrunched between two multi-story buildings. The sign above the door read, "God's House." Amazed, excited, overcome by joy, and hardly able to contain herself, she walked inside. With her mouth slightly open, she slowly sat down in a pew. Gleaming eyes, smiling lips and nodding heads turned toward her. People in the pew she sat in leaned forward and whispered, "Welcome." She had walked in during the end of the service, and shortly everyone in the whole church, it seemed, crowded around her to get her name, introduce themselves, and invite her back.

Every Sunday morning and Wednesday evening, which was the day of the church's mid-week service, Beatrice, Isaiah, and Peaches walked to "God's House." Isaiah made sure to bring a plate of food with him the second time they went to the church. After the service, the smell drew people to place orders for dinners. From that day on, Isaiah's family brought large shopping bags filled with dinners to be distributed after the church service.

***

"My Lord!" Beatrice stared at the house in front of her. She blinked her eyes, feeling the tears streaming down her cheeks and half expecting to wake up. Isaiah's warm chuckle filled her heart, and when she turned to him, she saw his eyes too were shiny. It was a large, two-story, single home, with the second level closing together at the top giving that level the shape of a triangle.

"We made it!" he said.

It had taken five years and a lot of work and sacrifice, but they'd finally bought their home in Queens. Its location, on a main street that was a mixture of a few stores along with private homes was perfect.

"C'mon," called Peaches, breaking their reverie, "let's go in."

Slowly they entered the house. The entry opened into an enclosed porch that ran the width of the house. They walked into the living room that opened up into the dining room. To the right of the dining room was the kitchen. They followed the stairway in the living room and looked into each of three good-sized bedrooms and a bathroom. After standing in the hallway for some time, they descended the stairway and stood in the living room. Beatrice nodded when Isaiah expressed his vision of redesigning the front porch to accommodate a take-out restaurant business.

Beatrice went into the kitchen. Isaiah and Peaches followed her. She opened up the back door. She put her hands to her face in joy. "Yes!" The word tumbled from her lips as her eyes scanned the large yard. She stepped down the one step and, holding onto Peaches, took off her shoes. Then she walked barefoot onto the earth. Isaiah and Peaches understood. Beatrice opened her arms wide and turned around making a complete circle just to feel the air. Her mind whirled with visions. She would spend Sunday afternoons shoveling into the earth, digging up weeds, and planting herbs, tomatoes, and a few vegetables. All summer long she'd gather up the herbs and veggies, and she'd use them in her recipes. In another area of her yard, she'd plant a rose bush and other flowering plants.

Within a month of moving to Queens, Isaiah hung a large sign outside the building: "Southern Kitchen." And they opened for business. The small take-out did so well that Isaiah left his job at the beverage company, and Peaches left her job at the hotel to work the restaurant. They pooled all their money together and paid off the mortgage in seven years.

As Beatrice was seasoning meat one morning, and Peaches was chopping up onions for the meatball stew they were making, the voices of Isaiah's associates drifted into the kitchen. They had gotten used to the men at their home, but now and then they'd hear a word or phrase that would push through their thoughts. Sometimes the group's movements vibrated into the kitchen. They were civil rights activists that Isaiah had begun associating with. He went to their meetings, and often he invited them to the house to hold meetings. Although Beatrice and Peaches were generally too busy keeping abreast with food orders to pay attention to the men's discussions, there had been times they had been completely distracted. Some evenings a man would bring a film projector and he'd set up a screen that'd show violent acts that had happened to Freedom Riders, which was the name given to men and woman who traveled to the South to protest racial injustice. Generally while the men watched the films, they'd become so quiet that Beatrice and Peaches would peek into the living room, and the pictures they'd see on the screen would frighten them. At times the men would shout and cheer. Then there were times they'd whisper throughout the entire meeting. Beatrice and Peaches admired the men, who were putting aside their lives to address inequality for Negroes in America. But they were also afraid for them because of the danger they faced.

Beatrice leaned back on the couch and placed her feet up on the ottoman. It was Sunday afternoon. It felt good being in her duster lounging around which was how life had been in the South. Church had been good. She looked over at Isaiah. He was reading the newspaper. Peaches was upstairs in her bed taking a nap.

Beatrice dozed off, but Isaiah soon woke her. "Mother."

Beatrice turned her head toward him, "Yes, son."

"As you know, I been meeting with the Freedom Riders. He paused

Beatrice tried to shut her mind from thoughts that were trying to form. She bit her lips.

"I'll be traveling with the group."

Beatrice felt as if a bolt of lightning had just shot through her body. Even the vibrant reddish undertone in her coloring left her. She then felt Isaiah hands over her hands. "I have to do this, Ma. I'll be leaving tomorrow early, and I'll return on Thursday. I'll be going to Mississippi. I'll be okay. I know how to take care of myself. I need you to believe in me."

Beatrice shook her head as the thought ran through her mind that something was wrong with Isaiah's thinking, though he functioned well in everything he did. It seemed that he had got past the horror of the ordeal he had suffered in Mississippi, but some part of his head had to be still damaged, because going back to confront racism was not sound thinking. It was more like some sort of death wish.

Her thoughts tumbled out of her mouth, "Son, you're the bravest man I know. I'm so proud of you. But I don't understand why you want to put your life in jeopardy by going to Mississippi protesting segregation. Don't you want to live? Do we give you too much pressure, me and your sister? I know how you look after us."

Isaiah shook his head. Then he turned his back toward Beatrice and lifted up his shirt. She jumped. She hadn't seen his back since he was eighteen. It looked worse than she remembered. It was horribly distorted. He had grown, and in that time the ripples hadn't gotten smaller, but had hardened into wide, raised rolls.

He put his shirt down and turned back to his mother. "That's why I go back. It's not about me anymore. It's about our children. It's about our children when they get here. It's about the young black boys and girls still down there. Somebody has to do this. I'm not waiting for somebody else to stand up. I'm doing what I need to do."

Beatrice never questioned him again. She nodded her head and tried hard to smile. She maintained her composure as Isaiah ran upstairs. She took tissues that she had in her pocket and wiped her eyes and blew her nose. Forcing herself to be strong, she went into the kitchen and poured out some tea into a cup. She sat at the table sipping and taking bites out of a donut. She then rinsed off her dishes and went upstairs to her bedroom. She couldn't be at the Sunday dinner table with Isaiah and Peaches. Up in her room, she read her Bible and prayed, "Please, Lord, change his mind. Please let my son not go with the Freedom Riders."

After a while, her children's sweet voices flowed in under her doorway, "Mother, dinner's ready."

"I'm not hungry. I had something earlier. You go on and eat." She had always eaten with them. Peaches' voice wavered. "Are you okay, Ma?"

"Yes, I'm okay." She heard Isaiah whisper, "Let her be, Sis."

Early Monday morning there was a soft knocking at her door. "Come in." She knew it was Isaiah. She had slept sometime during the night, for which she thanked God, but she had been awake most of the night. She'd heard Isaiah in the bathroom showering. Although turned away from him, she felt his large body overshadow her. He kissed her and whispered, "I'll see you Thursday."

She listened to his quick feet go down the stairs and heard the front door slam. Quickly she got up and looked out the window. She watched Isaiah get into the car that waited in front of the house.

Each day Beatrice fought off flashes of horrid visions of what could be happening to her son ... the bus getting turned over, torches thrown at him, beatings with sticks, hanging. She cursed the devil with each vision. She and Peaches refused to turn on the news so that they would not hear any bad news. Each new day felt like a victory because there had been no phone call. And although she thought it would never come, Thursday arrived. Around six in the evening, even through her cooking, Beatrice heard the front door open, and she nearly dropped what she was holding, as did Peaches. They quickly sat their bowls on the table and rushed to Isaiah and lost themselves in him.

They followed him to the couch and sat down, one on each side of him. Isaiah told then in a matter-of-fact way what had happened on his trip. "We stayed with families in the community. We met at churches and educated folks on the importance of voting and showed them how to vote. We went around the city putting up posters on racial equality. Yeah, people jeered at us and tore down the posters as soon as we put them up." Isaiah jumped up and bowed his back and curved his arm and started scratching up and down his belly and hoping around. "They called us gorillas!" Beatrice and Peaches couldn't help but laugh even though there was a tear in Beatrice's eye. "We just keep putting up the posters. They was trying to throw rocks, but the police stopped them. Men shouted out, 'You ain't never going to school with our daughters!' I wanted to say, 'I don't care if I never see your daughters, but our daughters are going to schools they want to go to.' We ordered at a segregated restaurant sitting in the 'white only' section. Sure we got spit on and received nasty insults, but no bodily harm.

***

Beatrice's eyes opened wide when, after his second week home, Isaiah announced that he would be going on another trip. She looked at Peaches, and she could see tears forming in her eyes.

"I'm leaving in the morning, going to South Carolina. I'll be back on Friday," he told them.

"Well, how often will you be going on these trips?" Beatrice had to know even though she didn't want to.

In his calm manner he answered, "About every other week I'll be traveling to a southern city in Alabama, the Carolinas, Georgia, and Mississippi.

Beatrice made sure she knew his schedule and had food prepared for him and the others he traveled with by bus, van, or car. She spent a lot of time in what she called her "prayer closet," closing the door to her room and praying on her knees to God. And when he was on a trip, Beatrice and Peaches used that time to catch up on everything they never had time to get to, because while Isaiah was gone they worked all day and nearly all night to keep their minds busy. They had to fight thoughts of Isaiah hanging from a tree.

Occasionally Isaiah would bring a new associate involved in the civil rights movement to the house to stay. That man would stay at their home until he got settled in a place of his own or until he returned to his home down South. Several of the men had expressed an interest in Peaches.

Peaches had shied away from the few men who had tried to start conversations with her. She and her mother were busy nearly all the time with the affairs of the restaurant. The kitchen had nearly taken over the house. Over the years they had remodeled the house so that what had formerly been the living room was turned into a huge kitchen. What had been the kitchen and dining room were remodeled into a living room, with a dining table and bureau in one area and a long, elegant white sectional couch covering nearly two walls across the room.

Beatrice didn't want the kitchen to take over Peaches' life. She thought that if Peaches waited too long, it would be too late for her to find a husband. One day she blurted out, "Peaches, it's time you get to thinking about marriage and a family. I got to have some grandbabies to cuddle up

North here. It seem your brother don't have time for settling down, but I see men looking at you, and you don't give them the time of day. Look, someday I'm going to die. And Isaiah, he busy coming and going. You got to look out for yourself. Stop turning your nose up at these men. Give a nice one a chance. Get to know him so you might get married and have your own family."

It wasn't long after her mother's comment that Peaches noticed a young gentleman who came into the house with Isaiah. He began to come to the house regularly for meetings. The men would talk, make phone calls, then leave. One evening after serving the men, as she walked back toward the kitchen, Peaches overheard the man she liked whisper to Isaiah that he would like to meet her. Isaiah put him off, saying, "This is not the time."

Weeks later, Isaiah and the young man returned from a trip to Alabama. Beatrice and Peaches, who had been cleaning up the kitchen, prepared food for them. As Beatrice was returning to the kitchen, she overheard the young man say, "I'd like you to formally introduce me to your sister."

When she didn't hear Isaiah's response, she realized that he must have fallen asleep. She went back into the living room and shook Isaiah's shoulder. "Isaiah," she said loud enough to wake him up. "This here gentleman has asked a question. I think you should answer him."

The young man repeated his request. "I'd like you to formally introduce me to your sister."

Isaiah got up and went into the kitchen. He had to tap Peaches on her shoulder to get her attention past the sound of clashing pots and splashing water. "Peaches, I want to introduce you to someone."

"Who, Isaiah? You see how busy I am."

"He's been asking me since I first brought him here, but I ain't answered him."

"Go on, Peachy," Beatrice said, coming back into the kitchen. She returned to pounding the dough for the next morning's baking. "Meet the gentleman. I'm okay."

Peaches placed her hands under the faucet, then dried them on her apron. "Look at me. I'm all sweaty. I'm a mess." Beatrice and Isaiah smiled at her. Beatrice could tell she was warming up.

Peaches followed Isaiah into the living room where the young man stood waiting. Beatrice couldn't stop herself from watching from the kitchen doorway.

"Peaches, this is Luther Elkton. As you know, Luther, this is Patricia, who we affectionately call Peaches." Peaches bowed her head and shook the hand that Luther extended to her.

"I'd like to know if I could take you, your mother, and of course, this crazy man here to dinner." Luther Elkton continued to hold Peaches' hand as he spoke. "I know you and your mother run this restaurant. I'm sure there's no finer cooks in all New York City. But maybe you can let me treat you so you can have someone serve you. I know a nice restaurant in Manhattan."

Peaches removed her hand from Luther's grip and burrowed it into her apron pocket. She looked at her mother and then at Isaiah, who said, "Don't you refuse my treat. Remember, I'm part of this too." As soon as she saw Peaches nod, Beatrice retreated into the kitchen, satisfied.

***

Six months from the day of their meeting, Peaches and Luther were married. Luther was an accountant, and he was gifted at making money expand and seeming to appear out of nowhere. He handled the finances for the Freedom Riders, securing vans and buses, and he saw that everything that was needed was in place. The day of their wedding Luther carried Peaches over the threshold into their home, which she had not known he had purchased for them. The wedding party and guests clapped as they entered, and the wedding celebration was held right there in their lovely home.

The marriage was a turning point in Peaches' life. She immediately got pregnant and was nauseated throughout the pregnancy. Beatrice had to hire help to keep up with the pace of orders at the restaurant. Before the first child was a year old, Peaches found herself pregnant with her second child.

The restaurant business began to suffer because hired help was not as dependable as family. So Peaches began bringing her babies to the restaurant. She, Beatrice, and Isaiah, when he was in town, would work nearly round the clock. At six in the morning, they would start preparations for the day's orders. They closed at nine o'clock at night. It took nearly two hours to wash all the huge pots, utensils, pails, instruments, and surfaces, and then sweep and mop the floor.

It was Isaiah who suggested that they close the restaurant. Even with hired help, an overload of work was always waiting for them. Isaiah said they had done well. They had enough money saved that, if they wanted to open another business later, they could. Luther agreed completely, and they made plans to close the restaurant, but they never agreed on a date.

Peaches had another baby. Now with three children—one boy and two girls—she juggled marriage, child rearing, and the restaurant. She pushed herself to get up early so she could get the babies up, dressed, and out with her. Luther would pick them up after work, but often the entire family wouldn't leave the restaurant until eleven at night. Peaches knew that Beatrice would stay up into the early hours of the morning cleaning up and preparing the next day's main courses if she wasn't there to help her.

One day, as Peaches had one arm resting on her hip and was using her other to stir the contents of a jumbo pot, she heard a strange sigh come from her mother. She turned toward her mother, dropped her stirring spoon, and cried out, "Mother! Oh, God! Oh, my God!" In a split second, Peaches had knelt down on the floor so that she could position herself underneath the upper part of her mother who had begun sliding down alongside the stove. Carefully she held her mother's head and lowered her onto her lap. The weight of her mother's body caused her knees to collapse so that her legs and hips were in an awkward and uncomfortable position, but she paid that no mind.

"Monica!" Peaches screamed. Monica, the hired help, who was upstairs getting the children to take a nap, banged down the stairs and rushed into the kitchen. She covered her mouth to smother her scream.

"I can get under this arm while you get under the other arm." Peaches panted as she struggled to move from under her mother's upper body and position herself under her shoulder to lift her. Together they lifted Beatrice out of the kitchen and sat her on the couch.

"Mother! Mother!" Peaches frantically called while gently tapping her face. There was no response. She ran to the phone and was barely able to focus on dialing for an ambulance, "My mother fell. I think she's unconscious. Please hurry," she shouted after giving her address. With trembling hands, she called her husband, crying as she spoke, "Mama fell. She's unconscious. I'm riding with her to the hospital. Call Isaiah."

Peaches then ran over to her mother. "Mama. Mama." She rushed into to the kitchen and got a cool towel and stroked her mother's face with it.

When she heard the sirens, she turned to Monica, "Monica, can you look after my children so I stay with my mother?"

"Yes, don't worry."

When the ambulance attendants approached her mother, Peaches broke down and cried uncontrollably as they lifted Beatrice onto a stretcher.

"She'll be okay," Monica whispered as she rubbed Peaches' shoulder.

"Are you riding with her?" The ambulance attendant's voice forced her to compose herself.

"Yes." Peaches shook her head as she responded. She felt empty as she followed the stretcher.

Isaiah and Luther were at the hospital within minutes of the ambulance's arrival. They joined Peaches in the waiting room. After an hour, a doctor approached them with distressing news. "Are you her son?" he asked, looking at Isaiah. Isaiah nodded. "And you're her daughter?"

"Yes." Peaches' voice was barely audible.

"I'm her son-in-law, Patricia's husband," Luther volunteered as he rubbed his wife's arm, knowing he was next to be questioned.

"Your mother's heart has failed. I need to run some tests to get a clearer idea about her condition. She's stable right now, but this is a serious situation."

"Can we see her?" Peaches was nearly crying.

"Of course."

"Peaches and Isaiah followed the doctor to Beatrice's bedside. Peaches wrapped her arms around her mother's neck and gently laid her head on her chest. Beatrice had regained consciousness, and despite her ordeal, her face looked rosy and bright. Peaches thought that the short time away from the restaurant had restored her mother to the freshness of youth, like the way she looked when they lived in Mississippi. Isaiah held his mother's hand and kissed her.

"How much, doctor?" Beatrice said with a strong, firm voice. "How much will the medicine and the tests cost?

Isaiah and Peaches looked at their mother. Immediately Isaiah intervened. He shook his head. "Please, Mother, don't be concerned about any cost. We'll handle the cost. You just get well."

The doctor had already called the billing office. Peaches saw her mother's eyes take on a distant look after the doctor quoted the cost. Beatrice closed her eyes and said faintly. "It would take everything we worked for. It would take all the family savings. No! No! I'm not doing that to my children." Her voice was firm, and she shook her head.

Isaiah tried hard to convince her. "We made the money. We can make it again. It's important that you get the care you need."

"But they say I won't be able to work the restaurant." Beatrice's eyes fastened on Isaiah's. "Look at me, Isaiah. I'm old now. I lived my life, and I'm satisfied." She smiled. "I have seen my children grow up nicely. I have seen my grandchildren. I have seen this family make good, and that's something not easy for our folks to do. Look at all our old neighbors living down there in them shacks in Mississippi. They still there. And we got nice homes and a business. If it's the Lord's time for me to join him, then let it be. Don't try to delay." She smiled. "You can't change God's mind."

Peaches tried to object, but her mother shook her head. "I had a good life," she whispered. "It's you children who made all the difference. I'm so happy with my family."

A nurse whispered, "We have to ask you to let her rest now."

As they walked toward the waiting area where Luther sat, Isaiah shook his head and said, "She won't agree." Peaches started crying and laid her head on Luther's shoulder. Moments later nurses were running toward Beatrice's room. A doctor came out and went to Isaiah while looking at Luther and Peaches as he talked. He seemed rushed as he said, "Your mother slipped into a coma. If we don't move quickly, we could lose her."

"Treat her! Give her the tests and medicines she needs," Isaiah said firmly. The doctor left, and within seconds a nurse came running toward Isaiah and handed him papers to sign.

***

The restaurant closed. It was not as difficult as they thought. They simply put a large sign out on the front door that read: Closed Until Further Notice.

Peaches was in the kitchen stirring the batter for the cake she was making to celebrate her mother's three-month milestone—the critical period after the operation she had undergone. As she stirred, she thought about how the doctors had told her mother that she would be on medication for the rest of her life and how they forbade her from doing any kind of strenuous activity, including restaurant work. Peaches stirred harder and harder as she thought of her mother's spirits being so low. As she was scrapping the batter into the pan, she heard a slight groan and immediately rushed to the living room. She saw her mother's body go into convulsions.

"Mother, Mother. Mama! No! Please, Mother!" With her hands shaking, Peaches picked up the phone and dialed for an ambulance. She screamed into the phone while staring at her mother, "My mother's having convulsion. She has a bad heart. We're at 1210 Bolden Avenue. Please hurry!"

The convulsions stopped. Peaches dropped the phone and ran across the room. Her mother's head was turned to the side. Her eyes were open and her mouth was slightly parted.

"Ahhhh," Peaches cried out. She wrapped her arms around her mother and started rocking. "No, Mother. Please. Please, Mother. Please, Mother, come back! Come back, Mother! Come back. Please don't leave us, Mother." She felt an arm on her shoulder firmly moving her to the side. The paramedics had arrived.

"How long has she been like this?"

"A few minutes," Peaches responded, her voice shaking.

"Move back!" the man shouted as he began pounding into her chest and alternatively breathing into her mouth. Beatrice's body heaved up and then air escaped from her lips.

"We got her!" The man yelled, and quickly both men moved her onto a stretcher and rushed her to the ambulance.

Peaches felt as if a huge force was tugging at her heart trying to pull it out. She called Luther, who left work immediately. She called Isaiah at the hotel number he had left with her. He said he would pack and board a bus back to New York. That night Peaches sat in the hospital waiting room, leaning on Luther's shoulder as she dozed off. The sun was just beginning to rise when Isaiah arrived, his voice jolting her out of her sleep. After their saddened hugs, she sat back down and drifted back off to sleep. Footsteps commanded her attention.

"Hello. I'm Dr. Alberto. This is Dr. Epstein." The doctor's voice was soft, and his eyes were compassionate. Even before the doctors' conversation turned to talk about her mother, Peaches knew in her heart that they hadn't been able to save her mother. Peaches and Isaiah knew that their mother had resolved that it was her time to go, and she had moved on to where she wanted to be.

"We're so sorry," Dr. Alberto said. "We were able to revive her three times, but she would not hold on."

***

Peaches was in the kitchen working, lost in reverie not believing that three years had passed since her mother died. She pounded at her bread dough when thoughts of Luther slipped in. She shook her head as her heart felt heavy, and she pounded harder so that she wouldn't feel the emptiness of that great hole that was in her chest. It was her children who kept her going. She made herself think of them so they would fill the hole. They gave her a purpose for living.

Sometimes it seemed as if Luther's handsome smiling face would appear in the kitchen doorway. She could almost hear him, "Peaches, you need to take a break now. You come on out of the kitchen and sit on the sofa with the kids. I'll wash those pots." Peaches nodded her head as her mind whispered, "It was good that Mama left before Luther was taken. It would surely have killed her to learn that her son-in-law, whom she regarded as her son, the father of her grandchildren, had been brutally murdered."

Tears slid down Peaches' face. She stopped her pounding and struggled to sit down in the chair by the table because her legs felt wobbly. Visions that she regularly fought flashed before her. A mob of men rushing toward the demonstrators Luther had been marching with. Men pulling Luther and another freedom rider into a car, laughing and drinking alcohol as they drove to a narrow landfill and pushed them into it. One of the men worked the levers on a backhoe, dropping scoop after scoop of dirt and debris on top of Luther and the freedom rider who was with him, burying them alive. "No ..." The word slipped out of her lips in a whimper. She sat down, wiped her eyes with her apron, and placed her arms on the table, allowing her head to drop into them. Rivers seemed to gush out of her eyes as her body quivered.

Peaches became just like her mother, working all the time. She moved back into the family home and reopened the restaurant. She got up early in the morning and generally didn't get to bed until past midnight. She hired help so she could be with her children when they returned from school, but her mind was always on the restaurant: what spices she had run out of, what items needed to be ordered.

"Momma, how many cups of water you need me to pour into the soup?" Sybrina had simply appeared in the kitchen and had grabbed the measuring cup.

"Four cups!"

Peaches' favorite child was Sybrina. Sybrina tried hard to please her mother and worked side by side with her, just as Peaches had done with her own mother. And Sybrina looked just like Beatrice. Peaches' son was nicknamed Skippy because he loved peanut butter. He would run into the kitchen just to grab something to eat and would disappear to his room. Her youngest, Missy, was just the opposite of Sybrina. She wouldn't go near the kitchen; her time was consumed with her friends and social activities.

Although one day seemed to drag into another, the years seemed to fly by so that one day Peaches turned around and looked at her children and they were grown. Skippy joined the Navy. Peaches knew he tried to distance himself as much as he could from the restaurant. He signed up for several tours in Vietnam before he was killed in action. Missy had become a nurse, and she joined the Peace Corps and married a native physician in Bangladesh where she was stationed. Only Sybrina stayed home, working as hard as Peaches worked.

Peaches was only forty-six years old when she died. Her heart simply stopped. The doctors said she had worked herself to death. Isaiah and Sybrina agreed to close the restaurant for good.

Sybrina married one of the young men Isaiah had brought up North with him following a civil rights demonstration in Alabama. After they were married, she moved with her husband to Alabama to live.

Chapter 11 Amos and Ellie

Nia strained her ears when her Grandma Vern's voice stopped. She listened for footsteps. The door to her room was slightly open. With her knees up to her chest and her arms clasped around her legs, she sat on the floor by the door opening. Sometimes she had been so intent on listening that she almost got caught. Most of the time, however, she'd scoot back and climb onto her bed whenever it sounded as if someone was coming. She was about to move, but then she heard Grandma Vern jubilantly ring out from the living room, "Now you talk about our folk and their history—let me tell the story about my mom and dad, old Amos and Ellie."

Nia couldn't pull herself away from the doorway when Grandma Vern was telling stories about her family. As she listened, scenes involving the people Grandma Vern talked about would come before her face. It was as if she was watching a movie. She kept the various family groups categorized in her head while she listened. She had questions, but she couldn't ask Grandma Vern. However, she found that as she kept listening many of her questions were eventually answered.

The telling of the family history would go on into the early hours of the morning. Even with all their smoking and liquor drinking, her relatives and their friends would get sobered up by the story telling. Sometimes other, older relatives would add their versions of the events that had happened. The listeners would become quiet as each speaker talked. Occasionally comments would slice through the atmosphere, "Yeah!" "I don't know how

I'd make it if I was living back then." "They was mean." "Well, at least she died peacefully."

When Grandma Vern told about her own mother, Nia could understand how Grandma Vern had become so mean. Grandma Vern's mother, Ellie, had four babies die right in her home. It was whispered among the town's women that the babies knew she really didn't want them so they chose to return to heaven. Grandma Vern's daddy, Amos, dug their graves and buried them behind the house. They'd have the minister over, and her family would gather around the small grave. Daddy Amos would plant a flower over each baby's grave. Daddy Amos was Beatrice's eldest son, the brother of Uncle Isaiah and Aunt Peaches. It took a long time for Nia to figure out that Daddy Amos was the same man Grandma Vern had said was Nia's great-granddad.

Grandma Vern told how her daddy used to work hard to make crops grow because that's what he did to provide for his family. He had worked for Mr. Thomas, who had given him a plot of land, so he worked that plot along with Mr. Thomas's land. Sometimes weather conditions ruined all his hard work. Those times when there was no rain, the crops stayed small and withered. One summer a big storm caused flooding everywhere. Daddy Amos was out in that torrential rain and raging wind trying to savage what crops he could, pulling them up and putting them into a big burlap sack that he dragged behind him.

Daddy Amos used to walk around with his head down. Grandma Vern believed that it was partly because he felt bad because there were days when his family went hungry. It was also because, in those days in Mississippi, it was disrespectful for a black man to look a white man or woman in the eye. He didn't want to chance having white men look at him and assume that he thought he was good enough to look them in the eye. Then too, Daddy Amos wasn't an attractive man. He didn't look like the rest of the family. He was short. Everyone else in the family was tall in stature. Amos's skin didn't have the reddish undertone like his family members had. His skin was a dull, listless, grayish-brown so that it always had an ashy look. Grandma Vern said that was why Beatrice had always shined him down with loads of lard when he was a child. He had lips that were too large for his face, slanted eyes that were too tiny for his face, and a broad nose that stretched too far across his face. He simply didn't look like his family. Actually, the secret that nobody talked about, but everybody knew, was that Beatrice wasn't Amos's real mother. Amos was two years old when his father and Queen Bee married. His father had been raising him because the boy's mother had died during childbirth. So, although Beatrice held him in her heart as if he was her son, his difference from her other children told another story. His walking around with his head down was more likely due to his not seeing himself as equal to other people in general, even the people in his own family.

Nia's Great-Grandpa Amos had worked since his youth on the plantation doing gardening and farming. He was a young man when he asked his mother to ask Great-Grandma Ellie's daddy if he could marry her. They were both young. He was eighteen, and she was sixteen.

Amos was too young to have any expertise with women. He couldn't see that Ellie, despite the fact that she worked from sunup to sundown picking cotton, had a spiteful disposition. It wasn't long after their marriage that she began acting sulky and sour tempered. When they first got married, they were living with her family. Then Amos asked Mr. Thomas for an old, abandoned, two-room shack that had once been used as slave quarters. Amos used what spare time he had to make it habitable, and then they moved in. They had to go outside to pump water, and the outhouse was a distance from the shack.

Granddaddy Amos did everything he could think of to please Ellie, but he couldn't stop the babies from coming, and she blamed him for each one. Things improved a bit when his mother gave him her house when she moved up North. Then Mr. Thomas died, and his children sold the plantation, so Amos lost his job. He was grateful that he was allowed to keep the land that their daddy had given to him. When the land wasn't yielding due to drought, Amos sought work as far as his feet would take him, and he took whatever was offered. He did everything from cleaning up gas spills to painting stores. Those jobs were unstable. He always was the first to be let go for whatever reason, or seemingly no reason at all. He couldn't get it in his heart to write his mother to ask for her help, although he'd heard that they were doing well up North.

When the land was good to Amos, his family ate well. He had taught his sons farming as soon as they could pull up weeds from the ground. He was a very organized man, and he had assignments all lined up for his children throughout the day at the level they were capable of handling. He was a thrifty man and had managed to buy some chickens, so he taught his children how to feed the chickens and how to clean their pens regularly. But Granddaddy Amos died young, at the age of thirty-two, in an explosion at one of the oil refineries where he had been working on weekends to bring more money into the household. They said Ellie slipped up after the funeral service saying to her sister that she was glad Amos was taken up so that she wouldn't have any more babies. Beatrice, Isaiah, and Peaches had gone down for the funeral, and they overheard her say that, and from that day on their family had nothing to do with her.

After Amos died, Ellie let herself go. Her beauty, which had been defined by her velvety, dark-brown complexion; her large, dark-brown eyes; perfectly sculptured lips; and a well-curved figure, dissipated. The change occurred because the frown that remained on her face pulled her cheeks down. Her rapid weight gain changed the contours of her body, and her sour disposition took the vibrancy out of her eyes.

Grandma Vern said that all she had ever heard as she was growing up was her mother talking about how she had made the wrong choice in marriage, because now she was poor and left strapped to a houseful of children. Ellie would tell her children that, when she was young, she could have married any boy she wanted, but she married their daddy because he had a job and worked hard, so she figured she'd be taken care of.

Great-Grandma Ellie would get angry whenever she thought about how her life had panned out. She would say that no one in his right mind would marry her now. As she'd move about her house, she would become frustrated by everything around her, and her temper would flare up no matter what she was doing at the time. If she was cooking, the children would hear the cast-iron fryer slammed onto the stove. They could hear her frustration in the heavy-handed way she'd mix eggs in a bowl. Grandma Vern said that, when her mother combed her hair, if she was angry, she would snatch the comb right through the knots so roughly that Grandma Vern's eyes would tear up. But she couldn't complain, because then her mother would smack her with the comb.

Ellie stayed mostly in her room and slept. When she came out, she wouldn't tolerate anything from her children—arguing, fighting, crying. Whatever object was near her would get picked up and used as a weapon against whoever was creating the noise. Grandma Vern's brothers had often gotten Ellie's huge black frying pan slammed against their heads.

Grandma Vern related how she was always getting beatings. She was one of the younger children, and Great-Grandma Ellie had no time for babies lingering. Once her babies began to walk, they had to learn to help out, or at least stay out of the way. Grandma Vern said that she usually didn't get out of the way fast enough so her mother frequently whacked her as she went past her fussing.

Her mother had thrown Carlton, her favorite brother, out of the house. Carlton was the only one who talked back to Ellie, and that happened only on three occasions that Grandma Vern could remember. Each time he was defending her.

Suddenly, Grandma Vern raised her voice. "I remember standing over that basket of clothes that was next to the kitchen table. I was only, I think, five years old, but I remember looking at those clothes, and I was trying to do what my moma showed me to do." Grandma Vern chuckled. She then continued. "It looked to me like she just took up something from the basket and pushed it together and put in on the table. Ellie came toward me screaming. She picked up that strap that she always kept nearby and started hitting me on my legs. I was crying, but then I saw Carlton next to Ellie. He said, "Ma, she can't fold them clothes right. She's just a baby. She don't understand, and she got baby fingers. Her hand too little." But when Carlton spoke, Ellie's face turned to looking like the face of a grizzly bear. She looked at Carlton and raised her arm with all the strength she could muster up and she brought that strap down on Carlton so savagely that his skin bore raised, swollen welts from the belt for days."

Nia had moved to the edge of the hallway, and she could see everyone in the room sadly shaking their heads. Grandma Vern continued, "Yet, Carlton spoke up for me on another occasion and got beat for doing so. The third time he 'defied' her, as Ellie called it, Ellie grabbed her shotgun, pointed it at him, and told him he was too grown to live under her roof. She cocked the hammer. Carlton ran out of the house with only the clothes on his back. He was sixteen years old."

Grandma Vern didn't see her brother Carlton until nearly seven years later, when she was twelve. He had come down for their mother's funeral as did her other two brothers who had left home when they were fifteen and sixteen. Grandma Vern became sad and reflective as she relayed that Ellie looked cold, hard, and aged beyond her years as she lay in the casket. But her children grieved sorely for her. They were gravely sorrowful because they believed that they had drained the life out of her, which was what she had always told them. She was laid to rest in the earth beside her husband.

Chapter 12 Grandma Vern's Move to New York

The family split apart after Ellie passed. When they went back to the house after the funeral, Vern's older brothers and sisters discussed how they would take care of the younger ones. Her eldest sister, who cooked for a rich white lady, offered to keep the youngest three siblings, which included Vern. She would take them to work with her, but they would have to sit quietly while she cooked. But her brothers felt that would be too much for her to take on. Carlton suggested that he take Vern back to New York City with him. He and his girlfriend would raise her until she was of age. That sat well with everyone, so Grandma Vern went with Carlton to New York City.

It turned out that Carlton was seldom home. He excused his absence by saying that he was working to "bring in the bacon." His girlfriend, Andrea, was already frustrated with Carlton. Now, in addition to caring for their own two children, she had his twelve-year-old sister to care for. She had no tolerance for Vern, whom she promptly and severely criticized for even the smallest mistakes. Consequentially, Vern stayed away from the house as much as she could. She'd stand along the schoolyard fence or sit on a bench until it began getting dark. Then she'd walk to the building where she lived and sit in the hallway. She would sneak back into the house when she knew that the younger children were in their beds and Andrea would be in her room. She would use the key that Carlton always managed to slip to her, no matter how many times Andrea would take it away from her.

Vern was twelve years old living in New York City without adult supervision. She had been put back two grades because the New York City school system assessed that she had received poor formal schooling. When her school day ended, Vern would stand against the school fence with a girl who had befriended her. This girl, for whatever reason, also avoided going home. Sometimes they walked to a park and sat on the benches until dark. A couple of boys in their class began to join them. They had fun with the boys, joking around, sometimes playing checkers and card games that the boys always had with them. A boy named Keith liked Vern. He would give her a kiss when he joined them, and she felt special around him.

One day Vern was walking home alone because her girlfriend had not shown up at school. Even Keith hadn't come to the park. She heard someone calling her name, and the voice sounded like Keith's voice. Normally, she wouldn't walk into a dark alleyway, but the voice called insistently, "Come here, Vern. Come on. It's me, Keith." Vern walked into the narrow alley, which was so dark that she could barely see her own arm and the book bag she carried. She didn't see anybody and felt scared. Then she heard an unfamiliar voice say, "Is that her?" She saw a face in front of her. Something hit her. When her eyes opened, she was on the ground, and she thought maybe she was in hell. Everything was still, and it was dark. She felt as if she was burning all over. She tried to get up, but stumbled, and she had to fix her clothes because they were all twisted around her. Quickly she picked up her book bag, which she found lying next to her, and she rushed, limping, toward the street. She didn't know if anyone was close behind her, so she ran as fast as she could even though she ached. Somehow she had gotten hurt, because there was blood on her arm.

After several attempts, she managed to unlock the front door to her building. She slipped inside, turned around quickly, and locked the door. Painfully, she climbed up the stairs, and with each step it seemed harder and harder to keep going. When she got to the third floor, she collapsed in the hall right outside her apartment door, but she heard Andrea ask, "Who's there? Is that you, Vern?" She thought that she replied, "Yes. It's me," but Andrea kept asking, "Who's at the door?" Then the door opened and Vern heard her say, "Oh my God! Oh my God!"

Andrea half-lifted and half-pulled Vern to the bathroom, sat her on the toilet, and held her with one hand while using her other hand to undress her. She turned on water in the tub, and the next thing Vern remembered was feeling cooling water around her and Andrea gently washing her. Then Andrea had her back on the toilet and was patting her dry and pulling a gown down over her. Vern walked, with Andrea holding onto her, past the couch, which was where she normally slept. Andrea put her in her daughter's bed. All Vern could think about was her brother being mad at her for going up into the dark alley. "Please don't tell Carlton," she whispered.

Vern didn't know whether Andrea told her brother or not, but although Andrea had taken care of her that night, the atmosphere in the house became even more strained because Vern refused to leave the house and would not go to school. She slept most of the day. It was only when Andrea threatened to call her brother and tell him what had happened that Vern got up and went back to school. She kept to herself and even stayed away from her only girlfriend. It seemed as if everyone was talking about her.

The day Vern turned thirteen, it appeared that no one knew or remembered that it was her birthday. At nine o'clock that night her brother called and wished her a happy birthday. When she handed the phone back to Andrea, she could hear her brother shouting over the phone. Then Andrea began to yell back at him.

Carlton would return home every few months, stay about two months, and then he'd be gone. It was the nature of his work was what he told them. Even when Carlton was home, Vern stayed out of Andrea's way, and she slept most of the day in her niece or nephew's bed until it was time for them to go to bed.

A few months after Vern's eighteenth birthday, she was walking home from high school daydreaming that she lived in a faraway country. She was envisioning herself in a fine palace when a voice sliced through her thoughts. A man she had never seen before was walking beside her. "Hello, lady. May I introduce myself?"

Vern stared at him. He was nice looking and well dressed.

"My name is Mike. May I ask your name?"

In a tiny voice, she responded, "Vern."

"May I accompany you on your walk?" He was already walking beside her. He talked well, and he had such confidence. Vern shrugged her shoulders, as she thought maybe he was part of her fantasy come to life. He kissed her hand when she got to her building.

The following day and the day after, Mike waited for her after school. He walked with her each day, talking as they walked, and he kissed her hand when they reached her house. On the fourth day, as he approached her, he pointed toward a car. "This is my car." Vern's eyes opened wide as her lips parted in surprise. She didn't know anybody who had a car. "I want to take you for a ride. Come on. I'm not gonna bite you. Instead of walking, we'll ride. I'll be sure to have you in front of your building at your regular time, okay?" He opened the door. Vern got in and watched him as he closed the door and walked around the car and got in on the driver's side. Vern thought of him as a prince who had come to rescue her from all the ugliness in her life and carry her off to his castle.

He turned to look at her. "I want to ask you something." Vern stared hard into his face. "I want to know if you'll be my girlfriend." Vern froze as she remembered how Keith had betrayed her. "What's the matter, sweetheart? You look terrified. I just asked you to be my girl. I'm not gonna hurt you. I'll treat you good. I'll show you. Come on. I'll take you for a ride and bring you right back." He did that for a few days. They would go for a short ride and then he would bring her back home. When they were out, he would buy her an ice cream cone or some other treat.

After she had been seeing Mike for about two weeks, as she sat in the car with him, looking at the lake and watching geese skim across the water, Mike turned to her, gently rubbed her face and said, "You're young. Men like girls young like you." She had no idea what he was talking about. All she knew was that she liked him because he was so nice to her.

"Isn't that beautiful?" he said. "Look at the water. It's so peaceful." She nodded agreeing with Mike's words and smiled as she continued to look at the water. "You have such a pretty smile. You should smile more often."

Mike turned the key in the ignition. Her heart thumped from disappointment because she didn't want to go home. She wanted to stay with Mike; she felt safe with him. He turned the radio on. A song Vern particularly liked bounced through the car and unaware of her movements, she began slightly swaying to its rhythm.

"Yeah, that's it—loosen up, baby."

Vern froze and focused on looking out the car window. Mike stopped the car in front of a building and turned to her. "This is where I live."

The building looked like a small mansion attached to other small mansions. Small plots of grass were in front of each building and trees stood in neat square patches of grass near the curb. It was a very rich-looking area. Vern held her head down. Mike pulled her chin up with his hand. "Would you like to see my apartment?"

"Yes." He was her knight in shining armor.

As they walked up the steps in front of the brownstone building, he hooked his arm around hers. After he opened the front door, he turned to the right and led her to the door of his apartment. When he opened the door, Vern was in awe. His living room was large, with the most beautiful furniture she had ever seen. An elegant white sofa and a matching lounge chair dominated the living room. Gold vases with silver and gold artificial flowers in them stood on the coffee and end tables. White venetian blinds hung over the windows and white curtains streaked with gold draped down along the sides of the windows.

"I'll show you around," Mike said as they moved further into the apartment. "This is the dining room, as you can see." A long glass table, with eight chairs around it, had a beautiful arrangement of flowers as its centerpiece. Plates were set out on the table. In Vern's mind, the silverware enclosed in napkins and the sparkling glasses next to each plate made the table look like the dining arrangement set for a king. The kitchen, complete with pearly white cabinets lining the walls, looked like one she could only imagine seeing in a magazine. A small room with a toilet that Mike called the "powder room" was opposite the dining room. Along the hallway there was a full bathroom on the right and a bedroom next to it. There were two bedrooms on the left. At the end of the hallway, a door led to another bedroom. Mike unlocked the door. A huge, king-sized bed took up most of the space in the room. To the right of the room were two doors. One led to a huge walk-in closet and the other to a full bathroom.

Mike sat on the bed and gestured for Vern to come to him. Vern stared at him and did not move. His voice became soft. "Hey, baby. I'm not going to hurt you. I just want to hold you." Hesitantly Vern moved toward the bed and sat down on it. Mike took her hand and kissed it. He than embraced her and began kissing her from her head to her feet. Vern experienced feelings surging through her that she had never felt before. Suddenly, Mike sprang up off the bed and said, "Okay, baby, we got work to do." Vern couldn't understand what he meant or why he had jumped up so suddenly. She didn't want to move. She wanted to stay cuddled in his arms.

"Oh, you want me to hold you, baby? You want to live here with me?" Vern nodded. "Well, it cost to keep up a place like this. Come on, we got work to do." Vern got up from the bed and followed him back to the living room. She sat on the couch while Mike went into the kitchen. He brought back a drink for her and one for himself. As she sipped from the glass that he handed to her, she listened to him talking on the phone, "I have a new girl, and I want you to train her. I should be there in about twenty minutes." He turned toward Vern. "So you like this place?" Vern nodded her head. "This is your new home now. You can see this apartment has four bedrooms. Other people live here, other ladies. Everybody who lives here has to work to help pay for expenses because this apartment is very expensive. You have to work too." Vern felt a rush of excitement through her body as Mike's words enveloped her: "This is your home now!" Her thoughts whispered, *This is a dream come true.* Then she focused on places she could go to look for work to help Mike pay for expenses.

"Come on! I'm going to take you down to where you're going to be trained. You're lucky because you're young. You won't have to work the streets. You gonna be trained, but after you trained, you'll just work from home. Clients will come to you."

Vern got back into the car with Mike. He was moving and talking so fast that she felt confused by the way he was acting. He had changed from being soft and comforting to talking and acting in a brisk, business-like manner. Mike stopped by a phone booth and then collected change from a small compartment on the dashboard of his car. "Get out. You gonna make a phone call, so we don't have no cops looking for you. Call your home and tell them you living with another relative and you're okay. Then hang up. Don't answer no questions. You got it?" The only relative Vern could think of was the one she had heard called Uncle Isaiah. Carlton was supposed to look him up in New York but had never gotten around to it. So Vern said the first thing that came to her mind. She told Andrea that she had found Uncle Isaiah and was living with him. She hung up before Andrea could get a word in.

Mike stopped in front of a group of women, and a tall, red-haired, pretty white lady came over to the car. "Go with her!" Mike instructed. Vern looked at Mike. "Go!" He leaned across her and opened the door. "She'll train you. I'll pick you up later." Vern hesitantly got out of the car. She had barely set both feet on the ground when the car door slammed, and Mike drove off.

The tall woman was friendly. "I'm Della, short for Delicious," she said as she walked her toward other woman who stood alongside a building. "This is Cookie. And this is Ebony. What's your name?"

"Vernetta."

"You called Vern for short?" Vern nodded in response to Della. "Well, come on, girl. Don't just stand there. Follow me and loosen up. Let me see you shake your stuff." The other girls started giggling. "Sway your hips when you walk, like this. Come on, put one hand on your hips and shake your booty." Della seemed fun loving and loose. She had an accent that Vern associated with cowboy movies. She was chewing gum and laughing while she walked with a swaying gait. Vern tried, but she just couldn't move her body the way the women could. "Little girl, you selling booty. You got to make it look inviting," Della said as a wide smile flashed across her face. "Oh, come on now. I know Mike ain't gave me a virgin to train. You a virgin?" Vern shook her head. Della took a deep breath and fanned herself with one hand. "Look, sweetie, let 'em know you got something hot!"

A car stopped, and the man in the car stared at them. One of the women shouted, "He wants her!" as she pointed to Vern. The man nodded his head.

"Well, see, honey?" cooed Della. "You just gonna get them anyway because they like young girls."

"And you look just like you come right out of the corn patch," Ebony said as the other ladies giggled.

"Now, you go with that man and you do what he tells you to do," Vern continued. It's important that you do exactly what he tells you to do. It's very important. Your life may depend on it. Here." She gave her a packet. "Tell him real sweet that you want to protect him. Make sure you say it like that and you give him this." The car horn beeped. "She's coming!" Della screeched.

Della turned to the other girls. "He look okay?" The other women were nodding their heads, and Ebony said, "Yeah, he okay. I know him."

Della yelled again, "Okay, okay, she's coming!" She tried to reassure Vern. "We're not gonna let you go with anyone who don't look right. See, you're our little sister now. We family. Come on." Della talked with Vern until they got to the car. She peeked in at the man, "Hi, honey." Her smile seemed to stretch from ear to ear. "I know you're gonna be good to her." She winked her eye at him and added, "It's her first day!"

Della turned toward Vern as the man reached over the seat and opened the door. Vern froze. She didn't like this job she found herself in, and she didn't like getting into the car with a strange man. Della firmly but softly said, "Get in, honey." Vern got into the car.

The man drove only a short distance and parked behind an old store. Vern was relieved that he wasn't taking her some place far away. He turned toward her and told her to get into the back seat. She did as she was told. She didn't get to say what Della had instructed her to say about the little packet. When they were both back in the front seat, the man looked at her and smiled as he said, "You about the age of my granddaughter." Tears that had flooded her head while she was in the backseat of the car now stood in the corners of her eyes. Someone she didn't even know had taken her. Now she was living a nightmare. The man handed her money.

The tears exploded when the man brought her back to the ladies. Della hustled her back to an area alongside a trash Dumpster. "Look, honey. This is what life is all about. Where's the money he gave you?" Della counted it and said, "Good! See, he liked you. Now wipe them eyes. I got to teach you some things. Let me see your packet. Just as I thought—you didn't even use it. You got to get bolder. The sooner you get bolder, the sooner Mike will take you off the street, and you'll work from the house. Wouldn't you rather do that? Stop crying. Wouldn't you rather be off the street?"

Vern whispered, "Yeah." But she remembered that Mike had told her she wouldn't have to work on the street at all. What had happened to her knight in shining armor?

"Okay," Della said. "Now we gonna practice. Let me hear you say, 'Honey, I want to be sure you're protected.' You look at him and smile and give it to him." Vern repeated what she said. "Now, you think you're strong enough to go back out there and get it right? If you get it right before Mike picks us up, you won't have to come back out here to the streets no more."

All Vern could focus on was "getting it right" so that she wouldn't have to be on the streets. By the time she got it right, she knew she was a different person. When Mike picked her up, she couldn't look at him because she understood that she had been a part of his game. She had been the hunted, and now she was captured in some kind of trap that had invisible nets that she would never get out of. When she walked into the apartment, she didn't feel the excitement she had felt hours earlier when she had first walked in. Now she moved along with the other ladies who talked excitedly around her as they headed for their rooms. With her shoulders hung down, she walked into the room that Mike pointed to while telling her it would be her room. The room had double beds, and she would be sharing the room with Ebony. She felt stale and soiled as she sat on her bed waiting her turn to use the bathroom.

Over the next four years Vern had four pregnancies that Mike quickly terminated. The fifth one she hid as long as she could, nearly up to the sixth month, because she thought that a baby would be a way out of the life she was living. But the day Mike found out about it, he knocked her so hard that she fell down onto the floor. He then kicked her.

"You pregnant bitch! You messing with my money and you did this on purpose. I'll kick it out of you."

She tried to stay out of his way because he'd assault her when he'd see her. The other woman tried to protect her, hustling her into her room when he was headed in her direction, but they had to be careful too because Mike had no tolerance for disloyalty. One afternoon as she rushed to her room from the kitchen where she had been making a sandwich, he ran behind her, pulled her out of the room by her hair, and banged her into the refrigerator.

"You want to eat up all my food? You want to stay her and get fat? You stupid whore." He slapped her.

Vern ran to the table and grabbed the knife that she had left there. "Leave me alone!"

"You holding the knife up to me, bitch? You better use it or you better put it down, because you gonna get hurt real bad if you think you gonna cut me with a knife." Vern's hand trembled as she put the knife down. Her insides cried as her mind wished that he would just love her. "I'm sorry." The apology trembled out of her mouth.

"You're sorry all right!" Mike lifted her up, opened the door to the apartment, and threw her out of the house. Her butt landed on the concrete steps, but in the momentum of the fall, she rolled over and scraped her leg.

Vern began a life on the streets. She ate at restaurants and used the ladies' room to wash. Her income came from servicing men, and she saved nearly every penny with plans of using it to get an apartment. One night a man she had serviced put a knife to her throat and told her to give him her money pouch. She unsnapped it from her waist. As he was taking it from her, he took his eyes off her for a moment. Seizing the opportunity, she kicked him as hard as she could as she knocked his hand from her throat. She rolled off the bed and fled from the hotel room. As she ran, she placed her hand over her throat and felt the slight cut from the pressure of the knife the man had held against her throat. She thought, as a shudder swept through her body, that she had escaped a horrible death. The man had been too big for her to take a chance on snatching the money pouch from his hands. So she had to start saving all over again.

Vern grew too big and heavy to continue her business. A woman saw her walking along the streets and took her to a shelter. A week after entering the shelter, she had her baby, a boy. But the baby had an enlarged heart and was sickly. The social worker at the shelter helped her to apply for benefits for the child and to get an apartment. Vern was back and forth to the hospital with her baby, quickly taking him whenever she noticed a change in his breathing pattern. She couldn't sleep through the night because she would jump up if her baby cried to check that he was not in distress. Even when she did go off to sleep, she could hear him breathing, and she would jump up if she didn't hear the sound of his soft breaths. The day came that he stopped breathing. Quickly she began CPR as she had been trained to do, putting her emotions aside. Her baby boy began breathing, but his breathing was choppy, and he seemed to be gasping for air. Vern ran out of the house with him, jumped into a cab, and rushed him to the hospital. The emergency room doctors worked on him but couldn't stabilize his breathing.

"Would you like to hold your baby?" The doctor, who was a woman, softly spoke to Vern as a couple of nurses and another physician stood next to the baby's crib. Vern nodded, biting her lips as she tried hard to hold herself together. The nurses pulled a rocking chair next to the crib. The doctor gently took the tube out of her baby's mouth and detached the other tubes from around his small body. Vern then lifted her son out of the crib and cuddled him in her arms. She sat down with him in the chair. As Vern looked at her beautiful baby, her tears fell on his face. She so carefully and gently wiped them off his face. She thought, *It has to be that God is punishing me for my sins.* Moments later, as she held her baby close to her heart while looking at him, her baby's tiny little chest did not rise. For the first time, from way down to the core of her being, she screamed, and her entire body heaved in and out as she cried. Vern lost all awareness of time and wasn't sure how long she'd been sitting with her baby before she felt a nurse gently take her baby out of her arms while another nurse knelt down beside her and held her.

The social worker made all the funeral arrangements because she was numb. The words of the minister just floated in and out of her ears. There was no family at the funeral, just the social worker and the nurses and doctors who had known her son. Days later, as she placed the urn with her baby's ashes on her bureau, she concluded that she was cursed and would never be loved.

The direction of Vern's life changed when Vern got a job working in a restaurant. She married a man she had met at the restaurant, Mr. Glenn, and had four children by him, two boys and two girls. Although he worked hard, he had a violent temper that was easily sparked, and he'd take his anger out on Vern. "You bitch. You tramp. You nothing but trash, and every man who rides up and down Washington Avenue knows you. You tricked me into marrying you, you tramp."

His temper frightened Vern so much that she bought a gun. She never had to use it on him because one day a man shot her husband to death. Mr. Glenn and that man had been coworkers, and the man, who was small and wiry, had just gotten laid off. He had put up with years of verbal abuse from Vern's husband on the job site. As the man walked past the house, Vern's husband, who had been sitting by the window, stepped out the house and shouted out, "You loser! You couldn't hold a job if your life depended on it! Punk!" The man pulled out a gun and shot Vern's husband in the head.

A numbness that had become familiar to Vern descended over her as she stared down at the man lying in the hospital bed who had been her husband. Tubes ran out of his nose and arms, and white bandages encircled his head. She gulped bile that rose in the back of her throat and felt as if the words and people around her in the room were far away, coming at her through a thick, gauzy veil and, though directed at her, had nothing to do with her. "A vegetable." Images of the beans in her father's garden so long ago filled her brain. And as her mind descended to her toddler-self, she watched the bright-green cylinders swaying gently in the sun, another part of her heard the doctor's words, "brain dead."

Someone held papers out in front of her face and banged a pen against them. "Sign here!" Suddenly she felt everything closing in on her, smothering her. She turned her face away from the papers.

"She needs more time." The words floated past her. The papers moved away.

Moments later, Vern emerged from a place of vagueness and looked around and saw that she was alone in the hospital room with her husband. She wondered how she would survive. She had four children and only a small income from the apartment on the second floor of their home. The restaurant where she worked had told her that business was slow; she had been let go.

As she stared at her husband, his eyelids began to flutter. It was as if he was struggling to open them. He never opened his eyes, but a raspy whisper emerged from his lips, "Call Sandy." Sandy was the name of the bookkeeper at his job. Then a breath of air flowed out of him, and his lips remained open.

Machines started to beep. The doctors and nurses rushed in. Vern moved out of their way and slowly walked out of the room. She kept walking. She was about to exit the hospital when someone called her name. "Mrs. Glenn! Mrs. Glenn!" She turned toward the woman.

"We were looking all over for you, Mrs. Glenn. I am so sorry. We were unable to revive your husband. I'm so sorry. I need you to sign these papers."

The afternoon that her husband died, Vern called Sandy, as her husband had instructed her. Sandy had her bring documents and sign papers, and from then on she received a check every week. It wasn't much—just enough to cover the mortgage on their two-family building and a few bills. Vern couldn't stop the bitterness from creeping into her, and she couldn't get rid of it. She knew it was from all the bitterness that had come to her in her life. She became like her mother, Ellie. When the children bugged her, she was quick to pop them. The housework annoyed her. She felt closed in. The only area in which she differed from her mother was that she never threw her children out the house. To deal with the pressures she faced, she retreated to drinking.

Vern used money she received from the tenants in the second floor apartment and even some of her food money for drinking. She felt comforted when she was drinking. It calmed her and helped her to enjoy her new freedom from abusive men. She didn't have to sleep with anybody or have to cook meals for anyone except her children, and, unlike her husband, they dare not fuss about what was prepared. In fact, she didn't have to put up with anything from anyone. If someone acted up while at her house, quietly she'd walk to her room, open her bureau drawer, pick up her gun, and return to the living room.

"Shut up or get out," she'd say, pointing her gun at them. If they were really obnoxious, she'd move closer to them, cock the hammer and whisper, "Leave—*now!*"

Guns were a language well understood in her community. Somebody got shot nearly every week. Even children got shot while sitting quietly on their front porches or playing in front of their homes, caught in the crossfire of bullets intended for someone else.

Chapter 13 Ty's Funeral

The intriguing family history that Grandma Vern presented sparked Nia's imagination so that she began to envision how catastrophes affect how people act. Then a sudden horrific occurrence left her feeling like a tidal wave had slammed into her, smothering the tiny, flickering flame of life that had been in her.

Nia fought to breathe as she sat in the first pew of the church overlooking the casket. In the next instance, she was angry at Ty for leaving her. Her heart pumped fast as a vision of her mother in the casket emerged. She shook her head. *No! No! No!* Then, even at fourteen years old, her mind moved into the vision she had held onto all the years … of herself sitting with her mother's arms around her rocking her.

People moved along a line viewing the body. She felt angry about that! Why would people want to look at him when he was in such a defenseless, lifeless state? He had always been so lively. New tears crept from her heart and burst through her eyes. Tyron had been killed. She wondered whether Ty's boss, who had ordered him killed, was there. She studied the faces of people as they filed past Ty's casket. She felt that she could look into their eyes and tell if they were Ty's killers. Drug bosses often showed up at a funeral if they thought their man was brave, even if they had ordered the execution. Nia knew that she could detect that cold, detached look in someone's eyes, which drug bosses had, because her own solitary, painful life had cast a cold stare into her own eyes. When she looked in the mirror she could see it. But at Ty's funeral, her eyes grew blurry from the tears constantly welling up, so she couldn't stay focused on identifying Ty's murderers. She bowed her head, overcome by the intensity of the pain and a feeling of betrayal.

Why couldn't he have listened to Grandma Vern, who had told him to stop doing drugs just like she had told him to stop running with gangs? Nia looked up and saw some of Ty's friends who were in the gang Ty had once belonged to. They passed in front of her and even nodded at the family as they moved along the processional line. She thought that it would have been better if Ty had stayed in the gang instead of becoming a drug dealer. Her mind took her to wondering how it was that boys always had to be involved with something out on the streets that wasn't right. The gang Ty had been in was made up mostly of boys on their block. Back then Ty had told her that belonging to the gang was their way of looking out for one another. If someone messed with one of them, they all went to war. Quite a few times, Ty had come into the house after having been beaten up. Vern and Tiffany would wash off his wounds and bandage him up. Grandma Vern would scold him about hanging out with, "them boys." She'd say, "You going to get killed out there. All that fighting! Why you hanging with them boys? You better than them. You smarter than them boys. You always been quick to learn! Stop hanging with them dumb boys!"

Grandma Vern would talk to Ty about his associations until her voice got hoarse, but it did no good. The gang members would come over and sit politely on the living room couch while they waited for Ty. Or they'd stand around outside in front of the house. When he would join them, they'd slap him on the back or playfully punch him on his shoulders. In their rough slang, they said things like, "Man, you's a warrior." "You knocked him out!" or "Yo, man! Ty, you don't run from a fight. You fearless! They had you cornered and you came out, man."

"You saved Jason's life, man," one boy had once shouted.

"You the man!" "You the man!" "Ty, you the man!" would tumble out of their mouths as they hugged him while they walked off together.

On one occasion, Ty came running into the house, jumping over furniture and other things along his pathway as he ran. He dashed into the bathroom and locked the door. He didn't have a bedroom of his own. When he turned thirteen, Grandma Vern had told him to sleep on the couch. She simply said that he was too old to sleep in the same room with the girls. That day he came running in and went into the bathroom, Grandma Vern kicked open the bathroom door and, holding her gun in her hand, yelled, "You not bringing no weapons in here!" All he could see was the gun. In one quick movement, Ty opened the bathroom window and jumped out. He stayed away for weeks.

When Ty returned home, he told his grandmother, "No weapons!" He held up his arms and spun around. "Search me!" Not even looking up from what she was doing in the kitchen, Grandma Vern replied, "Come on and get you something to eat, boy!"

At the funeral even oppositional gangs marched by the casket. Little boys she had seen wearing bandanas on their heads and sloppy pants were dressed like people—in shirts and creased pants. Most boys left the gangs as they grew older. A few graduated from high school, and the sense of accomplishment that went along with that achievement, plus the opportunities that were available for graduates, moved them away from gang life and into the work world. A few got caught up in the challenges of fatherhood and early marriage to their pregnant girlfriends. And some, like Ty, got lured into selling drugs.

Drug dealers had a sense for smooth, street-smart boys and gave them money, and then more money, for making drops. Nia had listened to Ty talk about how he was glad that he had gotten out of the gang because the gang had gotten into robbery and stealing cars. Nearly all of the remaining gang members were sent away to juvenile detention facilities. She knew Ty thought he had made it. He was selling drugs in school and keeping up his grades. He planned to graduate and was thinking about truck driving. Nia thought about how he had told her about all his plans, even about his guidance counselor calling him down to her office and keeping him after school talking to him about going to college. Nia had smiled then when she saw the expression of shock that was on his face even as he relayed the story. He had told the guidance counselor, "Nobody goes to college where I come from!" But his counselor kept calling him down to her office and insisting that he fill out application forms. She made him write the required essays while he was right there in her office. She'd tell him, "You need to see the bigger picture. There's a bigger world out there than the two-mile radius you've been running around in, like a hamster in one of those exercise wheels." Nia had laughed along with Ty. Ty said he had asked her, "Why you care so much?" His guidance counselor shook her head and looked him in the eye. Her eyes squinted, and her voice was a little above a whisper as she said, "I lost my brother and my cousin just last year. They were doing the same thing you're doing. I'm tired of our young black men dying in the streets!" Nia had felt sad after she heard what his counselor said. She agreed with his counselor.

Nia listened to some of the people who stood at the pulpit and talked about how good Ty was. Endless thoughts ran through her mind. She wanted to go up to the podium and tell how Ty saved her life, how he pulled her out of hell, but she knew she was not the loud, public-speaking type.

Nia's heart pained more as she thought how Tyron had known her so well and how he had looked after her. She had protested when he told her one day that he was going to teach her how to fight. He then explained to her that, because he stayed out on the streets more than he stayed at home, he knew the mindset of the boys in the "hood" when it came to girls. "You know I am a street thug." They had both laughed. He compared her to Tiffany. He told her Tiffany knew how to take care of herself. The word on the street—which was like gospel in the hood—was that Tiffany was the type that boys had to watch out for. They could get badly stung by her because she was street smart, cunning, pretty, and ruthless. Ty explained that "hood rats" knew Nia was quiet and timid. A bad, heartless boy would try to take advantage of that. Her heart fluttered when he said to her, "You're like a tiny, injured bird that can't defend itself." She remembered seeing Tyron as she went back and forth to school. He'd be standing along the fence or on the corner with a group of guys. Although he'd be laughing and talking loud with his friends, she knew he'd be watching her.

The words he added in his argument to teach her how to protect herself had stung her back then when he'd said them, and they stung her now: "I might not always be around to look out for you." So she went along with Tyron and let him teach her how to defend herself. He had even made her practice on him, and he hadn't been satisfied until she'd punched him hard.

New tears flowed from Nia's eyes as she heard a speaker talk about how good hearted Ty had been. Ty had always given her some of what he had. As he got older, he'd buy her clothes and give her money. Grandma Vern and Tiffany would corner him, "Tyron, where did you get the money to buy Nia that coat? You could have bought me a coat." Nia remembered when they'd see her come in with a new pair of shoes and they would look at Tyron. "Where did you get the money you gave to Nia?" Of course, they had nothing to say when he tossed a hundred-dollar bill on the table or pressed money into Tiffany's hand.

Grandma Vern would say, "Boy, you gonna get yourself sent to prison or killed messing with drug selling. Your uncles thought they was gonna get rich that way. You see where most of them is at now, either in prison or in their graves. God rest their souls. You should know better than to be selling drugs. Your own mother died from drugs."

Nia shivered as she thought of Aunt Tina. She had been found dead in her apartment. The investigation reported that it was a drug related crime. Her mind flowed back to the scene when Grandma Vern tried to 'talk sense into Ty' as she would say. And it was as if her talk was a warning, because it was the very next day that he died.

"Ain't you learned nothin', boy? You gonna finish me off and put me in my grave? That's where I'd be ready to go if drugs gets you too!"

Tyron shook his head, "Naw, I ain't foolish. I don't use the stuff. I just pick up and deliver."

"It's still criminal. What you gonna do when you get caught?"

"I ain't getting caught because I ain't greedy."

"They all get caught! You not smarter than your uncles. They all got caught!"

"I'm not saying I'm smarter than my uncles, but a man's got to eat. Nobody's gonna hire a sixteen-year-old. And, by the way, nobody said happy birthday to me last week when it was my birthday."

"You wasn't here, boy. How we gonna say happy birthday when you wasn't here? You was out there with your friends. So did they sing 'Happy Birthday' to you?" Grandma Vern said in a sarcastic tone with a wiry smile on her face.

"My point is, I'm just a boy in the world's eyes, and they ain't hiring me, and I ain't going around with no money in my pocket." Then Tyron broke big news when he said, "And talking about having money in my pocket, I'm about to be a daddy." Nia remembered his wide grin.

Everyone in the room stared at Tyron. It was as if time stood still. Tiffany's voice broke through the silence, "You got Navarna pregnant!"

"No!"

"Well, who then?" Tiffany had demanded.

"Simone."

"Simone! You can't be serious! Boy, you don't care who you lay up with! What is wrong with you? You really want her to be your baby's mama?"

"Come on, now. She's not that bad."

"She's dirty!" Tiffany insisted. "I saw her—"

"Come on, Tiffany," Tyron interjected before Tiffany could finish her sentence. "You just never got along with her."

"And what you gonna tell Navarna, who you say is the love of your life? Or are you going to tell her?"

"I'll handle it!"

"Boy ..." Tiffany shook her head. "I'm gonna tear up her behind. She did that to get back at me. She older than you. She's my age and raped my baby brother."

"Raped? Do you hear yourself? This your brother Ty you talking about!"

Tiffany screamed out, "I'm gonna kick her—"

Tyron abruptly cut her off. "No, you not! She not the same person she was when y'all was little kids fighting all the time. She don't say nothin' bad about you. And that's my baby inside of her. So you not gonna touch her." He looked at Tiffany with such intensity and coldness that both Tiffany and Grandma Vern were stunned.

"I gotta go," he muttered, and then he quickly left the house.

Tiffany shook her head as she paced the length of the kitchen. "I hate that bitch, and she gonna be my niece's mother. Oh, no. Oh, no ... I'm gonna get her! I'm gonna stomp on her!"

"And Ty will get you! I don't want no fighting in this here house," Grandma Vern growled. "I'm too old for all that nonsense. I'll shoot you both!"

Nia didn't want to cry as hard as she was crying. She was soundless, as she always was, but her whole body cried, and her shoulders shook from the impact. Couldn't that day have never happened? She was the one who had found Ty. That night, Nia thought she heard a strange sound. She opened her eyes in the darkness. Tiffany was sound asleep in the twin bed across from her. Through her window screen she continued to hear a slow shuffling sound coming from outside, somewhere in front of the house. She tiptoed out of her room and along the short hallway that led to all the rooms in the house. She looked into the living room. Ty was not lying on the couch where he usually slept. As she stood near the entry to her grandmother's room, which was across from the kitchen, Nia could hear her snoring. She peered into the dark kitchen. She then went through the living room and knelt on the armchair near the window so that she could peek out of the window. She saw something in the dark outside. When she pulled the curtain aside and looked out, she recognized Tyron's white sneakers, the name brand sneakers that Tiffany had gone into hysterics over when he had walked into the house wearing them. Nia couldn't see all of him. She rushed to unlock the door and then the main door leading to the steps outside. When she opened that door, she gasped. Tyron's body lay along the top of the steps. She stooped down and called his name over and over. "Ty! Ty! Ty!" She screamed out. "Grandma Vern!" She tried to pull Ty into the house, but she fell down, and his head flopped into her lap. His shirt was soaked with blood. She heard in the barest whisper, "Be strong, Nia."

When Vern came out of the house and saw Ty, she became hysterical. She woke up the whole neighborhood with her screams. "My boy! My boy! Somebody shot up my boy!" Tiffany ran out of the house and then ran back in and frantically dialed for an ambulance. She came back out and stared at her brother. They all knew it was too late. Tiffany dropped to the ground beside Ty and pressed her face against her brother's face. She let out an echoing cry, "No ... no ... no."

They never found out the real truth, but word on the street was that Ty hadn't handed over all the money he owed to his drug boss, and his boss got mad because it wasn't the first time Ty had shorted him. His boss had pointed a gun at his head and then told him to stand against the wall of the building. The man ordered his boys to line up in execution style to shoot Ty, but Ty took off, running in a zigzag pattern. Although it's often hard to hit a moving target, Ty was hit multiple times because the alleyway was narrow. Still, Ty kept running as he bled. Everyone said it was a miracle that he had made it home.

Ty's death was the talk of the community. Everyone had admired Ty. They simply couldn't help it. His teachers, the neighbors, his peers, certainly Tiffany, Grandma Vern, and even Nia, even if some kept their admiration silently in their hearts, as Nia did.

One of his teachers came to the house. When Grandma Vern opened the door, the woman presented her with an envelope and said, "I offer my condolences. We took a collection at the school. Tyron was very popular. He had so much potential. I don't think there was anything he couldn't do if he put his mind to it."

***

When the pallbearers placed Tyron's casket down over the grave, Nia looked at Grandma Vern. She looked small and withered as she stood beside the grave in her huge black straw hat, long black dress, and dark brown shawl. Nia strained to look into her grandmother's face to see if she was grieving for Tyron. It seemed to Nia that Grandma Vern had gotten caught up in the excitement of seeing her family, whom she hadn't seen for years, so that she lost sight of the terrible event that had brought family and friends together. But Nia couldn't get a clear view of her grandmother because there were relatives between them whose heads kept blocking her view.

Tiffany, who stood alongside Grandma Vern, had to be supported by her cousins, Grandma Vern's brother's sons, because she was so overcome with grief. She had lost too much. She had lost her mother to drugs and now her brother! Despite the tough image she usually projected, and as controlled as she normally seemed to be, Tiffany could not contain herself. She acted as if she wanted to fall into the grave with her brother. She slid out from her cousins' grip, collapsed onto her knees, and pounded the ground with her open palms.

Realizing Tiffany's extreme distress, the minister decided not to lower Tyron's coffin into the ground. After he had read the prayers, he closed with, "Ashes to ashes, dust to dust ... so he emerged to life ... so he will return to the earth. Amen!"

The crowd responded in one voice, "Amen!" Tiffany was lifted from the ground by her cousin and carried to a waiting car.

Nia felt more alone than she had ever felt, yet she didn't want to be with anyone. She walked alongside Grandma Vern and Tiffany as she was expected to. When they were in the car, Grandma Vern put her arms around Tiffany, who was still crying uncontrollably.

Chapter 14 The House Fire

Grandma Vern's small house was packed with folk after Ty's funeral. Relatives Nia had never seen showed up at the house days before the funeral. They came from all over the country, but most were from the South. For Nia, they were faces to the names of aunts, uncles, and cousins whom Grandma Vern had spoken about when she told stories about her family.

Folks were crammed together on the couch, doubled together in armchairs, and sitting on kitchen chairs that had been placed in the living room. People were sprawled out on the floor. Everyone seemed happy to see people they hadn't seen in years, and meeting family they had never met before. They looked through old photos and laughed and talked about "back in the day." Heads nodded as the rumble of conversation vibrated through the rooms. As they ate, everyone commented or smiled in agreement over how good the food was. The small house had never been graced with the tantalizing aroma of dishes that their relatives from the South brewed up in the kitchen. Even the food Nia had enjoyed making with Aunt Tina, good as it was, hadn't smelled so savory or looked so scrumptious.

Vernetta Glenn seemed to be basking in glory. It was as if she had done something phenomenally heroic. At one point, she called Nia. "Come here, child!" When Nia entered the living room, everybody's eyes were on her. At first they stared, but then smiles erupted on their faces. "This is Eva's baby," Grandma Vern said, and everyone looked at Grandma Vern with admiration.

"Vernie, what a job you doing raising chil'ren after raising your own," someone said. "You deserve a medal." Someone else said, "And I heard you snatched the child right from the hands of them foster care people who take our chil'ren away from us. You's a tough lady, Vern. They should have known better than mess with you and yours!"

Nia's eyes darted among the groupings of people – those surrounding the food table with plates in their hands and churning lips, those with stomachs rumbling with laughter that screamed out of their mouths, and those with shinning eyes and smiling lips exchanging introductions. She felt sickened by the gaiety and wanted to yell out, "Remember Ty!" Her Aunt Tina's funeral and repast had been far more sobering. It appeared that the only indicator that a funeral had occurred was the dark attire everyone wore.

Other than herself, only Tiffany was consumed with grieving. She was sitting on the floor in the living room with her back against the wall. Nearly everyone who passed by her tried to lift her spirits. People brought her small plates of food. One of their aunts from Mississippi said, "Open … open … open …" and although Tiffany really didn't open her mouth, the aunt popped into her mouth one of the small pastries that everyone was raving about. "See, I gave up mine for you, baby!" the aunt said. But Tiffany couldn't be made cheerful. She was quiet and polite to everyone, which was unusual because she was generally outspoken, sarcastic, and managed to make herself the center of attention among any group of people.

Nia knew exactly how Tiffany felt. She knew that no one or nothing could console Tiffany because her grief went to the core of her soul like Nia's own grief. Yet, she couldn't console Tiffany because Tiffany was part of the fabric of the family that Nia secretly hated. Only Ty had stepped out of that fabric.

Nia stayed in the kitchen helping her aunts from Mississippi prepare food plates as Grandma Vern had told her to do. Her mother, Eva, came into the kitchen and shouted, "Why is my daughter doing all the work?" Her comment made Nia feel awkward. She certainly had not done all the work. In fact, she hadn't cooked at all. She had been placing food on trays and taking them into the living room. She preferred to keep busy rather than sit around and feel obliged to answer questions from her relatives, who were all over the house, even in her bedroom. No one responded to Eva's question. Everyone kept right on working. Within moments, Eva left the kitchen.

Nia was surprised that she actually liked being around her aunts from Mississippi and Alabama. She was impressed by their friendliness and how efficiently they prepared different food dishes. They were coordinated and they flowed together as they worked, each addressing different aspects of the meal arrangements. Even though the kitchen was hot and their faces and necks were drenched with perspiration, they just kept on pounding, chopping, and throwing food into big pots or placing pies and cakes into the oven.

Nia especially liked Aunt Sissy, whom she learned lived somewhere in New York. The more she worked with Aunt Sissy, the more she admired her. It felt strange to Nia to find herself amid another great sadness, yet feeling good to be close to a member of her biological family. Aunt Sissy kept a smile on her face, and she was quick to giggle. She hummed as she stirred a huge pot of greens with a giant wooden spoon. She softly sang something that Nia didn't recognize as she cut brownies into neat little squares. She was so pretty. Her face was smooth and soft looking. Her cheeks were bright and rosy like the peaches that she rinsed off for the fruit salad she was making.

Each time Aunt Sissy finished with cooking utensils, Nia promptly whisked them away to the sink to wash them. When food was laid out on trays, and large bowls filled up, she'd carry them into the living room and place the food on a large folding table that had been set up. She'd make sure that enough cups, plates, silverware, and napkins were on the food table, and she'd empty out the trashcans that had been placed on each end of the table. When Nia returned to the kitchen, she would be careful not to get in Aunt Sissy's—or anyone else's. She would watch what everyone was doing so that she would not interrupt the flow of work. She would quickly wash bowls and pots as soon as she saw her aunts were finished with them. Sometimes, though, Aunt Sissy would lay onions or green peppers on the table, and in between her humming, she'd say softly, "Chop this, baby." Nia would chop the vegetables into small pieces. Aunt Sissy said to her, "You a natural! When you learn to chop up food like that?" Nia shrugged her shoulders. She didn't want to reveal that she had learned from Aunt Tina, because Aunt Tina was dead, and now her son, Tyron, was dead. It just didn't seem right to mention her name.

"You miss your mother?" Aunt Sissy asked. Nia looked at her and felt a strange burning in her heart. "I mean your foster mother. Do you still think of her sometimes?"

Feeling awkward, Nia nodded. No one in all the years since she had been separated from her foster mother—her real mother in her eyes—had ever asked her how she felt about being taken from her.

119

Aunt Sissy stood at the table beside Nia. Their shoulders touched as she picked up two onions, placed one in front of Nia and the other one in front of herself, and began chopping as did Nia. "The child welfare took my children." Nia nearly cut her finger as she turned to stare at Aunt Sissy, who continued to chop as she talked in a calm matter-of-fact manner...as if she had said a simple statement, like, "It's nice weather outside."

"They took all my children. That's why I know what you feeling. I been meaning to come over and talk with you, but I guess I can barely keep up with things at my own house." Aunt Sissy talked on and on, yet despite all her talking, she kept up her pace preparing food. They had to keep working because there were about a hundred people, both in the house and spilled out onto the street, so that preparing the afternoon meal flowed into preparing the evening meal. And between meals, snacks were consistently being prepared and set out on the tables.

The flood of faces emptied out of the house around eleven o'clock that night. Finally, the kitchen was closed down. All the leftover food was packed up and put away. Dishes were washed, dried, and stored. Tables and cabinets were wiped down, and the floor was swept and mopped. Aunt Sissy had opened the kitchen and the pantry doors, thinking that nice cross-breezes would offer everyone in the kitchen some relief from the heat. But they couldn't feel a breeze because the air that entered was hot and muggy.

"Come on," Aunt Sissy said, motioning for Nia to follow her. Nia followed Aunt Sissy out of the kitchen, and they sat on the back steps. "I see you like hearing about the family history. That's a good thing, especially since you seem like you still hurting and angry over what happened to you."

Aunt Sissy began telling her own family history. "My mother's name is Sybrina. And my mother and your Grandma Vern are first cousins. If you go back one more generation, my grandmother—they called her Peaches, but her real name Patricia—is the sister of Grandma Vern's father, Amos. Their other brother is named Isaiah. You may know him as Uncle Isaiah. Queen Bee was their mother. So your biological mother and Grandma Vern are from Queen Bee's son, Amos, and I'm from the line of her daughter, Peaches. So that's how we're related."

Nia's ears picked up at the mentioned of all those familiar names from Grandma Vern's stories. "Who are Isaiah's family line?" she asked.

"Isaiah never had no children. He was too busy taking care of all of us and fighting for our civil rights. And your Uncle Isaiah was here today at the funeral."

"He's still alive?"

"Oh yeah! He's famous. He been in the magazines. See, God says, 'Vengeance is mine.' Mm-hmm. All them evil men who beat him to less than an inch of his life are dead and burning in hell. But Isaiah, he still alive. He was born in nineteen ten, and he's still kicking. His mother, Queen Bee, was born in eighteen ninety, just twenty-five years after slavery ended."

As Sissy talked about the anger felt by people who had been accustomed to slavery and how that anger fostered hatred toward those she called "our folks," Nia found herself trying to picture that kind of anger. It was dark and solid and hovering. And it lingered in front of her as Sissy's words tumbled gently into the nighttime.

"They say she was a living nightmare." Sissy sighed and shook her head slowly. Nia had watched the dark ball of anger as Sissy had talked about their relatives and the conditions that surrounded their lives.

Finally Nia followed Sissy back into the kitchen, where Aunt Sissy kissed her on the cheek as she turned off the kitchen light. As Nia walked toward her bedroom, she could see a body sprawled out over her bed. She went into the living room, sat on the floor, and fell asleep.

***

A few months after Tyron's funeral, Nia nearly burned down the house. Her grandmother and her cousin Tiffany had gone out shopping. Nia sat in the armchair in the darkened living room. She kept staring at the curtains over the window. They were torn and needed washing. It seemed that her grandmother couldn't see dirtiness sometimes. Nia never said anything about it.

Before Ty died, Grandma Vern, in a dry voice that seemed to express perpetual disappointment, would say, "I got these three big children in here, and I can't get this house cleaned up!" Nia had always been left cleaning up behind the family, but because they were so messy, the house wouldn't stay clean. As Nia got older and entered her teen years, she decided that she wasn't going to clean up their mess. She wasn't rude, however, and she never spoke back to Grandma Vern. Grandma Vern had gotten older too and no longer hit her for her lack of enthusiasm or for any perceived insolence or disobedience. So Nia would do nothing unless she was told to, and her grandmother always let her know that she had done a "half-ass" job, with the exception of cooking. Soon she wasn't called on to do much of anything other than cooking. The dishes were always done, however, because Grandma Vern had a thing about dishes being left in the sink overnight, and Nia couldn't change her habit of washing dishes and cleaning up the kitchen as she cooked.

As Nia sat in the armchair, she watched the curtains curl and flow out into the living room from the slight breeze that entered through the window. Slowly she looked around the room. It looked cold and lifeless. The stillness and the quietness of the house engulfed her. She felt empty.

She was never included in anything. Grandma Vern hadn't asked her if she wanted to go shopping with them. She and Tiffany had simply left the house. Tiffany meant the world to Grandma Vern. Even the relatives had noticed, saying that Tiffany was the only person for whom Grandma Vern had a soft side. She remembered the first time someone said that. She began watching her grandmother respond to Tiffany. Grandma Vern was quick to agree with Tiffany, and went out of her way to get things for her, even when she couldn't afford them. Tiffany got away with nearly everything, and she came and went as she pleased.

Tiffany looked like a model. She was slender and had a pretty face that gave her that magazine-model look. What's more, she could sing. Her voice had a soft, unique quality that people couldn't quite describe but loved to hear. A couple of times she sang solo in the school choir. According to Tiffany, a man approached her and told her he was a music producer. He gave her his card and instructed her to call him. She called and met with the man.

Nia's eyes shifted as they took on a dim understanding. Tiffany had suddenly stopped talking about the man which meant that road hadn't led anywhere. Still, everyone in the family thought Tiffany was going to make it big as a singer. Many of the family members, particularly Grandma Vern, believed that Tiffany was going to be their ticket to riches. The family didn't even complain when Tiffany stopped going to school and began hanging out with an older man. Of course they didn't know she had gotten pregnant. Tiffany was astute about dealing with things like that. She found out where to get an abortion and got that taken care of early on. Nia knew because she had heard Tiffany talking to someone over the telephone making arrangements.

A darkened hue covered the room. She had spend painful years in this house. Hard as she tried, she couldn't remember when she had stopped crying herself to sleep at night, silently screaming for her mother. She thought of how she had to be cursed. She was fourteen years old. The two people whom she had loved had been taken from her. It had gotten harder and harder to get up in the morning, and her body began to feel heavier and heavier as she moved around throughout the day. Nia picked up a matchbook that lay on the table next to the chair. She pulled one match from the matchbook, struck it against the matchbox, and moved her hand toward the edge of the curtain. The curtain caught fire immediately. Just as she watched the flames leap toward the ceiling, the door banged open. It was Tiffany who began screaming, "Oh, God! Oh, God!"

Tiffany yanked the curtain off the window, hurled it to the floor. She grabbed the big throw cover from the couch and threw it over the burning curtain. She snatched a pillow from the couch and pounded it on the flames that leaped out from the corners of the throw cover. Grandma Vern ran in, grabbed another pillow, and tried her best to smother the flames. Together, they succeeded in putting the fire out. Nia sat impassively watching their frantic efforts.

Holding one arm with the other hand, Tiffany collapsed onto the floor and began to cry. When she began to cough, Grandma Vern yelled, "Go outside! Go on outside. Both of you get outside!" Grandma Vern struggled to open windows. Tiffany rushed outside. Nia followed her. They sat on the steps just outside the open door. The people who lived above them ran down the steps, coughing as they came. A few neighbors gathered on the sidewalk directly across from the house looking at the smoke coming out of the windows.

Grandma Vern went through all the rooms in the house opening windows as she went. When Nia heard her yell, "No!" she knew that Grandma Vern had found the open matchbook on the table in front of where she had been sitting.

Grandma Vern came out holding ointment and gauze and sat on the steps alongside Tiffany. One side of Tiffany's hand and forearm had been burned. As Grandma Vern began applying the ointment, a fire engine screeched to a stop in front of the house. Grandma Vern rushed toward the firemen, yelling, "We got it out! You don't need to pull no hose through the house to wet it down."

One of the firemen replied, "We won't take the hose in, but we have to make sure no flames are in the walls."

"It didn't get past the living room. Tiffany here was on it. That's why she got her arm burned."

An ambulance and a police car pulled up in front of the house. Police officers came to the bottom of the steps. "Who is Ms. Glenn?"

"I am," Grandma Vern said, standing up straight.

"You say your granddaughter started the fire?" the officer asked.

Tiffany hissed loudly, "No, Grandma ... no!"

But Grandma Vern was angry. "She started it. I saw the matchbook open and the used matchstick on the floor."

The officer turned to Nia and asked, "Did you start the fire?" Nia nodded her head. "How old are you?"

Nia did not respond. Grandma Vern answered, "She's fourteen. Old enough to know better."

"Has this happened before?" Now the officer directed his attention to Grandma Vern.

"No."

The officer scribbled some notes on a pad and then continued, "Any other behavior problems?"

"No," Grandma Vern answered.

The officer looked at Nia. "Why did you set this fire?" Nia did not respond. She simply held her head down over her chest.

"Does she talk?"

"No. She don't talk!"

"She is your granddaughter?" The officer questioned looking puzzled.

"Yes, she is."

"Where's her mother?"

Grandma Vern shrugged her shoulders, "Your guess as good as mine."

The paramedics approached Tiffany. One man had turned back and shouted, "Bring a stretcher!"

"I can walk," Tiffany was quick to respond.

"Never mind with the stretcher," the man said. Then he helped Tiffany to walk to the ambulance.

Grandma Vern yelled out to Tiffany, "Baby, I'll be there soon as the police done with me."

There was silence for a few moments. Then the officer turned to Nia and said, "You're going to have to come with us."

Nia stood up and, with a police officer on each side of her, she walked toward the police car. She was assisted into the backseat, and the door was shut. It locked with a loud click that caused Nia to jump. Her heart began pounding rapidly. It was dark inside the police car. A glass encasement separated her from the officers in the front seat. She felt totally alone. It seemed that the doors on each side of the police car were beginning to close in on her. Nia felt herself suffocating and began grasping for air.

Chapter 15 Family History

Every time Nia opened her eyes, bright lights glared at her and wide, red lips kept saying, "Wake up!" Someone was trying to pull her up from the bed ... or the chair. She wasn't sure if she was lying down or sitting up. Words floated through her ears, "What did you take? Tell us what you took!" Nia covered her ears with her hands. The room started to spin. Even though her eyes were closed, she saw her own body standing in the middle of the room. She could feel herself spinning around with the room, but her body didn't fall even when the room turned upside down and the spinning got faster and faster. Then there was a great crash.

Nia heard a soft voice. She opened her eyes. A woman in pink clothes was standing over her. "Well, hello," the woman said. "How are you feeling?"

Nia looked around. She looked at the white walls, the railing along the bed, and then at the woman who was talking to her. She knew then that she was in a hospital. Her mind flashed back to the time she had gone to the hospital when she was younger and her grandmother was in the room waiting to take her to home. Her heart beat fast, and her breath shortened as she looked around the room. She relaxed when she realized no one was in the room with her but the nurse.

"You had us worried. It's nice to see you back with us. Would you like some lunch?"

"No. I have to use the bathroom."

"Let me help you get up. You might feel a bit dizzy as you try to stand up. You've been out cold for three days."

Nia's stomach felt woozy, and her legs were wobbly. In the bathroom she forced herself to focus so she wouldn't fall. When she opened the bathroom door to return to bed, several doctors were in the room.

"Let me help you back into the bed," the nurse in pink said. "Do you feel dizzy?"

As soon as she laid her head on the pillow, one of the doctors shone a light into her eyes, and then placed a stethoscope to her chest. He mumbled some words to the group surrounding the bed, and then they left.

The nurse who had been in the room said, "Later today you'll be moving into another unit for observation. I ordered a plate of food for you. Try to eat something, sweetie. I'll be checking on you."

Nia wondered why they had saved her. She was not loved by anyone. She was a criminal because she had tried to burn down Grandma Vern's house, and she didn't care if she died. No one would even miss her.

She didn't know why she felt so dizzy, but then she remembered that she had put two pills into her mouth while she was sitting in the backseat of the police car. She had come across the pills while she was cleaning out Tyron's dresser drawers. Grandma Vern had instructed her to bag up all his things so she could donate them to a used clothing store. A few days before his death, she had overheard Tyron talking to one of his buddies. They were on the front steps, and Nia was sitting in the armchair by the open window. Ty had told his friend that he had powerful drugs in pill form that could take a person "to the other side."

His friend asked, "What other side?"

"Heaven or hell!"

"Yeah, man."

"You can't take but one at a time. I tried it. It's better than anything, man. It's worth a lot of money."

"Where you get it from?"

"Man, I can't tell that! I can't give away my source."

"Oh, so you stole it. If they so valuable, you better be careful, man. You might be in over your head."

"I can handle it."

They were quiet for a few moments. "Where you got it stashed?"

"Oh, I can't tell you that either, man."

The nurse brought in a tray of food and placed it on a wheeled table, which she positioned in front of Nia. Nia could tell that the nurse was trying to engage her in conversation. She talked continuously as she pressed a device attached to Nia's bed and raised the top of the bed so that Nia was sitting up. "Enjoy your meal."

When the nurse left the room, Nia pushed the table away from her bed. She pressed the device that lowered the frame of her bed and laid her head back on her pillow. With her eyes closed, Nia thought of where she might live. She thought of her Aunt Sissy. Aunt Sissy was warm and friendly, and she drew people to her. Nia knew that Aunt Sissy would have taken her in except that Aunt Sissy was absorbed with keeping child welfare people from messing with her family. When Nia had sat with Aunt Sissy on the back steps following Ty's funeral, she had seen the rosy tones drain from Aunt Sissy's face and her eyes fill with water as she talked about what had happened to her. Her voice had broken at times as she'd wiped the corners of her eyes. Nia couldn't imagine that someone as caring as Aunt Sissy could have lost her children to the child welfare system, because she had thought that only women like Eva had their children taken away. So Nia was interested in hearing about Aunt Sissy's past. Somehow her story had never surfaced in Grandma Vern's tales of the family.

Sissy was the youngest of three girls. She had always been sweet and accommodating. When everybody from the South had been trying to come up north, Sybrina, Sissy's mother, had gone south. This move had surprised the family because Sybrina's mother, whom everyone called Peaches, had always told stories of how in Mississippi they had to walk with their heads down when they were around white folks. Sissy's great-uncle, Isaiah, had also told Sybrina what had happened to him when he was a boy in Mississippi. The move south was precipitated by Sybrina's meeting a young man from Alabama. Her Uncle Isaiah had brought this bright young man with him when he had returned to New York from a trip to Alabama, where he had been registering Negro voters. Sybrina married that young man and went south with him. Uncle Isaiah had to tell the family, who were shocked by Sybrina's decision, that farming was in her blood, even though she had been raised in the city. It was true. Sybrina had been longing to live in the South. She wanted to be in open spaces, to enjoy warm weather, and to plant things because she loved watching things grow. So Sybrina moved to Alabama and stayed there in the house that her husband built for her, until he became ill and died.

After her husband died, Sybrina returned to New York City with little money because she'd had to use the profit from the sale of her house and most of her savings to pay her husband's medical bills. The hope that there would be better schools and opportunities for her children had motivated her to move back north. Sybrina and her three children stayed with a relative in Harlem for nearly a year before she obtained an apartment through public housing. She got a job as a domestic.

The relatives asked Sybrina why she would not marry. "It's not like you can't get a man," someone would inevitably say, because Sybrina was pretty. She had caramel-brown skin and dimples that emerged when she smiled. Her hair was naturally brown with reddish highlights. Even Uncle Isaiah, who didn't involve himself in idle family conversation, said to her as if he were speaking for her dead husband, who had been his own comrade, "Ain't no men good enough for you in New York, Sybrina? You ain't still in mourning for your husband, are you? How many years you think you need to mourn for him? We all know he was a good man. But if he could speak, he'd tell you to get married so someone can ease the burden of working and taking care of children off of you."

Sybrina shook her head very determinedly as she looked at her Uncle Isaiah, "I don't need a man. I don't need no worry a man bring with him. I ain't got time now to keep up with things the way I want. I don't need to add to what I got to do waiting on a man and answering questions about my whereabouts. Besides, I got three pretty daughters. You think I need to be worrying whether I married the right one?" When Sybrina had finished speaking, there was nothing more Isaiah or anyone else could say on the subject. Knowing that she'd made her point, Sybrina continued, "People change, you know. You think you marry this nice person and they turn out to be a monster, especially here in this big city with all its corruption! Sometimes men marry a woman for a showpiece. They don't even love the woman, and they don't treat her right, except in public when he's around other people, 'cause he's showing her off." That's when Uncle Isaiah told Sybrina that she reminded him of his own dear mother, Beatrice.

Although Sybrina had lived in New York before she married, she hadn't lived there as a mother. She hadn't known about the ghetto streets and how they seemed to devour children. Sissy and her sisters were mystified by city kids who talked fast and dressed stylishly. They were bold, acted unafraid of adults, and some even talked back to them. Sissy's oldest sister, Sandra, began to let a boy come to the house while their mother was working. She and the boy used to bring candy and give it to Sissy and her sister. Sandra would say that she wasn't really letting the boy in. She was just helping him bring in treats for them. "Don't tell Mother, or we won't get the treats, okay?" Sissy and her sister Sarah would nod their heads, rush to grab the candy, and chew on it while they'd sit in front of the television. Sandra and her friend would sit on the couch and watch TV with them.

Sandra got pregnant, but she got an abortion after her best friend's older sister told her how to go about it. She never told their mother, but as always seems to happen, Sybrina found out about it. When Sandra got pregnant a second time, her mother screamed at her every day, even slapped her at times. Sybrina told Sandra that she had better not get an abortion. "You was grown enough to lay up with that boy. Now you be grown enough to take care of the baby. No child of mine will kill a baby!" Sandra quit school without telling her mother and got a waitress job. She saved every penny and moved into her own apartment in time to take her baby from the hospital to her own place.

Sissy could hear her mother crying at night. She would go into her mother's room, get in the bed with her, and hug her mother around her stomach. "It's going to be all right, Mother. Don't cry. You'll see. Everything is going to be okay." Her mother would put her arm around her, and they'd both fall asleep.

Even though Sissy was the youngest, she would oftentimes tell Sarah, who was two years her senior, what they needed to do or how they should behave. One day she told Sarah that they needed to do exactly what their mother told them to do so they would never make her cry. She put up her pinkie finger and said, "Let's promise. We gonna listen to Mommy so we don't make her cry." Sarah smiled and hooked her pinkie around Sissy's pinky as they giggled.

Year in and year out, Sissy tried her hardest to make things easier for her mother. She had intently watched Sybrina cook so that, by the time she was nine years old, she would have dinner waiting when her mother came home from work. Sissy would watch for her mother coming down the street. Sybrina had become overweight, and her legs seemed as if they couldn't take another step. But she'd keep on moving, swaying from side to side, her hands often clinched around shopping bags full of groceries.

Sissy's mother worked for the same lady, Mrs. Waters, for twelve years. She spent her days cleaning the woman's five-bedroom, three-bathroom home: sweeping, mopping, vacuuming, washing dishes, washing clothes, and even washing windows. She would bring Sissy and Sarah with her on the days school was closed, and during the summer when camp ended. After what had happened to her oldest girl, Sybrina was careful about leaving her youngest two at home all day long. Sissy and Sarah hated to go over to Mrs. Waters' house because it was boring, and for eight hours they had to behave like little tin soldiers. They had to sit in the basement at a table and do schoolwork. Sybrina told the girls that Mrs. Waters was doing her a big favor by letting them come to work with her, so they had to be really quiet and still.

Sarah told Sissy that she didn't like Mrs. Waters. To her, the lady was nosey and mean. Once, Mrs. Waters had come halfway down the steps to the basement where they were playing. She was tall, thin, and appeared tense. She peeked down at their mother, whose back was to her because she was busy washing the small basement windows that looked out onto the lawn. In a high-pitched, quivering voice, Mrs. Waters said, "The house looks good, Sybrina. Don't forget all the curtains need washing too!"

"Yes, Madam," Sissy's mother answered without turning around. The woman turned and looked at Sissy and her sister, and it seemed as if she tried to smile, but the smile wouldn't stick to her face.

Once when her mother was in the basement dusting furniture, Sissy had jumped up to help her. She had picked up an extra cloth and started to dust, but her mother turned and spoke to her sharply, "Go back to the table and do some schoolwork!" Later that afternoon, as they walked to the bus stop, her mother took out a piece of candy for each of them. She hugged them both, kissed them on their heads, and whispered to Sissy, "I'm sorry, baby, for being sharp with you. I know you was trying to help me, but I have to do everything just the way Mrs. Waters wants. Besides that, I don't want you cleaning houses other than your own. I want better for you. You keep doing good in school so you can be somebody one day."

Sybrina's diligence paid off. Sissy and Sarah both finished high school and got jobs immediately following graduation. Sarah got pregnant, but Sissy's mother said, "She's of age. She's working." Sarah married her baby's daddy as her mother had suggested, but two years later she was divorced.

Having seen what happened to Sarah, Sissy was in no hurry to take the same path. Boys had always come to her, but even as she got older and found she was attracted to them as well, she was determined to do things just as her mother told her.

"Concentrate on school," Sybrina had said. "You don't need all this dating. God knows exactly the right man for you, and he'll send him to you … when he knows you're ready!"

As early as the fourth grade, boys had started to do special things for Sissy. One boy in her class gave her a box of chocolates. He told her it was for Valentine's Day. There were only four chocolate candies in the box, but she rushed home and ran to her mother holding the small box behind her back. Her mother had looked at her with a knowing smile. It was as if she were saying, "I know you're up to something, but I know it's something good!" Sissy presented the box to her mother. Her mother smiled wide as she said, "Now, Sissy! Where did you get these chocolates?" Sissy loved to see her mother smile. When her mother smiled, her whole face sparkled, and dimples appeared on her cheeks, and Sissy thought her mother was the most beautiful lady in the whole world.

Sissy told her mother, "A boy in my class gave the candy box to me, and I'm giving it to you." Her mother, who had been cooking, sat down at the table and said, "Well, we just gonna eat this together."

Sissy sat down at the table, and as they were enjoying the candy, Sarah came into the kitchen, reached into the small box, and took a piece of candy. "Where this come from?"

"A boy gave it to Sissy," Sybrina said. Sissy and Sarah started giggling. Sandra joined them in time to take the last candy. After they finished chewing on the candy and giggling as they ate it, Sybrina's voice became a bit stern. "Now, you girls be careful about taking gifts. Some people think you owe them something when you take gifts from them. So as you get older, be very careful about taking gifts from boys. Sometimes boys say, 'Well, you took my gift so can't I kiss you?'"

Sissy frowned quickly and said, "Ugh."

"Well, I'll talk about that another time. Just remember, it's not a good idea to take gifts from boys."

Sissy was pretty like her mother. She had the same golden, copper-brown skin and small dimples that showed whenever she smiled. She was shapely, as her mother had been when she was young. When Sissy got to high school, there were times when a boy would follow her around at school. Sometimes one was bold enough to follow her home. Sissy and Sarah would giggle about the boy who followed them as they walked home together. After about a week or so, the boy would stop following her, and she would never see him again, at least until Sarah would point him out to her.

Sissy kept her promise. She graduated from high school without dating. Some boys called her stuck up. But her mother told her, "That's all right. All that means is that they have a nasty attitude and they would have treated you mean after they got what they want from you. A lot of boys are real nice to you while they're trying to win you over. Then, when you give in to them, they don't want to stay devoted to you no more. They change like day and night. As you know girls end up having their babies and then they stuck having a baby from some nasty boy who won't even marry them. Most of these boys can't even help out with the money it cost to take care of their babies because they young and don't have jobs. So the girls have to find ways to get money to buy food and clothes for their babies while taking care of the babies."

The man Sissy married, Benjamin, had a hard time winning her over. He had to meet certain criteria before even being considered. He met the criteria. He was a steady worker. He had never been married, had no children, and had good moral standards. Sissy wouldn't even go out with Ben until after they'd known each other for a year. He would come over to their home and eat dinner with her family, and Sissy would listen as he and her mother talked. Her mother even invited Ben to attend church, so he went with her, even though he had never attended church before.

Ben had been the only child of a single mother. Like Sissy, he had always done exactly what his mother told him to do. It was rough in his neighborhood, but because he was taller than everyone else his age and looked serious, other boys never picked on him. He rarely talked. His mother had taught him, "It's better not to say anything than to open your mouth and have everyone laugh because they can tell you don't know what you're talking about."

When Ben was eleven years old, some boys in his class gathered around him as he walked home from school. They tried to get him to join their gang. "You big and nobody gonna mess with you," one of them said. Another boy said, "And you look mean. We probably won't even have to fight most of the time."

Ben kept walking, and they kept on talking. When he got to his house, he swung the door open and let it close behind him. He never even looked back. They never asked him again, although he'd nod to them when he'd see them, and they'd nod back. By the time he finished junior high school, two of the boys who were in that gang had gotten killed. Another boy who had been part of that gang had been shot in the back and was paralyzed from the waist down, so he had to get around in a wheelchair. As they got even older, he'd see that boy in the wheelchair propelling himself laboriously back and forth several times a day from his house to the liquor store.

Other offers came to Ben. Once, during track practice, he was by the fence near the track catching his breath. He was bent over with his hands on his knees when a pair of legs in shiny leather shoes materialized beside him. He looked up into the face of a man he had never seen before. The man leaned his back against the fence and said, "You fast as lightning. I can show you how you can use those legs to make a lot of money. And you cool, too. I see how you stay to yourself. You're a smart boy. Hey ... you smart enough to make some big money?"

Ben straightened up and looked the man directly in his eye. By this time he had a deep voice. He replied, "No, man. I ain't that smart!" And he jogged back toward the gym.

Throughout his junior and senior years of high school, Ben was a track star. His coach and his guidance counselor tried as hard as they could to get him to go to college.

His coach kept telling him, "You're wasting your talent."

Ben wanted to reply, "I don't want it. I'm not interested." But he knew that his coach wouldn't understand because running track was his coach's world.

Ben, however, wanted to work. He understood how his mother had struggled with her minimum-wage job. She was always afraid that she was going to be let go when business dropped back. He wanted to help out his mother so she didn't have to work overtime to keep up with the bills. Her regular weekly pay was two hundred and seventy-five dollars. She would save two weeks of her pay for the rent. Another week's pay was used to pay bills so she would have only about one week's income to pay for food, clothing, carfare, and any other things that came up.

Ben had wanted to help his mother out for as long as he could remember. During his junior year of high school he had gotten a job after school at a gas station pumping gas. He had been robbed at gunpoint twice when he worked there alone. Another time he had been robbed at gunpoint while coming home from his job after dark. It was evident that someone knew where he worked, and knew his work schedule.

After the third incident, as they were sitting at the table eating, his mother looked him in his eyes as she placed her hand on his shoulder, "I can't lose you, son. It's gonna happen again, and you might not walk away the next time. You got to let the job go." So Ben quit that job.

Benjamin was in his senior year in high school when he first noticed Sissy. He watched her and saw how she carried herself. He thought of her as a porcelain dish with gold-trimmed edges in a cabinet filled with plastic plates. He saw how she walked home with her sister every day. He also saw how other guys would look at her and how she wouldn't give them the time of day.

Ben didn't try to approach Sissy, but he thought about her a lot. He told his mother about her. His mother told him not to do anything. "If it's meant for y'all to meet, you'll meet," was how she put it.

***

The hospital room door suddenly swung open. Nia pretended to be asleep so she wouldn't have to answer questions. The nurse buzzed around her and left. Nia kept her eyes closed and giggled as she thought of the wide smile that had spread across Aunt Sissy's face when she relayed Ben's version of the day they met.

Some years after his graduation from high school, Ben went downtown to several stores searching for a ring for his mother, which he intended to give to her on Mother's Day. It took him a long time because he was slow about buying things. Sometimes he would vacillate between items for a long time before he'd finally made a choice. He wanted to be sure he wasn't making a mistake. As he intently looked at a ring in the glass case at one store, he saw the reflection of the salesgirl through the glass. Intending to ask her if he could see the ring, he looked up. At the sight of the girl, he froze, and his mouth hung open. It was Sissy. She kept saying, "Can I help you? Can I help you? Is something wrong?" Ben couldn't seem to get the words out. He finally got hold of himself. Although he had never stuttered in his life, he began to stutter. "Um …um …um … tha—tha—that ring." He felt so stupid as he pointed at the ring. Sissy was trying to follow his hand. "This one?"

He shook his head and said, "Naw."

"This one?"

"No, on the other side of it."

Sissy reached into the case and placed her hand on a ring. It was still the wrong one, so he said, "No. I'm sorry. It's the one next to that one."

She pulled out the ring and smiled as she looked at it. "This is nice. For your mother?"

He nodded his head and just stared at her. It embarrassed him to keep staring at her, but he couldn't take his eyes off her. She was so beautiful!

"Well, it's on sale. I'm going to figure out the discount for you. I'll be right back," she said brightly. He nodded his head while his eyes stayed fixed on her. He continued to stare even when she was mostly hidden by the cash register on the other side of the counter. Moments later she was back in front of him. "This ring is on a special discount this week. It's fifty percent off, so it currently costs only seventy-five dollars."

It was a lot of money, but Ben pulled out the cash and gave it to her. He tried to think of what he could say to her. Then he remembered that they used to go to the same high school. As she was giving him his change, he managed to say, "You used to go to Stanton High School."

"Yeah," she said, "how did you know? Oh, you see my ring." Then she seemed to look more closely at his face. Ben could feel his heart pounding. "Oh! You're that track star! It's because of you Stanton won all those medals that year. Are you in the Olympics now?"

"No, no." He could feel anxiety building up in him. "My coach wanted me to get into all that, but I needed to help my mother out. She been paying all the bills, so since I graduated I just been working." He could hear himself talking too fast, but he couldn't slow down.

"Nothing's wrong with that."

"Um, my name's Benjamin. Ben for short." He extended his hand toward her.

She clasped his hand in return. Ben quickly scanned her hand for a wedding ring and was encouraged that there was none on her finger.

"My name is Sierra," she said smiling. The way she said her name had his heart skip a beat as he stared at her. Her name sounded like a beautiful song, and he thought how perfectly her name suited her. "Everyone calls me Sissy for short."

Ben released Sissy's hand and let his arm drop to his side. He felt awkward, but he knew he had to step past his discomfort. He heard his voice tremble as he said, "I don't know how you feel about this, but I was wondering if I could take you to dinner sometime."

"Well, I don't really believe in dating. I'm a real old-fashioned girl, but if you like, you could come over to my house for dinner."

Ben felt excitement surging through him. "Yeah? Okay." He couldn't stop himself from staring at her.

Sissy pulled out a pen and wrote something on the back of the receipt. "Here's my address," she said. He took the receipt, and his legs felt weak as he walked away. He was sure she was watching him. "Ben!" she called. He turned around. She was holding up his package. Feeling awkward he went back, took the bag, and slipped it into his pocket. "Thank you," he mumbled, embarrassed, and kept nodding to her as he walked away turning around just in time to miss banging into a counter.

Chapter 16 Ben and Sissy's Wedding

Ben held his breath when the minister pronounced Sissy as his wife. Sissy looked radiant in her long, white gown and elegant, elaborate veil.

"You may kiss your wife," the minister announced. Ben leaned over to kiss Sissy. He knew how incredible it was that this was their first kiss ever. He didn't think anyone would believe him if he told them that. Ben was so overwhelmed that he swept Sissy into his arms and ran toward the doors at the rear of the church. Family and guests laughed and clapped excitedly as they rushed to follow them out of the church.

Ben eased his wife into the limo. As he was about to close the door, he yelled, "We'll see everyone at the hotel!"

When they arrived at the hotel, Ben and Sissy held hands as they ran into the building. Ben pulled Sissy, who had to run fast to keep up with him, into a waiting elevator.

"What are you doing, Ben?" Sissy whispered while trying to catch her breath. "We're supposed to meet our guests in the banquet hall on the main floor."

Ben answered, "I'm going to love you. I been waiting a long time, you know." Sissy started to giggle and couldn't stop. Another couple in the elevator smiled at them. On the eleventh floor, Sissy, still holding onto Ben's hand, ran behind him from the elevator and down the corridor. Ben stopped in front of a door to a room and unlocked it. He pushed the door open, lifted his wife, and carried her through the doorway.

It seemed as if it was only one giant step before Ben had Sissy in the middle of the king-sized bed. He began to ruffle through layers and layers of lace. His fingers kept getting entangled in the fabric as he lifted up each layer of the crisp material. After untangling his fingers for the fourth time, he became frustrated and heaved his body off Sissy's and lay beside her. They began to laugh, and laughed so hard that they rolled off the bed and onto the floor with Sissy landing on top of Ben.

When they finally stopped laughing, they smiled at one another. Ben slowly shook his head back and forth. "I love you. I love you. I love you so much, Sissy. Thank you for marrying me."

Sissy whispered, "Ditto!"

As they got up, Ben helped to brush down her layers of white lace. Sissy turned to the mirror above the dresser and adjusted her hair. They left the hotel room holding hands and ran toward the elevator to join the wedding party in the banquet hall.

Sissy was very fertile. She had a baby nearly every year for eight years. Her employer cut back her maternity leave because she was taking so much time off.

Ben and Sissy tried to save toward buying a house in a descent neighborhood, but they found that it was very difficult to save. Their two-bedroom apartment took a big chunk out of their income, and feeding and clothing their babies took nearly the rest of it. Oftentimes, because of their work schedules, they had to pay for a babysitter. In addition, even when they were able to save, something would happen that forced them to use their savings.

With their small place crowded with eight young children, Sissy found it impossible to keep the place in order. Often Sissy's mother would visit and spend her entire day straightening up the apartment. She would fold and put away clothing, pick up toys, throw broken toys into the trash, sweep the floor, wash bottles and dishes, prepare meals—all in between hugging, feeding and playing with her grandchildren. Sybrina even found it a never-ending battle. The minute she picked up an item from off the floor or from a chair, one of the toddlers would drag something else out of somewhere and leave it on the floor of the living room or the kitchen. To make things worse, the oldest boys were rambunctious. They liked to wrestle; beds would get broken and dresser drawers would end up splintered.

Sybrina began to put aside money that she intended to give to Ben and Sissy to help them buy a house. She figured that, if the boys had their own room, rather than sleeping on the couch in the living room, there would be less chaos because they would have a place to play. Since the other children followed the boys, who were the eldest, they would most likely gravitate to the boys' room, and perhaps the living room and dining room areas would remain straightened. Not telling anyone, Sybrina took on another job and worked at night to build up the savings faster. She had been working both jobs for two months when she collapsed at work. She was rushed to the hospital. The doctors diagnosed pneumonia. When Sissy was called, she immediately left her job and went to the hospital. From the hospital she called Ben hysterically crying. Ben informed his boss that he wouldn't be in that night and jumped into a cab to get to the hospital.

Sissy felt as if everything had crashed in on her when she saw her mother lying in a hospital bed hooked up to a huge machine that was breathing for her. The doctor tried to explain to her, "I am sorry but your mother is not responding to—"

Sissy placed her hand over her mouth and began shaking while whispering, "No! no! no!" She scarcely heard him as he said, "You need to gather your family together." She didn't even notice when the doctor left. She was still standing over her mother shaking when her sisters rushed in. Sandra put her hands over her face and broke out crying loudly. Sarah collapsed over the lower part of her mother's body and clung to her.

At Sybrina's funeral, Sissy felt as if a huge chunk had been taken out of her heart. She kept shaking her head while thinking of how unfair life was. Her mother had tried so hard to take care of her own children. Her personal comforts had been secondary to the needs of her girls. Then, after they had grown, when she should have been able to relax and enjoy herself, she was taken from this world.

Sissy fell into a profound depression. She stopped eating. She stopped getting up in the morning. She slept nearly all day and all night. She wouldn't even call in sick at work on the days that she remained home. Ben covered for her as well as he could. He'd call her employer and inform her supervisor that Sierra was ill. Ben took her to their doctor who referred her to a psychiatrist. Sissy was admitted to a state psychiatric hospital for observation and remained there for a month. Ben had to let the babysitter go because, without Sissy's income, they couldn't afford a babysitter. He took care of the children during the day and then worked at night, leaving the older children to care for their younger siblings.

As Ben and Sandra were leaving the building following a visit with Sissy, Sandra told Ben, "You can't keep doing this, Ben. You'll kill yourself working day and night, and then what will happen to the children? I'm going to take a few days off from work to find day care for the babies." She did just that and more. Sandra came over in the mornings to get the children dressed and fed and off to school or day care. She taught the elder boys how to prepare the babies for day care.

It was during the time that Sissy was in the hospital, that the oldest child, Donté, began to give his father problems. His teacher informed Ben that Donté was sullen and very uncooperative. When asked to follow instructions, he'd repeatedly say, "I want to go home." The school sent him for psychological testing. The psychologist reported that Donté's rebellion stemmed from anger that had been long in the making. He had been pushed through childhood because he was the oldest and had been expected at a very early age to help care for the other children. Sissy and Ben had always thought it was cute how smart he had been at responding to directives when he was only a toddler. They would point to the bag of pampers and say, "Get a pamper." He'd waddle over to the pamper bag, struggle to get one, and bring it to them. But then, with baby after baby coming, he had been expected to assist more and more. Donté had been so good at helping to care for his younger siblings that Ben and Sissy never realized that he hardly had any playtime of his own.

The psychologist stated that, in a sense, he was a little adult. He was angry with his parents because they were not at home anymore. His mother was in the hospital, and his Aunt was changing things around and had put his younger siblings in day care so that they weren't home when he got home from school. Then, in school, he was expected to be a child when in reality, according to the psychologist, he didn't know how to function like a child. At eight years old, his thinking was already aligned with that of the adults in the house. The psychologist recommended counseling. As the psychologist explained, if his anger was not resolved, his childhood would be repeatedly marred by defiant behavior.

Chapter 17 Breakthrough

"Good afternoon, Nia. You got to get up!" The nurse's voice was loud, interrupting her thinking about Aunt Sissy. "There's no sleeping allowed during the day." Nia sat up, although she felt tired and wanted to lie back down.

The nurse continued, "Why are you so tired? You're confusing the doctors. Can't be doing that. They're giving you uppers to get you alert and active, yet your body is responding like they downers, cause you sleeping and sluggish."

Nia decided then that she wasn't taking any more medicine. She was convinced that the doctors didn't know what they were doing. They weren't going to experiment on her. She took the pills as the nurse watched, but she pushed them to one side of her mouth with her tongue when she took the cup handed to her and gulped down a small amount of water.

"Okay," the nurse said. "Now, Nia, get up and get dressed, because you're scheduled for a group activity."

Nia had no sooner sat down on a bench outside of her room when she felt a huge body flop down beside her. The girl, who was still for a moment, began shouting, "Oh! I know you. Nia! Nia! I'm Tonai. What they got you in this crazy house for?"

Nia ignored her and simply stared ahead. Of course she remembered Tonai, who had befriended her at Stanton Family Counseling Services during their group therapy sessions.

"Oh, so you ain't talking? Oh, you want to talk to me, see, 'cause I'm the one who can protect you. It ain't safe in here. But I know what you in here for."

Tonai got up, stood in front of Nia, and wagged her index finger at her. "You tried to burn your house down!" Tonai started laughing. She jumped around excitedly as she talked. "See, I hear them talking. I listens. I said I want to come over here and see this brazen chick who tried to burn her house down. That's the way to go, girl! I remember … I 'member I went to visit you once, and this lady who answered the door yelled at me and slammed the door in my face. I'm glad you burnt that house down!"

Surprisingly, what Tonai said and how she said it struck Nia as very funny. Her belly exploded with laughter. It was the first time she had felt such a freedom to laugh since she had been abducted from her mother. *Abducted* was the word Nia felt best described how she had so suddenly and permanently been taken from her mother. She had never put words to her feelings, but now, being a little older, and having listened to Aunt Sissy talk, the truth to the trauma she had experienced seemed to be surfacing.

"Yeah! Yeah! Yeah! That's it. That's it!" Tonai responded excitedly. They both roared with laughter, and it seemed as if they couldn't stop. What was left of the pills that Nia had hidden in her mouth flew out. Tonai's face changed to a beet red coloring after she saw the pills shoot out of Nia's mouth. As soon as the pills hit the floor, Tonai placed her foot on them and ground them into the carpet. They laughed uncontrollably.

"Yeah, yeah, yeah," Tonai was saying. "You did. You got them back. You go, girl!" Nia laughed so forcefully that she could hardly catch her breath.

The nurses came over. They stared at Nia for a few moments. One of the nurses exclaimed, "Nia's laughing!" And indeed it was as miraculous as if someone had discovered gold in the water fountain.

Another nurse said, in a stuffy voice, "A patient seems to have brought her out of her depression."

Nia and Tonai couldn't stop laughing. Soon the nurses began laughing. They were still laughing as they went back to their station. Then, just as suddenly as Nia had started to laugh, she began to cry. Tears streamed down her face.

"No, no, no. Don't go that way!" Tonai said softly. But it seemed as if a floodgate had been opened, for Nia couldn't stop crying.

Tonai sat back down beside Nia. She put her arm around Nia's shoulder and drew her close to her so that Nia's head was on her chest. Gently she rocked her as she held her. "I know," Tonai whispered into her ear. "I know. I know, Nia. I know, baby girl."

It was a struggle for Nia to get up every morning because she just didn't want to face the day. The hospital was now her home. Consequently, everything she did was timed and planned. She had to look at the same people day in and day out, and they seemed odd to her. One girl rocked back and forth all day long. A boy who was about fifteen years old would stand immobile in the same stance every day, like a statue. All planned activities were redundant and boring. During the group therapy sessions, people complained about what they didn't like about the hospital. If it hadn't been for Tonai, Nia would have slept throughout the entire session. But Tonai would consistently burst out with something clever or funny.

A new therapist took over the group therapy sessions, a young white man in his mid twenties. He was a nice-looking man of average height. He had a friendly, almost humorous face, and he smiled almost all of the time. He was funny and made them laugh. He seemed to know how to make the sessions interesting and to get people to open up. "I'm here to help you," he said after the clinical director conducted introductions. He raised his arms and pointed both index fingers to his head, as he made a questioning look on his face. "Maybe you all can help me. I got issues!" Then he put his fist to his head and knocked on his head, "Hear that? I know. You can't hear anything because it's hollow!" As he sat down, he glanced into everyone's face, "But we'll do the best we can."

Nia listened and learned from stories told by others in the group. Her heart burned when the therapist turned to her. "And what might a lovely lady like you be doing amongst us 'social nut cases'?" he asked, putting his fingers up in quotation mark style.

"I was taken from my mother," she said quietly. This was surprising to the group because she had never said anything at all, and it was especially surprising to Nia, since things had shut down in her at the age of six. She talked slowly, and sometimes stopped to compose herself because of the pain, but she told her story.

Tonai became her cheerleader and responded in exaggerated shock and anger to situations Nia described. At times Tonai would nod and affirm, "Yeah, I know what you mean." Or she'd shift her body and exclaim, "They did that to you? Man, they better be glad I wasn't there. It would have been me and them." She would hold up her index and middle fingers in front of her face and move them back and forth toward her eyes and then away from her eyes, as if she was communicating with an imaginary person in front of her, all the while saying, "You see me. You got me. We understand one another, right?" She would arch her eyebrows and draw her lips tightly together. Then she'd slam one fist hard into the palm of her other hand and shout, "Bang!" Everyone roared.

"And you, Tonai, have talent enough to be in the acting business," the therapist said one day.

The group sessions helped Nia because everyone agreed that she had been abducted and abused. She felt such relief because, ever since she had gone to live with Grandma Vern, she had gotten yelled at and even hit when she'd said that her foster mother, Mrs. Patterson, was her mother.

She listened while the therapist explained to her that it was no longer about what had happened, but about how she would decide to act upon what had happened, to make something good come out of her life. He told her, during both group and private sessions, that she was a winner, not a loser. He looked intently into her eyes following a session and asked her if she was a winner. Nia smiled.

Chapter 18 The Children's Shelter

Near the end of the first week at the hospital, a nurse approached Nia and Tonia who were sitting in the activity room, "Nia, I need you to follow me."

"Where you taking her?" Tonai yelled.

"She'll be back soon."

Nia followed the nurse into a small room. "Have a seat." In the middle of the room was a square table with two chairs, one on each side of the table. As Nia sat down, a strange woman walked in and sat in the chair opposite her at the table. The nurse left the room and closed the door behind her.

"Hello. I'm Ms. Dorsey." The woman spoke warmly. "I'm a social worker with Child Welfare Services. How are you?" Nia remained silent.

Ms. Dorsey continued, "I'm working on finding a foster home for you to go to when you're discharged from here. So I'm setting up interviews with foster families. I have an appointment for you to meet a family tomorrow. Always have all your belongings with you when I come to take you to a placement meeting because, if a family accepts you, you'll go home with them. The plan is that you'll have a new home to go to when you're discharged from here." Ms. Dorsey stood up. "It was nice meeting you, Nia."

Ms. Dorsey was at the hospital the following day, and she took Nia to meet with prospective foster parents. During the interview, however, the couple informed Ms. Dorsey that they were unwilling to take Nia into their home because they noticed in her record that she had set her house on fire. They said flatly, in front of Nia, that they could not have any child in their home who set fires.

Other appointments were scheduled, and Nia met with other perspective foster parents. She always felt as if someone punched her in her chest when they rejected her. The foster parents would say that Nia seemed nice, but they couldn't handle a fire setter.

One morning, a nurse came into her room, pulled the blinds open, and told her, "You're being discharged today, so pack up whatever's important to you. Your social worker's coming to get you. I don't know what time she's coming, but you need to get up now and get ready just in case she comes early." Nia's heart began pounding. She had no home to go to! The day went by, and no one said anything about her leaving. She didn't mention it to anyone, not even Tonai whom she sat beside at breakfast and in group.

At group however, the therapist announced, "Well, we have some good news, however it will be sad for us because we'll miss her. Nia will be leaving us today."

Tonai jumped up and stood in front of Nia, "No, Nia. No! No! No!" She plopped back down in her chair and twisted toward Nia, "Why didn't you tell me?"

"She didn't know," the therapist solemnly interjected. "The decision came out of this morning's staff meeting. However, we will have a little celebration. If everyone can follow me in an orderly manner, there are some cupcakes and juice in the lunch room." As they walked, Tonai curled up her eyebrows as she looked at Nia, "Why didn't you tell me this morning at breakfast? Now we don't even have that much time together."

Nia shrugged her shoulders. "I didn't know for sure. You know how they do things around here. They say something, and then it don't happen. I don't have nowhere to go to so I guess I thought they made a mistake."

When they sat down, Tonai twisted around so that she was looking squarely into Nia's face, "You got to come by and see me, Nia. Will you come by and see me? When will you come see me?"

"I don't know. They didn't tell me nothing. I don't have a home. The social worker's coming to get me, but I don't know where she's taking me." She had barely finished her sentence when the social worker appeared in the room.

The therapist's voice rose above the noise in the room, "Let's say good-bye to Nia."

"Bye, Nia. Bye, Nia. Bye, Nia ..." The words vibrated through the room. Nia followed the social worker, who already had her bag of belongings in her hand.

"Is this everything you have Nia?" Nia nodded. As she moved toward the exit, she turned to look at Tonai, who had stood up. She turned back around quickly so she could hide the tears that were welling up in her eyes.

Nia stared out the car window seeing but not seeing as Ms. Dorsey drove. A large campus appeared before her view; several buildings were dotted along an endless, neatly shaved lawn. A black cast-iron fence enclosed the campus. Ms. Dorsey turned into the opening in the gate and drove up to a monstrous, two-story, rectangular, brown-brick building. She parked and got out the car. She walked around the car and opened Nia's door, "Here we are," she said brightly.

Nia stepped out of the car and followed Ms. Dorsey. Inside, they were surrounded by green concrete walls. There was a line of office doors, mostly open, and there was a small sitting area with a couch and chairs. A large metal door stood near the sitting area. Ms. Dorsey rang a bell that was on the wall beside of the door. She announced who she was through an intercom on the wall and then pressed a long handle when the door buzzed.

When they walked through the door, it was immediately shut and a thick, horizontal steel bar was slid across it. Nia's mouth gaped open as the thought that wisped through her head seemed confirmed with every step they took. She was going to jail for setting fire to Grandma Vern's house! The corridor was wide. Narrow doors with small glass windows were spaced on both sides of the dismal walls.

"Hello, Ms. Dorsey." A woman and a huge man stood in front of them. "I see they keep you busy. This must be Nia. Hello, Nia." The lady who greeted them stated that the building had once been a state asylum.

A boy who seemed to have come from nowhere flew to the big steel door and began banging on it and frantically yanking at the steel bar. The man who had been standing with them moved toward the boy. He was joined by a woman who yelled out the boy's name, "Eric! Eric! as she rushed towards Eric. Cautiously they grabbed his thrashing arms and kicking legs. They lifted him, the man at his shoulders holding his arms and the woman holding his feet together. Eric screamed as they carried him down the hall, "I want my mommy! I want my mommy!"

"These doors enclose rooms where children sleep." The lady was pointing to narrow doors along both walls. The end of the corridor opened up into a large room.

"As you can see, this is our multipurpose room. It serves as a cafeteria, gym, and activity room. Those long metal tables have benches attached to each side, and we pull them up after meals so that the room can be used for the other activities.

They followed the woman to the right of the multi-purpose room. "There are our resident bathrooms," the lady said, "one for boys, the other for girls." She opened the door to the girls' bathroom so they could see inside. There were several sinks, toilets, and shower stalls. A strange stench hung in the air at the shelter. Nia concluded that it was the slight scent of urine. As they followed the woman, she stopped at a door and unlocked it, "This will be your room, Nia."

The shelter was never quiet. It echoed with the sounds of children screaming, cursing, and fighting one another, or fighting the counselors who manned the facility in three shifts around the clock. Every now and then a child managed to sneak out of his or her room, or leave a group activity, run to the entrance door, grab the handle, and yank on it in a futile attempt to escape.

Chapter 19 Tonai's Story

"You'll see her again." They had thrown their paper plates and cups into the trash and followed the therapist back to their group location that seemed to Tonai to be in the middle of nowhere. Their chairs circled around in the open space that extended out from the nurses' station. Tonai had felt a shield of darkness descending over her as the door shut behind Nia. She felt sapped of energy as she sat down in the chair. Yet the therapist's words sliced through the darkness like a ray of light. She responded, "How you know that?"

"You and Nia have been running into each other all your lives. You know she feels just as sad as you feel. Why don't you tell us about things that happen in your life, Tonai? Maybe this is a good time to share your story."

Tonai threw her hands up and kept them up in the air for a few moments as she rapidly nodded her head, "Yeah, I guess so, 'cause this right here is the story of my life. Everyone I care about disappear from my life. My family disappeared from my life. Zap ... they were gone!"

Tonai shook her head, placed her hands on her knees, and leaned forward. Her eyes took on a distant look as if she was seeing something beyond them. "I remember that day. I can see it just as if it was happening now. Them social workers and policemen come into our home. They said they come to take the children."

Tonai shifted her position in the chair. "Social workers had come to our house before." Placing the palm of her hand on her thigh, she added.

"It all started because of the school squealing on us." Tonai shook her head, "It's a long, long story."

"We got time," the therapist quickly interjected, nodding his head.

"Now some of the story I got from my brothers and sisters 'cause I was real young." Tonai raised her eyebrows. "Mmm ... maybe two, going on three years, but I 'member a lot too. Well, my brothers was taking care of us in the morning 'cause my mom had to leave to go to work earlier than us, and my dad hadn't got back home. He worked nights. So when the alarm would go off, my brother Donté—he was the oldest, and he was the one who really took care of us—he would tell my other brothers to do things to help us, and they would do what he said. See, my three brothers were older than us girls. But Donté, he did a good job, and he was only a kid himself. He got us up and dressed—me and my sister, Rita. I was the youngest and Rita was next to me, so Donté had to dress us. He'd tell everyone else to get dressed. Desmond was the next oldest, but he always was a pain in the butt. Donté would have to yell at him sometimes to get him to do just what he said. Donté and Desmond would push our strollers and take us to day care while the others walked along, and then after they dropped us off at the day care, they'd go to school. Donté would be rushing everyone because they had to get to school early enough to get breakfast at school. He would give me and Rita cups that was like bottles except they had little holes on top. My mom had packed them in carry bags that was in our strollers. So me and Rita be sipping from our cups while they was pushing us.

"Then my brother Desmond got in trouble for taking lunch money from girls. He even knocked some girls down and took money out of their book bags. One girl told her teacher." Tonai raised her voice. "That got the ball rolling. Some other girls spoke up saying that he had done that to them too. Well then the teachers had a meeting. Some of the other teachers said that my bothers and sisters was getting to school late and weren't always dressed right. The school called Child Protective Services. That's when them social workers started coming to our home."

Tonai began breathing in rapidly as if taking in a scent. "They was snooping and sniffing around our home. One social worker lady walked right into our kitchen and opened the refrigerator and cabinets." Tonai shook her head. "No respect. She wrote notes on the tablet she carried with her. She went into my parents' bedroom, looked in the closet, and then asked to see the children's beds. There was only two bedrooms in the apartment. My mom and dad's room, which I guess was my room too 'cause I slept in the crib in their room. The other bedroom was my sisters' room. There was one large bed in that room. My mother told the lady that my four sisters slept in that bed. The lady asked my mother to open the door of the closet in that room. The closet was cluttered 'cause that was where all our stuff was—my brothers' clothes, my sisters' clothes, our toys. My mother explained that the boys slept on the pull-out couch in the living room. That woman made my mom open out the couch." Tonai stood up and pointed her finger out in front of her. Her eyes squinted and her voice deepened. "I just wish I was older at that time. They would have had to take me to jail 'cause I would have punched that lady dead in her face, treating my mom like that."

Tonai went on to explain that her mother had just recovered from an emotional breakdown following the sudden death of Tonai's grandmother. Her parents received a letter stating that the investigation found that the children were not receiving proper supervision, and that their small apartment was not safe for so many children. Tonai's parents were given two months to secure a larger place, and twenty-four-hour adult supervision for the children had to immediately be put in place. The children were to get to school on time and be appropriately dressed. The activities of the family would be closely monitored, particularly in light of the mother's recent hospitalization, which had confirmed her mother's emotional instability.

"My mom couldn't find no one to watch eight kids, so she took days off from her job. While we was at school, and in my case, day care, she'd go check out apartments. She wasn't able to find a landlord willing to rent to a family of ten." Tonai's voice lowered. "I remember that day they came and took us." Then she stopped talking. Her face lost its liveliness, and her eyes glared ahead.

Everyone in the group stared unblinkingly at her, some sitting on the edge of their seats. A still, nearly reverent atmosphere engulfed the group. She started talking after what seemed like an endless silence. Her voice was barely above a whisper. "We was sitting around in the living room watching TV when we heard these hard, loud knocks on the door. 'Police! Open the door!' My mother began trembling as she opened the door. She saw the social worker and started screaming, "No! No! No!" Donté and Desmond began kicking and fighting the two police officers. I was sitting in my daddy's lap. This strange lady put her arms out toward me. I buried my face into my daddy's chest. I felt like that lady was a monster trying to get me. I knew my dad's strong arms would save me from the strange people. But my father whispered in my ear as he loosened his arms from around me, "I can't help you, baby. We don't want anyone to get hurt. You have to go with the lady. You'll be back home soon. I love you always, baby."

Tonai told how she began to cry and wriggle desperately to get back to her father as the lady took her off her father's lap and strapped her into a stroller. As they were leaving, her mother rushed around trying to give a kiss to each of her children. As the policeman was closing the door to their apartment, they saw their mother standing in the middle of the room, her eyes drenched with tears, and they heard her agonized screaming. Even her father couldn't hold back from loudly crying.

Tonai began rocking back and forth and some of the other teens in the group began rocking back and forth. "They took us into this huge building and to a room that was noisy and was crowded with people, mostly children, and there was a lot of cribs. That lady who took me out of my daddy's arms put me in one of them cribs, and she put my sister Rita in a crib next to me. There was little table with chairs around it in the middle of the room. Children were seated around that table coloring in coloring books. Cartoons were showing on a TV that was on a cart by a wall.

People kept walking in and out of the room. A woman rolled in a tray with milk cartons and cookies. I watched them help my brothers and sisters to sit around the small table, and they began eating the cookies and drinking the milk. Then a pretty lady dressed in bright-colored clothing went over to my brothers. She took a seat and pulled it up to the table and sat with them and talked with them and laughed and smiled a lot. Then they got up and she took their hands, and they walked toward the exit with her. I screamed when I saw my brothers moving toward the door. Donté turned around and said to me, "I'll be right back!"

Tonai lowered her head. No one had ever seen Tonai cry or could even imagine her crying, big and brazen as she was, but her voice was low and muffled, and she swiped her arm across her eyes. "It was a long time before I saw my brothers and sisters again. Then another social worker came toward me and Rita, and she lifted Rita up out of the crib and put her in a stroller. Then she reached toward me and lifted me out of the crib and put me in the other seat of the stroller. She took us out of the building and strapped us in car seats in her car. I had been crying the whole time, so I guess I fell asleep, exhausted from crying 'cause next thing I knew the lady was carrying me up steps and into a house and was putting me down on a couch. A few minutes later, she brought Rita in. The lady whose home I was taken to laughed a lot. She laughed while she and the social worker talked. Then the social worker left.

The room I was in had poor lighting, and darkness projected from the rooms beyond that room. The lady sat on the couch beside me and Rita.

"My name is Mother Terry. What's your name?" I didn't answer. I started to cry and couldn't stop. I wanted my daddy. Mother Terry tried to comfort me. She held me tenderly and rocked me."

Tonai explained that the only one thing she wanted was to sit in her daddy's lap and to lay her head on his shoulder as he held her in his arms. This is what she had always done. She would sit on her daddy's lap until it was time to eat dinner. After dinner, after her mother had lifted her out of the high chair and placed her on the floor, she'd struggle to get back into her daddy's lap. She'd toddle over to the big armchair he'd be sitting in, and she'd hold her arms up toward him. He'd lift her up, and she'd stay in his arms while he watched TV until she fell asleep. She would always wake up in her crib, and her daddy would be gone.

Mother Terry was fussy. She'd complain, "They never bring enough clothes for the children. They expect us to go and buy more clothes, and then they don't want to reimburse us for all we spend." But Mother Terry was a good lady. Much as she tried to complain and show annoyance, she had a generous heart. She was a short, plump, pretty lady who loved to cook, and she cooked really well. She liked children. She had a daughter around ten years old who giggled a lot and kept herself busy just like her mother. Her daughter would pick out clothes for Tonai and Rita to wear. Sometimes she would change their pampers. On weekends she would bathe them and dress them under the watchful eye of her mother.

"That house was a huge house," Tonai said, stretching out her arms. Me and my sister had a room to ourselves, and we each had our own bed. All that room and space felt strange to us because we was used to our family always around us."

Tonai relayed that, as she got older, she heard what had happened during family visits. Initially, family visits were every other week. Their family meetings were held at the agency office. Tonai's family couldn't feel comfortable with social workers watching and oftentimes writing down notes. Tonai's parents were denied information on the families who were caring for their children. The social workers told them that, quite often, biological families become angry and vindictive, and cause trouble for foster families. So the agency's policy was not to let foster families and natural families know each other's contact information other than under certain circumstances, such as open adoption planning in which foster parents agree to allow the child's biological parents to maintain contact.

On one occasion, however, the social worker had asked Mother Terry to call Tonai's mother to try to secure documents she needed to get the children into day care. The social worker had said that Tonai's mother had not responded to her calls to get the documents.

Mother Terry was really nice to Tonai's mother. When Mother Terry called the number the social worker gave her, Sierra answered, and before they concluded the conversation, Sierra asked if she could visit her daughters. Mother Terry gave Sierra her phone number and address. They agreed to set up visits without involving the social worker.

A bright smile flashed across Tonai's face. "The first time my mother came see me, I ran the best I could, tottering and stumbling to her. My mommy scooped me up into her arms—both me and my sister—and she held us so tight. She stayed all day. Mother Terry just went about her business, doing things around the house. My mother pulled out our toys and she said to Mother Terry, 'This is Tonai's favorite toy, and this is Rita's favorite toy. I hope you don't mind, and I brought some of their clothes.' Now I know how my mother was trying to be strong for us. She was fighting not to cry, but while she held us and kissed us and smiled at us, tears drifted down her face.

"Mother Terry sat beside my mom. She said ..." Tonai turned her body sideways and cocked her head as if she was now this other person speaking ... 'Listen, baby. I'm a lot older than you. I know the system. Just do what they want! Whatever hoops they put in front of you, just jump through them, and you'll get your babies back!' My mom couldn't hold out no longer. She began to cry. I buried my head into her lap. Mother Terry hugged my mom and told her she could come see us anytime.

"When my mother stood up to leave, I clung to her leg, pressing my face against it. Mother Terry had a time prying me from around my mother's leg. She put me into the highchair. I kept my arms stretched out toward my mother, and I was kicking and screaming. My mother pleaded with me, 'Tonai, please stop crying. I don't want you to upset Mother Terry.'

"'Oh, don't worry about Tonai upsetting me,' Mother Terry was quick to say. 'I'm used to her crying.'"

Tonai went on telling of her past. Even when they had family visits every two or three weeks, things seemed to get stranger and stranger. "I could see the sadness in my mom and dad's eyes. And my brothers, Donté and Desmond, seemed to get angrier and angrier with each family visit. They would accuse my parents." Tonai pressed her lips together and spoke in a wining voice mimicking her brothers, "'Why haven't you found a bigger place so we can all live together? How come we don't have a nice house like these people we living with? Why aren't you doing anything? Why are we still living with strange people? Don't you want us to come home? You just don't want us back!'"

She shook her head. "And my youngest brother, Dayton, he seemed like he didn't even want to be around the family anymore. He wouldn't say anything. He'd let us girls hug him. He'd say hello to mom and dad, but he didn't want them to hug him. He wouldn't say anything to his brothers. Then Donté and Desmond began laughing at him and calling him a sissy.

"Then our visits with our parents were cut down to once a month 'cause the social worker felt that we wasn't getting along. They arranged special visits between Donté and Desmond and my sisters and me every two weeks. And Dayton and me and my sisters would have visits with our parents once a month."

Tonai took a deep breath, "Finally, nearly two years after we was separated, my parents got a house. Our family was reunited." Tonai stood up. Her face was beaming, and her mouth seemed to spread from one side of her face to the other side. "I'll never forget that day. We was all so happy. We couldn't stop hugging one another. My dad, my mom, and us kids was huddled together, bumping into each other as we turned around hugging whoever was next to us. Even sour-faced Dayton was smiling. Us kids started running through the house. Donté was heading the running train. We all streamed behind him in one line. I was the littlest, so I was the last one trailing behind them doing my best to keep up. We ran from one room into the next room. From the living room we ran into the dining room then into the kitchen. We circled around the kitchen table, ran back through the dining room into the living room. We actually ran alongside the walls of the living room, and then we climbed up the stairs. We were all so excited. It's like we were saying, 'This is our house!' We went into all three bedrooms. We'd run to the wall opposite the door we entered then turn and move back to the door to leave the room. We even went into the bathroom bumping into each other as we circled around trying to get out. When we went back down the stairs, my mom and dad was standing at the foot of the stairs, laughing. It was like me and my brothers and sisters just fell into our mom and dad's arms. The house was in Brinsdale—you know that's a descent neighborhood. It was attached, but we had a small backyard. My dad had put a little table and some chairs out there. Some evenings, my family would be sitting around that table playing board games. I'd be sitting in my daddy's lap, and Rita be sitting in my mom's lap."

Tonai sat down. "But the rent was so high that my dad and mom had to work a lot of overtime. They hired a babysitter, but Donté and Desmond tried to run things. They'd get mad if we wouldn't listen to them, and they'd fight us. They'd mess with Dayton a lot, make him serve them. Babysitters would leave 'cause they said it was too much for them." Tonai shook her head, "Our family wasn't the same."

It was a long story, but no one showed any signs of wanting her to stop. "Now, I learned most of what else happened from listening to my bothers and sisters tell our family story. Desmond got caught in the act of stealing from a clothing store, and since Donté was with him, he was accused as well. Child Welfare took them out of our home and placed them back in foster care. Social workers came snooping around again, and they reported that our home was unkempt and that the children were left unsupervised for long periods. They didn't take me and my sisters and Dayton out, but they would come around every week to see if things was right according to their eyes, I guess.

"My mom crashed and then lost her job. Without both incomes, they couldn't keep up the rent. We got evicted. I was walking along with the rest of my family carrying a bag of my clothes. We was all carrying stuff. We went to a shelter. They kept us for the night but said we couldn't stay there 'cause there was too many of us. We was placed back in foster care." She sighed. "There's more to my story. You'll still want to hear the rest?"

"Where are we going?" the therapist confidently said. "It's your day in group, Tonai."

"Where I was placed was a crazy house. It was way worst than my home. I mean it was clean and had nice furniture, but there were children of all ages and even another preschooler my age. Not one time was I hugged in that home. When my foster mother woke me up in the morning, she washed me up and took me to the kitchen and fed me. Then she took me to day care. When I got back home, she'd feed me, put me in my pajamas. Then for a little time while she got the other children changed for bed, I'd sit in the living room. But I'd soon be put to bed. At first I just stared at everyone, but the other kids would pick on me and hit me. A few times, I got smacked in the face with a toy. So I began to fight back, and I discovered that I could hurt other children, make them cry. I felt good."

"You felt empowered," the therapist interjected.

"Yeah. I felt better when I was fighting. I began to jump on other children and fight them if they had a toy I wanted. I would even fight my foster mother when she tried to move me when I didn't want to be moved, and even my foster mother would leave me alone.

"Then I changed. I got quiet again because, as I later found out, I was put on medication to address what the psychiatrist called 'my aggression.' Then I was put in a specialized day care for children with emotional problems.

"When I was thirteen, I began to avoid going home after school, mainly because I felt uncomfortable around my foster mother's son, who was seventeen. Once, he rubbed up against me the wrong way as I passed him on my way out of the bathroom. I elbowed him in his side as hard as I could. He yelled. My foster mother rushed out of her bedroom. As she bent over him, she asked him what was wrong, but he said nothing. She then looked at me accusingly. I went into my bedroom. After that, any time I saw my foster mother getting ready to leave the house, I'd leave the house too. I'd go over to my girlfriend Carrie's house. Me and Carrie would walk to the corner store and stand outside for hours watching everything going on around us.

"One Saturday morning I slept late because I had come in late the night before. I was awakened by the loud sound of my door slamming. It was my foster mother's son. 'It's just me, your brother,' he said.

"You're not my brother! Get out of my room!" I yelled.

"'I'm here to show you that you ain't as bad as you think you are. I gotta teach you a lesson.'" He reached toward me.

"I jumped up off the bed so I could fight him. He grabbed me, and I twisted around to get away from him. Then he hit me in the face. I yelled for help. He laughed and said, 'Nobody's here!' I tried to punch him, but he moved and then he punched me hard in my waist. I bent over holding my waist.

"'Don't go around here acting like you so bad,' he said. 'Now you see you ain't so bad.' He was pointing his finger at my face. 'This is my mother's house, and I don't like the way you talk to her sometimes. You just a foster child. Remember that!'

"Hard as I tried, I couldn't fight him off. He threw me on the bed. He put his hands over my mouth, and I thought he would smoother me."

Tonai stopped talking. The room was silent. Slowly she continued, "When he left my room, I felt so defeated. The pain way deep down inside was far worse than the physical pain in my body. His words stung my mind—'You just a foster child.' I wanted to cry, but I had made up my mind a long time ago that I wasn't crying no more." Tonai lowered her voice. "But I was crying inside. I held my stomach. I had tried so hard to avoid being alone around boys 'cause I seen my girlfriends, one by one, get plucked off. Next thing their belly all bloated up.

"I got up and wiped my face with my hands and then carefully opened my door and peeked out of my room into the hallway. I didn't hear no sounds, so I walked to the bathroom. It was hard for me to focus on washing because I felt so hopeless.

"Before leaving the bathroom, I stood by the door listening. Then, carefully I opened the door and walked to my room and closed the door. I tossed all my clothing into a plastic bag. I opened the door to my room and ran down the stairs and out of the house.

"Two days later the police picked me up at the corner store where I was hanging out with Carrie. As I sat on a bench in the police station, I laid my head back against the wall and fell sound asleep 'cause I hadn't been sleeping. Carrie had snuck me into her bedroom them nights I wouldn't return to that house. I slept in her bed with her, but I kept waking up, jumping up from nightmares. I was glad Carrie was a sound sleeper.

"'Hey, sleeping beauty. Someone's here to see you.' The officer's loud voice woke me up. I looked around and saw the child welfare social worker.

"'Let's go home, Tonai.' I just looked at her."

Tonai stood up. Her lips were twisted, her eyes were squinted, and her head was cocked to one side. Everyone in the group laughed at her expression. She continued to amuse the group, because she shifted positions acting as the one who was talking as she relayed the scenario.

"I'm not going back there!"

"'Tonai, that is your home.'" Her voice had turned high pitched and squeaky.

"No, that's the home you want me to be in."

"'You're older now. It's hard to place older children. If you're going to be defiant, you might be sent to a detention facility.'

"Whatever." Tonai looked up at the group. "I didn't mean to be rude, but that's how I felt." She then shifted her position to be the social worker who was talking. Her voice became high-pitched. "'Why don't you want to go back?'

"Because her son molested me."

Tonai sat down. She continued her story. "Everyone stood still. It was as if the whole police station had frozen in time. Then they came with questions and papers. The social worker wanted to take me to get an exam, but I told her, 'No!' I didn't want nobody poking at me. A couple of months later I found out nothing came out of it because my foster brother lied and said he didn't molest me. He said he wasn't even home."

Tonai abruptly stopped talking because something had just triggered an idea. She thought of how no one could protect her. She thought about how she had begun to devise ways to protect herself. She had deliberately gained weight. She used her height, weight, and rough mannerisms to remind people that it would be unwise for them to mess with her. It was why she dressed like a boy, in loose hoodies and baggie pants. Everyone either knew her or knew of her. She became a person whom some people avoided, which was what she wanted.

"I don't like nobody bullying someone else," she said. "I don't care who they are. I got a rep in school because of how I can't stand nobody being picked on. Even my teachers. You know how they can make a person feel so bad. Like this girl didn't have her book essay presentation. This teacher asked her what she was doing that she couldn't do her homework. I saw how she was embarrassed. She was the quiet type and wouldn't say nothing. I couldn't take it. So I spoke up."

Tonai stood up, stretching out her arms, with her lips poked out. In a loud, brazen voice she acted out the scene: "Yo! Ms. Petty. Oops, I mean Ms. Perkins. Don't you know it's rude to ask somebody their personal business? She don't have to tell you why she didn't do her assignment. She don't have to tell you what's going on in her life. I mean, she didn't do her assignment. That's it. All you got to do is give her the consequence or whatever, for not doing her assignment!"

Everyone in the group with the exception the therapist jumped up. Some stuck their fists up into the air and others just yelled, "Yo! Yo! Yo! Yeah, tell that teacher like it is. Be real." Laugher rippled through the group.

"Okay! Okay!" said the therapist. "Sit back down. Let's leave the storytelling to Tonai." He waved his arms in a calming down motion.

"I'd get sent to the guidance office," continued Tonai. "I'd sit there, pull my hoodie over my head, and get comfortable, 'cause they'd make you wait there forever. I'd think to myself, *Which is it this time ... detention or suspension?* Then I got sent to an alternative school 'cause they said I was disruptive in the classroom."

Tonai explained that she had been placed in two other foster homes before she was sixteen. She was old enough to refuse medication and quick to fight anyone she perceived as a threat. At sixteen, she was placed in a group home with five other teenage girls and round-the-clock counselors.

Her parents had two more children. They had gotten approved for public housing and were given a two-bedroom apartment unit.

Tonai told the group that she heard social workers talking about a phenomenon that sometimes happened to families whose children were in foster placement for lengthy periods of time. These families closed themselves into a new family unit, knitting themselves back together and leaving the child or children in foster care on the outside.

With her voice nearly in a whisper and her shoulders sloped down, Tonai said, "That happened to us. My parents started another family. They had two more children. There was no room for us in their home. When me and any of my sisters visited, we could feel our mother's tension. Her attention would be easily diverted to the children living with her. She'd keep asking us how long we were allowed to visit. Now, pretty much everybody but me aged out." Tonia swallowed hard. "And we all know what that means." Her eyes flared with rage as she thought of each of her siblings and how they'd fared once the system no longer cared about them. But then she bit her lip as the realization hit her that she wasn't so far from eighteen herself, and she turned away, not wanting the group to see the fear in her eyes.

"The system's certainly not perfect," the therapist said gently.

"It's messed up!" Tonia felt rage returning. "My sister, Rita, she living in a homeless shelter with two babies—babies! Ain't nobody got a place for her. Not even my mom can help. And you know why? Because of the 'system.'"

Everyone in the room knew exactly what Tonia was talking about. The faces of the teens took on pensive, saddened looks. When the money provided for a foster child's care stopped at age eighteen, many foster parents found excuses that allowed them to request the removal of the foster child, by then a young adult, from their home. Social workers would refer them to homeless shelters.

Tonai's voice erupted through the solidified pensiveness of the group. "My mom refused to let Rita live with her for a little while until she got back on her feet. She said that child welfare social workers were still breathing down her neck. She also explained to Rita that housing authorities were always monitoring families to ensure that only those individuals named on the lease were living in the apartment. They were quick to evict families who were noncompliant in any area of their lease agreement, because there was a long waiting list for public housing. My mom reminded Rita of how they used to struggle to pay rent every month. She expressed that for them to chance losing a public housing unit was a big risk because rent for their unit was based on a percentage of their family's income resulting in their paying affordable rent as opposed to the high rents in the private housing market.

"Rita pleaded with our mother, 'I'll keep the children quiet. Nobody has to know. It's only for a little while till I get a place.'

"'No!' my mom flatly told her.

"Me and my sisters know that she's afraid that child welfare will come and break up her new little family. She's so protective of her last two children, my little brothers. She walks them to school, and she's there when they get out."

Tonai took a deep breath, "Me and my sisters talked about how our mother has changed. She used to be so much fun, always laughing. She's suffered so much. We know she got caught up in the system, so we careful not to blame her. Joy—she's my oldest sister—said that what happened to our family was like we was swallowed by a monster whale and we couldn't get out until finally it spat us out. And by that time we smelled like sh … oops!" Toni put her hand to her mouth. "Sorry, gotta watch my mouth. So we real careful not to make our mom and dad uncomfortable.

"Donté and Desmond got out of the system their own way. They ran away from their foster home, and last I heard, they was living on the street. My mom said Donté calls her about twice a year, and a couple of times he showed up at her door." Tonai's thoughts flashed on Desmond, who never called or visited her parents, but she did not voice those thoughts.

"There's good news, though," she finally said. "Dayton got a good foster home." Suddenly Toni's face dropped, and she turned her face away from the group. In a low, muffled voice she said, "They adopted him." She jerked her head as if to shake off a thought. Then she said raising her voice, "He graduated from high school, and I heard that he's going to college."

Everyone in the group, including the counselor, was transfixed when Tonai stopped talking. Even Tonai sat motionless with her head down.

Days later, Tonai was discharged from the hospital. Her social worker drove her back to the group home where she'd been living.

Chapter 20 Family Unity

A few months after Tonai left the hospital, horrific news pulled her family together. It was Desmond's murder. It took the wind out of Tonai when she learned about it. She knew something was amiss when the counselor in her group home handed her the phone. It was her mother's voice. "Hi, baby. Are you sitting down?" She was standing up because the phone was on a wall in the hallway. The counselor seemed to sense that something was up. He brought her a chair. She sat down.

"Hi, Mom. Yeah, I'm sitting." Her mother had never called her at the group home.

"I know you strong, Tonai."

Tonai swallowed hard. Somebody died. It had to be her dad. He was older and having health problems.

"Desmond's dead."

Tonai fought to emerge from the crushing blow. She felt weak and couldn't stop tears from tumbling out of her eyes. Her mother's cries seeped through the long moment of silence.

"I'll talk to you when you get here." Her mother's voice was barely above a whisper.

***

It took strength to hold up through the funeral. Tonai smiled and hugged everyone like everyone else was doing. Maybe they, like her, were hoping they were all in a bad dream. The casket couldn't be opened because of the condition of the body. She had to fight off visions of his last moments of life because the police reported that he had been rigged with explosives before being thrown off a bridge.

Detectives were at the funeral. Tonai knew who they were. Their funeral attire couldn't disguise them. For one thing, they weren't family or friends. She'd stare at them, look them right in the eye. Their lack of emotion and focus on watching people, rather than the service, gave them away as being, 'on duty'.

The detectives were looking for Donté. They had been trying to catch up with him for years. They'd show up at family members' homes asking if they'd seen him. In addition to the death of the man he and Desmond had lived with after they ran away from their foster home, the police had been trying to pin other drug-related murders on him. They were sure that he was involved in a building explosion that had occurred a few days after Desmond's death. That explosion had killed members of a drug cartel that police believed were responsible for Desmond's murder.

Tonai's mind flashed to the scene at her parents' place where she had been before arriving at the funeral. She and her sisters, along with some close relatives, had sat in the living room. The group seemed too big for the room. People sat hip to hip on the couch and doubled up on the armchairs. A few people were in chairs that had been brought out from the kitchen. Her youngest brothers scrambled around on the floor, jumping up now and then, running to their room to get something, and sliding back down to their spot on the floor. Her dad wasn't there. He was in the hospital, but told their mom that, if he had to walk the whole distance, he was getting to his son's funeral.

Everything in the apartment was neat and clean. Beige and white colored the apartment—white walls, beige curtains, beige furniture, beige floor coverings. The word *sterile* ran through Tonai's mind. The kitchen could barely fit around the table that was in the middle of it. There was no dining room. A short hallway off the living room led to the bedrooms and bathroom. One bedroom had twin beds and a twin set of dressers. Beige curtains hung from that window. The other bedroom was nearly wall to wall with a large bed, matching dressers, and night tables. It was nice but too cramped. As she sat and looked around, Tonai wondered how the crowd that would come after the funeral would fit into the apartment.

Before they left the apartment to go to the funeral, Sierra had looked around at her children and said, "I just want it all to be over."

Tonai quickly scanned the faces of her sisters—Joy, Daisha, Ruby, and Rita. She saw hurt flicker through their eyes just as it had flickered through her own heart. Their mother's words made them feel as if she wanted them to disappear too.

When their mother left the living room, Rita calmly said, "She's talking about Desmond's funeral."

Indeed, their mother had said, over and over throughout the years, that she'd rather her sons be caught and imprisoned than be found dead. Tonai's mother had said that any day she figured she would get a call to tell her that Donté, her firstborn, whom everyone knew was dearest to her heart, had been found dead.

Tonia was relieved when it was time to go to the funeral. The tension in the cramped apartment was building inside of her.

When she stepped inside the church, her heart stopped. She heard a tiny gasp escape her. She didn't move. She just stared. There was Ben, her father, sitting in a wheelchair positioned in the aisle at the end of the first pew. The shape of him, the quiet way he sat—it was so intimately familiar. He was a part of her soul. Momentarily, she reflected on his strong arms around her, his gentle smile and slightly musky smell. Her heart fluttered, and she allowed herself to imagine that, even now, she could sit in his lap, just for fun.

She rushed forward, the thought unfreezing her frozen feet. Standing at his side, she stared at him in disbelief. He bore virtually no resemblance to the father she'd known. As she looked at him, she felt a blow to her chest so powerful like she'd feel if someone had kicked her hard in her chest, knocking the wind out of her. Her father had shriveled up! He was thin, his back was curved, and his eyes looked listless. She had been told that he was ill, but she hadn't known how ill. He looked up at her. His eyes swelled with tears, but none ran down his face. Tonai hoped desperately that he wouldn't cry. She knew the tears in his eyes went far beyond a reaction to his son's funeral. They were for everything that had gone wrong. Tonai bent down and gave him a lingering hug. Then she sat in the pew diagonally behind him and directly behind her mother.

Tonai's thoughts raced. Life was unfair. Her father had always been a good man. He had never hit his children. He had worked hard all his life, and now it seemed that it had all been fruitless. He had worked night after night for over twenty years, yet he hadn't even made enough money to take care of his family the way he wanted to. The doctors had diagnosed him as having lung cancer. He had never smoked, but he had been exposed to dust and soot at his job. As Tonai looked at her father, she could see his head jerk downward at times, and he'd press his lips together. She knew he was in pain. He'd been in and out of the hospital and had been in the hospital when he learned about his son's death. Despite the doctor's recommendations, he signed himself out to attend his son's funeral.

A tear escaped her eye. Tonai shook herself. *No tears!* She had vowed never to show emotion. But her eyes drifted back to her father. Thoughts whispered through her mind: *That's not him. He's not there. What has happened to my father? What has happened to the man who was always so strong and held me in his arms every evening?* She had been his favorite. She still had to be his favorite, all these years later. He was too weak to hold her youngest brothers. Tonai felt anger mounting in her. She couldn't stop the thoughts about her father. He'd never done anything wrong. He never drank. He never smoked. He did everything right, even when he was dating her mother. Sometimes in the past, when they had all still been together and sitting around the living room, he'd tell how he had courted Sierra. He'd say their mother was so tough that she would not even allow him to kiss her. He would laugh and say, "I would have settled for a kiss. That would have held me." Even though none of his children understood the full meaning of what he said, they'd all laugh because their parents were laughing. He'd follow that statement with, "But your mama was so beautiful and mysterious that she kept me anyway. And here we all are!" Tonai looked again at her father. His body jerked spasmodically as his hand began to tremble.

Tonai was the last of the immediate family members to follow the casket out of the church and down the steps. As she stepped onto the sidewalk and stood against the wall of the building, she thought she heard her name whispered. Tonai stood still. She heard her name whispered a second time, "Tonai!"

Glancing through the crowd standing outside the church, Tonai did not notice anyone who might be trying to get her attention. After a moment's reflection, she carefully cast her eyes down to look at the basement window. She saw a shadow move behind the dark screen over the window. Her heart raced. She knew it was Donté. She walked up to her oldest sister, Joy. "You have a piece of paper? You have a pen?" Joy was a great one for carrying everything in her pocketbook—just in case she needed it, she'd say. Tonai tore off a piece of the paper and scribbled on it, "I'll be back." She folded the note and acted like she put it in her bosom but she kept it in her palm. She handed the pen and the rest of the paper back to her sister, who had turned to talk to someone. Tonai took out a piece of gum, unwrapped it, and put the gum in her mouth. She chewed for a while, even popped a few bubbles. Then she took the gum out of her mouth and put it in its foil-coated wrapping in the hand in which she had the note. She moved toward her relatives who were near the basement window and joined in their conversation. As she brought her arms down after lifting them and hugging one of her cousins, she threw the wrapping, along with the note, on the ground near the window. She then joined her sisters as they all piled into the car that led the procession to the burial site. She said nothing about Donté to anyone.

The sun blazed down on the mourners gathered around the burial site, and the silence was broken only by the occasional call of a bird. Ben's gnarled hands clutched the arms of his wheelchair, and with a heavy release of wheezing breath, he pushed himself forward, not succeeding at first in his attempt to rise to his feet.

At first Sissy and the others around him urged him to stay seated. When Ben looked as if he was going to fall out of his chair, Sissy motioned for a few men to stand on each side of him. They helped him to stand. He stood over the casket that had not yet been lowered into the ground. Ben shook his arms to indicate to the men beside him to release him. Someone snatched his cane from the back of the wheelchair and positioned it in front of him. He leaned on it. Ben stood quietly for some time, his chin up, his eyes closed. Everybody understood that he was honoring his son. Then he bowed his head. All there reverently lowered their heads.

When Ben began to speak, everyone stood still, and a serene quietness hovered over the burial site, "You was a brave soldier, my son. You just didn't understand what was going on, but you was courageous and brave. May God have mercy on your soul." After the casket was lowered into the ground, Ben sat down. Tonai saw his head jerk sharply, but he continued to hold his chin up.

Following the funeral, family members and friends gathered at her parents' apartment. They wheeled her father into the apartment, and he sat at one end of the kitchen table. Tonai's mother gave him a pain pill, which relaxed him and caused him to doze off at times. Ben had adamantly refused to take any medications until the funeral was over. Tonai was happy to see him smile, even if it was interrupted by his dozing off.

The apartment was packed. There were so many people that even in the bedrooms, people sat in any spot that could be found on the beds, or they sat on the floor with their backs against the walls. In addition to her immediate family, nieces and nephews, aunts and uncles, and their children and grandchildren, as well as close friends of the family, were at the repast.

At one point, all Ben's children circled around him with the exception of Tonai's youngest brother, Dayton, and, of course, Donté. Dayton, who had come to the funeral with his foster parents, had sat in the back of the church with them. When Sissy saw them enter the church, she got up from her seat and went to the back and hugged him and greeted his foster parents. The few times she had met with his foster parents, she had expressed her gratitude that they loved her son and had been taking such good care of him. Sissy told Dayton that she looked forward to him coming to see her when he finished his schooling. He never responded, and he and his foster parents left immediately after the service.

Tonai watched all the babies being brought before her daddy, all his new grandchildren. Joy, the oldest girl, hadn't had any children, even though she was married. She had been the most sensible of them all, according to their mother. Although her brothers were older, she showed more maturity than they. She always thought things through and made decisions based on what would be best in the long run. She had finished high school and had married, and she and her husband were delaying children until they had met some goals. To Tonai and her sisters, Joy was a tower of strength, someone they could call or run to when things went wrong. But her three other sisters, Daisha, Ruby, and Rita, seemed to compete over who could have the most babies. Every year, one of them, or all three it seemed, became pregnant.

Sissy was always preaching, "Get the man to marry you. Make it legal! You need all the help you can get out here. You see how I had to suffer, even with a husband? What makes you think it's a joke out here?" Their mother would quickly add, "And don't bring no babies over here for me to babysit!" She'd shake her head and say, "I ain't taking care of no more babies!"

There was so much food being served at the gathering at Ben and Sissy's place following the funeral. The one thing Sissy always said she knew how to do well was to cook. Everyone agreed. When she put her mind to it, and when she had the energy and time, Sissy could, as they

166

said, "throw down." There was a huge turkey, a ham, smothered pork chops, fried chicken, potato salad, black-eyed peas and rice, candied yams, macaroni and cheese, collard greens, cornbread, and more. Tonai knew that her mother had stayed up all night preparing the food. It was her way of giving the best possible send-off to her son.

Everyone was quick to get a paper plate and pile food onto it. Lines formed on both sides of the kitchen table. People laughed and talked, especially about how well their children were doing. Ironically, because of the circumstance that had brought everyone together, everybody seemed to want to hear all the good news happening in the family. Everyone seemed to be doing well, according to their mothers' reports; one child got an art award, another won a sports contest, someone won the spelling bee, and another was a straight-A student. Tonai's eyes flitted from person to person as she listened to all the bragging. She knew that some of the children the mothers were bragging about had another side to them that had them "doing their thing" when they were out of the house away from their mothers' watchful eyes. Some were even doing drugs. But today she wasn't going to burst anybody's bubble.

The men tended to be less aggressive than the women about pushing into the kitchen to get food. There were too many women and children in there for their comfort! A woman would pile food onto a plate, grab a fork, and take the plate to her husband or man friend. Most of the men were huddled around a small TV watching a basketball game in Tonai's parents' bedroom.

After the men and children were served, the women carried their own plates into the living room and tried to find a space on the couch. Some even doubled up and shared a chair. A group of women stayed in the kitchen. They were simultaneously chewing and talking, saying, "Um, um, um, Sis, this sure is good!" "Oh, I miss your candied yams. They sure are good!"

After swallowing a mouthful of food, someone said, "Sissy, you got to give me the recipe for your baked macaroni and cheese!" They all agreed, and then shared how they made some of the dishes.

The ladies' conversations moved from topic to topic. After they compared recipes, they moved on to a discussion about knitting. As they talked and laughed, they cleaned up like an organized work crew. Women went around collecting discarded plates and cups. One woman reached into a cupboard and brought out a set of plastic storage containers. A couple of women began to scrape what food remained in pots into containers. Another went to the sink, ran some water into it, and squirted dishwashing detergent into the water. She began to wash the pots, utensils, serving bowls, and plates. Another woman, who was busy laughing at anything anybody said, picked up a towel and slung it over her shoulder and waited. She wiped the dishes, pots, plates, and utensils as soon as they were placed into the drainer, and set the dried items on the table. As each piece of kitchenware was placed on the table, someone would grab it and put it in a cabinet.

After everyone had eaten, the younger generation emerged as the entertainers. The adults were full and feeling fat and tired from everything the day's events had brought their way. The teens changed the music and began to dance. There was always one showoff clowning around. Tonai even jumped in and started to dance around the living room. Some of the older generation got up off the couch, threw their arms up, and began to sway as they tried to catch on to the dance. Of course, the older folks were hilarious because they were stiff and couldn't seem to follow the teens' quick dance moves. As everyone danced and hugged and laughed, Tonai laughed and felt warmed inside being with her family. She wondered why the child welfare social workers couldn't see her family now.

Of course somebody had to ask, "Sissy, have you heard from Donté?"

Tonai's mother, who was sitting on a stool next to the refrigerator, took a deep breath and said, "No. I ain't heard from him in about six months."

Aunt Sarah was quick to change the topic of conversation. "Well, Sissy, I got to give it to you. You got the strength of an ox. The work you put into this food layout is amazing. All these years, what you should have done from the jump start was open a restaurant!"

Aunt Sandra followed her sister's lead. "As a family we should pool our funds together and get a restaurant. We'd be rich! We were in the restaurant business once. Where's Uncle Isaiah? He knows. He had a restaurant."

"Uncle Isaiah went home after the burial. He's old, you know." Sissy smiled as she looked at her sisters and spoke of Uncle Isaiah. She was the only one who had kept in close contact with their uncle. "If he were here, he'd tell you that the restaurant business is a lot of hard work. From what I understand, restaurant responsibilities sapped the life out of his sister, our grandmother, as well as his mother, our great-grandmother. We never got to know either of them because they died before their time." Sissy shook her head. "I don't think I need that kind of burden in my life."

"Well, maybe they didn't have enough help," Aunt Sarah quickly responded. "We could get our children to work with us. I'd give them jobs" Everyone began to nod in agreement.

Uncle Gregory tuned into a bit of the conversation as he entered the kitchen and ran with it. Somehow, every time the relatives got together, the story of Uncle Isaiah's near lynching had to be told. And it seemed that everybody liked to hear it, no matter how many times they'd heard it before. So Uncle Gregory, who held a wineglass in his hand as he entered the kitchen, sat his glass on the table as he picked up a small paper plate and put a piece of cornbread on it. Alternately solemn and fired up, he told the story, occasionally sipping from the wineglass, which he kept refilling, or biting a chunk out of the cornbread. When his storytelling ended, Uncle Gregory twirled around and stumbled out of the kitchen, his hand clenched around his wineglass, on which he kept his eyes fastened as he moved through the living room.

In the kitchen, the tone of the conversation changed. One relative turned to the woman next to her and asked, "Did you hear about this new system they putting into the high schools?" As they talked about the new school policy, the women's eyes squinted, their eyebrows knitted together as their tempers rose, booming out through their excited voices and the sound of their hands slapping the kitchen counters.

Tonai walked into the kitchen, opened containers, and began piling food onto a paper plate. She carved off turkey and then went to the ham and added her carvings to the plate. She was piling food so high that her mother commented, "Tonai, that food's gonna spill off."

Tonai smiled, "I got this." She turned an unused plastic plate upside down and placed it over the food platter. Then she tore off a long piece of aluminum foil and secured it completely over, around, and under the plate. She put a fork on top of the plate, placed them both into a plastic bag, and tied the bag tight. Tonai kissed her mother and her father. "I gotta go," she said, smiling.

As she walked through the living room, her sister Joy looked at her with a slight frown on her face. Joy stood up and stepped in front of Tonai as she was about to pass her, and said, "This is your brother's funeral. Where you have to rush off to?"

"Yeah, his funeral's over, and he's in another world now, hopefully heaven."

"How can you talk like that? God forbid if it were you! How would you like one of us talking like that about you!"

"Hey! When I leave here, please just burn me up. Take my ashes and toss them in the wind. I don't want nobody going in debt paying funeral people over me. I don't want my body put in a casket in the ground and folks coming stepping on the ground where they think I am and crying. When I'm gone, let me be gone!"

"You ought to have more respect, Tonai."

"I am showing respect. I'm here. I been here all day. And he's here in my heart." Tonai pounded her fist on her chest. "He'll always be here in my heart. Now I got something to do. Do you mind? Excuse me!" Joy shook her head and moved out of Tonai's path.

Tonai walked out of the building. As she passed cars parked along the block, she peeked into the windows in the hope that some family member had come out for a smoke or just some fresh air and would give her a ride. She was lucky. One of her uncles sat behind the steering wheel of his Buick with his head laid back on the headrest. His eyes were closed, and his mouth was gaped open. She could hear him snoring from outside the car. She tapped on the window. Her uncle woke up with a start, turned his head, and looked at her. He rolled the window down a little. "How can I help you, Tonai?"

"Unc, can you take me to Eleventh and Cedar?"

"That's on the other side of town!"

"Yeah, Unc, I know. That's why I'm asking you for a ride." She looked around and blew cold air out of her mouth. "It's cold out here!"

"Get in."

Tonai had her uncle drop her off about a half a mile from the church where her brother's funeral service had been held. She didn't want to leave any room for her uncle to speculate where she was going. As soon as she got out of the car, she walked in the opposite direction from the church. When her uncle's car disappeared around the corner, she reversed her direction and headed toward the church at a fast pace. It had been nearly five hours since they had been at the church. Would her brother still be there? Donté was wanted for several murders. Why did he want to meet with her? She felt uneasy. Tonai looked around furtively in doorways and on rooftops to make sure that no police or detectives were still lurking around. As she walked, she wondered how her brother had gotten into the church with detectives there.

Tonai stopped when she got to the street where the church stood. There were several boys by a light post, their faces nearly covered over by their hooded sweatshirts. She walked slowly while watching them from the corner of her eye. Plain-clothes detectives knew how to fit into a neighborhood. In the area where she lived, she generally wore a black hoodie and hung out with boys standing on the corner. Now, although she was on the opposite side of the street, she listened intently to their conversation and determined that the hooded boys were the real deal. She passed a man sprawled out on ice-covered steps. Tonai thought that no detective would park his behind on icy steps and be spread out over two steps like the man was. Everything was okay. She quickened her pace.

She went past the front of the church and stood for a minute by the basement window where she had seen Donté's shadow. She lit a cigarette. She held it in her hand just like a man would. She went around the corner where the church stood and entered the parking lot area through an opening in the black iron gate that surrounded the parking lot. She was looking for the shadow of a figure at any window. There was none. She saw steps that led to the cellar. She went down those steps. As soon as she reached the concrete pad at the bottom, the door, which looked as if it hadn't been opened in years, squeaked open, just a little. She turned her body sideways and slipped inside.

She strained in the dark to see. The door shut. A man's figure stepped in front of her. Tonai's heart pounded. He whispered, "Little sis." The voice, even though it had deepened and had a rasp to it, was Donté's. Her mind flashed back years. For a moment, she was a baby holding onto the hand of her Donté, who had always given her candy or some milk to drink. Tonai hadn't even thought about how she'd feel when she'd see her brother. Tears welled in her eyes. He hugged her, and they held onto each other.

He took hold of the bag. "Is this for me?"

"Yeah."

"Thank you. Wait here a minute."

It was pitch black in the basement. The windows were either boarded up or covered with thick, dark curtains. He struck a match and lit a candle. She could barely see a table with a chair next to it. He went and placed the bag on the table.

"Come on. Follow me upstairs where there's light." He blew out the candle as he moved toward a stairway. They went up the stairway, and at the top he pushed open a heavy door that led to the church vestibule. Donté then held open one of the huge swinging doors to the sanctuary. Tonai walked into the church that hours earlier had been packed with people attending Desmond's funeral. She slipped into the back pew. Donté sat beside her.

"You been here all this time?"

"It's no biggie. It's what I do."

"How did you get in here, especially with all those detectives around?"

"I came the night before the funeral."

"But how did you get in?"

Donté smiled. His face looked rough, and despite a few scratch marks on his skin, his smile accentuated how handsome he was. Even in the dim light, she could make out his reddish-brown complexion and the high cheekbones that their mother had told them marked their American Indian heritage. He had thick, black eyebrows and deep-set eyes that seemed to bore right through her. His six-foot height added to the depth of the calm, authoritarian manner that defined his personality.

"I specialize in breaking and entry," he said at last. "I watched the detectives open up the church. I listened to their footsteps so I'd know where they were. A detective came into the basement, looking around and checking that the windows and doors were secured. I had already secured them. He had no real light, just a flashlight, so I knew he wouldn't be able to see me. I was behind the boiler. The detectives were here for three hours before the service started. They were watching for me to come to the funeral."

"While you were inside watching them?"

"Yeah."

"You didn't miss Desmond's funeral?" Tonai stared at her brother.

He lowered his head as he whispered, "No." When he looked up, his eyes looked glassy.

Tonai felt a deep sadness. They were silent for several moments. "They say you killed people."

Her brother was quick to respond. "They say you have a right to defend yourself if you're attacked."

"You killed those men who killed Desmond?"

"An eye for an eye and a tooth for a tooth." He stared at her for a few moments, and she felt as if his eyes were burrowing right through her. "You look just like your mother."

"She's your mother, too," Tonai said with her voice trembling. "I don't want you to die."

"I'll stay around just for you, baby."

172

"What about for yourself? Don't you want to have a better life?" Donté didn't answer. After what seemed like endless silence Tonai asked, "You have a wife?"

He shook his head. "No!"

"Children?"

"Not that I'm aware of. How's Daddy doing? I saw him in the wheelchair."

"I don't think he's doing so well. He has lung cancer." Once again neither spoke for a good while so that silence overshadowed the sanctuary. Tonai broke through the silence. "Don't you wish we could go back to how it was when we were all together?" She felt so much like a little girl again. "Do you think things would have been different if our family had all stayed together?"

He turned his face to one side. "That was a long time ago, baby girl."

Tonai smiled. "But you still calling me 'baby girl.' Can you tell me what happened all those years we been apart? How did you get so far out there?"

Donté took a cigarette out of his pocket and lit it. Slowly, as if sorting out things himself, he told the story of his and Desmond's journey. They were there for two hours. By the time he finished, Tonai had her hand to her mouth and tears streamed down her face.

"I want you to help me with something," he said.

"Me?"

"Yeah."

Tonai shook her head and leaned back. "Now, I ain't saying I'm an angel. I guess you can look at me and see that, but I can't hang with you, Donté. You too far out there for me. I go as far as kicking up a storm in school or in the home placements they put me in. I have stolen from stores when I was younger—candy, a bag of potato chips. Once I put on a jacket that was on a rack in a store, and I walked out wearing it. But I ain't crossing that line and doing something that's really criminal."

"I'm not asking you to do nothing criminal. I wouldn't ask you to do that."

Tonai was quiet. Donté continued, "I need you to take some papers to the district attorney's office. These papers are notarized, so they're legal documents. I wrote out what happened to the old man me and Desmond lived with. I informed about the drug cartel explosion. I gave names and dates and some pictures." He reached into his jacket pocket, took out a fat envelope, and handed it to Tonai. "I want you to hand this envelope to his secretary and get a receipt for it. You just hold onto the receipt."

Tonai sensed that there was no point in asking about what had happened to the old man and the specifics about the people who had died in the drug cartel explosion. She knew he would likely just kiss her on the forehead and say, "Just do it, baby."

"Okay, I can do that," she said.

"I knew you would. And I know you'll see to it this week … right, baby girl?"

Tonai nodded. She put the envelope inside her jacket and pressed her elbow against it to hold it in place. Donté stood up.

"Tell Mother, Dad, and my sisters that I love them. Tell them don't worry. I'm okay."

Tonai followed Donté out of the sanctuary and back down the steps to the basement. He didn't even bother to relight the candle. He knew exactly how to navigate through the pitch-black basement. Tonai kept her hand lightly on his back to keep up with him. Donté opened the basement door just enough for her to squeeze through, and then he stepped back. Tonai turned to look at him, but she didn't see him. She stepped out and ran up the steps. He hadn't closed the door. She knew he was watching for her to be clear of the church grounds. She knew that he was scanning windows, doors, and alleyways in the buildings across the street from the church for any type of movement, and looking around the church grounds for anything that looked suspicious. With heaviness in her heart that she'd never experienced, Tonai walked at a fast pace out of the churchyard, turned the corner, and walked along the front of the church. She felt as if some powerful force had scooped a hole out of her heart. She fought the thought that kept invading her mind. The thought was that she would never see Donté again.

Chapter 21 The Brothers' Story

Donté stood by the barely open door watching Tonai as she ran up the steps and as she walked out of the church parking lot. He picked up the slender branch that he had placed against the wall and used it to move the leaves back toward the cellar door, as the leaves had been displaced when he had opened the door to allow Tonai to enter. He then closed the slight opening of the door and sat on a stool that he had made out of crates. Donté reached out in the dark, grabbing binoculars that he had placed on a stand by the window. He peeked through the narrow slit in the shade that covered the window. He scanned the roofs, the windows, and the small backyards of the attached row houses that were lined up behind one side of the fence that boarded the church parking lot. He strained to identify any kind of movement. He could smell the food from the bag that Tonai had left. He had not eaten in two days, but he had learned to ignore his own needs as a tool for survival.

Donté moved to the other windows around the perimeter of the basement looking for any activity while watching Tonai as she walked past the front of the church and on down the block. He kept watching even after Tonai was no longer in his view until he was sure there were no federal marshals or bounty hunters still around. He knew that it was possible that one of them might have a feeling that he was in the church although it had been searched, and that man could be determined to outwait him and watch for his exit.

Satisfied, Donté reached into his pocket and took out his flashlight. The dim light was barely enough for him to see the bag on the card table. Donté sat on a chair he had placed by the table and put his flashlight down on the table so that it illuminated the food. He carefully took out the plate and searched the bag with his hand until he found the fork. Slowly he uncovered the plate and began to eat, his ears on alert for even the slightest sound. The aroma of the food reminded him of his family. He had disciplined himself not to think of them so that his emotions wouldn't affect his work, but talking to Tonai had made him reflective.

Every day he woke up was evidence of his survival. That's how life was for him now. He had crossed boundaries that were not supposed to be crossed. They were invisible boundaries, but everybody knew them, and they signified what was and what was not tolerated by mainstream society and even by the criminal world. He now worked alone, which he understood was extremely dangerous because he had no one to watch his back.

Donté studied how things went down leading to a mob-style execution often resulting in a body found in a river. Often the victim was a snitch who betrayed the man he worked for. The snitch had gotten a big payoff to reveal the whereabouts of his boss to a competing drug cartel. Drug bosses had to be smart and alert in the business they were in, always watching for cues and never trusting anyone. If a hit didn't go down like it was supposed to, the leader would quickly find out the identity of the snitch.

Donté found Desmond's killers easily because one of Donté's errand boys had purchased some big-ticket items—a big-screen TV, a computer, and some furniture. His boy never had money unless Donté gave it to him. Now he suddenly had a lump of cash that Donté hadn't given him. His boy had tried to stay cool for a few days, but the money began burning a hole in his pocket. Donté saw him through a restaurant window as the man was eating. He scribbled a note on a small piece of paper and took it to a waitress, directing her whom to give it to, and he handed her a hundred-dollar bill for her purse. He left the restaurant. The note read as if the drug cartel had sent it. He watched his boy read it and rush out of the restaurant. He followed him to the building from which the cartel operated. He knew he had to remain clearheaded to succeed in his mission. He suppressed thoughts of how they had tortured Desmond before they rigged him with explosives. That was how they did things. His brother's biggest strength was loyalty. Desmond wouldn't break because he knew they were trying to get to Donté.

It was the way of society to brand him a criminal. But the way Donté saw it, it was war. The big guys had come in and wanted to take over his territory. Donté had a good business area. Even though there were several large schools in his territory, he wouldn't let any of his people work the schools. When he had first started his business, he was twenty years old. When his people pressured him about selling at schools because of the profit it could bring in, he told them, "I have seven brothers and sisters. I'm the oldest. We not doing playgrounds! We not doing schools! There's enough business out there without taking in kids. When they reach eighteen, if they want a fix, we welcome them with open arms. If I find out anyone's working playpens—and I will find out—you'll be coming to see me!" There was always silence when Donté talked about someone being made to see him. He was good at what he did, and he quickly sensed when someone had gone sour. He could see a difference in how a person looked at him, or he'd notice when someone wasn't following his directives, or he'd see his man talking to someone he shouldn't be talking to. He had a calculating mind and quickly knew if he'd been shortchanged. Everyone else would know when someone had gone sour, too, because they'd find him behind a building, bones broken, and barely breathing.

Big players disrespected him by moving right into his territory, and they didn't care about the children or the community. They cared only about money. Donté had sketched out in his mind a plan of attack. He didn't need help. He had learned on his own about explosives. He'd sit and read books on them generally while he was waiting to make sure that no one was lurking around one of his residences or hideouts. He had tried out what he learned, first in a junkyard and then at a deserted factory. He hadn't even let his brother in on his ability to handle explosives. He knew that his brother wasn't as strong as he was. "De-Mon," that was the name Donté called his brother Desmond, and he said it with a Caribbean accent. De-Mon was hot headed and didn't think beyond what was happening at the moment. Donté had told him that, in their business, a man had to be cool headed so he could think clearly and change strategies quickly if necessary. And Desmond had another weak area. He obsessed over women. More than once Donté had to pull him out of some woman's bedroom because he wasn't where he was supposed to be to handle an assignment.

Besides schooling Desmond to be successful and survive as a drug dealer, Donté kept on him about controlling his temper and putting an assignment before his personal desires. Donté understood that Desmond had a lot of anger in him. Donté told him continually, "De-Mon, you got to let it go. What happened, happened!" But throughout the years, even after he became an adult, Desmond couldn't let go of being angry with his parents. He blamed his father for allowing people to come into their home and take him and his brothers and sisters away.

"A man's supposed to stand up and fight for his family even if it means dying," Desmond would mutter with his eyes squinted and his face taut. "A man don't let people come into his house and take his children. He should have fought for us. He should have knocked down them police officers, taken their guns, and then he should have shot them with their own pistols. But he didn't do nothing. He just sat there. He even let that white lady take Tonai—his precious Tonai—out of his arms. He let that bitch just reach on down and take our baby sis out of his arms."

Desmond had been mad at his father even before they had been taken away. He had hardly ever seen him. "He's working" or "He's sleeping" was all he ever heard when he asked where his father was. And then, in the little time his dad had when home and awake, he seemed to take an interest only in Tonai. Desmond would punch Tonai whenever he could because he believed that it was her fault that his father had lost interest in him. Until Tonai was born, he had been his father's favorite. He was the one his dad was always tickling, lifting up, and bouncing around. But his dad dropped him like a hot potato when Tonai came on the scene. He would snap at Desmond, just as he did with the others. So Desmond would pinch and hit Tonai, or sometimes kick her. He got away with it when he and Donté babysat the others. Everyone became irritated by her crying outbursts. He felt good, because he was really getting back at his father, until one day Donté punched him so hard that he burst out crying. Between his sniffles, he asked, "Why you hit me?" Donté grabbed him by his shirt and began to choke him. Then he said, "Whenever I hear Tonai burst out crying, I'm gonna bust you in your face!" Then Donté released him so roughly that he fell to the floor. Desmond never hit Tonai again. He'd just stare at her and try to scare her by making ugly faces. At first, Tonai would stare back, but then she began to laugh at him. Soon, the other kids would look to see what she was laughing at. They'd see Desmond's face and laugh at him too.

Desmond had begun to disrespect his parents by acting sulky and irritable around them and simply ignoring their instructions when they'd leave until Donté would get on him. Also, he was mischievous. He stayed up late after everyone else in the house had gone to bed. He and his brothers used to sleep together on the foldout couch in the living room. One night, Desmond shook Donté's shoulder and whispered fiercely, "Listen!"

"What you waking me up for?" Donté sheepishly replied.

"Shhh. They talking," Desmond said, giggling.

"What?" Donté asked, thinking that either his sisters were in the kitchen sneaking something to eat or were still up playing instead of sleeping.

"Listen!"

Donté heard low talking sounds coming from their parents' room. Desmond got off the bed and said, "Come on! I know how to listen."

Donté was quick to tell him, "We not supposed to do that."

"I'll give you my baseball card."

Donté was a baseball card collector. He had been trying to get Desmond to give him the card he had. Because the card was worth something, he had asked Desmond how he got the card.

"I found it," was all Desmond would tell him.

Listening to their parents talking seemed an easy thing to do in exchange for the card. "Okay, but be quiet so we don't wake up Dayton." Donté followed Desmond as they tiptoed to the closed door of their parents' room. Desmond placed his hand on the doorknob.

"You know we not supposed to open this door without knocking and they tell us to come in," Donté hastily whispered.

"Wait … wait … wait … look. I can open it without them knowing, 'cause I put this cardboard between the door by the doorknob, and the door opens a little but enough for us to listen. and it don't make no sound." Desmond slowly and carefully pushed the door just far enough for them to listen. They heard their parents talk about money in a jar on the top of their closet. Their mother wanted to keep on talking about money, but they heard their father yawning, and then they heard him snoring. Their mother began yelling at him and pushed him, but he kept on snoring.

Donté and Desmond clamped their hands firmly over their mouths because they couldn't stop laughing. Quickly Desmond slipped the cardboard out of the door. They ran to the couch, jumped on it, and buried their heads into the blanket to stop themselves from laughing out loud. After that, some nights they would listen to their parents talking. It was always funny to them. The nights they stayed up, they would be tired in the morning and wouldn't want to get up to go to school. Once at school, they'd fall asleep.

Desmond wanted to find the jar and take some money out of it, but Donté told him sternly, "No! They got to pay bills with that money. You find some other way to get money." And that's exactly what Desmond did.

He followed girls and tried to snatch their pocketbooks or their backpacks. They'd kick him or push him away. Desmond was sent to the principal's office with a note his teacher gave him that explained the reason he had been sent there. The school counselor had the school secretary call the girls' names over the PA system, and the girls who had stated he'd taken money from them reported to the principal's office.

Donté always went to Desmond's class at the end of the day to meet him, and then they'd both go to their youngest brother Dayton's class. The boys would then meet their sisters at a designated spot, and they'd all walk home together. That day, as Donté walked past the office on his way to pick up Desmond, he saw him in the office. He walked in and stood by him. The girls in the office were yelling excitedly and pointing at Desmond as they complained that he had taken money from them. One girl said that he had pushed her down and emptied out her backpack onto the ground and taken the dollar her mother had given her for snacks. The girls began pointing toward both boys, so the school counselor asked if it was both of the boys who had taken money from them. The girls kept yelling, "Yeah!"

Before the school day had ended, the girls' parents were calling the school with all kinds of threats that they would make good if the boys were not expelled from school. Child welfare authorities were contacted because the teachers also told the school counselor that the boys were sleepy when they arrived at school and were sleeping in class. That week a meeting was held at the school. Sissy, Donté, and Desmond were present as well as the school principal, the counselor, and a child welfare social worker. As his mother had told him to do when he had explained to her how he'd been wrongly accused, Donté spoke up at the meeting stating that he had never been around the girls. He told them that he'd go to each of his brothers' classrooms every day to get them, and then they'd go to the main entrance where their sisters would be waiting for them so that they could all walk home together. But the group began talking as if they hadn't heard him. When the social worker asked where they had learned about stealing, Desmond told them that they had listened to their parents talking about money. As they walked home behind their mother, Donté punched Desmond the entire trip, as their mother cried disconsolately.

When they were older, Donté told Desmond, "It's because of you that them social workers started messing with our family. You need to admit it. Because you took money from them girls at school, social workers began coming to our home snooping around. Then they sent Mommy a letter saying that our home was under investigation."

Donté continued to confront his brother because he had become annoyed with Desmond blaming their parents and not owning up to his own faults. "Mom was sitting on the couch holding the letter in her hand and crying. I looked at the letter. Mom told me what it said. It said that Mom and Dad was leaving us at home alone. We was not being supervised. It also said that our house was too small and a mess, and they didn't like our sisters sleeping on a mattress on the floor."

Desmond simply shrugged his shoulders, "So why they mad about all that? We was okay."

Initially after being taken out of his home, Desmond became happy when child welfare social workers told him that he would live with a nice family. He thought that he was going to live with rich people, and he imagined having all the things he ever wanted. He liked it even better when he found out that they were placing him and Donté together in a family without his other brother or sisters.

They were taken to a foster family who lived in a large house. Donté and Desmond had their own room together. For the first time each had a bed to himself. But after about two weeks, they talked to one another about how they missed their own family. Mr. and Mrs. Benton, their foster parents, had two sons who were a few years older than they were. The family was nice, but Donté didn't feel as if they belonged there. The Benton's were focused on their own sons. As they ate dinner together, Mr. and Mrs. Benton would encourage their sons to talk about what had occurred during their day at school. Whatever their sons mentioned became a topic of discussion. They would look at Donté and Desmond now and then and ask them a few questions, but the focus wasn't the same.

Unlike their mother, Mrs. Benton was strict. She had a routine, and everything had to fit in place with her routine. She didn't work, so she was at home all day. She would iron their clothes every day, put them on hangers, and hook the hangers on the doorknob on the closet door in their room. They would put on those clothes the next morning. She fixed a full breakfast in the morning. She made lunches for them to take to school. When Donté came in from school, Mrs. Benton had a snack for him sitting on the table. He was expected to sit at the kitchen table and do his homework after he ate his snack.

Desmond didn't return home until dinnertime. The stealing investigation found that only Desmond had stolen from girls in his class. Consequently, Desmond was transferred to an alternative school for

G.B. Jones

children with behavior problems. At that school he received therapy to help him understand boundaries so that he would not take what belonged to other people.

On school days they could watch one or two shows on TV, and only if they had completed their school assignments. It was hard on Desmond, but it was harder on Donté, who even though only eleven years old, was used to being in charge. He had handled everything going on in their home when his parents were at work or sleeping, which was nearly all the time. Donté told Mrs. Benton that he wanted to pick out his own clothes and that he didn't want to sit at the kitchen table and do homework like a first grader. He said that he wanted to do his homework in his room on his bed. Mrs. Benton agreed after reflecting on her foster parent training, remembering that she had been told that children in foster care come from deprived, chaotic, and unsupervised homes and that adjustment to rules often took a while.

Donté had only three days of doing his homework in his bedroom. On the afternoon of the first day, Mrs. Benton opened the door to Donté's room and saw him lying on his back on the bed waving a paper airplane over his head. The next day when she opened his door, she found him asleep in his bed. The following day she walked in on him reading a magazine. Mrs. Benton then told Donté that he had to do his homework at the kitchen table because he was not disciplined enough to do his homework in his room.

Donté would sit at the table and stare at his book. Mrs. Benton would tell him, "You been staring at that page for an hour now. You should know everything on it!"

Donté would act as if he was writing answers down. He'd tell Mrs. Benton that his stomach hurt after he'd been sitting at the table for some time.

"Your stomach don't hurt you," she'd tell him.

"How you gonna tell me my stomach don't hurt?" Donté would respond, pouting.

Mrs. Benton would point her finger at him. "Watch how you talking to me! Go to your room. If I get bad reports that you not doing well in school, you'll be on punishment."

Although Donté didn't focus on his homework at his foster home, he generally managed to get it done before class. His teachers found that he was good with younger children, so they made him a hall monitor and gave him other assignments.

Desmond's school was a considerable distance from his foster home, so he had to get up early every morning. It would still be dark when he left the house. He would return home shortly before dinner. After dinner, Mrs. Benton would have him sit at the table while she reviewed his schoolwork. He'd watch one TV program before Mrs. Benton would send both boys to their room for bed. Desmond, however, would stay up late playing with games that he'd contend someone at school gave him. He began to refuse to get up in the morning and would get angry with Mrs. Benton for trying to get him up. "I ain't getting up. It's too dark. That school's too far." He'd then add shouting, "Leave me alone!"

The social workers came to their home and tried to talk to Desmond. He was told that his unacceptable behavior was jeopardizing his foster home placement. He sat defiantly, slumping his body down in the armchair. He shrugged his shoulders. Mrs. Benton told him, "Sit up in the chair!" He straighten himself for a moment and then slowly eased himself back into a slouch. Mrs. Benton again said sharply, "Sit up!"

The social worker asked to speak to him in private. Mrs. Benton gave a look that indicated that she was disgusted with the social worker as well. She said, "You can go talk to him in his room."

The social worker assigned to them when they were first placed in the Benton home had left the agency. She had been a young black woman. She'd talk to them straight, saying, "I don't know how long you'll be in foster care. I'm not in the unit that decided that you had to be removed from your parents. That unit will decide when you guys can go back home. They work with your parents to get things in place for your return home. Just act right. Respect and listen to your foster parents. Do your schoolwork. Don't get into any fights. Then, when it's time for you to return home, there'll be no problems."

***

The candle began flickering, and Donté watched it quicken its pace as if gasping for air. It soon went out leaving Donté sitting in the dark in the cellar of the church, something he was comfortable with. Now at least his stomach was full. The lingering scent of his mother's cooking flashed memories of his past before him. His thoughts resumed, and he was there with his brother in their first foster home.

A young white man took over their case. The first time he came, he sat on Desmond's bed and asked them, "You boys being treated okay?"

Confused, Donté and Desmond stared at the man. He was acting as if he was trying to be friends with them. "I mean, you can tell me anything."

Donté shrugged his shoulders and said, "We being treated okay."

"So you like it here?"

Donté and Desmond exchanged glances. Desmond was quick to say, "She makes me get up too early. I be tired in the morning."

"Are they keeping you up at night?"

"It's just that the school's too far. When I get home, I don't have time to watch TV."

"I see," the social worker said. "Do you get your allowance every week?"

"Well, how much we supposed to get? Is ten dollars the right amount or are we supposed to get twenty dollars?" Desmond asked.

"Right now, ten dollars is the amount your foster mother is supposed to give each of you."

"Well, I need more than ten dollars. Ten dollars is not enough to cover my expenses, since I'm at school all day long and then ride the bus for almost two hours coming home. I get hungry!"

The social worker looked trapped. He said, "I have to go by what the state allows, and that's what's allocated for your age group because all your needs are taken care of through the money we give the foster parents for your care. Does Mrs. Benton make you enough for lunch?"

Desmond didn't respond. Donté spoke up. "Yeah, she does."

"You did recently get new clothing, didn't you?"

Donté couldn't take it anymore. "Look, they not mean to us or nothing. They try to do the best they can. We just want to be with our own mom and dad and our sisters and brother. When we going back home?"

Even at eleven, Donté knew that the social worker had not given him an answer. He was relieved when the man left. That man would come over every week and bug them. It seemed as if he was searching for something that the Benton's were doing wrong. He'd tell them that it was not their fault they had been taken from their home, and he would put down their parents, albeit in a nice way. He acted as if he wanted them to agree.

"Some people have a difficult time being parents. The challenges and responsibilities that go along with taking care of children are too much for them. The State steps in when children are neglected or abused. In your case, your parents had a hard time because there were so many of you. They tried their best."

Both of their hearts would ache when they'd hear words spoken against their parents. When the social worker would leave, they'd feel as if they were trapped in a box with no way to escape.

A change did come one day when Desmond outright refused to get up in the morning to go to school. The Bentons tried to talk to him. The social worker came over and tried to talk to him. Even Donté told him he had to get up and go to school. For four days in a row, he refused to get up and go to school. He would still be in bed when Donté left for school.

Then the unthinkable happened. Mrs. Benton turned off the TV that he had been watching in the living room. She told Desmond that he would have no privileges if he didn't attend school. She informed him that he would not be allowed to lie around and do whatever he wanted. Desmond jumped up and acted as if he was about to hit Mrs. Benton. He became verbally abusive, called her "bitch," and told her that she was paid to take care of him and that he'd watch whatever he wanted to watch on TV whenever he wanted to watch it.

Mrs. Benton called the police, the social worker, and her husband. They all came. The social worker pleaded with Mrs. Benton not to press charges for offensive language and threatening behavior. She agreed not to press charges if Desmond was immediately removed from her home.

When Donté got home from school, Mrs. Benton met him at the door. "I need to talk to you as soon as you put your things down." When Donté got to his room, Desmond wasn't there. The room looked neat. Donté looked into the closet. Desmond's clothes were gone. He pulled open Desmond's dresser drawers. They were empty. He rushed into the living room where he'd left Mrs. Benton sitting on the couch.

"Where's my brother?" Mrs. Benton patted the couch for him to sit down. He didn't want to sit down. Now they had taken everything away from him. They had taken his parents, all his sisters, and his youngest brother. They were not taking Desmond from him. He could feel tears welling up in his eyes. He was just getting used to things. He had gotten comfortable at his school. The teachers liked him and trusted him. He had some new school buddies. He had just decided that a foster home was not a bad place to be. He could barely hear what Mrs. Benton was saying to him.

"Honestly, I wanted you both to be here until you grew up, but your brother cursed at me and threatened me. I can't have a child in my home acting like that."

Donté wanted to say, "Parents are supposed to handle that." He thought of all the times that Desmond had snapped at his own parents.

They didn't throw him out of the house. Yet his mom and dad were being looked at as bad parents.

"I'm so sorry about this. Our family really wants you to stay. You're going to be a fine man one day, and we'd like to have a hand in your development."

"May I use the phone?"

"Of course."

Donté dialed the social worker's phone number. When he heard the worker's voice, he felt anger welling up in him. "Where's my brother?"

"Your brother is in another foster home. He's fine. He's calm. He admitted he was wrong. He's okay."

"He's not okay. I know him. And I'm not okay. You're not separating me and my brother."

"Now, you know this was not what I wanted either. Mr. and Mrs. Benton feel he is too challenging for them."

"Well, I'm not gonna be separated from my brother. You need to come and get me too so we can stay together. He needs me."

"Listen! I don't agree with the separation, but right now I can't do anything. I'll call you tomorrow to see what we can do."

Donté had never felt such loneliness and emptiness. He went into his room and sat on his bed, but he couldn't sit still. He couldn't even look over at Desmond's bed. Everything in the room seemed to tear at his insides, and he felt as if his chest was going to burst open. He ran out of his room and past Mrs. Benton, who was still sitting on the couch. He flung the door open so forcefully that it slammed back against the wall. Although his vision was blurry because of his tears, he continued to run past houses on his street until he ended up at a strip mall. Although hardly able to catch his breath, he ran to the back of the stores and down big concrete block steps that led to the cellar door of one of the stores. He sat in a corner on the damp pavement at the bottom of the steps and put his balled-up fists to his eyes. His elbows pressed into his stomach. His head touched his knees. As his body rocked back and forth, he let out a scream that emerged from somewhere deep within him as torrents of tears burst from his eyes.

Light woke Donté up. For a moment, he did not know where he was. Terror swept through him as he saw concrete walls all around him. Glancing up through squinting eyes, he saw more concrete blocks above him. He thought he was in a dungeon. Someone had thrown him into a dungeon! He put his head back into his hands. He mumbled, "Daddy!

Mommy!" In the next instant, he remembered how he had got there. He struggled to get up. His back and neck were sore.

***

It was like déjà vu. Here he was sitting on a stool in a church basement, surrounded by concrete walls, staring into the glaring blackness. He pushed his thoughts back to his childhood, unwinding his past. It was his memorial to his brother. He knew when he was done that the door would be shut, and he would never go back through it again.

He saw himself slowly climbing the huge concrete steps that led out of the cellar entry to the street. When he got to the top step the sunlight was so bright that he had to cover his eyes. He walked along the backs of the stores and out to the sidewalk. People were waiting at bus stops. He had no particular direction to go, so he just walked. Seemingly out of nowhere, a police car pulled up alongside him. He turned and stared blankly at the police officers. One of them asked him his name. He thought about running but felt too drained.

"Donté," he answered.

An officer got out of the car and came toward him. "Come with me, son." The policeman gently held his arm and helped him get into the back of the patrol car.

Donté was placed in the foster home that his brother Desmond had been moved to. The home was outside the city and required that he change schools. The majority of the children at his new school were white. Donté felt uncomfortable because he had never attended a school with white children. In addition, he didn't understand the work that the children in his class were doing. His brother didn't have to deal with adjusting to a new school, because he remained in the school he had been attending. Their new home was much closer to Desmond's school, so he didn't have to get up so early in the morning.

His new foster parents, Mr. and Mrs. Clement, differed from the Bentons. They were not at all strict. In fact, they were relaxed, spoke softly, laughed a lot, and allowed them to make most of their own decisions. Donté and Desmond thought that the Clements were rich, as their house was huge. There was a swimming pool out back, and lots of land around the house. They were each given a large, nicely furnished bedroom, but they told Mr. & Mrs. Clement that they would rather share a bedroom.

Donté was surprised when the Clements told them that they had grown children, because they looked so young. When they were all sitting around the living room and talking about their backgrounds, Mrs. Clement told them that she was half black and half Italian. She laughed as she warned them not to be shocked if they walked into the house one day and found the house crowded with Italian-speaking people trying to speak English. Her mother still lived in Italy.

Mr. Clement was tall and handsome. He had an executive job in a bank, and he was always talking about what he'd do when he retired from the bank. Mr. Clement loved sports. He would jump up out of his chair, and it seemed to Donté, Desmond, and Mrs. Clement that he was going to jump into the TV and run with the man to the goal line while they watched a football game. He'd have them all laughing. There was a basketball court on the property, and Mr. Clement would take both Donté and Desmond on, and he'd win.

When Mrs. Clement found out that Donté did not understand his schoolwork, she hired a tutor to help him. Having a tutor made a big difference. Donté's academic performance improved, but socially he felt alone and uncomfortable.

The home placement seemed good. Desmond got up for school in the mornings. Actually, he had no choice because Donté had told him he'd smash his head in if he didn't.

***

Donté heard a slight noise that immediately brought him back to the present and alerted all his senses. With a battle stillness, he listened. His ears scanned every area of the church cellar. A light scuffling sound emerged. He knew it was the sound of a mouse, which was good because it meant that he was so still that a mouse felt it could move about. One more day was all he planned to be there. His thoughts went back to tracking his and his brother's life together.

***

Donté and Desmond returned home from school one day after six months with the Clements to find their belongings packed in black garbage bags that were on the floor in the middle of the living room. Donté felt as if his breath had suddenly been sucked out of him, and it was a few moments before he was able to regain his breathing. He looked at Desmond and could see he was just as shocked. He than looked at Mr. Clement, who said with little emotion, "I wish you boys the best." The hurt he felt gave way to a fierce anger that he couldn't stop from rising up in him. His mind yelled, "Why are you doing this to us!"

The social worker arrived and indicated that they should carry their bags. They took their bags and followed the social worker to the van. All the social worker said to them was, "I have another foster parent who's willing to take you boys." Donté turned his head as he carried his bag so his brother wouldn't see the wetness in his eyes.

The foster home they were taken to was located in a rough neighborhood in the inner city. The social worker parked in front of a house that was in the middle of a long block of small, attached houses, each of which had a wood plank porch in front with four steps leading up from the sidewalk. Two huge teenage boys stood on the porch of the house where the van stopped. The boys came to the van, grabbed the bags the social worker handed to them, and turned and walked back toward the house. The social worker slammed the van door and walked behind the boys. Desmond and Donté followed.

"No school today?" the social worker questioned the boys.

"We had half a day," one of the boys answered as he opened the door to the house. He yelled, "Ma Davis! They here!"

A woman's figure emerged rushing toward them from the opposite end of the hallway, her skirt swishing from side to side as she walked. She was a heavy-set, coal-black woman with a pudgy face and pudgy arms that swung awkwardly as she moved toward them. "Come on in. Come on in!" Her voice sounded as if she was singing, and she waved her arm toward them as they stood in the doorway. They stepped into a narrow hallway.

The woman looked past the social worker and spoke to Donté and Desmond. "So you the boys who been causing all kind of challenges for foster parents."

Donté stared at her. He couldn't imagine what she meant. Why were he and his brother being labeled as "bad." Quietly he swallowed back a sadness that was welling up within him.

"Well, we'll see what we gonna do about that. I'm Ma Davis."

She looked squarely into Donté's eyes, "You are Donté?" Donté nodded. "Yeah you have the older child look." She turned her attention to Desmond. "So, of course, that means you are Desmond." She nodded her head as she said, "Pleased to meet you boys." As she was turning around, she gestured with her arm and said, "Come on into the living room."

An opening along the left side of the hallway led into the living room. Opposite the opening was the staircase leading to the second floor. The hallway ended at the entrance into the kitchen.

Desmond and Donté took hold of the large black garbage bags that sat alongside the stairway where the other boys had left them. They began dragging them when Ma Davis turned and said, "Leave those there. Nobody's gonna bother them."

The living room was crowded with furniture. There were two sets of couches and matching chairs, lamps, and pictures. Ma Davis sank into a big armchair. Donté and Desmond sat next to each other on a couch. The social worker sat in an armchair opposite them.

"You boys angry about being in foster care?" Ma Davis nearly shouted. Donté and Desmond exchanged glances.

"Oh, I know you angry. Everybody who comes here is angry. But I just want you to understand that I didn't have nothing to do with whatever you been through. But, I take care of kids here, and you are kids, so you gonna have to follow the house rules. You gonna have to do chores. You have to make up your beds in the morning, do some kind of cleaning on the weekend, and wash or dry dishes twice a week. Can you boys handle that? If you can't, tell me right now because you might as well leave back out of here if you gonna have problems following the house rules. I don't pick up after no child once they hit five years old, and you boys are what? Eleven and twelve? Can you follow these rules?" Donté and Desmond found themselves nodding and saying, "Yes, ma'am."

"Also, you must attend school every day there is school. And you have to get out the house on time in the morning. You have to be back in this house by six p.m. That's the time for your age. That way you can participate in after-school activities. You can hang out with your friends a little while … go to the store … whatever. That'll give you enough time left when you get home to eat, do your homework and your chores and watch a little TV before you go to bed." Donté and Desmond looked at one another. No one had given them that much time to stay out every day.

"Can you do that?"

They nodded in unison and said, "Yes, ma'am."

"Let me tell you. They bring me the kids who can't make it anywhere else. It's really up to you. I laid out how things are run here. Oh, one more thing, most important: no fighting, no cursing, no stealing. If you like fighting and cursing and stealing, you might as well go back out with your social worker 'cause you can't stay here. Oh, and no visitors in your room.

If you want to have visitors, you come to me. We'll work it out." The room was quiet for a while. "I know there's gonna be misunderstandings, but you come to me. I'm here all day long. I don't work. You kids are my work. So if you feel someone done you wrong, you come tell me about it. Don't let anyone tell you you'd be squealing. You just tell them that you doing what Ma Davis told you to do, 'cause this is her house. We have a group meeting when something's wrong, and we hash it out the best we can. I'm not saying everything is perfect here, 'cause it's not, but I try hard, and if you want to stay here you got to try hard. When summer comes, you boys working or going to camp. I don't allow boys to sit around in the house all day long. You got to be productive. Do you boys think you can hang?" Donté and Desmond nodded solemnly.

There were four other boys living in the home. Two of them were due to leave that week, so Donté and Desmond shared a bedroom with those boys for about a week, sleeping on a second set of bunk beds in the room. When the two boys left, Donté and Desmond joined Ma Davis and the other boys in moving the extra beds into the basement.

Ma Davis had a daughter who was five years old. She slept in the room with Ma Davis. She wasn't in the house too often because day care and visiting her father and other relatives took up most of her time. But, when she was home, Ma Davis kept her very close to her. Ma Davis was like a hawk. It seemed as if she could see right through people and know what they were thinking. They'd seen her jump in front of one of the older boys. "You don't mumble under your breath in here," she had said. The boy was sixteen and had a roughness about him that got him respect at school and on the streets. But Ma Davis stood facing him, looking him dead in his eyes, and it looked as if they were going to fight. In fact, she had said to them on more than one occasion, "They say we can't hit you, but don't think I won't knock you out and sit on you until they come. After you tell your story, I'll know what to say."

In the "hood," body language told everything about a person. The way Ma Davis carried herself suggested that she had no problem tangling with a person if it came down to that. She was sure-footed, confident, showed no fear, and she had a scar clear across the top of her forehead, which was generally covered by her hair, and another short scar under her chin. Big as she was, she was surprisingly light footed. There'd been times when she seemed to jump from one room to another catching up with one of them, and she was quick with her hands. When she confronted people, she looked them right in the eyes as she spoke. It was easy to imagine that, in her younger days, she had been in many a rumble, and that she had even gone toe-to-toe with men and won.

Even that sixteen-year-old boy that she confronted backed down. Ma Davis's voice boomed at him, "I said, did you have something to say?" He bowed his head a bit and waved his hand as if to say, forget it. He shook his head as he said, "Naw."

Ma Davis was a wise lady. She reached down into her bosom and pulled out a ten-dollar bill. "Here, go buy yourself a steak sandwich and fries. That's the way you blow off steam round here." The boy took the money and quickly left the house.

***

Donté couldn't stop the memories pouring out as he sat in the still darkness of the church cellar. Normally he wouldn't replay his past because he believed it could weaken him. But today he allowed it. He pulled out of his pocket the small case he always carried with him and opened it. He looked at the faded picture of him and his brother.

He had so much love for Desmond. He never thought about it because it wasn't something a person thinks about. It was just there. He and his brother had been together since Desmond was born. He was barely a year and a half old when he had begun to hold his little three-day-old brother with his dad's help.

There were times at night in a foster home when he would lie in his bed, reach his hand under his pillow, and pull out the photograph of him and his brother. His mother had taken the picture a few days before they were taken out of their home. She had put it in a little brown case and had given it to him. Even with all their moving and continually losing belongings in the process, he had managed to hold onto that picture. When he slept at night, he put it under his pillow. In the morning, he made sure that, as soon as he had put his pants on, he would reach under his pillow, pull out his picture, and put it in his pocket. Desmond didn't even know about the photo.

Ma Davis had a house rule that lights had to be turned off by a certain time. It wasn't long after they had turned off the light in their bedroom when Donté jumped over to Desmond's bed and punched him with all the anger that had been mounting up in him. Desmond yelled and began whimpering, "I'm gonna tell Ma Davis."

No one had said why they had been moved out of the home of Mr. and Mrs. Clement. But Desmond, with his big mouth, had given himself away. In the dark, they were talking, as they often did before going to sleep, when Desmond whispered, "Remember Mrs. Clement? I never saw anyone as beautiful as her." Donté immediately wanted to change the topic. "I just opened the door to listen to them talking like we used to do with mom and dad." Before he could finish, Donté had jumped on him and punched him.

Donté had gotten back into his own bed and tried to tune out his brother's voice. Desmond screeched, "You punched me hard. I didn't hear nothing. Mr. Clement, he came up behind me. I thought they was both in their room. Mr. Clement talked real harsh, like I never heard him talk before. He told me to go to my room."

"You not supposed to do that. That's their privacy. Don't you know the difference between right and wrong yet?"

"But it was fun!" Desmond said.

Donté could feel rage overtaking him, and he didn't like the feeling. He felt as if he would lose control of himself. He was so angry that he felt as if he could kill someone. The only thing that dissipated his rage was when he calmly and quietly told his brother, "If you don't shut up and go to sleep, I'm gonna kill you!" There was not another sound out of his brother. Donté soon regretted that he'd said that. But for the first time ever, the thought flashed through his mind that there was something about his brother—more specifically, something about the way that he thought—that wasn't normal.

Chapter 22 Desmond's Gang

Donté lit a cigarette. He was good at doing things in the dark. There were only a few people who could stay for days in a church basement. A good soldier does what he must do. Lacking discipline could cost a person his life. Hard as he tried, he had never been able to get Desmond to be still. He had told him over and over that when a person is still, just sits and thinks, even for hours, he will see things clearly. He was sure Desmond got caught because he would not follow the survival precautions he had tried over and over to teach him. Life for Desmond was running and rushing about in the excitement of the moment. In the dark, right after they'd turn off their room light, while lying in their beds, Desmond would talk on and on about what was going on with him out on the streets. He wouldn't leave anything out. That's how he'd always done … tell his big brother everything. Even as he'd listen to Desmond's activity, Donté would say, "That's too dangerous. That won't work. You can't depend on that!" Desmond wouldn't listen to him, because he liked the hype of street activity. Donté drifted off in thoughts about Desmond's gang involvements during their days of living with Ma Davis.

***

Desmond rushed into his bedroom and yanked open his dresser drawers. He rifled through them until he found his bandana, which he shoved into his pocket. He slipped out of the room, closed the door, and waited for the right moment to tiptoe down the stairs to the first floor. He knew how Ma Davis was, as he and Donté had been living with Ma Davis for over four years. Within that time, they had returned to their family for a while, but because they were together when Desmond was found stealing from a store, they were placed back with Ma Davis.

Ma Davis had been in the kitchen when he entered the house. Now, from the stairway, he heard her chopping. As quietly as he could, he took two steps down at a time. When he reached the bottom of the stairway, he looked down the hallway and saw parts of Ma Davis' long, red shirt moving in synch with her chopping. He could not see her face. Pumped up as he was from what was going on in the streets, he tried hard to calm himself. He took a deep breath as he prepared to take two big steps to get to the front door. He wanted to fly and could hardly contain himself. As he passed the kitchen door entrance, even though it was at the end of the hallway, Ma Davis's voice rang out like thunder. "Is that you, Desmond?"

"Yeah, it's me."

"You coming or you going?"

"I'm going."

Desmond had learned that he had to be really quick to make a move before Ma Davis did. So before she could engage him in more conversation, or, worse yet, try to stop him, in one quick move he leaped toward the front door, opened it, and was out of the house. He slammed the door behind him. He jumped down the front steps and ran across the street. As he joined two boys who waited for him, he pulled his bandanna from his pocket and tied it around his head. The group turned the corner and walked alongside an abandoned building. They went around to the back of the building. Desmond tapped on the door with their special code knock. The door opened, and cheers erupted. They entered a room furnished with old couches and chairs that had once been set out by neighbors for trash pickup. The boys had dragged them in from the street. Five boys between the ages of thirteen and seventeen were already in the room. A nervous energy filled the air. Several of the boys who were seated had their hands up waving in the air trying to get the gang leader's attention. A couple of the boys were standing, circled around the leader talking in loud, agitated voices. Finally, the leader said in his rough, commanding voice, "Everyone shut up and sit down!"

Someone shouted, "They zapped our man, just like that. So what we gonna do?"

The leader repeated, "I said, sit down!" Boys took seats, all the while shaking their heads and frowning. The leader continued, "Now, we got to calm down so we can make a plan. We got to put our heads together. We can't panic. You know they gonna be expecting us to do something to get revenge. So they on the alert. We don't want anything to backfire on us. We just can't go out there shooting, 'cause they got guns. They'll shoot back at us, and some of us could get hurt. We got to plan carefully and cover each other's backs. Now … the floor's open. One person speaks at a time. Myself, I think we need to have two people be spies, each to follow one of their men wherever he goes. If he goes to his home, our man follows him. When he comes out of his house, our man follows him. What we want is to find out where their gang meeting hideout is. We gonna catch them by surprise and close in on them."

Someone shouted out, "Bang! Bang!"

"Yeah! Yeah! Yeah! I like that," someone else yelled out.

Grinning and shaking, the boy they called Fidgety jumped up nervously, "I'll follow one man."

Little Man, who was more circumspect, put the plan in check. "They got guns," he said, and then added, "It seems too dangerous. How many us going get zapped?"

"Look," the leader said. "It's time we up our game. We all gonna have an assignment. We looking to hit them when they all at the same place, when they having a meeting, like we having now. One of us gonna spy on them and count as they show up for their meetings. We gonna know where they meet and how many there are of them. Someone's gonna be assigned to check out their meeting place so that we know all entrances. We going in with an automatic. Look, we can do this." He cleared his throat before continuing. "Eggie, I want you to go to a few gun shops and ask questions. And don't act ignorant. You go looking respectable. Go there in a suit. Find out about automatic weapons and the easiest ones to operate and how much they cost. You know, you fast about learning stuff. Ask them questions. There's a man on the street who sells all kind of weapons. Well, I'll be talking to him while you finding out about automatic weapons, so we make sure we making the right choice. We got to up our money because machinery like that cost. We gonna have to make a hit to get some money. Anyone got any suggestions? Something quick but will give us some heavy cash?"

"Tina's Place. They be rolling in dough, and it's just a bunch of women," someone said.

The leader was quick to respond. "You can't go by that because nowadays shop owners have guns on them. I don't want to lose nobody."

Turbo, who was a big, heavy-set, dark-browned-skinned boy with a deep, slow-paced speaking voice, said, "He right, man. That place keep a high cash flow. From the time it opens till the time it close, women be coming in there paying fifty, sixty, a hundred dollars and on up to get their hair fried. The owner, she locks up by herself. I cased that place a few times ... couldn't get myself to do it because ... well, you know, it's like hitting our mom, 'cause she's older."

"Don't get soft, Turbo. We ain't trying to hurt her. Hitting Tina's is our plan. Turbo, find out the time she leaves. I'll take it from there. Anybody got any problems with this plan?"

The room was quiet. "Anybody got any problems with our spy plan to snuff them out?"

Turbo broke the silence. "How we gonna be sure to get everyone counted at their gang hideout? What if someone comes up behind us and we never see them coming?"

"That's why we gonna have lookout men posted outside their place. We can do this."

"It's gonna take time to find out all about their meetings and who shows up," Little Man said, breaking through the silence that had rested in the room.

"We got time."

"Ain't they gonna get suspicious if we ain't doing nothing back to them since they downed our man?" Fidgety said in a nervous high-pitched voice tone.

"This is how we gonna play it. We playing low key. We acting like we in shock and we mourning the loss of our man. We gonna play it down. Everybody got that?" Heads were nodding. "In fact, I want half of you to take your bandannas off. You ... you ... you ... you ... No bandannas until I tell you. What that will do is make it look like we disorganized. We want to look like we stressed out and confused. I want Raj and Turbo to be spies. Like I said, you pick one of them and you stick with him like butter on bread till they lead you to their meeting place. You two know how to handle business. Once we know their meeting place, I'm gonna assign shifts to watch it and get a count of their boys. Because we need to get this done right, every day we meeting. Every day we hearing a progress report. Everyone got to keep eyes and ears open, and everybody got to watch each other's backs. I don't want anyone out there alone, and I don't want no mess ups!"

***

197

Donté nearly laughed out loud in the quiet of the dark church basement where he sat as he thought of how unsophisticated and disorganized Desmond's gang was. He shook his head as he thought of Desmond's refusal to listen to his advice.

***

Nothing went down as planned. Turbo was shot to death by the shop owner he attempted to rob. When he sneaked up on her as she opened her car door and tried to yank her pocketbook from her, she shot him several times with the gun she had in her coat pocket. The gang became discouraged and went back to what they knew. They jumped into a car, drove around until they spotted three members of their rival gang standing along a fence, and shot at them. That same week Desmond's gang lost another one of their boys, shot down while walking along the street.

That night, following the shooting of his friend, Desmond ran up the steps to his house and hastily unlocked the door. When he opened the door, Ma Davis was standing in the doorway. "We need to talk," she said sternly looking him in the eye. Desmond really didn't have time for Ma Davis. Things were too hot out on the streets.

"Yeah," he said, noncommittally as he slid past her and ran up the stairs. He yanked open the door to his room. He was rummaging frantically through his drawers when Donté entered the room and shut the door.

"You looking for these?" Donté said, holding bullets in his open palm.

"Yeah, man." Desmond jumped to snatch them from his hand but Donté closed his hand around them.

"Man, I need them," Desmond protested. "You don't understand. It's me or them."

"No, you don't understand. I'm not letting you go out there and get killed. You not going nowhere."

"Donté, man, I got to. My boys depending on me. I got to go. Give me them bullets."

"You gonna have to take them from me."

Desmond started toward Donté, but then stopped. He began to wring his hands and felt as if he were about to cry.

"Sit down!" Donté said as he pushed him down onto the bed. "We been together all our lives, and I'm not sitting around waiting for you to get killed. We're leaving here—now!"

Desmond's eyes widened as he said, "What you mean?"

"This is a dead-end street for you. We leaving now, so pack your things."

"I can't do that, man."

"You gonna do it, or I'll pack them for you."

Donté grabbed a huge suitcase that was near the door. He unzipped it and flung it open. He pulled out the dresser drawers and hastily threw their belongings into the suitcase. He then turned toward the closet and snatched clothing from the closet. He zipped up the suitcase.

Desmond's hands were nervously shaking in front of his body. "My boys gonna think I punked out."

"When they come around, Ma Davis gonna say the social worker moved you."

"But ain't she supposed to get the social worker to move us?"

"Ma Davis sticking her neck out for us. You know she don't keep no outright rebellious kids, and you outright rebellious. You been really messing up. You ain't been going to school. You stay in bed till you ready to get up. You leave this house, and you don't come back till you ready. You running these streets with your gang and ..." Donté stopped and looked deep into his brother's eyes. "I just hope you ain't killed anyone."

Desmond shook his head and said, "Naw, I ain't killed no one."

"Yet!" Donté interjected. "Look, man. Ma Davis had her phone in her hand to call the social worker. Then she looked at me and put the phone down. She said to me, 'You the only one your brother listens to. This is a dead-end street for both of you. You know they gonna separate you. He has no hope without you with him. You about to graduate from high school in two weeks. Two weeks ain't gonna change things from you getting your diploma. I'll tell the school officials something—like you sick or went down South for a family emergency. This is an emergency. I'll hold onto your diploma. You can come and get it when things cool down, or I can mail it to you. You take him out of the city.' Ma Davis went and got this suitcase and gave it to me. She sticking her neck out for us. Come on, we leaving here."

They could see Ma Davis sitting in the living room as they came down the stairs. She had an envelope in her hand that she put on the end table as they entered the room.

"I'm setting this here." She looked at Donté as she spoke. "You can take it or leave it. If it's gone when I come back into this room, as far as I'm concerned, I never set it there. It'd carry you a ways. Go on down to the bus terminal. Tomorrow, I'll report you both as having run away. God be with you."

Chapter 23 Tonai's Breakdown

Tonai pushed the door open and entered the group home. She had just dropped off the envelope that Donté had given her at the district attorney's office and had gotten a receipt from his secretary. She looked around the living room. No one was there, and the room looked cold, like an institution, not a home. The couch took up most of the living room as it was long and wide, made to accommodate a group. It was covered with a hard, dark plaid material that didn't easily show spills. The light was always too dim in the living room. Tonai suspected it was so that handprints wouldn't show on the dusty-looking, light-brown walls. The green rug was a rough-textured, indoor-and-outdoor material designed to survive hordes of children's feet.

Tonai walked into the bathroom and looked at herself in the mirror. She pulled off her hoodie and stared. She looked deep into her eyes and whispered, "Who are you?" Her hair was in short, fat braids. She scanned her face. It looked rough. There was a scar where her foster brother had punched her. Her thoughts told her, *You're too tall, too big. You're fat!* She looked down at her clothing. It was loose and bulky. She smelled an odor on her body. It wasn't the kind of odor that someone else could detect, but she could smell it. She looked back at herself in the mirror. Her heart squeezed in her chest as she whispered, "I don't know who I am. I'm not a boy. I'm not a girl." Then she thought of how Donté hadn't acted as if she were a freak. He had treated her just as he always had. She was his baby sis. He saw past all her oddness and even told her that she looked just like their mother.

But her thoughts shouted back at her, *You're afraid. You hiding behind this tough façade because you're afraid to be you!* Suddenly Tonai felt weak. She leaned against the wall. She wanted someone to hold her. She wanted to be in her daddy's arms. She wanted her family back. She thought about her dad and her mom having a new family and how she no longer fit in with them. Her sisters had their own families. She didn't fit in with them either. Her two oldest brothers had had each other until Desmond died. Even Dayton had a foster family who had adopted him and considered him as their own. The foster homes that she had been placed in had not been homes to her. The group home where she now lived was not home either. It was just a residence with other "placed" girls. There was no love there. In fact, it was a crazy house. Most of the girls were rough, quick to argue and fight. With the exception of one girl named Rosie, none of the girls in the group home was trustworthy. They'd smile at a person while plotting to steal something that person had. Some girls simply took things from weaker girls and would give those girls looks that dared them to go to a counselor

Only the girl named Rosie seemed normal. She was a short, petite, quiet girl who stayed to herself. Yet, she seemed confident about who she was, and she showed no fear. She'd look people in their eyes when they spoke to her, and she'd never flinch no matter how big they were or how bullish they acted. She'd talk in a soft, calm voice. The girls at the group home liked and respected her, although they didn't know the right way to show it. They'd ask her if they could borrow a few dollars or an item of clothing. She'd respond in a sweet voice, "I got something to do with my money." Or she'd say, "I don't want my stuff messed up." They'd suck their teeth as they'd walk away from her, "Rosie you never give up anything." Much as Tonai wanted to be friends with Rosie, Rosie wouldn't let her in.

As Tonai looked at herself in the mirror, she slowly shook her head. She saw that her eyes were puffy and reddened as tears streamed down from them. She heard herself say, "You don't belong anywhere. You have no one!" The sudden realization terrified her. She could feel her breathing become labored. She should have asked Donté to take her with him. She could tell that he still had a soft heart for her. "No! No! No!" Her mind nearly yelled as she shook her head and said, "I don't want a life on the run like that." Tonai's thoughts raced back over to her father. *Please hold me, Daddy!* She could feel herself screaming inside.

Tonai placed both hands around her head because her head began aching. It felt as if a hammer had begun to pound on it. She started screaming. Sudden banging on the bathroom door intensified her headache. The bathroom door burst open. Counselors approached her.

"Can't I have some privacy!" she yelled as she tried to push the counselors back out of the bathroom. The words, "We're here to help you," floated past her ears. Tonai fought the counselors until finally three of them wrestled her to the floor. Every time they asked, "Are you calmed down yet?" she started fighting again.

An ambulance transported Tonai to a hospital crisis unit. She was in the hospital for three days before she got up out of bed. She knew because she had counted how many times a nurse had come into the room and opened the blinds to let sunlight in. They medicated her with a drug that kept her asleep nearly all the time. On the third day, when she woke up, she felt calm, and her head felt clear. She told the doctor that she didn't want any more medicine. When the doctor left her room, she shook her head and muttered to herself, "I'm okay, I'm okay."

A nurse bustled into the room. "The doctor has prescribed this for you," she said standing over Tonai.

Tonai looked at the woman. "I'm okay. I'm not taking any more meds."

"Now, you want to take your medicine," the nurse insisted.

"I said I'm okay," Tonai repeated in a rough, raised voice. The nurse left.

As she began blinking from the bright sunlight that entered through the window and cut across her eye, Tonai regretted having spoken rudely to the nurse. She thought of what she had learned in counseling about how it is unwise to be hostile toward people you depend on. She got off the bed. She was dressed in a hospital gown. Pulling the back of her gown together to cover her backside and holding it firmly with one hand, she left her room and approached the nursing station. Tonai looked down at a nurse whose head was buried in a chart. "Is that my chart?"

The nurse looked up and said, "Well, good morning. Breakfast is on the way."

"Where am I?"

"This is the Crisis Unit at Malvern Hospital."

"Malvern Hospital! Why am I so far away from the city?"

"This is where they brought you, sweetie."

"I'm ready to leave," Tonai said in a firm voice.

The nurse stood up. She was as tall as Tonai. She looked into Tonai's eyes as she said, "I will inform the doctor when he comes on the floor. He'll be in to talk to you."

"Can I get my clothes back? I'm not comfortable walking around in this sheet."

The nurse laughed. "Your clothes are in the cabinet in your room. You can put them on."

Tonai made herself the ideal patient. She ate her meals, was conscientious about her hygiene, dressed neatly, forced herself to tone down, nodded her head in agreement to whatever anyone said. But secretly she would not swallow her pills. She kept the ones that wouldn't instantly dissolve in a corner of her mouth. Then, when the nurse she'd been smiling at left, she'd spit them into napkin and she'd throw the napkin into the trash.

"Hi, Doc. My name in Tonai. I know you're Dr. Beard." Tonai extended her hand, shook the psychiatrist's hand, and sat down. Dr. Beard smiled and stared at her. Tonai turned her head to the side and closed her eyes to help herself maintain her focus and composure so that she would not spread herself all over the place, which is what past therapist told her she did. She took a deep breath, "Just because a person gets mad doesn't mean she's crazy, does it Doc?

"No, it does not. However, it's how the person acts out her anger that might be looked at as a problem. Why don't you tell me what made you so angry and resulted in your fight with the staff at the group home?"

"Doc, I don't mean no disrespect, but did you ever go into the bathroom in your home and just want to be left alone?"

Dr. Beard chuckled. "Certainly. Go on."

Tonai pursed her lips together, and she felt as if steam was rising up in her. She breathed softly, reminding herself to release the steamed-up feeling. Softly she said, "That's all that was happening, Doc. I wanted to be alone." Tonai hiked up her shoulder. "I just needed a moment, alone. I needed alone time, me time. I was dealing with some bad news happening in my family. I needed to let it out. Yeh, I yelled out 'cause I needed to release the tension that was in me." Tonai spread her mouth from one side of her face to the other as she said the word *release*. "That's all. You ever wanted to scream Doc?"

Dr. Beard did not respond. He looked intently at her.

Tonai's eyebrows curled. "Oh you don't have to answer, Doc. 'Cause I know you have. We all have. But see, you can do what you want to do in your home, but when I do something, three counselors got to pull me down and sit on me and then bring me to a crisis unit. You know what my crisis is, Doc?" Dr. Beard did not respond. Tonai calmly said, "These authority people come messing with my family, splitting us apart. My mother was a most loving mother. She just had too much to do. Well we all messed up now. I been in and out of foster homes, raped, beaten, unloved. My best friend in the whole world was taken from me. So one day when I scream, it's all about how hurt I am, and I'm brought to Crisis."

Tonai was discharged ten days after Dr. Beard's assessment. When they told her she was discharged, she stomped her feet and raised her fist into the air. "Yes! Yes! Yes!" she hollered.

Chapter 24 Finding a Family for Nia

After Nia had been at the shelter a few weeks, a counselor informed her that she'd come to escort her to the reception area. The reception area was on the other side of the huge door with the metal bar across it. It was the area where children met with family members or other visitors. As soon as Nia entered the reception area, she saw her social worker, Ms. Dorsey.

"I have a meeting scheduled for this afternoon," Ms. Dorsey said. "Go get all your clothes and come right back."

The counselor walked her back to her room and helped her pack. After placing all of her belongings into a black garbage bag, Nia followed the counselor back to the reception area. She then followed Ms. Dorsey into a room. Ms. Dorsey sat at one end of the long conference table and motioned for her to sit in a chair adjacent to her. Soon there was a knock on the door. Ms. Dorsey got up to open the door.

A man and a woman stood in the doorway. "Hello, we're Mr. and Mrs. Walker," the woman announced.

"Hello, Mr. and Mrs. Walker," Ms. Dorsey responded as she extended her hand and shook hands with each of them. "Did you have any trouble with my directions?"

Mrs. Walker smiled as Mr. Walker said, "No, not with your directions ... with my wife's interpreting your directions!" Ms. Dorsey and the Walkers laughed.

Ms. Dorsey turned toward Nia. "This is Nia. Nia, this is Mr. and Mrs. Walker. They wanted to meet you to see if they feel they can provide a home for you." Mrs. Walker smiled at Nia as she and her husband sat in chairs opposite her at the table.

Ms. Dorsey continued, "We set up this meeting to introduce you and to enable you to ask questions to find out more about each other." She passed a folder to Mr. Walker. Together he and his wife flipped through the pages. Mrs. Walker pointed out to her husband something on one of the pages in Nia's folder. Mrs. Walker and her husband kept their eyes fixed on that page for a few minutes.

"Feel free to ask questions ... anyone?" Ms. Dorsey said, a little too brightly.

Mr. Walker looked at Nia as he spoke. "You look like such a nice young lady. How old are you?"

"Fourteen," Nia answered with her voice barely above a whisper.

"It says on your information profile that you set a house on fire."

Nia bowed her head and stared at her hands.

Ms. Dorsey interjected, "That happened only one time."

Mr. Walker continued, "I know you probably been through a lot, but what would cause you to start a fire in your home?"

Nia continued to stare at her hands, but said nothing. Several moments of silence ensued. Mrs. Walker pointed to something else in the folder, and from where she sat Nia could read the words, "severe depression, suicidal." Mrs. Walker's hand drifted down the page to the school performance section and stopped at the phrase "intellectually gifted." She pointed out that section to her husband, and they exchanged glances. She then spoke. "We think we would like to have you in our home, but I think you can understand that we want to know you wouldn't set our house on fire."

Ms. Dorsey interjected, "As you can see, Nia doesn't talk much."

Mr. Walker scratched his head as he said, "But we got to hear her say something so we can try to understand what she feels. Now, I'm a pastor, and I believe all children can be worked with, although some take more time than others. Young lady, I have to know. See, we have two children. They're eight and nine years old. I need to know if you set fires when you get angry!"

They were staring at Nia. Nia barely shook her head as she continued to look down. A tear drifted from her eye.

"Do you think you would like to live with younger children?" They stared at Nia, who continued to hold her head down. She nodded her head.

"It says here she's a good student." Mrs. Walker said enthusiastically.

Ms. Dorsey smiled and said, "Yes. She maintains good grades and always has had good conduct reports."

The room was quiet for a while before Mr. Walker turned toward the social worker. "Do we have to make up our minds right now?"

Ms. Dorsey smiled as she answered, "I'm afraid so."

"Then would you please excuse us for a few minutes? We'd like to talk it over," The Walkers stood up and left the room.

Nia continued to look at her hands. She didn't want to have any conversation with her social worker. Ms. Dorsey was a young, white, professional woman who had no idea what it was like to live as a foster child. Ms. Dorsey would always tell her how nice a particular family was. She would get her hopes up, then, the family would reject her. Ms. Dorsey seldom had much to say after a family rejected her.

Following their last meeting with a perspective foster parent, a single mother with two children, who had flatly stated, "she's dangerous," Ms. Dorsey told Nia that she would apply for a group home residence. She would live with about five other girls rather than a family. Nia had overheard other children at the shelter talk about the horrors of group homes. When Ms. Dorsey had told her to get all her belongings after the counselor had brought her to the reception area, she thought that Ms. Dorsey had come to move her to a group home. She had gotten excited at the possibility that she would go to live in the group home where Tonai stayed. Nia shrugged her shoulders as she thought that, if the Walkers rejected her, she would ask to be placed in Tonai's group home.

Finally, the Walkers returned. They sat down and looked at Nia. Mrs. Walker said, "We would love to have you come live with us, Nia."

Ms. Dorsey couldn't contain herself. A wide smile spread over her face, "Great!"

Mr. Walker stated, "We're parked right out front. Where are her bags?"

"She only has one bag," Ms. Dorsey responded.

Mr. Walker put out his hand toward Nia. She wasn't sure if she was supposed to shake it, but then she realized that he wanted the black garbage bag that contained all of her belongings. She handed it to him.

Mrs. Walker's voice seemed stressed as she spoke. "Why does this child only have one bag? It can't contain more than two or three outfits."

Ms. Dorsey explained, "We tried numerous times to contact her grandmother. We left messages for her to bring Nia's clothes to our office so we could get them to her, but she never responded."

Mrs. Walker sounded almost indignant. "Now, we all know a fourteen-year-old girl needs a wardrobe of clothes and personal items."

"I will make out a clothing voucher tomorrow," Ms. Dorsey said. "It has to be approved by my supervisor, but I don't think it'll be a problem."

"I intend to register Nia in school tomorrow, so we need to shop for her this evening. Will we get reimbursed?"

"Yes, up to one hundred and fifty dollars."

"She has nothing!" Mrs. Walker protested. "It's going to take a lot more than a hundred and fifty dollars to get her wardrobe up."

"I will speak to my supervisor and request a special clothing voucher, and I'll explain the circumstances."

"Thank you." Mrs. Walker said as she put her arm around Nia and guided her out of the room.

"Good-bye, Nia, and good luck!" Ms. Dorsey nearly shouted as Nia walked between the Walkers toward the building exit.

***

Nia adjusted quickly to her new home, mainly because she was kept so busy. The Walkers were church people, and their church had lots of activities for children. With her foster mother's prompting, she joined the usher ministry and the choir. At her high school, she was involved in an after-school homework program and a writing workshop. In addition, her social worker picked her up weekly and took her to therapy.

One day, after four months of living with the Walkers, Nia received an urgent call from her social worker. Ms. Dorsey told her that her biological mother, Eva, had called informing her that Nia's grandmother was gravely ill and in the hospital and that her family would be meeting at the hospital. Nia promptly told Ms. Dorsey that she wasn't going to visit her grandmother, and that she had no family. About an hour later, the social worker called back. Aunt Sissy was on the phone as well. As usual, Aunt Sissy was sweet and charming, but she was very insistent that Nia get to the hospital. "Grandma Vern wants to see you, Nia. I'm going to met you and take you to the hospital."

Nia reluctantly agreed. She knew Grandma Vern had been the center of her family, mainly because she was such a no-nonsense person. The relatives would laugh about past times when they were children visiting Grandma Vern. They'd say that Grandma Vern had a quick backhand that knocked them down to the floor when she thought they had talked disrespectfully to her.

Eva was the only one who had ever confronted Grandma Vern. Nia used to lie on her bed when she lived at Grandma Vern's house and listen to Eva and Grandma Vern's arguments.

"Don't you treat my daughter different from the others," Eva had yelled out. "That's my daughter, your granddaughter, not no stranger! And don't be beating on her. You got something you don't like she's doing, you tell me about it. I'll get with her."

"You ain't been able to get with her all her life 'cause you had no time for nothing but searching for the next high," Grandma Vern had screeched back.

"And why do you think I started getting high? It was to get away from you and this house."

Nia had thought there was going to be a big fight. She had never heard anyone speak to Grandma Vern that way. In one sense, Eva was like Grandma Vern because she didn't try to cover up anything. But unlike Grandma Vern, Eva was kind and sensitive to other people's feelings. As Nia grew older, she sensed that, underneath Eva's living-only-for-the-moment gaiety, resided a deep sorrow.

That day Eva and Grandma Vern had argued, Eva said, "Yeah, I signed those papers for foster care because I didn't want her growing up here. I wanted to give her a better life. But no ... you couldn't leave things alone. You had to go complaining that you wanted your granddaughter with you. The only thing you really wanted was that little bit extra money added to your welfare check that taking care of another child would get you. Oh, you can't fool me, Mother. I know you!"

Neither would back down. "You been a headache since you was a baby. Now you's a migraine!" As Grandma Vern said that, Nia imagined her waving her hand dismissively as she always did when she had a certain tone in her voice. "Go on and get back to your drug-dealing friends. You can't even help yourself or your daughter, so how you gonna come over here and tell me how to handle your daughter?"

"My daughter's unhappy, Mother. Can't you see her pain? Oh, why would I expect you to see it? I forgot. How could I forget? You can't see pain. You hard as a rock. You never hugged me, Mother. Not one single time. Children need to be hugged, Mother!"

"Well, let me see. I don't remember ever seeing you hug your child," Grandma Vern responded in an icy voice. Eva then rushed out of the house and slammed the door.

***

At the hospital, Nia's family members were gathered around Grandma Vern's bed. Nia tried to stay at the back of the crowd because she didn't want Grandma Vern to see her. But almost as soon as she and Aunt Sissy entered the room, the other relatives opened up a path for them to join the group. Grandma Vern wanted her to come closer. "Nia," she barely whispered. Someone pushed her forward. A voice rippled through the room, "She wants to speak to Nia alone." Nia felt panicky as everyone turned to leave the room. She stood before her grandmother, but looked at the floor. She couldn't look into Grandma Vern's face. It occurred to her that somehow Grandma Vern was going to hurt her. After all, the last time they were together, Nia had tried to burn down her house.

"Come close," Grandma Vern rasped. Nia wanted to turn and run out of the room. She slowly moved closer. Grandma Vern looked as if she had shriveled away to the point where there was nothing left of her under the sheet that covered her. "Child …" she began and then stopped and took a labored breath. "I just wanted all mine home. I got this cancer, and I'm dying." Grandma Vern closed her eyes. The moments of silence were nearly unbearable to Nia. Her grandmother's low-toned, labored voice emerged, "You don't think I cared for you … but I cared. I was rough, I know, but that's how I am." She stopped to rest, than pointed her chin at the bedside table, "Open that drawer." Nia looked intently into her grandmother face. "Open it," Grandma Vern whispered. "I ain't got no time left."

Nia slowly opened the drawer in the little table beside the bed. Inside she saw a worn-out Bible with tattered edges, a comb with some missing teeth, and a wrinkled white envelope. Grandma Vern coughed, and her chest heaved. Her face hardened into a grim expression as she gasped, "See that envelope? Take it. It belongs to you."

Nia took the envelope. A prolonged bout of coughing overtook Grandma Vern, and she seemed to be choking. Nia turned around to call a nurse when her grandmother said, very clearly, "I was waiting for the right time to give it to you." Grandma Vern seemed to force words out between labored breaths. Nia turned her attention back to the envelope.

"The address inside is your foster mother's." Grandma Vern had barely finished her sentence when Nia moved away from her bed. The room seemed to empty itself of everything including her grandmother. Nia rushed out of the room, past her family, and ran down the hall. She vaguely heard Aunt Sissy behind her, saying, "Nia ... Nia ... wait! Where you going? I got to take you back."

Nia ran outside. It was raining. She clasped the envelope in both hands. As she ran, tears exploded over her face. Nia ran along the street, passing people walking under umbrellas. She took shelter underneath the awning of a building where a few people stood. She wiped her eyes and her nose with her wet sleeve. She trembled as she opened the envelope. The paper inside read, "143 Cedar Street." She turned toward a man who was also standing under the awning. Calming herself to speak clearly so that the man could understand her, Nia spoke to him in a trembling voice. "I'm trying to get to this address. Do you know where Cedar Street is?"

"Oh, yeah. It's on the other side of town. You have to take the B3 and get off at the terminal and transfer to the N116."

Nia ran out into the street and held up her arm. A cab pulled over. She opened the rear door, jumped in, and slammed the door. "I need to go to 143 Cedar Street." Her hand was shaking as she placed the paper back into the envelope.

Hard as she tried to keep track of landmarks along the way, when she looked out the cab window, everything was blurred because of the wetness in her eyes. The cab driver had taken an expressway that she didn't recognize. As he moved onto an exit ramp, she managed to read the name of the exit. It sounded familiar. Nia's heart started to pound as the driver turned off the main street and began to drive down side streets. The cab slowed. Nia's mouth dropped open. She recognized the street! The cab stopped. Nia opened the cab door.

"Miss, I'll take the fare now," the driver said. Nia got out of the car, walked up the steps, and rang the doorbell. The cab driver opened the cab door, stood up and shouted at her, "Miss, you have to pay me now!"

Nia yelled back, "I'll be right back with it."

The cab driver sat back down into the cab. Nia took a deep breath as the front door of the house opened. A lady she had never seen before stared at her. "Can I help you?"

"Yes. I'm looking for Mrs. Audrey Patterson." Nia could barely get the words out. "My mother."

"Well, she doesn't live here."

Nia's heart sank. "But I lived here years ago."

The lady looked confused. "Well, I've been living here eight years. What's your mother's name again?"

"Audrey Patterson."

"Oh! She's the lady we bought the house from. I don't know where she lives now. Good luck," she said and shut the door.

Nia returned to the cab. "Eighteen dollars," the driver shouted. She had fifteen dollars in her pocket. She handed it to him. "It's all I have." He turned his head as if annoyed, clicked his meter, and drove off.

Nia turned around and looked at the house. She saw the curtain move. She began to walk down the block. The door opened again. "Young lady! You can come in here and use the phonebook if you want to see if your mother's name is listed. My computer's down. If you see your mother's name, you can call her from here." Nia quickly rushed back toward the house and up the steps. She walked into the house as the woman held the door open. She waited while the lady locked the front door, and then she followed her into the house.

The rooms—the front room, the living room, the dining room—were just as she remembered, except that everything looked a lot smaller. The steps leading upstairs curved. She remembered sitting on the top steps holding her doll named Titi.

"You can sit right here," the woman said, pointing to a little table with a chair attached to it. There was a telephone on top of the table. "The phonebook is right underneath."

Nia lifted the telephone book and flipped through the pages until she found the listings for Patterson. She ran her index finger down the list to find a match with her mother's first name, but there was no match. She went over the list again. She could feel her heart fluttering as she closed the phone book.

"You didn't find your mother's name?"

Nia slowly shook her head.

"Are there any relatives who can help you find your mother?"

"No," Nia whispered.

"Were you taken from her?"

"Yes."

"I'm a teacher," the woman said, "so I've had some experience with the child welfare system. Sweetheart, it's raining. Maybe you should go home now. It's not a good day to be out. But I'll tell you what. Another day you might want to come back and ask the neighbors. You might find someone who has kept in contact with your mother."

As Nia got up, she asked. "Do the Franklins still live next door?"

The lady shook her head. "I'm sorry."

Nia heard herself thanking the lady as she opened the door. She felt her body shiver as the door shut behind her. Nia walked to the next house and went up the steps. She rang the bell and knocked, but no one answered. She went to the next house on the street. A man opened the door. No, he didn't know a Mrs. Patterson. She rang the bell at the rest of the houses on that side of the street. No one came to the door at most of the houses, and when people did answer, they didn't know anyone named Audrey Patterson.

Nia crossed the street and started inquiring from house to house along that side of the block. At the third house she tried, an elderly gentleman answered. He opened the door slowly.

"Yes, I remember you." He responded when she asked him if he knew Audrey Patterson. Nia's heart raced. "I used to watch Audrey drive off with you. Why don't you step in out of the rain?" Nia entered the foyer of the house.

The man closed the screen door. "So you that little girl. Everybody liked you. It's fun watching a lively child who's respectable behaving." He looked Nia up and down and said, "Well, you ain't grown too much. Tiny thing still. What happened? One day you was with her and the next day you was gone."

Nia simply stared at him. Then the man said, "I guess things happen."

"Can you tell me where my mother is?" Nia intently searched the man's face.

"Oh, yes," he went on, almost as if he hadn't heard her question. "Mrs. Patterson was a good lady. Well, I'm sorry to tell you. I guess you hadn't heard. She had a stroke right after you left, and I heard they sold her house to pay the nursing home."

"What nursing home is she in?" Nia's voice trembled as a chill wavered through her body.

The man shook his head as he placed his hand on his chin. "Now, I don't know that. I'm sorry. That was about eight or nine years ago. People say she was heartbroken. Oh, now I remember. Them people from the child services come and took you. Taking her baby away like that. Them people need to be stopped. Now, look here." Nia saw compassion in his eyes. "I been around a long time, and I done seen a lot of things. You got to go on with your life. It's not good to hold on to the past if it hurts bad, as it seems like it's hurting you. I can see the pain in your eyes. Don't get me wrong, that's a good thing. So many of the young people these days don't even care for their parents … treat them bad. But you trying your hardest to find your mother. But … you don't know what you'll find. Eight, nine years is a long time. The Lord may have taken her up by now."

Nia pursed her lips tightly to keep herself from crying. The man opened the door, and she walked through it. "You need to get out of this rain, child," he said as he was closing the door.

Nia couldn't leave the area. Going from house to house, she knocked on doors and asked if they'd known her mother. Just as had occurred on the opposite side of the block, either there was no answer, or the person who answered hadn't known Ms. Patterson. Thoughts of her mother being in a nursing home raced through her mind. She had to get to a library to find addresses of nursing homes. As she walked, she tried to remember the cab driver's turns so that she would return to the main street. Somehow, she got there. She approached an older woman asked where the nearest library was.

"It's two blocks up the street, but it'll be closing soon," the woman responded and then added, "Baby, you're soaked. You need to get out of the rain."

Nia ran as fast as she could toward the library and was relieved to find it still open. She asked at the desk where the computers were, but was asked for a library card, which she didn't have. The woman directed her to telephone books in response to Nia's inquiry. Nia was surprised to see a whole bookcase filled with phonebooks from cities all over the country. Locating the phonebook for her old neighborhood, she flipped to the heading, "Nursing Homes." There was a page listing nursing homes, and she tore that page out. She held the page to her chest and closed her eyes as she whispered, "God, please let me find my mother." A moment later she folded the page in half, then in half again, and again, and put it in her pocket.

Nia walked out of the library. She had no idea where to go and just started walking. It was still raining. All she could think about was finding her mother. Her mind flashed back to the last time she had seen her. Her mother had found out where she lived, but Grandma Vern wouldn't let her in. Nia knew her mother had looked desperately for her. Her mother loved her! She had suffered, just as Nia had, and now she was in a nursing home. Nia covered her head with her hands and started to run. She ran to escape the words of that man who said her mother could be dead. According to him, it had been about eight years ago when her mother had a stroke. That had to be right after Grandma Vern had shut the door denying her mother from seeing her.

"Nia!" a man's voice shouted out. Nia slowed down and looked back. A police car came up behind her. She stopped, and the policeman got out of the car and walked toward her.

"Nia Glenn," he said sharply. "Do you know people are looking for you, young lady? Come on!" He grabbed her elbow and guided her into the back of the car. He shut the car door and sat back down in the front seat. "You picked a bad night to wander around the city. It's a good thing your grandmother remembered the address she gave you. I'm taking you home."

Nia grabbed the handle, flung the door open, and jumped out of the patrol car. She ran blindly across the main street, oblivious to cars that swerved and came to screeching stops to avoid hitting her. Seeing a subway entry, she ran down the steps. Having no money for the fare and noticing that the man in the fare booth was occupied with a long line of people, Nia rushed into the entry gate behind a lady going through and dashed onto the platform. There was a train waiting with open doors. She heard a voice shout behind her "Hey, get back here!" just as she rushed onto the train. The doors closed, and the train left the station.

Nia sat down and took out the paper that listed nursing homes. She fought back new tears. She moved closer to a lady who was seated next to her on the long bench that ran the length of the wall between two doors.

"Can you help me?" she asked the woman as she pointed to the name of the first nursing home on the list. "Do you know how I can get to this address?" The woman looked at the page and shook her head. Nia pointed to the next address. "Do you know how to get to this one?" The woman looked at the address and shook her head again. She turned her head away and then she turned back toward Nia and took the page from Nia's hand. She scanned the listings and then pointed to an address at the bottom of the page. "I know this one ... Sacred and Caring Hands Nursing Home. But it's back the other way. You have to get off at the next stop and go to the track for the southbound train. You take the E5 to Hampton Street. It's about three stops. When you walk up the steps to the street, you'll be on Hampton Street. Turn right and walk two blocks. Turn right again. That street is Irving Street. You'll see the nursing home. It takes up the whole street. Well, this is your stop. Good luck."

Nia quickly folded the paper, stood up, and slid it into her pocket as the train slowed to a stop. "Thank you," she said. Then she exited as the doors opened. She ran up the stairway leaving the northbound tracks and rushed down the stairway leading to the track for the southbound trains where she waited for the E5. Several trains that were not her train passed, and she began to feel anxious. She felt her clothes and noticed that they had dried out. Nia was relieved to see, in big, bold letters, E5, on the front of an approaching train. When the train doors opened, she got on as fast as she could. The train was packed, but she found a seat next to a large woman whose body took up nearly half of Nia's seat. Nia sat at the edge of the seat so as not to disturb the woman.

The train's horn sounded as it slowed to stop. Nia struggled to catch a glimpse of the station name on the yellow wall. It wasn't her stop. The woman next to her moved her shoulders as if irritated by Nia's constant movements. Nia leaned back in her seat when the woman turned and looked at her.

When the train pulled into her stop, Nia let out a sigh of relief as she had begun to wonder if she had been given incorrect directions. Nia hurried off the train and ran up the steps exiting to the street. She barely noticed that the rain had stopped. She ran down two blocks along Hampton Street until she saw the sign for Irving Street. The nursing home was just as the lady told her. She ran up to the main entrance and walked in. There was a big reception desk. She stood in front of it until the woman behind it noticed her and said, "Can I help you?"

"I'm trying to find my mother."

"Does she live here?" the woman asked.

"I don't know," Nia responded.

"You don't know where your mother lives?"

Nia felt tears welling up in her eyes from a mixture of anger and fear, but she held them in. "I was taken away from my mother," she said.

The woman was silent for a moment and then asked gently, "What's her name, honey?"

"Audrey Patterson."

The lady typed the name into the computer on her desk. After a few moments she typed in something else. Then a few seconds later, she typed again.

She looked up. "I'm sorry, sweetie. She's never been here."

"Can you look up to see if she's in another nursing home?" Nia felt her heart pound.

"I'm sorry. I can only look up the residences that are part of our healthcare system. I've looked up the six nursing homes we have in the city."

Nia took out the pages from the phonebook. "Can you tell me which ones you looked up so I can cross them off the list?"

"Let me see the list," the woman said. Nia handed over the page. The woman browsed through the names of the nursing homes and crossed off the ones that were associated with hers. She handed the page back to Nia and said, "I hope you find your mother."

Nia thanked her, folded the page, and put it into her pocket. Quickly she retraced her steps to Hampton Street and walked toward the subway entrance. She approached a man standing at the corner about to cross the street. She held the paper up to him. "Can you tell me if any of these nursing homes are near here?"

"Yeah. This one's right up the street."

"No! One that's not crossed off."

The man browsed through the listings. "Well, yeah, this nursing home is one stop north from here. It's actually right on this street. See?" He pointed to the address.

Nia asked, "If I was to walk, about how many blocks uptown?"

"Oh, that's a hike. Maybe seventeen blocks."

Nia began to walk as she folded up the page. Then she ran. She ran about three blocks before her knees felt as if they were burning. When she spotted a police car on the opposite side of the street, she slowed her pace and walked alongside other people. The walk seemed as if it would never end. She counted the blocks. Nia got a burst of energy when she passed her fifteenth street. When she got to her seventeenth street, her heart sank as there wasn't a nursing home in sight. She fought off feeling panic and continued walking. After walking a few more streets, Na saw a huge building and quickened her pace.

The name on the sign in the front of the building in big gothic style lettering, read, Tabor Rehabilitation Home. Nia walked inside. There was a little booth over to the left. She walked over to it. The lady on the other side of the glass window slid the window to one side.

"How may I help you?"

"I'm trying to find Audrey Patterson. I want to know if she's here."

"What is your relationship?"

Nia's heart pounded. "I'm her daughter," she said struggling to fight off a sudden feeling of dizziness.

"What's your name?"

"Nia Glenn."

"You're not on the list of visitors."

"She's here?" Nia could feel her mouth drop open.

The woman looked at her. "We don't normally give out information on our patients."

Nia couldn't help herself. "She's here?" she said excitedly.

The woman nodded and said, "Yes. She is one of our patients."

Everything inside Nia exploded. "Can I please see her?"

"I have to follow policy. She has to approve your visit. She isn't in right now. She went on a trip along with a few other patients. Our visiting hours end at nine p.m. They won't be back before then. I can't promise you anything, but come back tomorrow and we'll see how we'll handle this."

"Thank you! Thank you!" Nia practically shouted, and ran outside. She stood on the sidewalk and stared hard at the front of the building, as if to commit it to memory. She didn't mind that it had started to rain again, but she didn't want to be wet when she met her mother, so she got under the awning that extended from the building entrance. After standing for some time, she ran out to the curb to ask the time from a man who had parked his car. She learned that it was seven forty-five. Nia returned to her spot under the awning and sat on the concrete ground. She suddenly felt drained, and crossed her arms over her knees and laid her head on her arms.

"Hey! Hey girl! Chu can't stay here." It was a short Hispanic man wearing large gloves and holding a black garbage bag. "Ees not allowed. Chu have to go somewhere ... not here." Nia got up and started to walk down the street. She crossed over a side street and approached a building with a narrow recessed doorway. She stepped into that doorway area. She could still watch for the people returning from the trip. Nia became sleepy and slid down into a sitting position with her knees bent in front of her. She rested her head on her arms that she had folded over her knees. Immediately she fell off to sleep.

"Well, hello, darling."

Nia looked up. A thin white man stood over her. The street was chillingly black. The man smiled. "Ain't you a sweet young thing?" He grabbed her arm and pulled her up before she could react. "You're coming with me." Nia twisted to escape his grip, but he grasped her arm more tightly. "See this?" He pointed at her with what looked like the tip of a knife. "If you fight anymore, I'm gonna cut you up."

"Help!" Nia screamed as she twisted frantically.

"Oh, nobody's around," the man said, shaking his head. "Nobody's coming to help you. This part of the city is dangerous, and nobody's on the streets after nine but you and me. Nobody's gonna miss you, or you wouldn't be here. You coming with me, and we gonna have some fun." They turned off the main street as Nia continued to struggle. In a split second, the man whipped out a knife and cut her on her arm. She didn't realize he had cut her until she saw her own blood. Her surprise caused him to laugh and he said, "Oh, I'm gonna have fun with you." Nia squirmed violently, and the man cut her arm again. "Chop chop" he said teasingly.

Nia yelled as she kicked him as hard as she could and yanked her arm free from his grip. She ran screaming down the street unsure of how close the man was behind her. She turned the corner and ran out into the main street. Blood trailed from her arm. Desperately, she ran toward the sound of a police siren. The police car swerved toward her and stopped short in front of her. She pointed down the street as she yelled, "That man cut me!" Two policemen jumped out, and one asked for a description. "He's white and skinny," Nia shouted. "He's around the corner!"

Nia saw the taller officer pull out a gun as he took off running in pursuit of the man. The other officer called for an ambulance and backup as he reached into the patrol car and grabbed a first-aid kit. "Let me see your arm." Nia held out her arm. The officer took out large cotton pads, which he quickly unwrapped and firmly placed on Nia's arm. "Hold this down," he said as he used other pads to wipe blood from her arm. An instant later, he changed the pads on her cuts and wrapped gauze around the pads and secured it with tape. He then gently guided Nia into the patrol car.

The other officer emerged from around the corner with the man who had attacked her, in handcuffs. "That's him!" Nia yelled. "That's the man who cut me."

"He's got blood all over him," the officer who made the arrest said to the one who had tended to Nia.

"Lay him on top of the car," the officer who had bandaged Nia's arm instructed. The other officer slammed the man against the front of the police car. The man yelled in pain as his head thumped loudly on the metal hood. "We've been looking for you," the officer yelled.

By this time, a small crowd had gathered, mostly men, whom, Nia guessed from the looks of their faces, their clothes, and the sacks they carried, were homeless. Someone yelled, "Punk! She kicked your ass. You little punk!" Someone else added, "Too bad she didn't cut you all up."

Another said, "Yeah! We ought to tear you apart. She just a little girl, and you cut her. You child molester! You pervert!" Another police car rolled up, and the officers jumped out. An ambulance came and parked a few yards in front of the first police car. As the policeman helped Nia out of the car, the crowd applauded.

The ambulance crew quickly assisted Nia into the ambulance. By the time they reached the hospital, one of the paramedics had taken off the pad the officer had placed over her lacerations, washed and disinfected her arm, and wrapped it with fresh cotton patches and gauze. They took her into the emergency department, where she received stitches on each cut. Finally her arm was bandaged.

Nia gave her name when they asked her, though she was at a loss as to what address and telephone number to give. Resignedly she gave her foster family's information when they pressed her. It was around three in the morning by the time the doctors and hospital staff finished treating her and completed all the necessary paperwork.

***

"Nia! Nia!" Nia opened her eyes and saw Ms. Dorsey standing over her. For a moment she wasn't sure where she was. In the next instance, however, she remembered what had happened and realized that she had fallen soundly sleep.

"You have to get up now. I have to take you home."

Nia shook her head. "I'm going home with my mother."

"Your mother's not able to take care of you at this time. She admits to that."

"No, I mean my real mother! The one you took me from when I was six."

"Well, we'll talk about that once you're home," Ms. Dorsey said.

Nia shook her head, "I'm not going with you."

Ms. Dorsey sat down and pulled her chair up to Nia's bed. "Nia, you are fourteen years old. You're still a child, and the child welfare system looks after children. I'm sorry you suffered because you were taken out of your foster home and placed with your natural family. But that's how it works. Families have a right to their children, even if they aren't the greatest families. If they want their children and they can take care of them, they have a right to have them. Now, I need you to get up so I can get you back to your foster family. Don't try to run, Nia. What happened

220

to you was because you were out on the streets on your own. The streets are a dangerous place for adults, let alone children. Your foster mother will take care of you. She'll tend to your cuts to see that you don't get an infection. You don't want to end up losing your arm. People have lost arms and legs by not taking care of their wounds. Come on. Let me help you up so we can leave. The doctor has given me your treatment orders and prescriptions."

"I found my mother," Nia blurted out. The social worker stared at her. "She's in a nursing home, so she's not so well." Nia looked at her social worker. "Will you help me to go see her?" It seemed to Nia that social workers had all the power over her life.

"I can't promise you that. I'd have to check with my supervisor."

Reluctantly Nia got off the cot and followed Ms. Dorsey.

Chapter 25 Nia's Birthday Party

Nia knew that her foster parents tried to make her feel at home. The Walkers were good people, and Nia liked them, but she didn't feel at home. The Walkers were already a family unit before she had joined them at age fourteen. Mrs. Walker took wonderful care of her arm. She recorded the story of the capture of Chop Chop, the serial killer, from the TV news. The news did not disclose Nia's name because child welfare authorities did not approve of her name or her picture being broadcast on national TV. So at the time of the broadcast, no one other than her social worker and her foster parents knew the identity of the brave fourteen-year-old girl who had fought with Chop Chop, even after being cut, and led the police to him. Her foster father, Reverend Walker, used that event to talk to Nia about angels watching over children.

Things were whirling around Nia so quickly that she hadn't had time to plan a strategy to see her mother. The social worker continually put her off by saying that she still awaited her supervisor's response. The social worker called Mrs. Walker on the afternoon of Nia's fifteenth birthday and told her that she was on her way to pick Nia up. Mrs. Walker assumed that the social worker was taking Nia somewhere special for her birthday, so she hurriedly brought out a cake she had made and called the family into the dining room.

"I don't know what your social worker has planned," Mrs. Walker exclaimed as she sat the cake down on the dining room table." She seemed rushed, talking quickly and nodding her head as she spoke. "We don't know when we'll see you back here. So we have to celebrate your birthday a bit earlier than we planned. We wanted to take you out to dinner, but it looks like that can't happen. So, here are your gifts." The family presented gifts to Nia. As they gathered around her, they sang the birthday song and then shouted at the top of their lungs, "Happy Birthday, Nia!"

Nia was surprised by the family's attention to her. Mr. and Mrs. Walker and their children were so excited. Their faces beamed with anticipation as they wondered if she liked the gifts they had gotten her. She opened package after package and felt such gratitude that it barely mattered what was inside the boxes. The last time she had a birthday celebration, she had been with her mother. She had been six years old then. At the thought of her mother and the birthday gifts, Nia broke down and cried.

"Why is Nia crying, Mommy?" Mrs. Walker's daughter asked. "Doesn't she like her gifts?"

"She likes them. She's just happy," Mrs. Walker answered as she hugged her daughter.

Ms. Dorsey interrupted the birthday party. When Nia was settled in the car, the worker told her, "Your mother's meeting us at the office. I might as well tell you, she's been calling the office requesting that you be returned to her."

Hearing reference to her mother had Nia's heart leap. But as the social worker continued, her shoulder sloped down as she realized Ms. Dorsey was talking about Eva.

"She claims she's drug free."

When they arrived at the Child Welfare office, Eva was sitting on one of the benches. She stood up when Nia came in and smiled brightly. "I heard about that ordeal you had. Quiet as you is, nobody can punk you. That's my girl. That's what I said when they called and told me the circumstances around you being cut. After I heard how you fought, I said, 'Like mother, like daughter!' How you doing, baby? Let me see your hand."

Nia held out her arm and said, "It was my arm."

"Oh! Look at that! My lord! I wish I was there. He wouldn't have legs to stand on when I finished with him. Oh, by the way," Eva smiled, "Happy birthday, baby."

Nia thanked Eva. The social worker interjected, "You can go into my office to talk." The social worker closed the door as Nia and Eva sat down in the two armchairs in her office. For a brief moment Nia stared at Eva who was dressed in a red leather jacket, a short black skirt, black tights, and big spiked red heels. Her hair, dyed a dirty blond color, hung straight down onto her shoulders. She was chewing gum and spoke with her lips turned to the side. "I'm glad she left," Eva said. "She makes me feel uncomfortable. Here I am, a grown woman with a near-grown daughter, and I got to be sucking up to her." She turned to Nia and smiled, "How you doing, baby?"

Nia shrugged her shoulders. Eva pressed her, "I mean, how you really doing?" Nia dropped her head. She felt no bond of love for this woman who was her biological mother.

Eva continued to talk, "I really came here to tell you Grandma Vern died yesterday. I didn't want these people telling you that your grandma died, so I came to tell you myself. The funeral is Saturday."

"I found out where my mother is," Nia blurted out. "She's in a nursing home. I want to go to her. I asked the social worker to help me, but she ain't helping."

Eva's expression turned sarcastic, "No, baby. They ain't gonna help you. They don't understand about us loving each other. They don't even care. They think they saving a child by putting them in a ..." Eva made quotation marks in the air with her fingers. "'Nice home' with people who have more money than us and ain't so stressed out. But you can't buy love. The way I see it, these social workers have two things against them. For one, they mostly young, single, and don't know anything about raising children. And the second thing is, they don't love the children in their care." She leaned back. "I may have love, but I can't handle things, right? But they have no love and they screw up children worse. They ain't saving children. They the real monsters. I mean, maybe they help a few children whose parents are real nightmares, 'cause they really crazy in the head and hurt their children. But, see, the system don't know the difference between people who love their children but need a little help, or maybe a lot o help, taking care of them, and parents who ain't there for their children at all, maybe because they on drugs or their mind's blown. And since social workers ain't got love to give them, they mess them up, send them to one foster home after another. That's all messed up. Children need to grow up in a stable home with people who love them. That's the way God made it to be." Eva looked closely at Nia. "But I heard you got some nice foster parents." When Nia nodded, Eva continued, "Then, baby, maybe you should stay with them till you finish high school. You hit gold if you have some nice foster parents who really care for you in their hearts." Eva shifted her position, "I wanted you to come and live with me, but I think you be best off finishing high school with your foster parents.

"I want to see my mother."

Eva was quiet for a moment.

Nia continued, "I found out where she's staying. She's at Tabor Rehabilitation Home."

The silence in the room was nearly unbearable. Then Eva placed one of her legs on top of the other as she sat, and she began swinging the leg on top almost uncontrollably. She suddenly stopped moving her leg and leaned toward Nia. "I'll help you, baby. I have nothing against the woman who raised you from a baby. She did a good job with you, and it wasn't her fault that they took you from her. I'll take you to her. I'm gonna ask the social worker if you can come to my house on Friday and stay over for the funeral the next day."

"I don't want to go to the funeral. I would rather spend the whole day with my mother."

Eva turned her head away from Nia. She closed her eyes as she dropped her head. "I understand," she whispered. Moments later, she turned her head back around and looked at Nia. "Yeah, that's okay. I'm gonna help you."

Nia felt her heart pounding. "I went there. The lady at the desk said I have to be approved."

"I'll talk to Aunt Sissy. She knows how to maneuver things. Huh! She should by now. They took her children from her, but she said they ain't taking no more."

The social worker pushed open the door without knocking. "You guys have a nice talk?"

Eva looked up at the social worker as the woman walked into the room. "I told Nia that her grandmother passed yesterday. The funeral is this Saturday. She wants me to take her to her Grandma's funeral."

"Oh, I'm sorry to hear that," the social worker said. "Yes, of course she can go to the funeral."

"I can meet Nia here Friday," Eva said loudly.

"But isn't the funeral on Saturday?" the social worker questioned with a puzzled look on her face.

"Yes. But our family starts coming in, from wherever they coming from, days ahead, and I have to accommodate them. I think it'll be hard on me to come here on Saturday to pick up Nia with the funeral being on Saturday and all I have to attend to. See, I'm my mother's only living child. I'll bring her back on Sunday."

"Are you comfortable with that, Nia?"

Nia nodded and softly said, "Yes."

***

Friday couldn't come fast enough for Nia. That day at school she couldn't focus on anything. She was happy when the bell signaled the end of each class period. Her mind kept drifting to her mother. She was alive! Nia could feel her heart pounding. Then she tried not to think about her mother. Hadn't something always happened to stop her from getting to see her? Nia squeezed her eyes closed, and even though she made no sound, somewhere inside her a voice screamed, "No! No! No!"

As she entered her last class for the day, Nia sat in the seat closest to the door. She was the first one out the door when the dismissal bell rang, and she rushed toward the school bus. She became irritated as she watched girls talking and laughing while standing outside the bus rather than boarding the bus. There had been times when she had stood outside the bus talking and laughing with her friends. But this day, she thought they were inconsiderate to all the other students who were already on the bus and wanted to get home. Finally, the bus driver started the motor, and those girls strolled toward the bus and got on.

After the bus dropped her off, Nia ran down the street. Her girlfriend, whom she usually walked with yelled out, "Nia! What's going on?"

"I gotta go!" Nia shouted. She ran as fast as she could. She hadn't said anything to her friend because she knew she wouldn't understand. Nia knew that she was not like the other children she now went to school with because they had always lived with their parents and had good, happy lives. Even the disagreements they had with their parents were within the framework of loving, stable families.

Energy was pumping through her and seemed to be controlling her as she unlocked the side door to her house and walked through the kitchen. She couldn't contain the smile spreading over her face as she rushed down the hallway and passed the dining room and living room entrances. Mrs. Walker's voice brought her consciousness back to the present. Mrs. Walker was sitting at the dining room table with a newspaper spread out on the table in front of her. "What happened? What's up with you?"

Words tumbled out of her mouth as she continued to walk toward her room, "Grandma Vern died, and Ms. Dorsey is coming to take me to Eva, who's at the agency waiting for me. Eva's going to take me to her house. I'll be with my relatives for a few days." She stopped speaking abruptly. She wanted so much to tell Mrs. Walker that she would get to see her mother after nearly nine years. But she knew she couldn't share that with Mrs. Walker because, if Mrs. Walker said anything to the social worker, the visit with Eva would be cancelled, and the social worker would arrange to take her directly to the funeral and then return her to the foster home.

As she entered her room she began to pack her overnight bag. The bag was part of a luggage set that her foster family had given her for her birthday. Nia began to hum, and despite herself, the words to a song emerged from her lips. Her foster mother came to the doorway of her room.

"You have a beautiful voice, Nia,"

Nia stopped singing. She hadn't realized she'd been singing.

"You need any help?"

"No."

"I'm gonna make spaghetti and meatballs for Sunday dinner, and peach cobbler, your favorite dessert, just for you." Nia didn't respond. "Well, I'll let you alone," Mrs. Walker said then left the doorway.

The social worker picked Nia up, and as they drove to the office where they would meet Eva, she commented on how well Eva was doing. Eva had been attending a day-treatment program for substance abusers, and daily testing had shown that she was staying clean. She had moved into Grandma Vern's house, as Grandma Vern had left the house to her.

When they arrived at the agency, Eva was already waiting. After they sat down in the social worker's office, the social worker expressed that her only concern was that Eva had a boyfriend. The social worker told Eva that her boyfriend could not stay overnight during Nia's visit, and that at no time could Nia be left alone in the house with him. As the social worker talked, Nia thought of how she would love to stay with her mother overnight.

"Nia will have to be back here Sunday at noon. I will meet you here, and I will take her back to her foster home then." The social worker looked at Nia. "You have my cell number. You call me if at any time you feel uncomfortable. You understand?"

The realization came to Nia that this woman did not respect Eva. In fact, she treated her like a child who needed watching. For the first time, Nia felt irritated by her social worker. She had never felt that feeling before, although she had seen how quickly other teens got irritated with their social workers. Nia reasoned that being fifteen was what made her able to feel irritation. But she didn't like the feeling.

"You understand?" the worker repeated.

"Yeah." The word pushed out of her lips as a smirk flashed on her face.

The surprised expression on Ms. Dorsey's face made Nia turn her head. Thoughts rippled through her mind. *Just what is she going to do? Try to take me to the funeral herself? She better not bring her white face up to Grandma Vern's house, around them people, talking like she's someone's boss. All that anger pent up in them folks from years of being beat down and not being treated with dignity by people in authority positions, and now here comes this lady disrespecting the family funeral proceedings by talking child welfare business. She'd be lucky if she made it back to her car in one piece.*

My condolences to you both." The social worker's comment brought Nia back from her drifting.

Nia stood up when Eva stood up. Together they walked out of the worker's office and out of the agency.

Chapter 26 The Reunion

It was as if Nia was living a dream. As she sat on the train next to Eva, she whispered, "God, if you're really there, please let me see my mother." While they were riding, Eva gave Nia directions to get from Tabor Rehabilitation to her house. After they exited the train and climbed up the steps leading out of the subway, they walked north on Hampton Street.

"This is where you were attacked?" Eva asked as they approached the area near Tabor Rehab.

"Yeah," Nia responded.

"Honey, I'm over twice your age, and I been on the streets nearly all my life. I wouldn't be caught down here at night. When you visit Mrs. Patterson, please don't be out on these streets after dark."

Nia took a deep breath as she faced Tabor Rehab Home. As they entered and walked to the reception booth, Nia felt her heart pounding so hard that she thought it would burst through her chest.

The receptionist smiled as she opened her window. "You're Nia."

Nia's eyes opened wide. "Yes ..." The response barely escaped from her lips.

"Well, you can sign in right here. Take the elevator to the second floor. When you get off the elevator, walk straight ahead to the nursing station. Someone there will direct you to Mrs. Patterson's room." Nia and Eva were both so excited that they held hands and jumped up and down.

Nia hugged Eva as tears began to flow down her face. Then she cried out, "Thank you. Thank you. Thank you."

"Go on, now," said Eva. "You have the tokens. You know how to get to the house when you're done. Leave before dark. Someone will be at the house to let you in." Eva then turned and walked toward the door.

Nia quickly stepped into the elevator. She wiped away her tears and felt around her face to make sure that no hair hung out of place. On the second floor, Nia stepped off the elevator and walked straight to the nursing station. "I'm here to see Audrey Patterson." She couldn't stop her voice from trembling.

"She's in room two seventeen. That room is on the left about halfway down the corridor."

Nia's legs wobbled as she walked down the hall. She turned left and entered the room. Her eyes opened wide when she saw a woman in a wheelchair. She moved toward the wheelchair. The woman's head was slumped down onto her chest. Questions raced through Nia's mind: *Is she dead? Is she the right person?* She stood in front of the woman and whispered, "Mother … Mother … Mommy …"

The woman raised her head. Nia looked into the face of her mother. She slid down beside the wheelchair until her knees touched the floor. She put her arms around her mother. Her whole body went limp as she held onto her mother.

Mrs. Patterson softly said, "Girl, why are you crying?" Nia looked up into her mother's eyes. Audrey Patterson cried out, "Nia! Nia! Nia! My baby! My baby!" She bent her head down touching Nia's face and her arms closed around Nia's body. "Oh, God. Oh, God. My baby! My baby!"

Nia's voice echoed the pain of years, "Mama! Mama! Mama!" Her body shook. She could hardly catch her breath because of the depth of her crying. She couldn't help how loud she was. Her tears soaked her mother's dress. She could feel her mother's tears misting her cheeks. Nia and her mother held tightly onto one another, their hearts pulsating from the pain of their separation and the ecstasy of being together.

A nurse came to the door and looked in. "Is everything all right?" Then she yelled out, "Oh, my God!"

Another nurse came to the door and gasped. "Mrs. Patterson's hugging her with *both* her arms! She's moved her right arm!"

Hearing the commotion, other staff members came to the room and quietly stepped in. "Oh my gosh! Look at her arm!"

"It's her daughter," someone whispered.

Tears seeped out of the eyes of some of the nurses. They reached into their pockets and got tissues and patted their eyes as they remembered the many times they had heard Mrs. Patterson talk about her daughter being taken away from her. Sensing their need for intimacy, the nurses drifted from the room. Their excited talk flowed to the nurses' station where they shared the news with other nurses.

Nia lifted her head from her mother's chest and looked up at her mother. "I'm not going to leave you, Mama."

"My baby! My baby! How ever did you find me?"

Nia told her everything—almost everything. She didn't tell about the attack.

"Oh, my baby! Thank God you still my strong girl. Thank you for coming back to me. Look at you! You just about grown. You go to school?" Nia smiled and nodded. Then she sat back on her knees and gripped her mother's arm. "What school?" her mother added.

"Linden High School."

"Oh, that school's in a good neighborhood. You not with your family no more?"

"No. I'm with a foster family."

"Now look at that. You mean to tell me they took you from me and you still ended up in a foster home? Them people would not let me visit you. I begged and I cried. I knew your mother had been on drugs, so I asked a friend of mine who worked in one of them drug rehab places if she could track your mother down. She gave me your grandmother's address. I went by there. Your grandmother wouldn't let me come in."

Nia's heart prickled with pain as the scene became vivid in her mind as if it had just happened yesterday. She whispered, "I was coming to the door, and she shut the door. I ran and looked out the window and saw you." She put her head back down on her mother's lap and began to cry again. Her mother rocked her as she held her arms around her. Nia heaved her body even closer to her mother. She felt so warm, so complete, so fulfilled. She had found her way home!

***

Nia and Mrs. Patterson were awakened by a nurse. "It's time for your medication, Mrs. Patterson." Nia stood up and moved away from her mother's side. When the nurse finished administering the medication, an aide wheeled in a food tray and set it in front of Mrs.

Patterson. Nia's mother shook her head and looked at the nurse. "I'm not hungry."

"Oh, Mrs. Patterson. Now, you want to get real strong because of your daughter. Do you know that you moved your right arm?"

"Did I?"

"You had it around your daughter. We all saw you hugging your daughter with that arm. Let me see you lift it up." Mrs. Peterson slowly raised her arm.

"Oh my goodness! You broke through, Mrs. Patterson! Just wait till the doctor and the physical therapist hear about this. They'll be in to see you." She looked at Nia. "You're definitely good for her." As she was leaving the room, she looked back at Mrs. Peterson and smiled as she said, "Enjoy your meal."

Nia watched her mother eat. She ate some food off her mother's plate because her mother insisted. They laughed as Mrs. Patterson talked about so many funny memories she had of Nia.

Nia stayed for hours. She moved to the other side of the room while the staff attended to her mother. After they assisted her into bed, Nia moved a chair up to the bed. She held onto her mother's hands. At times, she laid her head on her mother's arm. They talked about what had happened during their lives apart. Nia told her mother how it had been in Grandma Vern's home.

Her mother shook her head and cried as she said, "I could tell that lady was mean. I felt so uncomfortable when I went up to that house. I said to myself, 'This is where they put my baby!' My heart was so grieved. I couldn't focus on anything after they took you away from me. I know it's why my blood pressure went through the roof, and I had a stroke."

Nia put her face beside her mother's. "I love you, Mama. All these years I couldn't think of anyone but you. I hated everything." Mrs. Patterson put her arm around her daughter and stroked her head gently.

"I had so many plans for you. You were going to music school to learn piano so you could play with the city orchestra. You were about to take ballet lessons when that woman snatched you away from me. You told me you was going to be a doctor to help sick little babies. How are you doing in school?"

"Okay."

"Just okay? Baby, you need to do good in school. It's a way to have a better life. I'm an old lady now. I can't take care of you."

Nia shook her head. "You're not old, Mama."

"I'm fifty-two years old. I was up there in age when you was with me. I'm so happy that you came back into my life. But you're still a child, and we don't want social workers coming around and messing up things again, so you got to do things right. You got to finish school. While you working on school, I'm going to work hard on getting myself together. How's that for a plan?"

Nia smiled. "But I can visit you, right?"

"You my daughter, and you asking if you can visit me? You better visit me!"

"But I don't know if the social worker will allow it," Nia said solemnly. They were both quiet for a while.

Then her mother spoke, "Well, this has to be our secret. Your mother—"

Nia interrupted Mrs. Patterson and said, "Eva is not my mother."

"Baby, she is your biological mother. If she don't mind you calling her Eva, then I don't have a problem with that either. But maybe Eva will help us. Maybe she will agree to you visiting her, and she'll let you come here."

"I can't go to that house." Nia shook her head. "I can't ..." Nia continued shaking her head.

"Baby, I been sitting around here for years. To tell you the truth, I didn't feel much like going on. I don't have no family. You know I was an only child, and my mother been gone a long time now. I had only one child, and he was killed in the war. You were my life." She bent her head down and fresh tears welled up in her eyes. "I don't want to put you through no pain. We both been through too much already."

Nia stood up and hugged her mother's neck. "I love you, Mother. I'll be here every day. I'll find a way."

"No, Nia. Please listen to me, baby. You in a good foster home. I can tell by the way you look. The way you dressed. You fifteen now. Oh ...," she said, stopping herself. She twisted toward Nia and said, "Happy birthday, baby."

"Thank you."

"It was three days ago, wasn't it?"

"Yes," Nia said, smiling brightly.

"I'm so sorry I don't have a birthday gift for you. I'll have to work on something."

"Mother, being with you is the best birthday gift ever."

"Oh, baby." Mrs. Patterson stretched her arms out and closed them around Nia. "Do you remember how we used to rock together in that rocking chair?"

Nia wiped fresh tears away so she could speak. Her voice wavered. "Yes, I remember."

"You big now, but we'll make up for the time some kind of way."

Nia nodded her head and whispered, "Yes."

"But I need you to stay in school. Now I want you to listen to me. I have to work on me and you have to work on you, and maybe if we work hard, we can get a home together again if that's what you want."

"Yes, Mother, that's what I want more than anything. I'm so happy."

"So am I, baby."

A nurse entered the room and told them that Eva was waiting downstairs. "I don't know why she's here," Nia said, frowning. "I was supposed to catch the train to the house."

"Maybe she wanted to see that you safe. Look how dark it is. Time slipped by us. Bring Eva up. I want to meet her." Nia stood still and began to shake her head. Her mother said solemnly, "Baby, Eva may have problems, but she seen to it that your name got on the visiting list, and she brought you here, didn't she?"

Nia smiled, "You're right, Mommy. I'll get her. Mommy, can I stay overnight with you tomorrow? The funeral is tomorrow, and with all the company that will be in the house, I'd rather be here. I have to leave early Sunday because Eva has to have me back at the agency at noon."

"I'll ask the head nurse while you go get Eva. I know there have been times family members have stayed overnight. I'll have the answer when you return, and of course, Eva would have to agree.

Nia looked back at Mrs. Patterson as she was about to exit the room, "I'll be right back."

When the elevator door opened on the lobby floor, Eva who had been standing in the receptionist area, rushed toward Nia. Nia immediately asked her if she would like to meet her mother. Eva smiled and nodded as she whispered, "Yes."

They did not speak as they rode up in the elevator and as they walked toward the room. When Nia entered Mrs. Patterson's room, she walked over to Mrs. Patterson and stood next to her. There was not a sound or even any movement in the room for a good while.

Then Eva spoke. "I appreciate what you did for Nia. I know you took good care of her. I'm sorry about how things happened."

Nia's mother held her index finger up and put it to her mouth. "Shush! You didn't do nothing wrong by me. It wasn't your fault. You meant to do the right thing when you put your daughter in foster care. But that's not why I wanted to speak to you. I want to thank you for bringing Nia to see me today."

Eva seemed uncomfortable and touched her hair with her hand. "Sure."

"What I want to know ... well, what *we* want to know is whether you would ask the social worker if Nia could visit you on the weekends, and you would allow her to come here."

"I don't have a problem with that, except it would probably have to be one day and not the whole weekend. Either Saturday or Sunday. I think two days to keep up with things is a bit much for me. I don't want to mess things up. See they would hold me responsible for anything that might happen ... like Nia getting back late." She twisted her lips and added, "Like today. I could handle one day. But it's really up to the social worker to say she can visit me. I'll ask her. I could teach Nia how to take the train from the station nearest to her foster home and how to return. But I told Nia she got to leave this area before it gets dark, 'cause this is a really bad area. It's nearly nine o'clock."

Eva looked at Nia. "When I called the receptionist, she said you had not signed out, so I knew you was still here. You can't be walking around these streets at night and standing down in the subway station by yourself." Eva redirected her attention to Mrs. Patterson. "I got someone to drive me here to pick her up. This is where she already got attacked."

Mrs. Paterson's eyes widened. "Nia, you didn't tell me you were attacked."

"I'm okay. I didn't want you to worry," Nia was quick to respond.

"Oh, my girl kicked his a—" Eva caught herself and put her hand to her mouth. "Oh, I'm sorry." She looked at Nia. "It's dark now. I had to get Rick to drive me over here because you wasn't at the house when we got back from the viewing."

"I offer my sympathies for your loss," Mrs. Patterson said in a low, soft voice.

"Thank you. Well, Nia, we got to get going."

"Ms. Eva, Nia asked if she could stay overnight with me on Saturday after her day visit. She said you're taking her back Sunday morning. I checked with the head nurse, and they said they would allow it. They would put a cot in my room. We really don't know when we'll see each other again." Nia and her mother held each other tightly.

"I guess with all that's going on at my house, it would be okay. I mean this is something the social worker would normally have to approve, but we all know this visit here wouldn't be happening if we waited on the agency's approval. It's okay with me. But, Nia, you have to be downstairs waiting at ten thirty on Sunday morning. If I don't get you back on time, the social worker will not trust me, and your visits will not be allowed. That means you wouldn't be able to visit Mrs. Patterson like we're planning."

"I'll be downstairs," Nia said excitedly.

"I'll see that she's downstairs on time on Sunday. Thank you, Eva.

Nia hugged her mother. "I'll be back in the morning."

"Okay, baby. Remember what I told you. We both got work to do."

"Yes, Mama."

***

As she rode in the backseat of the car, Nia took deep breaths and kept telling herself that she had to be strong for her mother's sake. She would walk into Grandma Vern's house and go right to Grandma Vern's old room where Eva told her she could sleep that night.

Nia was grateful that the house was quiet when she entered. It just wasn't the same as when Grandma Vern was living there. Tiffany wasn't home. A few older men she didn't recognize were sitting in the living room slouched down on the couch and in armchairs. Eva said a loud enough greeting for both of them. Nia followed her, seeing silhouettes of woman's figures shadowed on the wall as they passed the kitchen entry to get to the bedroom.

"Get some sleep," was all Eva said as she closed the room door. Nia stood still for a moment. It was an eerie feeling getting ready to sleep in Grandma Vern's old room. She forced herself to be strong, to focus on her mother. Nia quickly changed into her nightgown and got into the bed. She lay in the bed with her eyes open and planned her strategy for the following morning. She would get up early before anyone got up because they would sleep late, as that was the way of Grandma Vern's people. She would find Eva, who would likely be sleeping in an armchair, and tell her she was on her way to Tabor Rehab. She would stay with her mother all day and overnight. They would watch TV and talk. She knew her mother would talk about when she was little, and they would laugh. They would eat their meals in the dining room, which her mother had said they would do. Her mother had told her that Saturday nights there was special entertainment with professional performers in the community room. The presentations were always good. They would enjoy that together. In the midst of her thoughts, Nia fell asleep.

Chapter 27 Living on the Streets

Tonai crossed off the last name on her list of people who could give her a place to stay. She had been sitting at her kitchen table for hours thinking about people and then writing down the names of the ones she figured could possibly help her; her sisters Joy, Daisha, Ruby; her mom and dad; Uncle Isaiah; Aunt Sarah; Aunt Sandra; Great Aunt Terry, her Daddy's Aunt; her first foster mom whose name she couldn't even remember. A shudder riveted through her as she crossed off names as she defined the reason each person couldn't offer her a place to stay. Two of her sisters were already doubled up because her sister Rita had also lost her apartment, and she and her two children had moved into Joy's small, one-bedroom apartment. Her sisters Daisha and Ruby were living with their boyfriends. Tonai envisioned them shaking their heads when she'd knock on the door, their children screaming and running around in the background. She could hear them, "You know, Tonai, I would let you stay here, but my man, he already told me that he don't want anyone but me and my children living here. Rita already been here asking, so I know what his answer would be. I'm sorry." Their pretty big brown eyes would have a sad puppy dog look in them.

She gulped hard as she looked at the line across her parents' names as the buzz of the partially broken refrigerator seeming to grow louder. Her mother had made it clear that government housing forbade anyone not listed on the lease to move in, and there was a long waiting list for government housing. Authorities were quick to evict those who were out of compliance with their leases. Tonai and her siblings knew how devastating eviction would be to her parents after all they'd been through. As she went down her listing of her relatives, Tonai's heart sank. None of them could accommodate her because they all struggled financially. Her few friends all lived with foster parents or in group homes, so she couldn't stay with them. Tonai sat back against the chair as she crumpled up the list and tossed it into the trashcan.

Tonai sat at the narrow table that was against the wall at the end of her kitchen and looked at her apartment. The extent of the kitchen, which was to the right of the apartment entry, was a single cabinet that stood above a basin-like sink, a narrow stove, and slender refrigerator that appeared to lean heavily against the stove. The boundaries of the kitchen were defined by a change in the floor covering from white linoleum to the brown carpeting that covered the rest of the unit. Her living room, which was also her bedroom, had one window against the wall opposite the kitchen. A day bed, which she kept covered with a quilt and four throw pillows, was against the right wall adjacent to the kitchen. An old-fashioned brown end table with a short leg slanting out from each side stood alongside the end of the bed and completed the furnishing in her apartment. A lengthy, wood-paneled closet that had two sliding doors ran alongside the wall to the left of the entry door, stopping at the bathroom. This small square of space was her home. She had become comfortable in her tiny apartment. It felt like her.

With her elbows burrowed into the table, she placed her hands over her head. Her mind kept beating on her. "Why you keep messing up?" Her thoughts moved through the drama of the previous months. She had returned to the group home following her hospitalization. She managed to get a part-time job as a cashier in a department store, which kept her busy and off the streets. A few months before she turned eighteen, the usual age of discharge from foster care, her new social worker applied for a grant. The grant assisted young adults' transitions from foster homes or group homes to apartments, provided they were completing high school or had completed high school and were working. The grant provided down payment and monthly rental payments until the person completed school and had been employed for a few months. Tonai had seen the sad outcome of young adults who were not accepted into the program. When they turned eighteen, they were told the name and addresses of homeless shelters and discharged from child welfare services.

Tonai had exploded with joy when she found out that she had received the grant. She had located the small efficiency apartment in the inner city that was not far from her job.

Tonai reflected on how she had ignored the social worker's warnings that completing school was essential to keeping the grant. She had put her job first, picking up hours. When the school year ended, she had failed three of her courses and was not allowed to graduate. She decided she couldn't handle another year of school and officially dropped out. Consequentially, she lost the rental assistance grant. After several months of working, she got fired from her job. Having no savings to draw from, she could not pay her rent. Despite her landlord's letters demanding that she leave, she stayed in the apartment because she had nowhere else to go.

Tonai picked up the court papers that she had put on the table. She was ordered to appear before a judge to defend herself against her landlord's eviction demand. She didn't go to court because she felt there was no point in telling the judge that she didn't have the money to pay her rent. A few days after she missed the court hearing, she returned home from job hunting to find posted on her door an ugly notice with the word *evicted* printed across it in large, bold, red letters. She ripped it off and read the date that a city marshal would come and dump her belongings onto the street.

At nine o'clock on the morning of the eviction, Tonai hastily packed her essential belongings as compactly as she could in a black garbage bag, which was how she had packed her things all her life. She had no money. She had gone to a welfare agency weeks earlier, but had been told that she didn't qualify for financial assistance because she didn't have a disability or dependent children. After she had told the worker that she could not pay her rent, as she had no job, the worker gave her the location of a shelter for homeless people.

Tonai laid her house key on the table. Leaving dishes, pots, and other possessions that she couldn't take with her, she solemnly walked through the door of the small, furnished efficiency that had been her home for six months. When she shut the door, the slight click of the lock sent a flicker of fear through her as she walked toward the building exit.

Following directions she got from people she asked as she walked, Tonai climbed the steps of an old brick building that looked like it might have once been a church. Inside, the lighting was dim, and her eyes had to adjust from the bright sunlight she had just left. The walls were concrete and painted white. The floors were wood boards. Big, closed double doors were ahead. A scent was in the air that she had never quiet smelled before. It reminded her of old people's stale clothing. To her right was a chest-high counter. She looked at a woman sitting at a desk behind the counter. The woman appeared absorbed working at a computer.

"Where can I put my things down, 'cause I have to look for a job?"

The woman looked up with a surprised look on her face. "The shelter is only for overnight sleeping. It opens at eight." For a few moments, an empty stillness filled the space between them. The woman then said as she stared at Tonai. "It's first come, first served, and we only have so many beds."

Tonai felt unable to move. She nearly shouted with a trembling voice, "Can you tell me where there's a shelter I can get into now?"

The woman slowly shook her head. Her eyes seemed to sadden. "There's no shelter that's open during the day unless you have children. Then you go to a women and children's shelter. Do you have children?

Tonai began backing away from the desk. She turned around and nearly ran out of the shelter.

Tonai spent the day going in and out of stores and restaurants in a futile attempt to find employment. She was limited to employers who would hire her on the spot because she had no phone or address. She had no choice but to carry her sack with all her belongings into a building with her and leave it where she could keep her eye on it during an interview. Tonai told the people she spoke with that she'd take any job they had. The response was generally the same—no openings. On the few occasions when she was referred to a manager, the manager would ask about her last job, but when she'd say that she had held that job for six months, the manager would lose interest in her.

She was hungry, but since she didn't have any money, she couldn't even buy a bag of potato chips. Tonai always thought that she was tough, but she found herself looking longingly at leftovers on people's plates when she'd go into a restaurant seeking employment. She began to think of ways to get food. She could go into a restaurant and take a napkin and quickly scoop food from plates that had not yet been removed from a table. It wasn't illegal. She could cut off the parts where the person had bitten. Hungry as she was, however, she couldn't get herself to eat leftovers from strangers' plates.

After an exhausting day, Tonai made her way to a park. It was one of the few places she'd be allowed to sit. When she used to ride home on the school bus, she'd look at homeless people and wonder why they hung around parks. Now she knew why. She was now one of the sad street people that she used to see and pity. She was one of the destitute people with shopping bags, sacks, or shopping carts full of black bags.

She asked the person beside her on the bench—a thin, older, Caucasian man—"Do you have the time?" He nodded but didn't tell her the time. "Are you waiting to get into the shelter for the night?"

The man looked up, squeezed his eyes half-shut, and said, "Yep."

"Do they feed people there?"

"No! Are you dumb or something? They give you food at the Mission. You better hurry. It's about to shut down for the day."

"Where is it?"

The man stood up, squinted with his eyes, and pointed, "Over there, down that street."

Tonai tried to follow his hand, but she wasn't sure which street he was pointing to. "Which street? What's the name of it?"

The man got upset. "You ask too many questions!" He grabbed his sack and rushed off.

Tonai walked in the direction the man had been pointing and thought about how he had said that she had to hurry. She asked a woman who was standing in front of a trashcan, staring into it, "Can you tell me where the Mission is?"

"Sure can. Come on. I'll take you there." The woman walked very fast. "We have to hurry." They walked about three blocks, and Tonai saw a line of people outside a building. A plaque over the building read Northside Mission. The lady stood with her in the line. They had almost gotten to the door when a male voice hollered out, "that's it!" and the door shut.

Tonai moved to the front of the line and banged on the door. The woman who had led her to the Mission raised her voice, "Don't do that! They won't allow you to ever come here if you cause problems. That's how I lost my privileges. They said I was stealing food. I was. I was putting food in my bag here 'cause I'd get hungry later, 'cause they only serve one time a day. You have to remember this. See? Read the sign. It says, Sunday, ten a.m.; Monday, Wednesday, and Friday, five p.m.; Tuesday and Thursday, twelve noon. They don't serve on Saturdays. I guess that's their day off. There's some other places that serve the homeless all week, but you have to walk far. Sometimes my legs won't take me."

Tonai sat down wearily on the doorstep, but the woman stopped her and said, "You got to get up. It's time to start walking to the East Street Shelter so you can get a bed for the night. Do you know where it's at?"

Tonai nodded her head as she stood up. "I was there earlier. I thought it was a place to stay, but it's only for sleeping."

"You got to start walking now to get on line to get in. They only have so many beds you know."

"You're not going there?"

"Noooo. They steal my stuff. I'm a hard sleeper. I can't sleep with one eye open, and they don't let you sleep on top of your things. You have to put your things underneath your cot. The cots are so close together that it's easy for someone to reach under your cot while you sleeping and take your stuff and put it into their bag. I lost everything twice. That was enough for me … had to start all over collecting things."

Tonai moved her sack in front of the door and sat down on it so that her back was against the door of the Northside Mission. "I'm staying here. I'll stay right here till this opens tomorrow afternoon."

"Yeah, I've done that before. Well, see you later."

"See you later." Tonai stared at the woman for a moment. Then the full reality of her situation hit her like a sledgehammer. At eighteen, she was homeless. Suddenly she had a strange feeling she had never experienced before. She felt a suffocating fear, as if something were sucking the life out of her. She struggled to catch her breath.

"Oh, God, help me," she whispered. She caught her breath and spoke to herself, "Don't panic, Tonai. Don't panic." She buried her face in her hands. "Think, Tonai, think!" She forced herself to think how she could get back on her feet. She thought of everyone she knew or had even met, even the foster parents she had lived with. She quickly mulled over her relationships with them and whether they had room. She came up with the same answer every time. There was no one! She thought of where she could go to get work. Then she thought about going back to her old job. She knew the work and did it well. Even her supervisor had said so. Her problem was with being supervised, doing exactly what she was told to do. Tonai nodded to herself. Friends, even her teachers, and school counselors had told her she was too stubborn, as she always thought she knew the best way to handle a situation and had a problem taking orders. Now look where she was. She would swallow her pride and go back to her old job. She would look her supervisor in the eye and sincerely apologize to her. Then she would ask for her job back. She would go the next day after her meal. Tonai thought about how she would go about getting an apartment after she got her job back. She kept her mind busy because she knew it was all she had left.

The streets quieted as the night hours past. Tonai was glad because she didn't have to deal with people walking by and staring at her. Around midnight she fell into a deep sleep.

Tonai's eyes widened. She was standing in front of a huge, blue-paneled house that had a front porch that ran into a large deck. She felt confused as she walked up the steps because she knew in her gut that it was her family's house, yet she couldn't understand how this could be real. She became overjoyed when she saw Dayton. He was sitting on a lounge chair on the ivory-white deck, his nose in a book. Donté and Desmond were playing catch. She went into the house, almost as if she was floating. She peeked into the living room that had a long sectional couch and big-screen TV. Daisha was lying on the couch looking at TV. Next, she passed the dining room and saw a long mahogany table with seating to fit her whole family. The kitchen was so much like her mother---happy looking, bright cherry colored cabinets all around, some with doors open. Canisters, plants, and small porcelain figurines covered the counter surfaces. Joy was in the kitchen placing seasoned chicken in a bowl. She rushed out the kitchen door. Tonai followed her. She saw everyone. It was a huge yard. Her mother was taking the meat that Joy brought to her and placing it on the grill. Her dad was healthy and vibrant emptying an enormous bag of ice into a cooler that contained cans of soda. Ruby and Rita were giggling while swaying in a two-seater swing. Donté and Desmond began wrestling on the grass. Dayton and Daisha emerged in the yard likely from smelling the food. Everyone was there. She was just getting ready to run up to her mom and dad when sounds began cutting through her head.

"Get up! You have to leave!" A rough loud voice and confusing background noise agitated her. She couldn't understand where the noise was coming from. She struggled to stay with her happy family, but the noise grew louder and louder. Brightness from the sun and sounds of cars pierced through her consciousness, and her eyes opened.

A police officer jumped out of his car and was shouting while waving his hand, telling the people who stood, sat, or lay in front of the Mission that they had to leave.

"Come back at noon. No squatting on the sidewalk is allowed! This is a public street. You people can't clutter up the street. People need to get to work."

Tonai struggled to get up. She followed the slow-moving little group as they strolled away from the Mission. She heard people saying things like,

"Just walk until they leave. Then we can turn around." "Shhh ... shhh." "Is he gone?"

Tonai kept an eye on the police officer and walked more slowly than the others, staying a bit behind the group. She had reasoned that, when the group turned around, she would be in front of the line and would have the best chance of being the first one back at the Mission door. They had all turned the corner. She noticed that people on the sidewalk moved out of their path. Then someone whispered loudly, "They're gone!" Tonai turned and ran back around the corner. Already a few people were at the door. Tonai plopped her bag down and sat on it. She was starved. Before she realized it, her anxiety burst from her mouth, "The cops gonna come back and recognize me and put me in jail for defying an officer!" She threw up her hands.

"The cops not putting you in jail." A thin, young white girl who was in front of her had turned around. Although there was a shadow of prettiness, she looked sad and defeated. Her lips turned down as she talked, and her voice was low, shaky, and sour. "You must be new out here. I haven't been out here long either. But I learned that they don't see our faces because we're an embarrassment. So they'll never recognize you."

Tonai looked at the tall buildings that ran up and down the streets and the bustling people. They walked quickly past them, their faces lifted, their eyes seeming to have shutters on them. She sensed they were holding their noses from breathing as they passed them by.

A slender, wiry looking older man stepped out from behind Tonai and stood beside her joining their discussion. His stubby, blondish-brown hair was disheveled and stuck out around his head. There was an absorbing sadness in his eyes. "They should not be snubbing us. I worked all my life. Then my wife got real sick." The man coughed, and Tonai turned her head away from him. Sounds of people passing by talking loud and laughing drowned out his voice. The man raised his voice. Tonai turned her head back towards the group but kept looking down at the ground.

"The doctors took all my money." The man took a deep breath, held it, and let it out slowly as he continued to speak. "I couldn't keep up with my mortgage. I was trying to save her life. She died anyway. Lost my home. Lost my job 'cause I took so much time off, so I guess they realized they could do without me."

Tonai looked behind her and saw the line flowing down the block alongside the buildings. She felt anxiety rising up as she thought about the police coming and breaking up the line, and then she'd have to fight through all these people to try to get a close spot. She didn't want to hear the man's story. She just wanted to get inside and eat.

"It's hard looking for a job keeping crisp-looking clothes and a clear head when you living out of your car." Placing his head on his chest, the man mumbled, "Then they took my car ... hauled it of to the car pound. I watched them. I couldn't get it out ... had no money.

The man's voice broke. He began to cry. Slowly he moved back behind her.

Tonai tried hard not to think. She didn't want their words pulling her down. She didn't want their desperation and hopelessness. She didn't want to become one of them. She placed her head firmly down on her chest to discourage any more conversation. Seemingly coming from nowhere, breezes that brought an offensive odor kept brushing past her. She was hoping she'd get used to the smell, but she began sneezing.

"Hold your nose, girl. I can't afford to get sick. I don't want your TB," a woman's voice screeched. Tonai kept sneezing.

"You have to get out of here!" a rough voice bellowed out.

Echoing voices yelled at her, "You too sick. You got to leave, now!"

Someone handed her a tissue that she really didn't want to take because she didn't know where it had been. She took the tissue and held it over her nose. Tears welled up in her eyes. Desperately she fought the tears from running out of her eyes and onto her chest. She was Tonai, strong Tonai. But she had no home and nowhere to go. She was on the streets, and she had to scuffle to get a cot to sleep on overnight, and she had to scuffle to get a free meal. And now, the homeless people were rejecting her and trying to throw her off the food line!

The man behind her patted her on her back as his voice bellowed out. "She don't have TB. She's too young. She's a teenager." The crowd quieted down.

A loud scraping sound brought on jubilant cries from the crowd. It was the doors of the Mission opening. Tonai followed the people in front of her. She was so relieved when she passed through the archway into the Mission. She got a tray and received plates of food from servers behind a counter that had a glass shield in front of it. The people serving wore white plastic masks over their faces and rubber gloves on their hands.

Tonai followed the person in front of her and sat at the same table. She didn't even notice if it was a man or a woman. She placed her black garbage bag containing all her belongings on the floor between her legs. She began to eat. The food tasted better than anything she'd ever eaten. Slices of turkey with gravy, mashed potatoes, green beans, salad, a dinner roll, juice, milk, a piece of cake. She ate everything too quickly. When she asked if she could get a second helping, she was told that, after the Mission closed its doors to incoming people, she could get in line for second helpings—if there was any food left. She waited until the doors were closed and got in line again for seconds.

It was a Thursday. Tonai asked a lady sitting near her, whom she heard someone call Evelyn, where the best places to sleep were if a person didn't want to go to a shelter. Evelyn giggled.

"The best place is the New Castle Hotel or a penthouse apartment at the Executive Suites." Evelyn stopped giggling when she saw the solemn look on Tonai's face. "Well, you have to be careful that you don't be in someone else's spot. Under the bridge still had room last time I looked. There at least you protected from the rain. You might be able to get a big cardboard box from the back of a store that sells big things like furniture or washing machines, 'cause sometimes they put big boxes outside before they break them down. If nobody else is at a spot, you can put your box there, and everyone will know that's your box."

Tonai left the Mission with Evelyn. They walked together with all their belongings to the back of a warehouse. Tonai found a large box and carried it over her head.

As they walked, Evelyn keep talking about surviving on the streets. "You got to keep one eye open, even while you sleeping in your box, 'cause some people are mean to us. There's some people who like to kill homeless people because they think nobody cares what happens to us. Sometimes members of gangs try to kill us to prove how tough they are. People die every day out here."

Evelyn stopped talking. She seemed absorbed in her thoughts. Tonai wondered how much farther they'd have to walk. She looked at Evelyn, who didn't seem to mind walking. Evelyn started up again. "Even if you don't get killed by a crazy, there's all kind of diseases a person can catch that can kill you, 'cause you live on the street where all the germs is. You ain't protected from people coughing on you or spitting on you, and they might have TB. And a lot of us die from pneumonia because in the winter we never warm enough. When it rains, you get wet even if you under the bridge, and you can feel dampness in your bones. You got to be so careful."

Evelyn talked until they got to a spot under the bridge. Evelyn pointed at the ground, "This is the spot nobody claimed." She seemed to be absorbed in her thoughts. Then she said, "It's safer if you have some buddies—friends who become your family. That's the safest way. You all stay together, live together, sleep together in the same huddle of boxes or in the same box. That way, someone in the group can be the lookout person so that some freak can't just sneak up on you."

Tonia put her box down and crawled into it. Evelyn handed Tonai her large bag, which she had been carrying for her. She smiled as she waved at Tonai and walked away. Evelyn amazed Tonai because she was a small, thin, pale white lady, yet she had carried both her own bag as well as Tonai's the entire trip to the bridge. Tonai laid her head on her black sack.

***

Day in and day out, Tonai followed the same pattern. In the early hours of the morning, before sunrise, she'd walk several blocks to a gas station to use their bathroom. She'd brush her teeth, splash water on her face, and then wipe her body off with a washcloth that she kept in a small plastic bag inside her black trash bag. She'd wash her washcloth and ring it out real good and put it back in the plastic bag. Once a week when it wasn't raining, she'd sit her washcloth on top of her box and let it air dry.

Leaving the gas station carrying her large bag, Tonai would walk to the Northside Mission or to a church that served breakfast. She'd sit on her bag and wait for the doors to open. After she ate, toting her bag of belongings, she'd go to stores and fill out job applications. She'd spend the entire day looking for a job. She had gone to her old job, but the lady who had been her supervisor was no longer working there. When she went to the personal office, she was told they weren't hiring. In the evenings, after a long day of job searching, she'd walk to a mission that was closest to where her job search ended and wait in line for dinner.

On Sundays, she'd get up while it was still dark and take the long walk to the Eastside Shelter. They had shower stalls that were available to homeless persons during the hours of six to nine on Sunday mornings. The shelter provided towels, and they'd give her clean clothing and take her soiled clothes which they'd wash, dry and give back to her before she left. She would then rush to get to the Northside Mission for breakfast.

Weeks on the street turned into months. Tonai continuously tried to suppress the fear that kept groping at her mind that she would be living on the street for the rest of her life. One Sunday morning, however, she made a decision that changed the course of her life. On that particular Sunday, Tonai walked to the Northside Mission and stood in line hours before it was scheduled to open, which was her usual pattern. As she sat on her bag containing all her belongings, sounds of people singing erupted into the air and became louder and louder. As the singers approached, they shook hands with people standing in line in front of the Mission. The singers were nicely dressed and very pleasant, smiling as they sang and as they greeted people. They seemed oblivious to the fact that they were talking to homeless people. Tonai stared at them. She used to laugh at people who went around in groups toting Bibles, going from house to house or standing in a park shouting about God. They seemed desperate to push their beliefs onto people, and nobody wanted to be bothered—or so she thought when she was in high school walking with her friends. Tonai and her friends used to cross the street and walk in an opposite direction from wherever they were assembled. The Bible-toting people would be so insistent. They'd call out to them, "Jesus loves you." Her response had always been, "Yes, I believe there is a God … somewhere. And no, I don't want to hear you talk to me about Jesus!" Now, as Tonai looked at them, she could almost hear her heart pleading, "Please help me!"

There were six singers. One of the men shouted out, "You don't have to live this kind of life. God didn't intend for you to be homeless. He made the earth. He made man to dwell in the earth. He made everything for us. And he said, after making everything, that everything was good. If your life is not good, something is wrong! It doesn't line up to what God intended. So how did things get out of line with God's plan for you? Do you think it's God's fault or man's error? Do you have a relationship with God, your creator? If you don't talk to God every day and even throughout the day, you don't have a relationship with him. And that's what's wrong! We're supposed to have a relationship with our heavenly Father. To ensure that we have a relationship with God, who is holy, God sent his son Jesus to pay for our sins because man was so disobedient and rebellious. So after Jesus died for our sins, we have a right to all blessings, including having a nice home to live in."

People applauded as the speaker continued. "If you believe that Jesus died for your sins, raise your hand." Nearly all of the people in the line raised their hands. "Most of you believe. So why are you here?" No one answered. "You are here because God is a nice thought in your mind, and Jesus is a nice thought, but you really don't have a relationship with God. If you have faith in God, you will see him open up doors for you, and he'll walk you through them. I'm not saying that the road is smooth all the time, because it's not for anyone, but if you really trust God, you'll see his handiwork in your life. You won't be homeless," the man said, holding up his Bible, "because it says right here in his word those who trust in him will never be without. God takes care of those who trust him."

The man went on, seeming to gain strength from the power of his own speech. "You've been through a lot. You tried everything else. Why not try God? Why not see if what he says is true? You can come with us now. We're on our way to church to learn more about God so we can get closer to him."

Tonai eyes were fixed on the speaker. She had never seen other "Bible people" act like him. It was as if he really cared about them. Then the man yelled out, "If you want to get off these streets, God will get you off these streets. Put him first. We'll show you how." Tonai stepped forward with her bag.

"Well, you're making a good decision, young lady. What's your name?"

"Tonai." Tonai then added, "I think you should know that more people would probably come, but if they leave their spot and come to your church, they'll probably miss getting into the Mission, and they'll have to go without a meal." Even as she spoke, she saw people in line moving forward filling in what had been her spot.

A woman with a radiant face smiled and nodded her head as she spoke. "We know. But, Tonai, you have already given God a sacrificial offering by putting him before your own comfort. God honors those who sacrifice for him with a pure heart. You're going to be richly rewarded for your great sacrifice. Watch and see." The other church members nodded and looked at Tonai with beaming smiles. Another man from the church group stepped forward and said, "I'll carry your bag for you, Tonai." For a moment Tonai held onto it. Then she handed it to him. "I'm Brian," he said. "I'm one of the ministers from Fellowship Church."

The man who had been speaking to the crowd continued. "Do you know that, if you were to die without having accepted Jesus as Lord and Savior of your life, no matter how good you think you were, you would go to hell?" He looked at the crowd. "Your life now is hell. Do you want to live on earth in hell and then live for all eternity in an even more tormenting place? Accepting Jesus as Savior of your life means you believe that Jesus died in your place for your sins so you won't go to hell for your sins. Accepting him as Lord means you follow him by letting him guide you in your journey through life. It costs you nothing to accept Jesus as Lord and Savior of your life. He looked at Tonai. "Are you ready to accept Jesus as Lord and Savior of your life?"

"Yes," Tonai responded as she stared at the minister.

"All those who want to join this daughter of God in publicly confessing that Jesus is Lord of their life, repeat this prayer along with her. When you say this short prayer, it means you acknowledge that Jesus is the Son of God, and that you believe He came to earth to die for your sins, and you give Him the right to be Lord of your life. You submit to his will even over your own. You know this world would be a beautiful place if everyone submitted to following Jesus? Jesus is the Prince of Peace. Accepting Jesus as Lord and Savior of your life is beginning a new journey. It's a journey of love for God and for one another. It's a journey of being a peacemaker, refusing to argue or fight, even when a person treats you badly. Instead of fighting with your enemies, you pray for them. If they come to know the truth, they'll be set free from all bitterness and hatred, and they'll walk in love. Then you won't have any enemies anymore, but friends. So pray for your enemies. Submitting to God is a journey filled with God's truth, and watching God triumph through you. Everyone who's ready for a journey with the Lord, which means being committed to following Jesus, in the sincerity of your heart, repeat after me."

The minister spoke slowly, pausing after every few words as everyone recited what he said: "Lord Jesus, I believe that you came to earth for me. You are the Son of God. You are perfect in holiness, and you took my place, dying on the cross for my sins. With my mouth I confess and with my heart I believe that, Jesus, you are my Lord and Savior. I choose to follow you, Jesus."

The group from the church clapped their hands, shook tambourines, and sang. They moved among the crowd and handed out cards. The minister spoke again, "Everyone who confessed that Jesus is Lord of their life should be at service on Sundays. We invite you to Bible study on Wednesdays, or just come to the church and commune with God in a peaceful place. Our church doors are always open. We are handing out cards with the church name and address. The church is just a few blocks uptown. Remember, you just said Jesus is Lord of your life. Now you have to show Him that He is Lord of your life. You have to do something. We've seen people's lives miraculously change after accepting Jesus into their lives. You got to work at getting to know God just like you have to work on any other relationship. I assure you, you will never regret taking a stand for Jesus. Let us join together in song and prayer."

The minister began singing, "This little light of mine. I'm going to let it shine." Everyone joined in. The minister prayed for everyone. Sniffing and soft sobbing could be heard among the crowd. Even though the minister invited everyone to join them for church service, only Tonai joined the group. But people nodded their heads, and some mumbled that they would be at the next Sunday service.

A young woman put her arms around Tonai. "My name's Alicia," she said. She was about the same height as Tonai and not much older, yet she seemed so strong and confident. Tonai walked a few blocks, and the whole time Alicia talked and asked Tonai questions. Almost before she realized it, Tonai had spilled out most of her life story, but somehow she didn't feel embarrassed around Alicia.

They approached the church building that took up an entire block, and they entered through one of three sets of huge double doors that covered the entire front of the building. The inside of the church was like a gothic temple. A high ceiling, which was painted with colors, mostly hues of blue and yellow, looked like the heavens opening up. Tall stained-glass windows with pictures of angels decorated the side walls. Statuesque white columns were elegantly positioned around the sanctuary. Three sections of long mahogany wood benches flowed from the pulpit nearly to the door.

A reverent quiet filled the sanctuary even though the pews were filled with people. And people were praying in various positions. Some people were sitting in the pews with their eyes closed, some were kneeling with their heads down to the floor, some were standing looking upward, and others were slowly walking up and down the aisle.

"They are all praying to God in their own way," Alicia whispered into Tonai's ear. Alicia placed her hand alongside Tonai's arm and gently rubbed it as she guided her to the first pew in the church, where they sat down. Tonai felt uncomfortable in the front row; it was as if she was in the spotlight. She looked behind her. People shook their heads and kept their eyes closed. Some people held their hands up as they looked toward the ceiling.

"The service will officially begin in a few moments," Alicia whispered. "Perhaps you have something to say to God, or maybe you'd simply like to thank him." Alicia knelt down onto the floor, put her hands over her face, and bowed her head to the ground. She swayed back and forth slightly. Tonai could hear her sniffling. Tonai turned around. She had never seen people acting the way these people were acting. They didn't seem to care who was watching them.

Tonia closed her eyes and tried to figure out what to say. "God, I guess you're real," she whispered awkwardly. She figured he must be if this lady could hug her, bring her all the way up to the front of the church, and not be afraid to sit beside her. "I'm homeless," she heard herself say. *I don't look like these people*, she told herself as she glanced around at all the nicely dressed people in the pews.

A loud voice echoed through the room. Alicia got off her knees, sat in the pew, and whispered, "That's Pastor William Thompson." Pastor Thompson asked everyone to stand in reverence to God and to lift up his or her arms in a posture of praise. Tonai couldn't seem to lift her arms. She looked at Alicia, whose arms were lifted above her head. Her eyes were closed. Tonai looked around. Arms were lifted to different heights. Keeping her elbows close to the sides of her body, Tonai closed her eyes and lifted her arms.

Tonai felt a gentle breeze on her face. She opened her eyes and looked at the windows. They were closed. She looked toward the back doors. They were closed. She closed her eyes. The gentle breeze was still there. Everything in her, even her thoughts, became calm and peaceful. Tonai felt as if something had been released somewhere deep within her. She didn't understand what she was feeling. She heard her own voice softly whisper, "Jesus. Jesus. Jesus."

"The Holy Spirit is moving in this place right now." The pastor's voice echoed through the room. "Oh, we praise you, God. Oh, we thank you, Jesus."

A woman's melodious humming became a gentle song. People joined in singing along with her. A pianist and other musicians entered from a side door below the stage and took seats with their instruments in an area near the piano and began playing. People in long blue gowns marched in from the back of the church, down the aisle, and up onto the stage as their voices thundered in song. Tonai joined everyone clapping and swaying to the music. She was surprised that she didn't become bored or annoyed with the repetition of some of the songs, but she kept moving her feet and clapping her hands.

As the songs ended and the choir sat down, the pastor moved to the pulpit and began preaching. Tonai's lips parted as she listened. As the pastor talked, it seemed as if he was helping her to put together pieces to the puzzle of why things had happened to her.

The pastor held up the Bible and shouted, "Only what God says is truth. God is truth. Everything that isn't lined up with what God says is a lie. If your life is a wreck, then you need to reference the Bible, God's roadmap for our lives. Check out what areas of your life are not following this roadmap. You can be blessed only if you honor God. God is the creator. He is Alpha and Omega, the beginning and the end. We are the creatures created. The state of affairs in this world is a mess because man is not in alignment with God's will. God is love. He created us to love him and to love one another. He made everything on earth beautiful for us. Look at all the variety of foods that come out of the earth. Look at all the life forms. Look at the trees and the flowers. This planet is a tapestry of God's love. Jesus tells us that all the commandments or requests of God are summed up in these two sentences: 'Love God with all your heart, mind, body and soul,' and 'Love your neighbor as yourself.' For those who need clarification about who your neighbor is, everybody is your neighbor. Anyone in need is your neighbor. The family in Africa, China, Russia, Iraq, or in a rundown community in America is your neighbor. Does the world look like it's following God's commandments? No! It does not! Greed and selfishness dominate. Yet we say we care about other people. We say we help others. But if you helped people in a godly manner, you would never judge the people you're helping or have derogatory thoughts toward them. You don't help people by making them feel like they're failures or focusing on their mistakes. They might have missed it, but as a child of God, you lift them up. That's what Jesus did. He lifted us up. He got underneath us by allowing himself to be tortured and to be crucified as a sacrificial offering for our sin. Can you sacrifice for others? Will you put a smile on other people's faces? Lift them up instead of tearing them down! Truth be told we all made mistakes, some of them real bad, so who are we to judge anyone!"

Tonai felt as if she could listen to Minister Thompson for hours. His voice was soothing. "Let's bow our heads. And with your heads bowed, I want you to think of how you missed it. How you missed an opportunity to put a smile on someone's face. How you missed it by not offering a helping hand. How you missed it by not ministering to people about how God loves them, no matter what they've done. I want you to talk to God, to ask for forgiveness, and to ask him to use you to demonstrate His love."

The sanctuary became very still. The pastor's head was bowed. Tonai could see that Alicia's head was bowed. Slowly she turned her body to look at people behind her. They sat motionless with their heads bowed. Even children were pin-drop quiet. She bowed her head and closed her eyes. She thought about the homeless crowd she moved around with. She couldn't imagine making someone smile. Suddenly it struck her that she didn't smile anymore, that she had no more humor. It struck her like a blow to her chest. She wasn't Tonai anymore.

A voice broke through her thoughts: "Please set your hearts to give offerings to God."

Tonai looked up recognizing the voice of the minister who was with the group who had brought her to the church. She watched the people, with heads still bowed, walk to the front of the church and place money or envelopes on the altar.

After the offering, Pastor Thompson said, "We always like to welcome our guests. If anyone is visiting this church for the first time, please stand." Tonai felt her heart pound hard in her chest. Alicia patted her on her shoulder. Tonai stood up.

"We welcome you. Your name please?" Pastor Thompson asked.

"Tonai."

"Tonai, we welcome you and pray we have blessed you."

Immediately, people came up to Tonai and hugged her. Some shook her hand and nearly shouted, "Welcome. Glad to have you with us."

She was stunned, felt frozen in time as faces appeared in front of her and bodies hugged her. She couldn't respond even though her arm was being swung from person to person in a handshake position.

After the service ended, Alicia turned to Tonai. "Would you like for the pastor to pray for you? He's an anointed man of God, and sometimes he makes prophesies over people. I have seen what he says come true." Tonai nodded as the thought flew through her mind that she needed all the prayer she could get. Alicia took her hand and led her a few steps to the pastor.

Pastor Thompson's eyes seemed to pass through Tonai as he said with a broad smile, "Welcome." He put his hand on her head, and as he did, two men moved toward her and stood behind her.

"You are a daughter of truth," the Pastor began. "I pray, Lord, that you bless your daughter with revelation of truth. As you well know, Lord, this daughter of yours has been kicked about, and the enemy of her soul has tried to put heavy weights on her to keep her bound in a web of deception and lies. She has already seen the lies that have been acted out in her life and brought her to a place where she has nothing and no one. But you, who are Lord of our souls, see that she has a heart of love, and you provided angels around her to see that she was not destroyed and did not lose her mind. You, Lord, sent your ministers to bring her out of darkness into your marvelous light. And now, Lord, I'm asking for your Holy Spirit to dwell in her life so that the anointing of God leads and guides her from this moment on."

Tonai felt her body weaken. She began to fall backward. The men behind her caught her and gently lowered her to the floor. She then lost all sense of her surroundings. She felt a stream of water flowing over her. As the stream of water flowed over her, she saw herself embraced in loving arms. It was a far better feeling than the warm feeling she had felt as she had lain in her father's arms as a toddler, a memory she had forced herself to hold onto. Her thoughts and her body motions were stilled in this place of perfect peace.

Finally, after being motionless on the floor with her eyes closed, Tonai became aware of sounds. She could hear the pastor praying for other people. As she attempted to get up from the floor, church brothers, as she heard other people in the church call them, immediately assisted her and helped her to sit back down in the pew. After a few minutes, she opened her eyes. Alicia whispered, "You were slain in the Spirit. That means that God's Holy Spirit is in you. The Holy Spirit has confirmed your confession of Jesus as Lord and Savior of your life. Whatever you were doing out there in the world that's not godly, you won't be able to do anymore. You won't feel comfortable doing wrong. You'll find yourself eager to learn about Jesus, and eventually you'll be working for the Lord." Alicia smiled and patted Tonai's hand.

Tonai felt at peace as she listened to the minister praying for people and watched them get slain in the Spirit. A murmuring began among the people in the sanctuary. The sound grew louder and louder, and soon she could hear individual voices. They were speaking words she could not understand. Alicia stood up and began to speak in this strange language. Tonai looked at her and saw the sincerity in Alicia's face as she muttered what sounded to Tonai like words in the Arabic language. Tonai began to rock back and forth.

"Help me, God, to know how to pray," Tonai whispered. She picked up the Bible that Alicia had lain on the pew. She opened the pages and began to read. She kept reading until she realized she heard no talking, or any other sound at all in the sanctuary. She looked up and there was no one around except Alicia, who sat beside her.

Alicia smiled and said, "It's time to go. Church is over." She stood up. "You can keep the Bible."

"Thank you," Tonai whispered. As they walked, the reality of her situation hit her. "Where's my bag?"

"It's in the hallway closet," Alicia responded and added, "Are you hungry?"

Tonai nodded as she responded, "Yeah."

"Come on and join us downstairs. Mother Beverly's got some good victuals laid out. She's the church cook."

Alicia led Tonai down some steps that opened up to a huge dining area. The pastor, the people who had sung in front of the Mission, and a few other people were eating. Following Alicia, Tonai sat at the table where Pastor Thompson, his wife, and Minister Brian, the young man who had carried her bag from the Mission, were seated.

The food was succulent, just as Alicia had told her it would be. It reminded Tonai of her own mother's cooking. The dining room area was warm and comfortable. Tonai found herself continuously laughing as the pastor and Minister Brian told humorous stories about things that had gone on at church social events. When Alicia and Tonai had nearly finished eating, Minister Brian politely excused himself.

The pastor and his wife looked at Tonai. His wife was a short, chunky, yet elegant-looking woman. She had light brown skin, and there were dark-brown freckles dotted across her pleasant, plump face. She looked at Tonai and said, "We know we don't know you, and you don't know us, but we'd like to think the Lord might want to use us in his plan to take you in a new direction." Tonai stared at Mrs. Thompson. She forced herself to pay attention, though she was already beginning to think about getting to a shelter so that she could stretch out on a bed for the night, rather than sleep crumpled up in her box.

"We have a room in the basement of our house. And there's a bathroom down there. It's humble—just a bed, a dresser, and a small writing desk—but if you want, you're welcome to stay there until you get back on your feet. Would you like to stay with us?"

Tonai's mouth flew open. Her eyes widened as she stared at Mrs. Thompson. She could hardly believe what she was hearing. "Yes," she finally breathed out.

"You can use the kitchen in the mornings to make breakfast. Just clean up afterwards. We invite you to join us for dinner in the evening, which we have right before we go to church."

Pastor Thompson added, "We don't ask just anyone to live with us, but we recognize when God's hand is on a person. His hand is on you, daughter." He smiled at Tonai. "We do have a few stipulations. They might be major because of the lifestyle you been used to. Can you handle a few rules, Tonai?"

Tonai barely whispered, "Yes, sir."

"No smoking. No drinking. No loudness. No company. Keep your room and bath clean and tidy. No sleeping in during the day except Saturdays. You have to go out every weekday and look for a job. You have to go to church on Sunday. Everyone in my house goes to church on Sunday. It's how I run my house. Is this too much constraint for you?"

The image that had been periodically cropping up in her mind of her rushing to the homeless shelter shattered. She felt such joy that she could barely clear her throat to say, "No, sir."

Chapter 28 Nia's Graduation

Nia walked across the platform and shook hands with her high school principal as he handed her a diploma. Although the auditorium was packed with people, and looking at the audience she couldn't distinguish one person from another, in her mind's eye she could see her mother clapping for her. She walked down the steps to exit the stage and followed the line of graduates walking in front of her back to her seat. She was happy that the ceremony was ending.

"Congratulations!" was the last word the school principal said, and students threw their caps up into the air. Nia quickly rushed to the aisle and ran toward the handicapped section, where her mother sat. She intended to get to her mother before the aisles flooded with people. In her long, black graduation gown, she maneuvered through people, darted away from friends who tried to get her attention. She told them, "I'll talk to you later."

Her mother was seated in the handicapped section because she walked with a cane. Also seated in the row with her mother were Nia's foster parents, the Walkers, and her foster sister and brother, Esther and Ezra, who were about to enter high school themselves. To Nia's surprise, Eva was sitting next to her mother, frantically waving her arms at her. Nia ran toward them. They came out into the aisle so that, as she approached them, they circled around her hugging her and kissing her. Esther had the graduation program pamphlet opened to a page where names were listed and was excitedly pointing out Nia's name to everyone.

They left the building together walking slowly so that Nia's mother wouldn't be rushed with her cane. On the steps in front of the high school, Mrs. Walker said that she wanted a picture of Nia and her mother. Next, Mrs. Walker took photos of Nia and Eva. Eva took the camera to take pictures of Nia and the Walkers.

Ezra exclaimed, "Wow! How many people have three mothers?" Like a flash of lightning, it hit Nia that the mothers in her life loved her.

Mrs. Walker then asked a total stranger to snap a final picture of the whole group. Nia smiled as she stood between her mother and Eva. Mr. and Mrs. Walker stood on the step above them while her foster brother and sister were crouched down in front of her.

Nia felt full inside. She thought of how good her foster family and even her natural mother, Eva, had been to her. Nia looked at Eva. She knew it had taken everything in her to make it to the graduation. She found out that Eva had called the Walkers and asked if they could pick her up from the train station and allow her to ride with them to the graduation. She had requested that they not mention her coming to the graduation, as she had wanted it to be a surprise.

The Walkers had learned that Nia was visiting Mrs. Patterson under the pretense of visiting Eva, and they assisted any way that was needed so that Nia could visit her mother every week. The agency social worker, who wasn't aware that Nia was visiting Mrs. Patterson, but thought she was visiting Eva, had denied her visit to Eva on several occasions. Once, when Nia had been placed in detention for walking out of a class, the social worker had denied her a Saturday visit. Eva had called Mrs. Walker, and they had talked about it. Mrs. Walker then drove Nia to her mother's nursing home, enabling her to visit her mother that Saturday. She had waited until the visit was over, reading and doing crossword puzzles in her van. Following that weekend, early Monday morning, Eva went to the agency's office, cursed the social worker out, telling her that a child should not be prevented from seeing her parent as a form of punishment. But because of Eva's outburst, visits were officially stopped. The social worker told Eva that she needed to attend several counseling sessions on behavior management before visits would resume.

Mrs. Walker set up her own arrangement so that Nia would be able to visit her mother. On Saturday mornings, Mrs. Walker would drive Nia to the train station where she would catch a train that transported her to a major transit depot where she transferred to the train that took her to the neighborhood of the nursing home. Nia would spend most of the day with her mother. She would leave late in the afternoon to take the train back. Mrs. Walker would pick her up from the train station.

"The graduation luncheon is on me," Mr. Walker thundered. "We're going to Lobster Island and eat our hearts out!"

A new excitement hung in the air. The children piled into the backseats of the van. Nia sat in the middle section between her mother and Eva. Eva began talking about the graduation ceremony, and she had everyone laughing as she expressed how she thought that the guidance counselor would never end his speech.

Nia looked at Eva for the first time it seemed. She saw that she was a pretty lady and a lively, talented person. Nia put her head down onto her chest because grief overtook her for a moment as she thought of how Eva could have achieved anything in life if she had pursued it.

Her mind shifted to the interaction she had with Tiffany less than two weeks before her graduation. Tiffany had called her. She had found her number in Eva's purse. Although she felt a strong impulse to hang up the phone, she listened as Tiffany talked. Tiffany told her that Eva was back on drugs and had stolen house money to buy them. She had paid none of the utility bills, so the electric company, the water company, and the telephone company had threatened to disconnect services.

As Tiffany talked, an image popped into Nia's head of Tiffany crying out, "No, Grandma ... no!" as Grandma Vern told the police that Nia had started the fire. Then she smelled the pungent, acid odor of the burned curtain.

A few days after Tiffany's call, Nia had gone over to the house. She had taken the train there after visiting with her mother at the Tabor Home. She had talked to her mother about Tiffany's call. Her mother had told her to see what Tiffany insisted was so urgent that she had to talk to Nia in person.

As she walked along the street toward the house, it appeared as if the entire street had decayed. The houses were jammed together, and most seemed barely able to stand. Instead of grass in front of many of them, there was hard, dry ground. Dirty ornaments hung over some porches. A couple of houses on the street were boarded up.

When Tiffany opened the door, she looked like a shadow of the cousin Nia had grown up with. She was alarmingly skinny, and her eyes looked as if someone had gouged out the sockets but left the eyeballs in them. Tiffany had always been taller than Nia, but they were now about the same height. Tiffany's confidence and vibrancy—her most prominent traits when she was younger—had vanished.

"Hey, cousin," Tiffany said. She looked as if she was trying to smile, but Nia saw sadness imprinted on her face. "You look good, girl. Look at you. Nia, Nia., you as tall as me now, and you look like one of them models." Her voice was low, just above a whisper, and shaky, so that Nia had to strain to hear some words. "Come on in. You not gonna play cold to your cousin, are you?" She had her arms out, and she hugged Nia, but there was no strength in the hug.

Nia followed Tiffany into the house. Although it was daylight outside, because the curtains were closed, the house had a darkened hue. Nia saw that the place was a total wreck. A couple of the cushions from the couch were on the floor. Trash spilled from every bucket and ashtray within sight. Nia regretted she had come to the house. She walked behind Tiffany into what had been her grandmother's room. Eva lay across the bed.

"She's gone back," Tiffany said. "She's not doing anything but getting high. We about to lose this house 'cause of her not paying the taxes." Nia looked at Eva's back. Her fully clothed body lay across the bed. Her feet hung over the edge of the bed with shiny green leather high heels clasped around them. She had her head turned sideways, and it was pressed against her green purse. Her eyes were closed, and her mouth was slightly open. Nia began to wonder why Tiffany wanted her there. She could not help Eva. She had nothing to say to her.

Nia shook her head. "I can't help her." They left the bedroom and stood in the hallway near the kitchen entrance. As Nia looked down the hallway, she could see the room in which she had slept as a child. In a moment, painful visions invaded her—visions of ghosts moving along the wall, Ty climbing out of the window, Tiffany prancing around like a queen, Grandma Vern beating her with a strap. A taste of bile rose up in her throat, and her eyes went blurry as she was overwhelmed with a need to flee. Quickly she walked out of the hallway into the living room.

As they entered the living room, Tiffany lit a cigarette. Nia was astonished. "I didn't know you smoked. You always said that, because of what happen to your family, you would never put a drug to your mouth!"

"There's a lot you don't know," Tiffany retorted grimly.

Nia realized how things could turn around. Standing in front of her was Tiffany, the one everyone considered so beautiful and talented, the one the family believed would become a big star. And now there seemed to be nothing left of her. She had gone down, down, down. From her looks, Nia knew she was on drugs.

"I was thinking," Tiffany said. "Now that you about to get out on your own, you could come stay here. You could have Grandma's room. You know your mother. She ain't home most of the time. We can all give you so much each month, and you can pitch in too." Tiffany bit her lips as she searched Nia's face waiting for her response.

Nia shook her head. "I can't. I'm getting a place with my mother when I graduate."

"You and Mrs. Patterson could stay here." Tiffany's voice rose sharply. "You can stay in Grandma's room."

"I can't, Tiffany."

"Remember this?" Tiffany held her arm out. Nia could see the skin pulled together and darkened where she had been burned. "It's almost invisible now," she whispered.

Nia looked Tiffany straight in the eye. "I can't," she said abruptly. She wanted so much to say, "Don't call me no more," but she held her tongue as she walked toward the door.

"You ain't no better than us," Tiffany yelled as she followed behind Nia. "You could never accept us." She pointed toward the back room. "Your mama right back there on that bed. That's where you come from. Don't act like we ain't your family."

Nia could feel rage rising up in her. She imagined an ugly scene in which she was fighting with Tiffany. Just as quickly, the thought flashed through her mind that she was going to graduate in a week and a half. If she fought Tiffany, the cops might be called, and she could go to jail. She rushed out the door and slammed it behind her. She almost fell down the steps in her haste to leave the property. She was sure that Tiffany would throw open the door and scream curses at her, but when she realized that the door had not opened, she slowed down.

A bump in the van ride brought Nia back to the present. She smiled as she felt her shoulder pressed against her mother's. She was overwhelmed as she looked at her graduation gown flowing onto the floor. She had graduated high school!

"A penny for your thoughts," Mrs. Patterson said as she looked at Nia.

Nia looked at her mother and then rested her head on her shoulder. She could feel her mother smiling, and she felt her stomach giggling with laughter. Then she began giggling. They understood. They had made it. They had worked hard just as they had planned. Nia had stuck with school as her mother had told her to do, even during really tough times. Upholding her part of their agreement, Audrey Patterson had also fought hard, suffering through pain and discomfort as she underwent physical therapy to get back on her feet.

They were working on reaching their goal of getting a place together. Nia would get a job. Mrs. Patterson had Social Security disability checks coming in every month. They had already begun to look for housing. The social worker at Tabor Home gave them information on applying for government subsidized housing so that most of their income wouldn't go toward rent. Nia had wanted to take a one-bedroom apartment that was available, but Mrs. Patterson disagreed

"You need your own room, baby. You're grown now, and you need your own space. I need my own space too. We love each other, but we need our own space and private time. We need a two-bedroom apartment.

Nia had even gone further and said, "We'd be better off if we had a house."

Her mother had responded, "I'd love for us to have our own house. Don't have to worry about the landlord's rules and all." She then turned her body more toward Nia and sighed as she said, "But, baby, you gonna get married one of these days, and there I would be stuck with a big house with no one in it but me."

Nia had shook her head, "I'm never getting married. Never! Never!"

Her mother had laughed. "I think you're going to get married soon. A tall, dark, handsome man will come into your life and you'll say, 'Mommy! Mommy! I'm getting married!'" Still laughing, her mother added, "And that's what I want for you." But Nia looked forward to moving into the house she knew they would find.

Lobster Island was packed with other graduates and their families. As a waitress approached them, they focused on the menu. When the waitress began to speak, Nia looked up and stared into the young woman's face. "Tonai!"

"Nia!"

Each blurted out the other's name at the same time. Nia stood up, and she and Tonai hugged each other tightly.

"I'm so happy to see you, Nia," Tonai said as they hugged. As they loosened their embrace, she looked Nia up and down, "Look at you, girl, with your graduation gown on. Look at that hairstyle. Ah, sookie! Sookie! Oh, Nia, I'm so happy to see you doing good. You such a special friend."

Eva yelled out, "Ain't you Ben and Sierra's daughter?"

Tonai looked at Eva and responded, a bit defensively, "Yeah, they my mom and dad."

"Well, girl, you and Tonai seem to be good friends."

"Yeah, we go way back ... like being in the nuthouse together," Tonai nearly shouted.

"Shhh," Nia said quickly.

"Well, guess what?" Eva squinted her eyes so that they looked as if they were closed. She was quiet a moment, and everyone at the table stared at her sensing that she was about to say something important. "Y'all related. You cousins."

Tonai and Nia looked at each other, and then looked at Eva for an explanation. "Nia, Tonai is Aunt Sissy's daughter. She been in foster care since she was a baby, so she ain't been around the family much. Tonai, I'm Eva, Nia's birth mother, and me and your mother are cousins." Tonai's mouth dropped open. "Oh, I heard about you, Aunt Eva. I think I seen you before, but you look different.

Nia stared at Tonai as they both put their hands to their mouths. Eva kept her focus on Tonai. "I saw you when you was a baby." She turned to Nia and said, "You know your Aunt Sissy—you always helped her cook. Give me a minute. Let me figure this out, because it goes way back. Your Aunt Sissy is not really your aunt, Nia. She really your second cousin because she my cousin. Because she's much older than me, I was brought up calling her Aunt Sissy. Tonai, Uncle Isaiah, who your mother calls Granddaddy Isaiah or Granddaddy I. because he's so old and always looked out for the family, is really your mother's great uncle. Tonai, your great-grandma, Peaches, and Nia, your great-grandpop, Amos, Grandma Vern's daddy, were brother and sister. I mean, you two are down-the-line cousins, but you still cousins."

Mr. Walker scratched his head and said, "That's too much genealogy for me!" Everyone laughed.

Tonai said excitedly, "I knew there was a reason I always liked you!" Nia and Tonai began laughing as they again hugged each other. Tears rolled down their faces.

Nia's foster father extended his hand to Tonai and said, "And I'm Mr. Walker."

Nia quickly said, "Oh, I'm sorry. These are my foster parents, Mr. and Mrs. Walker, and these are their children, Esther and Ezra. Eva has already introduced herself. And this special lady is my mother, Mrs. Patterson."

Tonai was still for a moment then began scratching her head as she said, "Now I'm for real, for real, confused!" Everyone laughed. Looking at Mrs. Patterson, Nia said, "She raised me from birth until I was moved to live with my biological family."

"Oh! Okay, I got it." Tonai smiled broadly and said, "Oh! Pleased to meet you all." Tonai quickly added in a lowered voice, "Let me take your order now. I don't want to get fired for chatting with ... family."

Even after bringing their food orders, Tonai came back to the table several times. Before the group left, she wrote down her address and phone number on a napkin and handed it to Nia. Tonai and Nia lingered while the others walked ahead.

"We having a church jam tomorrow night," Tonai said to Nia.

"A church jam! What's a church jam?" Raising her voice and curling her eyebrows, Nia added, "And you, Tonai, go to church?"

"Yes, I do. I'll tell you about how that happened one day soon."

Nia stared at Tonai. She looked really good. What hit Nia suddenly as she looked at Tonai was that she didn't have the old rough mannerisms and the street-slang-laden speech. And she didn't wave her hand around when she talked the way she used to. She had lost weight, and she wore a clean white shirt and a neat black skirt, even if it was her uniform. During Nia's last encounters with Tonai, all she had worn were hooded sweatshirts and baggie pants.

"Listen, Nia, church people—real church people—have more fun than people who ain't into God. I been on both sides. Believe me. I know! We don't party like how you know to party ... but we party hard with God and, like I said, we have more fun because it's not fake fun. You know how it is out here ... everyone trying to look cool and fit in and get mad and want to fight if they think someone looked at them the wrong way. Those parties are all about show-boating." She took a deep breath. "This church jam is for young people our age. And, girl, or I should say cuz, I guarantee you gonna have a good time. There's gonna be a play, a band, and singing and all kind of food. You got to come 'cause I got to talk to you. Where you live? I'll pick you up."

"You have a car?"

"No, but I know someone with a car who will drive me to come and get you."

"Oh, on Saturdays I'm with my mother all day. She stays at Tabor Rehab Home."

"Yeah? I know that place. But wait. What's wrong with your mother? She seems like a live wire."

"No, Tonai." Nia's slightly raised voice had annoyance in its tone, "When I say my mother, I'm talking about Mrs. Patterson, the lady using the cane. She was actually my foster mother, but to me, she's my mom. She raised me from infancy."

"Oh, yeah. I apologize. Don't jump on me. I understand. Believe me, I do understand. Well, our church holds services at the place where your mother lives. Several of our ministers go there during the week to talk with the residents. I've even been there with them ministering to the folks. I can pick you up from there."

***

The play at Tonai's church held Nia's attention because it was about family and acted out various crises that pull families apart. Tonai sat with her at the beginning of the play, but kept getting up, disappearing, and then reappearing. When the play ended, Tonai led Nia to the food tables in a back room where they got plates and helped themselves to pizza, drinks, and snacks.

The dining area was packed. As they held their plates of food and looked around for seating, Tonai cocked her head to the side, in a follow-me gesture, as she said, "Let's go sit outside."

As they ate their meal on the top step of the church entrance, Tonai began talking. "I was homeless when these people brought me to this church. Don't look so surprised, Nia. It could happen to anyone, especially kids like us who been in foster care. It's because they separate us from our families and put us in these artificial families. I call them artificial because they ain't taking care of you unless they getting paid, and they don't love us."

"Some are good homes," Nia quickly added.

"Yeah, I stand corrected. There are a lot of good foster parents. But a lot of them ain't going to care for you unless they getting that money. So when we turn eighteen, poof!" Tonai opened and closed her hands. "We're told we're on our own. Shi— Oh, excuse me. I'm still working on my mouth. Long story short, that's how I became homeless. I'm afraid to think about what would have happened to me if I hadn't joined with the church people that day they showed up at the Mission. I mean every day I had to fight off something. Sometimes it was my own fears, but most of the time it was real danger, like men trying to molest me. Yeah, that happened one time too many. These ministers saved my life. Now I feel so free. I don't have that hurt that was in me, churning all around my insides."

"I know what you mean," Nia quickly interjected. "The foster family I live with, they're ministers. They helped me a lot."

"See how God works? I know you go to church with them."

"Not always. But most of the time."

"You were blessed to have those foster parents, but I wasn't so fortunate. My foster mother couldn't care less what happened to me. Her son molested me. Then they put me in a group home. That's where I was living when we was in the hospital. That was a cold place. Them girls will steal the gold out of your teeth while you sleeping."

For moments they sat quietly. Tonai broke the silence. "But, hey, girl, I see you found your way to your mother, and you surrounded by all your mothers at your graduation. Only God pulled that off for you. Only God! All the anger you had in you, back when I knew you, that seems to be gone."

"Maybe it just seems to be gone," Nia said. "I didn't invite Eva to my graduation. She called Mrs. Walker and found out about it."

"But didn't it feel good having all them there for you?"

Nia turned her head and looked down, "Eva's back on drugs."

"But she was at your graduation. That's a big effort for her if she's strung out. It's like she had to fight against strong impulses going on inside her to get to you. That tells me she could overcome drugs. She just don't know it."

Nia started to get up. "I gotta go."

Tonai put her hand on Nia's arm. "Chill, cuz. We—me and you—family. Now, I can talk to you straight … okay?" Nia sat back down. Tonai went on, "You don't ever want to be where I been, all tore up inside with anger, raped, going against my own natural body sex—you know, dressing and acting like a dude, penniless, homeless, and going downhill fast. But I had something happen to me that changed all that. God got hold of me."

Nia tried hard to be respectful, but she couldn't stop a smile from emerging on her face. She bowed her head as her thoughts spun. *It couldn't be Tonai talking about God like one of those Bible-toting religious fanatics. She had to be joking.* She sobered herself and looked up at Tonai as she thought, *I'll wait for the punch line.*

"When I came into this church," Tonai continued, "I felt a soft breeze touching my face. I'm telling you, I felt it. I didn't even know what it was at the time, but I got changed. My heart changed."

Nia stared at Tonai. She was dressed like a normal person. She wasn't jumpy and loud. Nia nodded as she agreed that some kind of transformation had happened. Tonai's voice pushed through her thoughts. She sounded like a minister. "I learned it was God's spirit. It's called the Holy Spirit. Then that same day Pastor Thompson and his wife took me in. The same day! I was homeless, and they took me into their home. Now that's a miracle! I know people don't want to believe in miracles. God works through people, you know, puts things into their hearts to do. I think people don't want to face up to there being a God because then they can't do any old thing they want to do.

Nia's thoughts drifted to the meanness of people, tearing her from her mother when she was little and defenseless, putting her with abusive people. Where was God then?"

Tonai's voice rose above her thoughts. "We got to be good." Tonai sat back, leaning her elbow on the step behind her. Nia followed suit and slouched back. The middle church door opened, and music jumped out. Two young men walked down the middle section of steps. The men and Tonai and Nia smiled and nodded. The cousins watched the men fade into the darkness.

"See how they just flowed into the darkness?" Tonai commented.

Nia laughed. Then she tried to adjust her mind to this new, philosophical Tonai.

"I'm serious," Tonai continued. "We got to love and harmonize with everything around us. See, here in America, we don't want to harmonize. People from the East know how to harmonize with their environment and each other. African people harmonize with their environment. Indians harmonize with their environment. We here in America can't harmonize. We don't flow with the breeze. We don't stick together and pull each other up. Instead, we pull each other down. Too many people are about whatever they can get for themselves. That's why the air is polluted and the climate is all out of whack—because greedy people clog up the air with soot and trash trying to make all the money they can make. I guess you're thinking, 'Well, if God was so with you, why didn't he get to you before you was homeless?'"

Nia shook her head. "Yeah I was wondering why bad things happen to good people."

"Well, for me things happened the way they happened because probably I would not have been ready to hear God."

The air was relaxing because it was the perfect temperature. A sweet summer breeze flowed around them now and them. They both became reflective for a few moments. People sporadically walked past, some of them couples. Nia liked to see couples. It suggested love was still alive.

Tonai broke through Nia's reflective quietness. "I still live with Pastor Thompson. I have my own room and bathroom. They told me to get a job and don't act up. Now I know how to be humble and grateful. I got a job, and I play by the rules."

A thought tickled Nia's mind. *Tonai playing by the rules?* She looked at Tonai and smiled.

"Yeah, girl. I read the Bible. Don't get me wrong. Everything's not how I want it. You know we'll always have challenges or have to confront something we need to deal with. But, Nia, God will let you know He's with you."

"What is being saved?" Nia interjected. "I always hear about being saved, but I don't know what it actually means." With this question, she consciously acknowledged Tonai as an "expert" in religion matters.

"Being saved means believing in your heart and saying out of your mouth that you accept Jesus as Lord and Savior of your life. You know He died hanging on a cross. The way He saves you is through your believing that He is the Son of God, believing that He came to earth specifically to die in your place for your sins—past, present, and future sins."

Nia turned toward Tonai. "Well, to tell you the truth, Tonai, I don't know Jesus. I mean I know he's a spirit, but I never felt him around me. Up until recently, I wouldn't know how to believe he exists, because I seen nothing but evil all around me."

Tonai was still and attentive as Nia talked. Then she said, "Sin is being evil, going against how God tells us to live, which is rebellion against God, who is good. Those people you lived with was against the truth, living how they wanted. They had no consciousness of God's will."

Nia nodded her head. Like a flash of lighting, it struck her that her Grandma Vern and Tiffany were full of anger and fear. That's how they could be so mean. Eva and even Ty were filled with anger and fear, but they turned it on themselves by mutilating themselves, destroying themselves. They were sinning. Nia's thoughts moved quietly to her lips, "Why would God put me with them?"

Tonai's raised voice brought her back. "Jesus took our sin debt so we wouldn't have to go to hell for our sins when these bodies we're in die. When you believe and accept Jesus as your Lord and Savior, you're saying that you acknowledge Him as dying in your place and going to hell in your place so God sees you as holy because you have no sin. Jesus is the door to being before God. That's why we always have to end our prayer or conversation with God by saying, 'In Jesus's name.' His life on earth was an example of love and giving. And we're to follow His example, which is what we mean when we accept him as Lord of our life." Tonai's voice lowered. "He helps us. We change in how we think and do things."

Nia's heart pumped fast. She didn't want to be like her natural family. She wanted to get rid of the anger and bitterness.

Tonai continued sprouting out words like a ball of fire: "I know it don't sound real. I mean, how can one man die for all of us? Well, that one man was really God come to earth. All of us together don't equal the greatness of God. Anyway, it's something we can't figure out, and to tell you the truth, we just don't need to figure it out. Our job is to accept what God says is true. Our job is to have faith in God, in Jesus. You have to read the Bible to understand more. I'm still learning. This I do know: Jesus is so good to us that, when we say his name and believe that he's real, we can have victory over everything. Jesus is love because God is love. He wants us to walk in love. All this fussing and fighting among people, fussing over different religions, hating different races, all this bickering, greed, and selfishness—it's not God's way. It's man's way. It's man's rebellious way. It's man wanting to be in charge."

It was as if Tonai was in Nia's mind, hearing her thoughts.

"But God is the real boss," Tonai continued, "and as the Bible tells us, God is love. We should have His nature. We should always help one another. We should always give. Give, give, give, and not try to keep, keep, keep, everything for ourselves. Giving can be in any area. Sometimes it's as simple as a smile that might reach into the heart of people who feel that no one loves them or cares about them. I know about that."

Nia's thoughts drifted back to the days when she hadn't been able to smile. Her heart fluttered with joy as she thought of how she had found her mother, and her smile had returned.

"Sometimes it could be just listening to someone who needs someone to talk to. Sometimes it could be giving someone a few dollars. Give it to them instead of loaning it to them. If people honored God and followed Jesus, we wouldn't have all this antagonism and warfare. It's greedy, power-driven leaders who jeopardize everyone's safety with their godless ways, even if they claim it is for God that they want to kill other people. God is love. Who else could make such a beautiful place for us to live? His love is all around us."

Tonia turned and pointed to a tree. "Look at that tree," she said. "Look at how beautiful the wood is. How strong it looks. Look at the leaves, a beautiful green, and they provide shade for us anytime during the day when we want to get a break from the sun. Think of all the different varieties of flowers. Better yet, think of all the variety of food that grows in the earth and on the trees to feed us! Look up at the blue sky!"

Nia looked up. It was mesmerizing. She felt that she could be drawn into the depth of its endlessness.

Tonai pointed up. "Look at the stars, Nia. Can't you see their beauty? They're like sparks of light in the sky. And the vastness ..." Tonai stood up and stepped up the two steps to the landing. She stretched her arms out, and she held them out as she turned around. "And the vastness of the sky. See that moon? So cute sitting up there like a smile. And to think people all over this earth can see that moon just like us. Isn't that enough to know there is a God? Can't no evolution fit everything in place so perfectly. You can see it's the enemy of God who wants to destroy God's beautiful creation."

Nia's mouth was open. Tonai's new manner and powerful way of expressing herself was amazing. Tonai had barely stopped for breath, but Nia was the one who felt breathless.

Tonai stepped back down and sat beside Nia. She took Nia's hands and held them. "Nia, I know you suffered a lot, but I want you to have forgiveness and joy in your heart. You'll feel such freedom. Do you want to be saved?"

"Yes. I mean, I thought I was saved. I said the words at my foster dad's church, but I was just talking, and I didn't really understand what I was doing."

"Well, now you can be saved with your whole heart. The heart is what God relates to anyway. People can say anything out of their mouths, but God goes right into your heart to see what the real deal is. Repeat after me what's called the prayer of salvation, because your words will be saving your soul if you really mean what you're saying to Jesus. You're speaking to Jesus telling him that you believe that He, who is God's son, came to earth and suffered torture and died in your place for your sins, and that you acknowledge Him as Lord and Savior of your life and will follow him. If you don't accept that He did this for you, you'll stand before God when you leave this earth and be judged for your own sins. That's just the way it is!"

Nia repeated Tonai's words

"Come on, get up," Tonai said with a laugh. "You got to meet your family." She held Nia's hand as they ran into the church, and she was beaming with excitement as she brought Nia to Pastor Thompson.

"This is Nia, Pastor Thompson. She just received Jesus as Lord and Savior of her life."

Pastor Thompson looked straight into Nia's eyes and said, "Well, welcome! You made a smart decision, young lady. You'll never be the same. You have a good big sister. She'll look after you."

Nia followed Tonai out of the church, and they sat back down on the steps. They talked on through the night and into the next morning. Tonai explained to Nia that she now had a new heart. "But I don't feel any different," Nia responded.

"It's not a feel thing," Tonai was quick to say. "You just go about your business, and God works on the inside of you. You just have to do some things that strengthen your relationship with Him, like have a special time every day to talk to God, come to church, read your Bible. Watch and see if God doesn't take care of all issues in your life, especially your heart.

Chapter 29 The House

They stood outside their home staring at it in awe the day they got the keys. Nia jiggled the keys in the air then rushed to open the door. The house was a townhouse in an upscale neighborhood that had flowers in the yards and trees nicely positioned along the streets. The real estate agent had told them it was a popular neighborhood for professionals primarily due to its closeness to the inner city.

Nia hooked her arm into her mother's arm as they stood inside the house. They had been in the house before. They had even placed supplies there, and even a ladder, but now it was actually theirs. The front door was still open. "This is not a dream, is it, Mother?'

Mrs. Patterson smiled so wide that her whole face glowed, and her eyes sparkled. She shook her head as she looked at Nia. "No, baby, it's not a dream. It's a dream come true!"

Nia felt her heart beating rapidly as they walked through the house. A door opposite the main entrance led to a powder room that had a marble sink and a mirror covering the entire wall above the sink. The light blue toilet matched the walls and flooring. They walked through the living room and dining room and then stood for a while in the elongated kitchen that ran the width of the house. Cherrywood cabinets with brass knobs surrounded the kitchen. A door leading to the backyard stood midway along the back wall. Next to it was a sink with a window above it. Two other doors were along the wall entering the kitchen, one lead to the basement, the other opened to a huge shelved closet. Excitement bubbled within them as they walked back toward the front of the house and went up the stairs, which were to the right of the front door.

Nia placed her hands over her mouth as they moved from room to room. There were three bedrooms and a bathroom on the second floor. She gasped and whispered, "Everything is so perfect."

"Yes it is," Mrs. Patterson said while nodding her head. "Now ... let's see how we're going to decorate our home."

They went back down the stairs. Nia followed her mother outside. They picked up their overnight luggage and a duffle bag that they had dropped outside in their excitement to enter the house. The duffle bag was full of paper plates, plastic cups, two small pots, a frying pan, a couple of utensils, and some canned and frozen food items. After wiping down the kitchen table, which the previous owner had left, they placed the items from the duffle bag onto the table, except for the perishable foods, which they put into the refrigerator.

Audrey Patterson's artistic talents, which had long been dormant, surfaced as she paced back and forth through the kitchen, dining room, and living room. She raised her arms as she loudly said while pointing in different areas of the rooms, "Mellow yellow, dazzling orange, brazen green, dancing red, pungent purple, brilliant blue."

Nia could feel the excitement in her mother as she looked at the walls, and she knew that her mother was making mental calculations of the dimensions of the rooms. Her mother went to a closet area under the stairs and pulled out paint cans. Nia rushed to help her. The previous owner had told them that there was paint in that closet. If they could use it, they could have it. Her mother had been quick to respond, "Yes we can use it."

Watching her mother now caused her to flash back to her childhood when suddenly her mother would get up from the couch where they'd been sitting together reading a storybook. She would go to the closet. Nia would hear her rumbling through the closet. Her mother would emerge with paintbrushes and buckets of paint and determinedly go up the stairs and into Nia's room. Nia would rush to keep pace with her. Her mother would push the teddy bears away from the wall. Next thing Nia knew, that wonderful animal that she had gotten excited about in the storybook would come alive on her bedroom wall.

"How does this sound? Beige for the walls in the living room with one wall, the main wall that the couch will likely sit in front of, having a foot-wide, mocha-brown strip running from the top left of the wall to the lower right bottom of that wall." Her mother's arm swung up to help show her design plan. Mrs. Patterson moved into the dining room. "Plum red for the walls in the dining room. Mellow yellow for the kitchen."

"Yes!" Nia's face beamed as she clasped her hands tightly together.

"Let's get to work!" Her mother's eyes sparkled.

Time escaped them as they rolled paint onto the walls. They laughed, sang, and even danced a step of two while painting. Nia worked on the higher areas that required a ladder. They had the radio on, and sometimes a song caused a momentary change of focus.

An oldie came on, and Mrs. Patterson said, "In my day, they did a step like this." She put the paint tray down. Modestly she took a step or two and swayed her body.

Nia could not contain her laughing. She was up on the ladder, but she wanted to hug her mother. "You're so much fun." A tear escaped from a corner of her eye because, for a second, she mourned the years she had missed the "fun" of her mother.

"Well, let me see what the young people are doing these days."

"Okay," said Nia. "When something comes on that I can relate to, I'll show you." Her mother shook her head as they resumed painting the wall.

A rough rap song bombarded the room. "Come on, Nia. It's your turn. Show me how the young people are doing it. Nia giggled and shrugged her shoulders. "I never danced to that type of music, Momma. I don't know how to dance to that."

"Oh, you just don't want to dance. Where's my strong daughter who's not afraid of anything?"

Nia got down off the ladder, turned the radio off, and rushed toward the area where they had put the overnight bags. She grabbed her computer and rapidly typed. Moments later, music invaded the room. Nia danced as she moved back toward her mother, pouncing with the beat, moving her arms and legs in unison ... to the right, to the left, twisting her waist. Even her elbows were up in the air.

Mrs. Patterson swayed toward her. "I can do that too!" She waved her arms and turned around. They laughed, and when the song ended, they fell into each other's arms.

"Now I'm out of wind," Mrs. Paterson huffed. "Anyway it's time for lunch."

Together they made sandwiches, giggling at nearly everything either of them said. Nia talked about her job. For a moment she felt she just wanted to sit, eat, and talk with her mother.

Mrs. Patterson put them back on task. "Come on now. Let's get back to work so we don't have to look at this job tomorrow." Her mother winked at her as she added, "Yes I know we accomplished a lot, but let's aim not to have painting to do tomorrow."

Nia's mouth opened in amazement and she stared at her mother because her mother had read her mind. She had just been thinking that they had done enough painting for the day and they could continue the following day.

As they worked, all sort of thoughts flowed through Nia's mind. She had Tonai to thank for this dream becoming a reality. Nia thought how Tonai acted more like a big sister because she looked out for her. Tonai had introduced her to a lady—a church sister was how Tonai referred to her—who was a teacher at an elementary school. The lady helped Nia through the application process for a position of attendance clerk at her school. That same week the principal called her in for an interview. She got the job!

It was Tonai who convinced Nia to enroll in a home-ownership seminar. Nia had never thought of a house as an investment. She learned that if she were to buy a home, when she was ready to sell the house, she could get back all the money she had put into the house. She also learned that, if she didn't want to sell it when she was ready to move, she could rent it and would have income coming in from the rental. So she began saving nearly every penny she made toward buying a house. It was a dream that she shared with her mother. Although it took nearly a year from the time she got her job, Nia and Mrs. Patterson were able to purchase a home.

Mrs. Patterson stopped her work. "Time for me to get dinner ready." She looked up at Nia. "You doing a good job, baby. Keep on painting." She went over to the bathroom and washed her hands.

Nia listened to the sounds of her mother moving about in the kitchen. She could hear the refrigerator door opening and her mother unwrapping the food that they had placed there hours earlier. She heard the sounds of her putting pots onto the stove.

The scent of her mother's cooking floated her back to the days of her early childhood when she would sit at the table and her mother would set a plate brimming over with food in front of her. Her mother would sit down, and they'd bow their heads in prayer as her mother would say the blessing. Then they'd eat, talking and laughing through their meal.

Early the next morning, light-brown carpeting was installed in the living room and dining room. They walked barefoot over it enjoying its softness while awaiting the delivery of their furniture. The bedroom furniture came first which they were happy about, figuring they could lay down and nap when they felt exhausted. Later the same day the furniture they'd picked out for the living room and dining room arrived.

They had the most fun decorating the main rooms. Adjacent to the two bay windows in the living room, they placed their new plum-red, soft-cushioned sofa. They positioned a matching lounge chair catercorner to the couch. They put bright-white end tables next to the sofa and chair. On top of the end tables, they placed large lamps with multi-colored globes. They hung a huge picture in a red, white and beige design on the wall opposite the couch.

An island theme was the focus of their dining room. A wicker table and chair set was placed in the middle of the room. Nia put a short black bureau along a wall and hung a picture over it. She put a large bamboo plant in one corner of the room. Together they painted the kitchen walls yellow, matching the refrigerator and stove, choosing a mellow shade of yellow to complement the brown cabinets. They hung two green plants over the kitchen window and placed a square table alongside the wall with a chair placed at each end. Each designed her own bedroom. The spare bedroom was made into a den.

The front lawn was small, but Nia thought that the bushes and flowers the previous owner had planted had the look of a celestial garden. The backyard was likewise small, but it was ringed with rosebushes. Immediately outside the back door there was a concrete patio area with a barbecue grill on it.

***

Just as her mother had predicted, Nia became interested in a young man who worked in the school office as a guidance counselor. His name was Winston. They often ate lunch at the same table with a few other workers. Several times Winston had asked Nia if he could take her out to dinner, but each time she had turned him down. Then, one Sunday, he showed up at her church and sat beside her. After the service, Nia introduced him to her mother, Tonai, Pastor Thompson, and some of the church members. He stayed for the meal following the service. Winston's visit to Nia's church changed the direction of their friendship. They began to sit together during lunch at school, and weather permitting, they walked outside, talking and laughing. Nia liked Winston's easy manner and humor.

***

"I love you, Nia." Winston had turned toward her as he looked at her. There was a kind smile in his bright eyes. They were sitting in a two-seater swing on his back porch. He put his arm around her shoulder. "I want to share my life with you."

Nia felt confused. Her head seemed to be slightly shaking from side to side as her mind echoed, *No!*

They had been at Winston's family's church earlier that day. She had met his parents, Mr. and Mrs. Kingston, his younger brother, and some of his relatives. After the service, his relatives had gathered around the pew where his parents sat. Winston's parents and younger brother had gotten up to greet their relatives, and they then stood in the aisle. Nia was still seated next to Winston. Uncles, aunts, and cousins approached with arms open wide, hugging Winston's mother, father, and younger brother. Some of them rocked back and forth while holding one another as they were embracing.

"I'm Aunt Simone," a voice jumped at her. "I'm Winston's favorite aunt."

"No you're not!" another woman's voice said, and the crowd laughed.

"And you must be Nia!" Aunt Simone exclaimed.

All their smiling eyes focused on her. She felt uncomfortable. Nia nodded and tried to smile.

"Well, you're pretty and sweet," Aunt Simone said as she bent down and hugged her. Winston stood up, and as he did so, he tapped her elbow. Nia stood up and stepped out into the aisle following Winston. All his family gathered around her and hugged her.

"Everyone's invited over!" Mrs. Kingston's voice rose above the crowd.

"You got food warming on the stove … greens, macaroni and cheese, sweet potatoes, and fried chicken?" Aunt Simone's voice hissed when she said "fried chicken."

"Actually, I do!"

"Well I believe I'm going to beat you home." Laugher burst through the group.

Nia looked at the faces of Winston's relatives as they sat around his dining room table. They were such a warm and loving family. And their laugher was contagious.

"Are you going to spoil Nia like you spoil your little brother?" Aunt Simone giggled as she looked at Winston. "You're going to be a poor man one day because your heart's so big. You know, Nia, Winston was an only child for a long time. Then when his little brother came along, you would think he was his father. He takes him everywhere. Buys him everything he wants."

At first Nia felt a little uncomfortable when they mentioned her name at the table, but she found herself laughing and flowing with the acceptance they extended to her. She watched how much they cared for one another.

Winston took her hand as he moved away from the table. They had finished eating and were listening to jokes and pretentious fussing. She was trying to take her plate up as well as Winston's, seeing his mother beginning to clear the table. But his mother came over to her with plates in her hand. "You stop that," she said. "You're my guest."

Nia put the plates down and followed Winston as he led her to their back porch. She followed his lead and sat next to him on the swing.

The afternoon air was so perfect; breezes flowed warmly over her arms. She watched two birds flying back and forth together. As she listened to their tweeting, she wondered if they had a language and talked with one another.

Winston's words—"I want to spend my life with you"—echoed in her head. Nia stiffened, and suddenly she felt smothered as if the air was thickening and closing in around her. She stood up. "I have to go. I got to get home. Can you take me home?"

Winston looked baffled. "Yes. Of course." He stood up and walked alongside Nia toward the driveway.

***

Nia began to avoiding Winston because the thought of being in a close relationship with a man frightened her. She really didn't want things to change. She and her mother were very close. She felt warm and protected around her mother. Nia would sit on the couch next to her mother as they watched television, and sometimes she'd lay her head on her mother's shoulder.

Tonai confronted Nia as they sat at the kitchen table in Nia's house. They were eating ice cream and talking about their jobs, the house, and church activities when, seemingly out of the clear blue, Tonai asked, "Why are you avoiding Winston?"

The early evening sun was shining brightly through the window over the sink, sending a slice of light across the floor and along a portion of the cabinets and making the cabinet knobs twinkle like gold nuggets. There was a calming mellow hue in the kitchen.

Nia shrugged her shoulders.

Tonai got up and she stooped down in front of Nia, whose head was bowed. She took Nia's hands. "You feel safe now. You're afraid of letting someone else in your life." She touched Nia's chin and lifted her face until Nia looked up at her. Softly she said, "But you know Jesus now. You can always lean on him. Winston has a good job. He has a career. And most important of all, he has faith in God."

"I can't," Nia said, shaking her head vigorously.

"You think you'll lose your mother?"

Nia simply stared at Tonai. Tonai went on. "Listen, I love you, Nia." She shook Nia's hands, which she was still holding. "We been knowing each other since we was kids. I listened to them therapists, even though it seemed like I wasn't. I kept their advice in the back of my head. You can't beat yourself up. You have to say you deserve good. You can't be afraid to move on."

Tonai stood up and walked two steps backward and sat back down in the chair. She took a huge spoonful of ice cream, and as she swallowed, she looked up at Nia. "I think that's why I found a way out. I mean, I might not have known it consciously, but when a way opened, I followed that path. It's the road that saved my life."

Nia had stopped eating, and her head was bowed once more. Her eyes watched the dimming of the sun's ray. She felt no desire to finish her ice cream.

"It's obvious that this man loves you, because he wants to marry you!" Tonai moved her own bowl aside. She reached across the table, grabbed Nia's bowl, and placed it where hers had been. She began eating Nia's ice cream.

Between her gulps she continued talking. "At least consider him, Nia. Can't you imagine that he had to pass up other girls to get to you? There's a black male shortage out there, in case you haven't noticed. He's an educated black man and handsome. And like I already said, he's a Christian man with values. He's not like a lot of these men out there who are nice till they get what they want from you, and then they toss you to the curb. He's not like the kind that'd string you along—constantly telling you he loves you and continually hurting you 'cause he won't do right. That type really love themselves, not their woman. Cousin, and my best friend, my baby sister, you need to recognize the hand of God in your life. God's given you a gift of a wonderful man. He's blessing you. It's like he's giving you back the intense love you need. Your mother likes Winston.

She's real okay with it, as any mother would be. Oh, you don't believe me? Well, let's ask her."

"No, no, no. You don't understand," Nia responded anxiously. She put her head down onto her arms, which were folded on the table. "You don't understand."

"What don't I understand, Nia? Tell me. Tell me. I'm listening. You know I'm a good listener." They were both quiet for a while.

"I don't think I can love like that," Nia finally said.

"That's not true, Nia. You love your mother. You love me." Tonai's eyes opened wide and she tilted her head. "Don't you love your cuz, Nia?"

"Yeah."

"So, what's up?"

"I don't feel no love for people I lived with as a child. I'm not sure I feel love for the Walkers, as good as they were to me. I feel appreciation toward them." Before she could realize what she was saying, she blurted out, "I tried to burn a house down!"

"That's all in the past, Nia. You were a hurt kid then. But that's not who you are now. You love your mother. And you loved Ty, Nia. All you told me about him, I know you loved him. Remember Ty, Nia? He was from that house."

Nia smiled, "Yeah."

"Well, that corrects that thought. You might not have felt love toward people who abused you, but if you search down inside, you'll find love there."

"I had no love for Grandma Vern. I didn't even go to her funeral."

"You a Christian now. Not only a Christian because you say you are, but by acting like a child of God." Tonai leaned toward Nia, and in a loud, forceful whisper said, "You got to forgive. You got to forgive your Grandma Vern and all them folks who hurt you."

Nia shook her head. Tonai lowered her voice and slowly said, "I agree with you, then, about the marriage. You right. You can't go into a marriage with bitterness and anger in your heart." Nia was shocked by Tonai's statement.

"You know I'm right, Nia. You got to set things right. You can't carry around anger, bitterness, or deception in your heart. You got to own up to the fact that Eva is your biological mother, and Tiffany is your cousin. Actually, if you don't forgive your family and accept them as your family, then you dismiss me, too, because you wouldn't be acknowledging me as your blood cousin."

Nia's eyes widened, and her mouth opened because of her surprise over Tonai's statement. She whispered, "No, Tonai. You my heart. I love you."

"You need to go to Eva and Tiffany and ask for their forgiveness," Tonai said staring at Nia.

"What! Why I gotta ask Tiffany for forgiveness? She's the one who treated me like dirt when I was a child and defenseless." Nia twisted her lips in annoyance and turned her head away from Tonai.

"Look at me, Nia," Tonai said in a low yet demanding voice. "Tiffany was only a child then. And haven't you given your life over to God? You do say that Jesus is Lord and Savior of your life, right? That means you will follow Jesus. You know Jesus was called the Prince of Peace. Following Jesus means giving up yourself—all the negative feelings you have, even feelings from being treated wrong. You supposed to take a servant's seat for the sake of peace. Jesus' signature is forgiveness. Remember what Jesus said, after they hanged him on the cross? Jesus said, 'Father, forgive them. They don't know what they're doing!'"

Tonai intensely looked at Nia as she nearly whispered, "Your people didn't really know what they was doing. They was selfish and mean, just like the people who crucified Jesus. They have to answer to God for that. But don't let the wrong way they acted be in you. If you really, really didn't like the way they were, don't be like them."

Tonai raised her voice, holding out her finger as if making a point, "But ... you do have to love them."

Nia looked up, not really seeing anything. But her ears were open because, deep in her insides, she knew Tonai was right.

Tonai's voice broke through her thoughts. "God tells us we're to love our enemies and pray for them, especially for those who spitefully used us. Why? Because if we pray for them to change from hatred and meanness to love, then we won't have enemies anymore. We wouldn't have people killing one another because they're offended or because people don't believe what they believe. Love makes people respect and honor other people." She paused. "Do you think Eva meant for all this to happen to you?"

Nia was startled, and her heart beat rapidly. She didn't respond.

"Actually, you even told me she was trying to keep you from the chaos of the family by placing you in foster care. She knew she was an addict and couldn't take care of you." Tonai lowered her voice. "That doesn't mean she didn't love you. I know you don't want to hear that because it makes things difficult. It seems like you got to choose mothers, but it's not like that. Nobody ever gave Eva credit for being smart. She has accepted you identifying with your mother, and she even helped you be with your mother as best she could. Nia, Eva loves you. It's time for you to reach out. You will be so relieved. It's easy to be bitter and angry. It's harder to go to people who you think hurt you and genuinely forgive them. But actually, if you really look deep into a person's past, you can usually understand his or her negative actions. When you understand, you can forgive them … and after you forgive them, you can help them."

Nia's mother had walked into the kitchen. Clearly, she had heard much of what Tonai had said. Walking with her cane, she moved slowly toward the refrigerator. "Free you heart, baby," she said. "It won't take nothing from us. We in this forever. You got to forgive them."

Nia stared at her mother. Then she put her hands over her face. "I don't know how. I don't want them in my life. The last time I was over there, Tiffany cursed me out. It was near the time of my graduation, and I felt like jumping on her. Imagine me going to jail and messing up my life over some dumb stuff. She's on drugs. I don't need that drama in my life."

"But addressing drama was what Jesus's life was all about!" Tonai exclaimed. "We're here to address the drama in people's lives. Just like other people have helped us, we have to reach out to others in need. We don't have to get caught up with them, but we have to help show them a way out."

Tonai was silent for a few moments before continuing. "I'll go over there with you. You can invite them to church. You know how people think of us as crazy Christians? Don't worry. They not gonna want to hang around you. The devil don't want to be around Christians. Be up front with them. Tell them you ain't giving them your address or phone number until they clean, 'cause you don't need their drama spilling over into your life. You tell them you'll have someone pick them up anytime they want to come to church, 'cause God is their way out. We need to try to bring them to Jesus. Who knows? Maybe all you've gone through was to save those people over there in that house!"

Nia's lips parted and her eyes widened. Tonia continued, "Talk to Winston. Tell him what you got to do. If he's the man we think he is, he'll wait for you."

Chapter 30 Eva's Death

Nia and Tonai walked up the steps to Grandma Vern's house in silence. As Nia knocked on the door, she noticed that it was newly painted. After waiting a few minutes, she turned around and looked at Tonai who was standing on the step below her. Tonai gave her a look and a head nod that told her that they weren't leaving and that she should knock again. She knocked. Nia noticed a slight movement of the curtain in the front window and a face peeking out. It was Tiffany.

The door slowly opened, and Tiffany and Nia stared at one another. Tiffany looked amazingly different than she had looked the last time Nia had visited her. She looked older and appeared to have matured, as she had a serious look on her face, a look Nia had never seen before. A small boy, about two years old, came out from behind Tiffany and grabbed hold of her pants.

"Is this your son?" Nia asked, staring at the child.

"Yeah."

"He looks just like Ty."

Tiffany smiled. "Everyone says that. That's why I named him Tytoo, and we call him Little Ty." Nia raised her arms toward Tiffany, and Tiffany raised hers. They embraced and held onto each other until Little Ty plopped down onto the floor at the foot of his mother and let out a cry. Tiffany let go of Nia, lifted him up, and rocked him in her arms. Nia wiped a tear from a corner of her eye. "Come on in," Tiffany said. She looked at Tonai and added, "Are you Aunt Sissy's daughter?"

"That would be me," Tonai said, grinning.

"You look just like Aunt Sissy," Tiffany said as she closed the door behind them.

As they walked into the living room and sat down, Tiffany said, "I'm clean. I had to clean up when I found out I was pregnant. I wasn't having no drug addict baby and have Child Welfare take my baby away from me." Quickly, she put her hand over her mouth. "Oh, I'm sorry, Nia. I didn't mean no offense."

"I'm fine," Nia responded. "That's all in the past." Then she blurted out, "I wanted to say I'm sorry how I acted all those years." Nia knew that if she had taken a moment to think about apologizing, she wouldn't apologize.

"You sorry?" Tiffany said, wide-eyed with surprise. "Oh, baby cousin … sister. You don't owe me no apology. I owe you an apology. I look at my son, and I think, *What if he gets taken away from me?* You know for our family that's real! Look at him on my lap now. He follows me all around the house. He always wants to be with me. If someone came and just snatched him from me, he'd go crazy, and so would I. We couldn't understand what was going on with you when you came to us. All we knew was you was sour and crying all the time, so we—no, I'm gonna say *I*, yes, *I*—rejected you. I'm owning up to my part. I treated you mean, Nia. I treated you like you wasn't even a person. You was right to turn your back on me the last time you was here. I was all messed up." Tiffany was silent a moment. Then she added, as she looked at her son, "I hope he's like Ty. I mean I hope he's like Ty except the drug and gang part. I hope he has a good heart, I guess is what I mean. I'm gonna try my best to raise him right."

"You look good Tiffany."

"Well, you remember when you last saw me. It wasn't me. The man I was with then got me strung out. I got a good man now. He's Tytoo's daddy. We gonna get married. He works. He got goals. He say we gonna move out of this neighborhood."

A heavy, choking cough came from the back room. "He lives here with you now?" Nia asked.

"Yeah. He's why the place is fixed up."

"The house does look a whole lot better," Nia commented.

"That's 'cause my man painted all the rooms. He been fixing up the kitchen. He do that kind of work. He's good with his hands." Tiffany turned toward Tonai. "So, what you doing these days, cousin? You have to excuse me. You my own cousin, and I hardly know you."

"Well, that's 'cause I wasn't raised at home, so you never seen me around."

"I seen pictures ..." Tiffany said.

Nia heard the cough again. She interrupted Tiffany and whispered, "Oh, your man works at night and sleeps during the day? I guess we disturbing him."

"No, he's at work. That's Aunt Eva coughing."

"How's she been doing?" Nia quickly asked.

"She ain't doing so good. She been in bed for three days now, coughing a lot, and she won't eat."

"I need to say something to her."

"She back there in Grandma Vern's old room."

Nia walked along the hallway and entered the bedroom. A dusty grayish hue hung over the room. Heavy, ceiling-to-floor, dark-green curtains covered the windows. Eva was under the covers, although the room was warm, almost hot. Nia looked at Eva's thin outline under the covers. She whispered, "Please God, deliver her from drugs. Please free her."

Nia turned to leave the room when she heard, "Is that you, Nia?" Nia turned around and stared at Eva. She didn't sound like herself. Her voice was raspy and labored. "I heard you a Christian."

Nia moved toward the bed. "Yes."

Eva struggled for a moment and finally managed to raise her body a little so that she supported herself on one elbow. Her entire body was trembling.

"I heard you doing real good." Eva coughed, and her cheeks ballooned out as if she was holding something in her mouth. She slowly reached over to get a cup from the nightstand, and she spat a thick glob of mucus into it.

Horrified, Nia put her hands over her mouth and gasped, "What's wrong with you?"

"Cancer. I got the cancer ... lung cancer. I only got a few months, a few weeks, a few days. Who knows?" Her body collapsed back onto the bed, and she took labored breaths. "They tell me something different every time I go." She sighed. "I ain't told Tiffany. She doing good. I don't want to worry her. She think I got pneumonia. She keep trying to get me to go to the hospital. I tell her I ain't going. She don't know I been to the doctor. He told me what's up. He wanted me to go through chemotherapy and all kind of treatment. I told him I already been through enough hell on earth and walked out his office." Out of breath, Eva laid her head back down on the bed. She took several long, deep gasps, than whispered, "God answered my prayers."

Nia stared at her. She couldn't imagine Eva talking to God. Eva's frail hand reached toward her, and she patted the bed. Nia sat down on the bed.

Eva raised her head. "I asked God to bring you around to see me." She wheezed then continued. "I know it's hard on you to come here." She put her head back on the pillow and closed her eyes. She struggled to turn her body. Then she reached under her pillow with one hand. Even though she seemed barely able to breathe, and her hand was shaking, she kept reaching for something under the pillow.

"I'll get it for you." Nia thrust her hand under the pillow and pulled out a wrinkled envelope.

Eva lay back, breathing with short, uneven breaths. "Give it to Uncle Isaiah."

"Uncle Isaiah is still alive?"

Eva kept her eyes closed and said nothing.

"Where would I find him?"

"Ask Aunt Sissy," Eva whispered. The conversation exhausted her as she began taking short, quick breaths as if trying to catch hold of air. Moments after her breathing calmed, she opened her eyes and strained to raise her head again. In a small, scratchy voice she said, "Don't discuss it with no one. Put it in your pocket now." Eva's face crumpled, and she winced as if she was in extreme pain. Then her head fell back onto the pillow. She looked at Nia steadily and then whispered, "I want to ask you to forgive me. I didn't know no better."

Nia's eyes flooded with tears. Before she could think, she cried out, "Mother, please forgive me for not honoring you as my mother. I didn't know no better either." Nia put her arms over her mother's body as she laid her head on her chest. "Thank you for life," she whispered.

Eva gently placed her hand on Nia's head. She then let out a rough cough, and Nia felt her mother's body collapse. Nia raised her head and stared at her. Her coloring had changed to a dark, smoky gray. Nia jumped up and screamed, "Tiffany!"

Tiffany and Tonai came running into the room. Tonai rushed toward Eva, seized her by her shoulders, and shook her violently. She yelled, "Eva. Eva! Eva!" Eva opened her eyes as Tonai screamed at her, "Do you accept Jesus Christ as Lord and Savior of your life?" Tonai continued to shake her as she shouted in Eva's ear, "Do you acknowledge Jesus as dying for your sins?" Eva nodded as a breath escaped her lips, "Ye ..." But before she could finish, her lips stopped moving and her eyes fixed on the ceiling. Nia screamed. Tiffany ran to the phone and dialed 911.

Tonai closed Eva's eyes and straightened the bedcovers. She turned toward Nia, who stood trembling. Tonai put her arm around Nia as she guided her out of the bedroom and into the living room. She moved a pillow off an armchair and sat Nia in the chair. Tonai sat on the arm of the chair consoling Nia as they waited for the paramedics to arrive.

Tytoo was shrieking from all the commotion, and Tiffany could not focus on attending to him. She held him in her arms as she talked with the paramedics when they arrived. Nia kept her eyes closed as Tiffany answered questions and signed papers. The men went back to Eva's room and moved her body onto a stretcher. Tonai gently put her hands over Nia's eyes as the men carried Eva's covered body past them. When the men stepped outside the house, Nia, Tonai, and Tiffany ran to the doorway. Nia felt as if a hole was being dug out of her heart as she watched the paramedics place Eva's body into the ambulance. The men slammed the doors and drove off.

Solemnly the three women went back into the house and sat in the living room. Tears gushed from Nia's eyes, and she couldn't quiet the sound of her pain. Eva's dying seemed unreal to her. Eva was supposed to be around forever, always messing up, but always around. Nia was suddenly hit with the realization that she had loved her natural mother.

Tiffany stared blankly, as if in shock. Though her son tried to climb into her lap, she did not respond. Tears trickled out of her eyes.

Tonai finally broke the silence. Softly she asked, "Tiffany, do you know of a funeral home so we can begin making arrangements? Tiffany. Tiffany. Tiffany!"

Tiffany turned her head toward Tonai. Through her tears, she whispered, "What?"

"Do you know of a funeral home so we can begin to make arrangements?"

"Yeah. The one that buried Grandma Vern. They worked with us, 'cause we didn't have all the money up front."

"Did she have insurance?" Tonai pressed. When Tiffany looked blankly at her, Tonai quickly added, "You just tell us what you want us to do. If you feel comfortable making arrangements, just tell us who to pay. We both working. We know you good at negotiating things, and you look out for family."

***

It was a small, quiet funeral held in the parlor of the funeral home. Only three cars made up the funeral procession. One was Winston's. Nia, Mrs. Patterson, Aunt Sissy, and Tonai rode with Winston.

"She's gone to heaven," Tonai whispered as they stared at the casket.

Nia realized that her face must have revealed her surprise because Tonai exclaimed, "Oh, you can't judge anyone. Only God knows the whole story of a person. He's big on people's hearts being in the right place even if their lives are a mess. Remember we covered her with the prayer of salvation. She confessed her belief with her dying breath." Tonai smiled broadly. "She's in."

Nia wasn't even sure if Tonai was talking to her; it was almost as if she was talking to herself. Tonai continued, "Yeah, she made a mess of the life given to her. She wasted it. But she's now spending eternity in the land within the pearly gates of heaven. Hey, she's happy now."

An old man whom Nia didn't recognize was at the burial. He was dark and tall, with two deep lines on each side of his face. He was slightly stooped and walked slowly with a cane. Just before the coffin was lowered into the ground, he pushed some dirt onto the coffin with his cane. He mumbled something Nia couldn't quite make out, then he slowly turned and made his way from the burial ground. Nia stood staring at the casket after everyone began walking away.

Tonai tapped Nia's arm. "There's Uncle Isaiah. Come on! We got to catch up with him before he leaves."

Nia rushed alongside Tonai. Aunt Sissy was up ahead, walking and talking with Uncle Isaiah. As she and Tonai caught up with them, Nia sensed that there was something very unusual about him. He looked like everything there was to know about life was in him.

As they reached the hearse, Nia watched Uncle Isaiah position himself to get into the passenger side of the front seat. Tiffany and her son were already in the backseat. As he pushed back onto the seat, one hand on his cane, the other holding the dashboard, Aunt Sissy said to him, "This is Nia, Uncle Isaiah. She's Eva's daughter."

The old man stopped his efforts. He leaned forward on his cane, his legs still planted on the ground. He examined Nia for a moment before speaking. Then he said, "Yes. I remember you. You was a fussy baby. 'Course, you couldn't too much help it. Look like the Lord blessed you anyhow. What you want?"

His abrupt question startled Nia. She opened her pocketbook. She stared at the envelope inside for a quick moment and then took it out. She felt uncomfortable because Uncle Isaiah seemed so distant. As she handed it to him, she said, "Miss Eva, when she was dying, told me to give this to you."

"Miss Eva! That was your mommy girl! She was a good lady. My favorite niece … real sweet … do anything for anybody … give you the shirt off her back if you asked for it." His voice rose a bit. "She just couldn't get loose from them drug demons that had hold of her. But she free now." He put the envelope into the breast pocket inside his jacket and then sat back into the car. He slowly moved one leg and than the other into the car and placed his cane between them. "I'll let you know," he said as he grabbed the door handle and shut the door.

Chapter 31 The Deed

Uncle Isaiah was just as Nia had imagined him when she had listened to stories about him told by Grandma Vern and Aunt Sissy. Somehow he was bigger than life even at his great age. Aunt Sissy and Tonai brought him over to her house. He entered not looking to the left or to the right, unlike most people who would turn their heads as they walked while complimenting she and her mother on the job they had done decorating the house. Uncle Isaiah acted as if he was familiar with the floor plan of the house, because he walked right to the kitchen, sat in a chair that leaned against the wall, took his hat off, and hooked it on the corner of his chair. His sat erect, holding his cane in front of him. They took seats around him at the table – Mrs. Patterson, Nia and Tonai. Aunt Sissy sat a short distance from him in a chair Tonai had quickly dragged from the dining room when Aunt Sissy had entered the kitchen.

Immediately he began talking. His voice was amazingly strong, deep and unwavering. His entire manner drew them in. They looked like they were in a trance listening to him. "I stood up the whole time of the inauguration. I stood at attention, old as I am. I stood up the whole time. I believe, if the good Lord kept me this far, it was to see this great happening. I was there two days ahead of time so I could be right up front. Oh, there was a lot of people out there too, sitting on grass, sitting on concrete. Crowds kept wavering in, but I stood my ground. I had my bag on my shoulder with my water bottles, sunglasses, and wind jacket. Oh, I know how to travel. I stood in the first line to see with my own eyes the election of a black man as president of the United States. I had to see it. You all don't know what it was like when I was young. Why, down South they could take a black man and string him up to a tree if they felt so inclined to do so. There was no real investigation. Black man's life wasn't worth nothing back then. As you know, I got beat real bad 'cause they thought I might be smarter than them. I was just a kid."

Uncle Isaiah shook himself as if moving away from horrid memories. "After I got healed, I moved up North. No one thought I'd ever go back. I went back. I joined up with a group of men and women who worked to fight bigotry. When we'd get the word that someone was in trouble, we'd go down there. We'd bring that person out under the cover of night. Sometimes we'd bring whole families out. Of course, there were things we did in the open, like protest segregation. We'd march, and we'd picket. Sorry to say, there was many died for the cause. Mean, horrid deaths. God rest their souls."

An eerie silence overshadowed the room. Sissy broke the silence. "Well, Daddy I., we always heard about how you a real hero. You never got caught 'cause you been doing civil rights work for a long time."

Nia realized that she must have looked confused, because Sissy added, "That's what we call our Great Uncle Isaiah, Granddaddy I., or, just Daddy I. for short. The *I* stands for Isaiah. We call him that 'cause he done outlived everybody, and he looks out for all of us."

Uncle Isaiah hiked up his shoulders as he raised his voice: "Oh, I got caught a few times.

But I'd remember how they tied my arms around that tree and beat me senseless. Then I'd get a mighty strength."

He became still. His eyes widened and stared into the distance. Everyone knew he was reliving a scene: "When I got caught, it was usually one or two who snuck up on me, 'cause you can hear a group coming. I knew I had to shut them up before they called to their troops. It's only the Lord that strengthened me. I fought for my life and for the lives of the folks I was trying to help.

"It was me or them. But generally, when a few men were coming, I'd know 'cause somebody gonna mess up. You hear a tree branch snap. Or you might hear crackling because one of them steps on leaves. Now with a group, they all fired up, so they can't be quiet. But the secret to survival is you got to stay calm. Staying calm, so you can think clear, that's how you don't get caught. I mean, a few freedom fighters did get caught. I know sometimes there's strange happenstance. But for me, I think what worked was staying calm like nothing was happening, so I didn't panic and make a dumb decision. Then, too, I had a praying mother.

"There'd been times me and another freedom fighter, or sometimes a whole family, be in a hole in the ground underneath a cabin, and they be standing right on top of us. We would leave the back door open and drop a jacket on the ground so it'd look like we was running. They'd run out the back door. The rest of the group would be too fired up to think, so they'd go rushing behind them. They didn't know the woods like we did. And don't think we let them dogs sniff us out. We'd sprinkle red pepper around the cabin. Them dogs would start sneezing, and their noses would be burning so they'd start yapping, and that was that. Them men would tie them up somewhere and move on. And I got better as time went on, so we wouldn't get discovered helping someone. See, we didn't want to hurt nobody, 'cause if we hurt one of their men, all the black folks in the town would be in danger."

Uncle Isaiah's voice became deeper. His eyes squinted, and his face looked intense. And the eyes of everyone in the room were glued to him. "See, we knew if we hurt them men and then left that town, white men would take revenge on any 'nigger,' as they called us. And they'd string somebody up and leave him dangling from a tree. So we tried our best to be careful no one got hurt. There was one time we came real close to getting caught. We had almost half the black folks who still lived on an abandoned plantation with us. There was twelve of us hiding in a trench made from a tree falling down over a ditch. They was right above us, and a baby waked up and let out a cry. Men was standing right above us. Jimmy put his hand over the baby's mouth and, sad to say, we all knew we'd have to smother the baby right in front of his mama and daddy and sister. It'd be the baby, or all of us including the baby. They was on a nigger hunt. They'd drag our bodies behind their vehicles for all the other black folks to see what happens to niggers who help someone who they say committed a crime. It wasn't no crime committed, just race hatred acting against us! But you know a mother's instinct to save her young-un. In a split of a second she put her breast over her baby's mouth, and the baby started sucking. The men on top say, 'What was that?' And one of them say, 'It sound like a mountain cat.' Then another one said, with his voice shaking, 'We lookin' for niggers, and lions looking at us, and they's hungry. They's sneaking up on us from down in the ravine. You know they strike fast.' Someone else said, 'We better get out of here.' So they left out from there running and

293

scared. I say it was the hand of God looking out for us. So now my life has come full course when I stood and watched a black man being sworn in as president of the United States."

He took a breath and looked over at Nia. "But I came here to see you, Nia, because the letter you gave me is really for you. I think your mother, Ms. Eva, knew that I would see to it that things were in place the way she wanted them to be in her will."

Isaiah smiled, and his face relaxed. His voice softened. He looked reflective as if he was talking to himself. Suddenly he looked at Nia. Nia felt frightened for a moment. Tonia got up and turned on the kitchen light, as the dusk of evening had moved in. Uncle Isaiah shook his head. His whole body seemed to breathe out. He whispered, "Eva was my favorite of all the babies I seen come into this world. She was the prettiest baby. She had big, dark-brown eyes that sparkled; small, ruby-red, heart-shaped lips; and a little button nose. She had the puffiest rosy cheeks I ever seen. You wanted to squeeze them cheeks. And that's exactly what everybody did. She had soft black curls that swept all around her chocolate-brown face. Her body was round and plump. She smiled and giggled all the time. You just wanted to hold her and hug her. I think that was what was wrong. Everybody was always holding her. So everybody had a hand in spoiling her. That is, everybody except her mama. Now her mama's ways is what I believe caused the big clash in their personalities."

Uncle Isaiah shook his head as lines burrowed into his forehead. His voice became rough, "Her mama—your Grandma Vern—was heartless. I'm gonna say it: hateful as snake's venom. She got it from her momma. I told Amos not to marry Ellie. All he could see was how fine looking she was." Isaiah shook his head and looked sorrowful for a few moments. "My brother died young. He couldn't keep up with what she wanted. No! You can't go by looks. But that was all he was going by, and that was all he got! I'm telling you young people, you can't just stop with the outside. You got to look deep inside a person you planning on marrying. She worked him to death. Forty-one years old, and went to his grave leaving twelve children fatherless! He didn't listen to me. See, my mama didn't raise no fool. I ain't never married 'cause of what I seen and heard, and I couldn't afford to be slowed down because of the mission I was on. I almost got snagged by the marriage trap once when I was young and my hormones was racing in me. This good-looking, finely shaped, sweet gal was determined to hook me in. I was young, but I was strong, and I left town."

Tonai giggled. Nia smiled. Isaiah continued: "Amos's wife died young, too, and not too long after him. I guess she died from bad nerves. She couldn't handle being poor, having all them kids, and then no husband 'cause she ran him to the grave. She couldn't see no way out. So she died. They say she used to beat them kids something terrible. So that's how your Grandma Vern got off to a bad start. Many of Amos and Ellie's kids didn't do so good, the boys mostly. They come north to the big city, ended up selling drugs or on drugs. Most of them died before they reached thirty. The ones still alive is in and out of prison. I guess if Amos could have looked into a looking glass and seen all this havoc passing down through his heritage, he would have never married Ellie. You young girls, listen to your old Daddy I., as Sissy's generation calls me. Don't up and marry no man in a hurry. Be around him for a while. See how he acts around his mother. Do he get impatient with her or do he treat her like she's a queen? How does he act with his money? Is he smart and saves some of his money, or does he spend it all as soon as he gets it? And when he spends, does he share or does he spend it all on himself? In fact, most important, does he have a good heart? You don't want no sour ball. Oh, you better watch these things. What's in place and not in place is what you get. Actually, truth be told, having children, bills, and responsibility will bring out a person's true colors.

"But Eva, she had a good heart. She was the opposite of her mother. That's why they clashed so much. Eva would give you the coat off her back if you asked her for it. She was always giving away stuff. That's another way she got into trouble with her mother. Her mother would see her coming down the street—no coat. She'd go into the house and get her strap, be waiting at the door. 'Where's your coat, Eva?' Then Eva would say as a matter of fact, 'This girl didn't have no coat. She just had a sweater on. So I gave her mine. She said she'll give it back to me when her mother buys her one.' Whew! She'd get beat from the outside steps on into the house. Even neighbors would be banging on the door to tell her to stop whipping the child. It couldn't seem to register with Eva what her mother meant by, 'I bought that coat for you, and you costing me more money 'cause I gotta buy you another coat.'

"I remember once some white racist men had tracked us up here to New York City. See, we had made three consecutive trips down to the same town. They was vicious in that town. They hated black folks. And they especially hated us 'cause we was rescuing families."

Tonai interrupted Isaiah, "Uncle Isaiah, where would all these people you'd bring up here live?"

"We'd double them up. In them days, people wasn't selfish. Two families would live together till they got on their feet. All it took is the man getting a job, 'cause it didn't cost so much like now to get a place. Then, too, we had people working with us who had influence. They would put some families we brought up North into the projects, or sometimes they put them up in hotels.

"But that time when them men was on my trail, I didn't want to put my mother and my sister in jeopardy, so I came to Vern's house. I knew sure enough them men wasn't coming into no black ghetto, 'cause they knew they'd be the ones to get lynched. Vern answered the door. She said, 'No!' flat outright and slammed the door in my face. We stood there a moment and then started back down the steps. I heard, 'Psst, psst!' from a side window. I turned around and saw this little hand motioning me to come to the back door. The lights throughout the house were out, but Eva opened up the back door. 'You can come stay in my room, Uncle Isaiah,' she whispered. I said, 'Oh, no, honey. I don't want to get you in trouble.' I could barely hear her when she said, 'There's no one else in my room. They all gone down South. Aunt Ester came and took them down South with her for a few weeks. Mommy went in her room and closed the door. She ain't gonna get up because she been drinking.'

"Eva was about fourteen then. We followed her through the kitchen, and we went into her room. We stayed there three days. I said she's my little angel. She snuck and brought us food. She stayed out in the living room at night reading a book or doing homework till she fell off to sleep on the living room floor. Vern was in her room drunk. I don't think her mother ever found out. In fact, I know she didn't, 'cause we would have heard how bad she beat the child."

Isaiah shook his head and then nodded. Everyone nodded with him. "I never forgot that. After that I made sure I always sent her something for her birthday, even if it was just a card with a dollar in it. It didn't sit well with me that she would defy her mother, but I was running for my life."

All the listeners in the room seemed mystified as they envisioned the scenarios Uncle Isaiah presented. Their bodies heaved in as they saw Uncle Isaiah's wind seemed to leave him and his face draw down as if great pain had hit him. Slowly he shook his head. It was as if he was crying ... inside. His voice was slightly muffled when he spoke, "I told Eva when we was leaving, Baby, I know things is rough for you, but please be careful. Listen to your mother. Also, don't do everything everybody wants 'cause it might hurt you.' I didn't know how else to help her. Maybe it was just too late because of the mess she was born into."

The room was quiet. Isaiah went on, "Eva got caught up in things real young. Ran off with some boy, and next thing she was on drugs and pregnant." He looked up at Nia, "One good thing she did, she didn't have no more children. Oh, I don't mean no offense, baby. I mean, she knew she couldn't take care of children, so I think she got her tubes tied or something. At least that's what I heard."

Uncle Isaiah cleared his throat. "Well here." He handed Nia an envelope that he had placed on the table when he first sat down. "This is really for you."

Nia opened the envelope, pulled out the neatly folded paper, and slowly unfolded it. She had expected a personal letter, but she could see that it was some kind of legal document. Nia felt her heart flutter. Isaiah put his slender, firm hand on her arm. "Your mother left the house and everything in it—all her belongings—to you, Nia. The house is already recorded in your name."

It was as if everyone in the room was paralyzed. Finally, Nia said in a voice barely above a whisper, "Tiffany lives in that house."

Isaiah shook his head. "You own the house!" He turned toward Mrs. Patterson and said, "I have enjoyed meeting you, madam. Sissy, I'm ready to go." Uncle Isaiah got up, put his hat on, and grabbed his cane, which was leaning against the table. Sissy stood up and kissed everyone, and she and Isaiah left the house.

Nia was still staring at the letter when the door closed behind Isaiah and Sissy. Tonai jumped up and screamed, "Hallelujah! As the Bible says, Satan meant it for bad, but God turned it into good!"

Nia's hand began to tremble as she held the paper. She let go of the paper and let out a loud cry. Mrs. Patterson gently put her arms around her and drew her close to her as she said, "It's all right, baby." Nia wept as she pressed her face against her mother's body. She looked over at Tonai, who had an intense, questioning look on her face. Finally, through her sobbing, Nia said softly, "I tried to burn that house down!"

Mrs. Patterson began to rub Nia's back as she softly said, "Sometimes we don't understand everything going on around us, and things seem out of control. We feel like a little ant that has no voice, and we feel snuffed out. That's what happened to you, baby ... and to me."

Tonai ran to get a box of tissues and gave them to Nia. Nia blew her nose. Tonai than got a wastebasket and placed it on the floor in front of

Nia. Mrs. Patterson lowered her head and murmured in Nia's ear. "Now I can see what the Bible means by 'Wait on the Lord.'" She looked directly into Nia's eyes. "To you, I was your mother. You never accepted anyone else filling in that place, not even your real mother. So you could never see the love she had for you, even if she didn't really know how to show it. The little she had to give, she gave to you. And all she had when she left this world, she left to you. She loved you, baby."

Nia blew her nose again and wiped her eyes. "I'm calling Tiffany," she said. "I'm gonna tell her about the will." Nia blew her nose again. "And ... and I'm gonna let her have the house."

Mrs. Patterson beamed, and hugged her. "I'm proud of you, Nia."

"No!" Tonai shouted. "You know she's gonna sell it. She told us her man's looking for a place in a better neighborhood. It could be you who sells it and keeps the profits."

"If she sells it, she sells it," Nia replied. "But I'm not gonna put her and her family out of the only home she ever knew. Tiffany's been in that house since she was born. I'm not gonna do that to her, and I could never charge her rent. I know what you're thinking, Tonai. If the situation was reversed, and I was in the house, she would sell it out from under me. But I'm not reacting to who she is. I got to react to who I say I am. Thanks to you both, I'm okay. I'm gonna make it. She needs the help. Besides, I'm not playing into any demonic family curses. Is that how you say it, Tonai? I want to be free from all that manipulation that's been a part of that ... part of my family. Giving, not taking, is a way to be free."

"You go, girl!" Tonai shouted exuberantly. Mrs. Patterson kissed Nia's forehead.

Chapter 32 Premarital Counseling

Winston and Nia went to Pastor Thompson to schedule their wedding. The pastor informed them that he would not sign a marriage certificate without premarital counseling. Looking directly at them, he flatly said, "Love ain't enough to sustain a marriage. There's too much unexpected drama. And if you come with baggage, it's even harder because all that baggage gets unloaded into the marriage. A marriage can make love turn sour because most people getting married don't have real love. They love the pretty face, the shapely body, the money their partner has, and so on. Real love gives ... not takes! You see, we're mostly a selfish society. It's me ... me ... me! You have to forget about it being all about you once you're married. You need to be able to share simply because you now share everything, even space in a house."

The Pastor's words sunk deep inside of Nia. She knew in her heart that she had a fear of marriage. That was why she had run when Winston had first told her he wanted to marry her. She had seen nothing but tragedy in marriages in her family. And she knew that life throws curve balls. But the phrase the pastor used—"unexpected drama"—sent a flicker of fear through her mind. What dramas would she and Winston have to go through?

Nia took a quick look at Winston. She wondered if he was strong enough to make her feel safe. Could he stand up and protect her from whoever or whatever tried to knock her down? He'd had such a sheltered upbringing—a happy childhood, completely different from hers. His father and mother were still together. He had only one brother, who was seven years younger than he was. He had been happy during all the years that had been tragic for her.

The pastor's booming voice commanded Nia's attention. "When you young, and so, so, in love, you can't even begin to understand the real deal with marriage. Oh, it starts with the pretty part—the hugging and cuddling and the sex. Believe it or not, that quickly takes a backseat to other things going on in the marriage. The things that come at you, once you're married, are so rough that nearly half of all marriages don't make it. It might be even more than half now."

Nia shivered. Winston rubbed her arm as if to warm her up. Nia nodded, letting Winston know she was okay. She knew she shivered from the pastor's words slicing her consciousness. *Was she able to really be a godly wife? Could she be a helpmate to her husband as the Bible dictated? Or, would she pull this happy man, who always had only love in his life, down?*

She could see the pastor's lips moving. Then her ears began to focus on his words. "Marriage needs to be able to get through things like the illness of a child, the loss of a job, the serious illness of a partner. Don't pledge to marry if you can't be there for each other when the storms hit. Trust me, there will be storms! I'm a pastor, and I'm married to the same woman for nearly thirty years—twenty-eight and a half years to be exact. There were times life hit us so hard. I'm telling you, the hit was so hard that even I, with my position as pastor, which I've had nearly as long as I've been married, looked at my wife and I thought, *I can't take this no more.* There'd been times we both looked at each other, and our eyes were saying, 'This ain't gonna work.'"

The pastor suddenly stopped talking. He placed his hand to his chin. It felt odd and uncomfortable to have no sound in the room with the pastor. Nia looked around at his office. It was paneled all around. It was a comfortable size ... not like those mega millionaire preachers who had more like an office suite with a bathroom and small den attached to their office. And those rich preachers' actual offices were more like living rooms with couches and lounge chairs opposite their desks. But Pastor Thompson's office was humble—just a normal-sized desk, wood floors, and two comfortable office-type chairs opposite his desk.

"Children, what I'm trying to explain to you is that marriage is a job." Nia's thoughts stilled as the pastor's voice rolled back into the atmosphere. "You got to make up in your mind that you won't abandon the marriage.

You got to think of your marriage as God's arrangement. God arranged your natural families. Messed up as some of our own kinfolk can be, and as mad as we can get at them, we don't abandon them. They're forever our sisters and brothers, cousins, whatever. Marriage needs to incorporate that binding tie. No matter what, it stays in place, with, of course, the exception of extreme things like abuse. But see, those marriages should have never happened. But just think of how different the world would be if partners didn't give up and abandon marriage. Think of how truly selfish it is for a partner to walk out of a marriage, particularly when children are involved. It's extremely hurtful to the children because children love mommy and daddy unconditionally."

Pastor Thompson's voice softened. He rubbed his chin as he looked at them. "First of all," he said, "marriage has to start out on some common ground. You two do have a starting ground. You both share the same faith. You both are active in the same church. You both have good jobs. That's good ground. Do you both believe in saving money? You got to save to cover yourself for six months or even a year because one of them hardballs that can hit you is loss of income. Don't think that, because you have a job, everything is set in steel. In a moment's time, you can lose your income. You go to work one day and your boss calls you into his office and tells you he can't use you no more. Oh, he might say that the company is shutting down your department or reducing personnel. Same thing!"

Pastor Thompson smiled at them. "You both too young to have gone through real hard-hitting storms." His face turned serious as he added, "Unless your family had a bad crisis."

"I been through storms, Pastor." Nia's voice trembled as she told him about growing up in foster care. She was surprised at how her voice caught when she mentioned her mother's drug addiction, and an image of Eva, smiling and radiant, floated gently through her mind. She was even more surprised at her desire to follow that image.

The pastor was quiet after Nia had spoken about her past, unable to keep the hurt and defiance from her voice as she told him about her grandmother's abusiveness. When he began speaking, he spoke slowly, carefully selecting his words. "If you've been in foster care, young lady, then you have to work very hard not to follow ways that your family had that caused you to be placed into foster care. You have to make sure all that anger built up in you, which is a natural consequence of children who experienced what you been through, is gone! You have to work to gain good parenting skills."

301

Pastor Thompson stared at Nia for a few moments and then added, "Nia, you have a special mission from God. It's between you and God what that is." He shook his head. "Nobody who is a child of God coming from your past can escape using that background for ministry. It may not be now; it may be ten, twenty, or thirty years from now." The pastor looked sternly at them knitting his eyebrows together. His eyes burrowed deep into Nia's. "You have a special assignment waiting for you. But for now, young lady, I need to know that all that bitterness, which is a natural result of your experience, is out of you and will not be transferred into this new family you and Winston are intent on beginning. I need to know that you will not mistreat or abandon your children."

Nia's heart pounded so hard that for a moment she thought that it would burst through her chest. "No, Pastor, I could never do that!" she responded with tears welling up in her eyes.

Pastor Thompson looked at her calmly and said, "Yes, this is hardcore. You came from chaos. The only one who could fix you is Jesus. He is the repairer of hearts." Then he looked at Winston and asked, "Were you aware of her background?"

"Yes, sir, she told me."

Pastor Thompson looked at Nia again. "That's good, daughter. But I need you to do something that might be the hardest thing you have ever done. I need you to go to your biological mother and tell her you love her. Can you do that?"

"My mother passed about two months ago, Pastor. I sat on her bed. I didn't know she was dying. I put my arms around her and thanked her for giving me life."

The pastor handed Winston a box of tissues, and Winston held the box out in front of Nia, who kept taking tissues to blow her nose and wipe her eyes.

"My daughter, you have forgiven your mother. But make sure your heart is free from all bitterness related to your past. I want you both in here undergoing counseling until I'm convinced you're both ready for marriage. I want to see you for at least six sessions. I'll determine whether you need more after that. I will not marry you until I'm convinced that you have enough faith coming into the marriage, and that you have true love, which means you love the other person as much as you love yourself. When imperfections begin to surface in either of you, and they will, I need to be convinced that each of you is able to love the other person past his or her faults and shortcomings. And, of course, I need to hear the Holy Spirit tell me you both are ready for marriage. That's when I'll marry you."

The pastor looked at his calendar. "Saturdays I'm booked with meetings, and Sundays I'm here trying to teach you folks something. Monday is Bible study. How's Tuesdays at six in the evening?"

Both Winston and Nia quickly nodded. He placed their names on his calendar at that time for six consecutive Tuesdays. Pastor Thompson got up and stood in front of them. "Well then, I'll see you two next week to begin our sessions."

***

Pastor Thompson was a good-looking man. He was tall and had a deep-brown complexion; shiny, black hair with a crunchy-curled texture; thick eyebrows; and a thick, black mustache that matched his hair. His eyes were so powerful they seemed to burrow right through a person. Sometimes a woman mistook his staring at her for lasciviousness, and she'd walk toward him with an inappropriate intent, generally at the altar-calling part of the service. But Pastor Thompson was a true man of God. He could see faultiness in a person's heart, and he'd expose the woman's intent no matter how pretty or innocent-looking the woman was. He'd raise his hand dramatically, then bring it down and point at the woman. In a commanding voice, he'd say, "Come out, you foul demons of lust and manipulation! I say, in the name of Jesus, release this woman and let her go!" The woman would go limp and fall backward into the arms of deacons, who would have positioned themselves behind her. They would ease her to the floor. Usherettes would be quick to place a silk sheet over whatever area needed to be covered so that the woman would not be indecently exposed as she lay on the floor. When she began to get up, ushers would immediately lift her up off the floor. They'd hand her tissues, which she'd use to pat her eyes as she was guided back to her seat. There had been times when Pastor Thompson commanded the devil out of a lady who had such a sweet disposition and innocent look about her that Nia would feel bad for the woman. She shared her concern with Winston. Speaking calmly and confidently, Winston had responded, "He's been a pastor a long time, and he's a serious man of God. He has the gift to discern spirits."

Regardless of whether Nia agreed with Pastor Thompson's methods, she had to admit that no one ever questioned his intentions. Pastor Thompson would say he had been called by the Lord to be a pastor. He'd tell his congregation that he was God's servant, and therefore he did everything in "fear and trembling" under the watchful eyes of God. So Pastor Thompson took his calling seriously and didn't stand for any foolishness from his congregation. If he knew someone was messing up, he would approach that person and extend himself any way he could to help that person get back on the right path. He'd tell the congregation, even from the pulpit, "We getting one shot with our time here on earth. The enemy of our soul wants to make us blow it. My job is to help you understand how to be strong, walk like Jesus, and therefore have victory over the devil, the enemy of your soul."

Nia thought about the pastor's strong words about forgiveness as she rode in the car with Winston. She thought about Tiffany. Tiffany had never even called her after they had met to transfer ownership of the home. She had seemed nervous and kept yelling at her son during the meeting. Months after the deed transfer, Uncle Isaiah had told Sissy who relayed it to Tonai who told Nia, that Tiffany's boyfriend had left her because she had started getting uppity and putting pressure on him to get new furniture and remodel the outside of the house.

"What for?" he had responded. "We're moving out of this neighborhood! We'll be selling the house and moving into a better neighborhood. I don't want our children to be raised up in this neighborhood with boys selling drugs on every corner."

"This is my house!" Tiffany had told him. "And it's paid for! Why would I want to sell it and have to make payments on another house? Wherever you thinking to move is gonna cost us something."

Tonai told Nia that Uncle Isaiah shook his head as he said, "He's gone, and she's still living in that house all by herself with her son, of course. I thought she was smarter than that. She had a way out, and she didn't take it! She had a good man and would have had money through the house sale, but she couldn't see it. She couldn't let go of her past and move on. Now bitterness is creeping up on her, 'cause it's hard for a woman raising a child all by herself. I heard she yells at her son something fierce sometimes."

"A penny for your thoughts," Winston said as he stopped in front of Nia's house. Nia shook her head. I was just thinking about Tiffany."

"And what did Pastor say?"

"Forgive them. Love them. Give them your house." They laughed for some time.

Nia and Winston went through six grueling counseling sessions in which Pastor Thompson had them role-play various marital crises situations. During one such scenario, Pastor Thompson told them that they had three children, and Nia was not employed when Winston's boss called him into his office and told him that, because of the economy, his company was closing down Winston's department. Their income was suddenly gone!

Another scenario Pastor Thompson had them role-play dealt with the sudden illness of one of their children requiring the child to be hospitalized. Even during the role-playing, Nia and Winston began to argue over decisions. As the sessions continued, Nia and Winston began to gain understanding of the complexity of marriage.

During the last session, Pastor Thompson emphasized walking in love, using as their model Jesus's walk on earth. The pastor stood before them and waved his hands at them, as if they were his congregation and he was delivering a sermon: "Jesus tells us to love one another at the cost of our own well-being. Oh, we Christians can't grasp that! Jesus tells us that, if your brother is hungry, feed him. If he is thirsty, give him something to drink. If he has no clothes, clothe him, even taking off your own coat and giving it to him."

Nia's mind drifted to Eva and how she gave to others even as a young child. For the first time ever, it dawned on her that her own biological mother had had a godly heart. Nia's eyes flickered as she forced herself to hold back a tear that formed in them.

"Now, Jesus didn't qualify our giving, like asking the person if he has been looking for a job. In fact, Jesus said, if someone asks you to walk a mile, walk two miles with him. Jesus told us never to hurt anyone. If a person slaps you, turn the other cheek, so he can slap the other cheek. Jesus says you can teach a person better through love, which you demonstrate through helping him and giving him what he lacks, rather than through cursing him and rejecting him. Do you realize what walking in love really produces?"

Pastor Thompson stopped and seemed to be waiting for their response. But both Nia and Winston sat staring at the pastor not sure whether they would answer the question correctly.

"It can change a person's heart," said Pastor Thompson. "It tells the other person that you're not his enemy. It disarms the other person from his evil intent. It means walking in humility, which means that we don't think we have all the answers, but we understand that everyone has a right to choices. In our responses to others, we should always ask ourselves whether our intended action will hurt people in any way or inhibit their freedom to choose."

The pastor's voice became surprising gentle, and he even smiled warmly as he looked at them. "Jesus came to teach us a higher way of life. It's time we rose to this way of life. Jesus taught that, even if it kills you, you're to love. And Jesus demonstrated this. He allowed men, acting just as I described, to torture Him and finally nail His hands and feet onto a cross. Can you imagine Jesus, God, nailed to a cross for us? Don't you know the weight of his body was tearing His skin, pulling tendons, muscles, and bones out of place while He hung there all those hours? Even while dying, being innocent of all accusations, He asked God to forgive people for killing him. He was teaching us love even as He died."

Winston bowed his head as he mumbled, "I'm sorry." The pastor didn't hear him, but Nia heard him.

"Be conscious of following His example," said the pastor. "Always work to bring people into God's kingdom. We call it saving souls. God honors your work to save souls, because you save people from burning in hell in response to their own sins when they leave this world, which would happen if they don't accept Jesus as having paid for their sin debt. Can you, my children, walk in love outreaching to people?"

Nia and Winston glanced at each other and then smiled. At the same moment they said, "Yes, Pastor."

Pastor Thompson came from behind his desk and placed his hands on their heads. "I love you, children. Remember that your first ministry is your family. Always ask God to help you make the right decisions. Walk in the beauty of love right in your home first. We'll set a date for the wedding with my secretary."

Chapter 33 The Wedding

Uncle Isaiah walked Nia down the aisle. She knew how difficult walking was for him, but he had insisted on giving her away. He grasped his cane firmly with one hand and hooked his other arm around Nia's arm. With each step he struggled gallantly to move his body forward, and Nia could tell that he took great care not to put any of his weight on her. Everyone had doubted that he could do it because lately he had been wheelchair bound. Nia knew that it was important for Uncle Isaiah to present her to Winston because of Eva, who still held a special place in his heart. And Nia felt a surge of love and appreciation for this extraordinary man who was her great-great-uncle. She bowed her head as she walked and whispered, "Please, heavenly Father, give him strength."

As Nia walked, she felt the warmth of the sun coming through the stained glass windows, shining on her face and arm. Winston stood waiting at the altar, smiling expectantly. When she got to the altar, he extended his hand to her to help her balance as a couple of men assisted Uncle Isaiah into his wheelchair, which had been placed near the altar. As she stood facing the minister, Nia quickly looked at Tonai, who was her maid of honor. Tonai looked gorgeous. Winston's best friend stood by him as his best man. Mrs. Patterson sat proudly in the first pew on the left side of the church with Aunt Sissy beside her.

Nia had wanted a small wedding, but the guest list kept growing as people in their church expressed excitement over the wedding. Winston was outgoing and had invited his many friends and all his relatives, even distant ones. So the church was packed, and people spilled out into the vestibule. Neither Tiffany nor any of Nia's relatives from Grandma Vern's linage, whom she really didn't know well, showed up at the church, although Nia had included a note with Tiffany's invitation stating that all family were invited. However, in her heart, Nia was glad that no one from her family had come other than Uncle Isaiah, Aunt Sissy, and Tonai.

The minister's words echoed through Nia. "Do you take this man as your husband through riches and through poverty, in sickness and in health, in happiness and sorrow, till death do you part?"

Winston looked extremely handsome as he stood facing her. He was tall, brown like the earth, and had a beaming, gentle smile and sparkling eyes, which Nia thought was because he laughed so easily. He was like a huge mahogany tree hovering over her—strong, firm, and protective. Nia closed her eyes and whispered, "I do."

After Winston said, "I do," Pastor Thompson's words rang through her ears: "I now pronounce you man and wife!"

When Winston kissed Nia, it seemed as if water were being poured all over her—soothing, calming water. She felt warm, sparkling feelings surge through her. The congregation exploded into applause as Winston and Nia held hands and walked down the aisle toward the rear of the church. Winston would stop every few feet and lift up his arms while firmly holding Nia's hand and wiggle his body in a hilarious dance motion.

Gaiety rippled through the pews as the congregation followed Nia and Winston outdoors. The day was beautiful; the sun seemed to be smiling, and the sky was a powder blue. Nia yelled, "I'm throwing the bouquet!" It was a beautiful bouquet, a huge display of bright yellow, purple, and pink flowers. She held the flowers over her head. Women and girls rushed down the steps of the church. Nia looked at Tonai, turned, and aimed the bouquet in her direction. Tonai caught it, and the crowd whooped in approval.

As they ran down steps to the curb, the congregation threw confetti over them. Nia heard someone say, "What a beautiful couple." They posed for numerous pictures orchestrated by the photographer. A new wave of laugher ripped through the crowd as Winston and his best man jokingly made humorous facial expressions and postures as the photographer was setting the camera to snap a picture.

As soon as the pictures were done, Winston grabbed Nia's hand, "Come on! The limo's waiting." She turned and saw Pastor Thompson at the top of the steps. He smiled and waved at her.

As the limo moved down the street, Winston planted soft, tender kisses over Nia's face and on her lips. Moments later she gently laid her head on his chest.

The reception was held at a club called Riverbend. Water poured down a simulated mountain near the building's entrance, changing colors as it flowed. When they entered the room, it was already packed, and the crowd cheered for them. A hostess led them to their table, and Winston's best man offered a toast after the wedding party was seated at a long table in front of the ballroom. Forks and knives clinked against wine glasses, which kept Winston kissing his bride following the age-old tradition. Faces beamed as talk ran through the room about how lovely the wedding was and how delicious the food was.

The disc jockey called out, "And this is for the bride and groom!" Nia heard the first notes of her favorite love song as Winston took her hand and led her to the middle of the floor. They danced nearly the whole song before other couples joined them. The music changed to an up-beat tempo, and soon nearly everyone was on the floor dancing.

Winston's parents, brother, and his favorite aunt shared one huge round table with Nia's mother, Uncle Isaiah, Sissy, and Tonai. Uncle Isaiah made comments that had them all laughing. Then Winston's father joined in and told jokes. Nia could not stop laughing as she and Winston stood listening. Everyone seemed to become funnier and funnier. Winston's dad grasped his wife's wrist, pulled her to the dance floor, and began to dance something that looked like a cross between Indian guru moves and an old popular dance called the jerk. He held his arms up into the air and thrust them down at the elbows while yanking his stomach in. He was smiling, and his thin body seemed to twist in every conceivable direction. Nia burst out laughing. She understood where Winston got his sense of humor. She looked around and saw that people's eyes sparkled and their cheeks glowed. She felt warmed inside for the happiness everyone had for her. Someone tapped her on the shoulder. Nia whirled around to find Tiffany standing beside her holding onto her son's hand. Nia reached her arms out and hugged her tightly. She stooped down and hugged Tytoo.

"I'm glad you made it," Nia said warmly. Winston quickly pulled two chairs up to the table.

"You look beautiful, Nia," Tiffany said, a bit shyly. "Look how things ended up. I never even thanked you for the house. I guess I had a hard time, with the way everything was happening. I want to thank you for giving me the house."

"It was always your home."

Tiffany smiled as she let go of Nia's hand responding to Winston's guiding her to the seats he had placed next to Tonai, who greeted her warmly.

"I'm making another toast," a man called out above the music. Nia recognized him as one of Winston's older cousins. Everyone raised his or her champagne glass. Nobody cared that a toast had already been offered. "To the bride and groom," Winston's cousin said. "May the blessings of God flow through their lives. May they have health, long life, and prosperity, and may their children be blessings to them."

Winston turned toward Nia. He was beaming. He whispered in her ear, "I'm ready to go." Nia smiled as he pushed the tip of his tongue into her ear. It tickled, and Nia giggled. She whispered back, "Another hour. This is so much fun, and my cousin Tiffany just came."

Some boys went out onto the floor. They recited words to a rap song. They folded their arms and heaved their bodies energetically from side to side.

Nia's mother called out encouragingly, "Go on, babies. You do your thing."

The photographer wove through the crowd snapping pictures. The wedding party moved outside onto the lawn, and the photographer took more pictures.

"This is our exit," Winston said, as soon as the picture session ended. He seized Nia's hand, and they ran to the limousine, which was waiting to take them to the airport. They entered the backseat of the car. When Winston pulled the door shut, the automatic locks clicked loudly. Nia jumped. It was pitch black inside. In an instant, seemingly coming from nowhere, fear surged through her. She began to sweat and even tremble. It had been dark like that—almost black—in the backseat of the car of that social worker who had taken her away from her mother. She had banged on the door and tried to get out. She had screamed and screamed.

Through the flood of her emotions, she heard a soft, kind voice. "What's wrong, Nia? What's wrong?" Nia turned and looked into Winston's face. As suddenly as the feelings had swept over her, they were gone. Nia didn't answer him. He began to gently rub her shoulder. She slipped her feet out of her shoes and folded her legs underneath her. Then she placed her head on Winston's lap and instantly fell asleep.

CPSIA information can be obtained
at www.ICGtesting.com
Printed in the USA
FFOW03n1534260717
38186FF

9 781477 281369